Darkmage

M.L. Spencer

This is a work of fiction. All of the characters, organizations, and events portrayed in this novel are either products of the author's imagination or are used fictitiously.

DARKMAGE

Map by M.L. Spencer

STONEGUARD PUBLICATIONS

Cover by Claudia McKinney and Teresa Yeh
phatpuppyart.com
Edited by Morgan Smith

ISBN: 978-0-578-41393-8

First Edition: November 2011
Second Edition: January 2017
Third Edition: November 2018

Printed in the United States of America

The Southern Continent

Praise for Darkmage

IRDA Award for Fantasy

"One of the best fantasy stories I've read this decade."
BookNest

"Betrayal, lies and destruction follow across every page."
Grimdark Magazine

"A masterful story."
Readers' Favorite

"Dark and Thrilling."
The Fantasy Inn

DARKMAGE

M.L. Spencer

THE RHENWARS SAGA

Darkstorm (Prequel)
Darkmage

Prologue

Aerysius, The Rhen

Thunder ripped the sky, amplified to a throbbing din by the stone walls that rimmed the square beneath the Hall of the Watchers. Meiran Withersby felt the sound of it physically in her chest. Sheets of rain poured from blackened skies, pounding down on the roof of the cloistered passage above her. She glanced out through the narrow arches that lined the walkway but could make out nothing. Just a thick, choking blackness so complete that it seemed as if a dark pall had been draped down over the entire city, perhaps the entire world. The only light was the dim glow of the lantern that dangled from her fingers.

Lightning crackled and, for the briefest instant, Aerysius winked into existence around her and then disappeared again as abruptly. Meiran hastened her pace, wrapping the black cloak she wore more tightly about herself. Her feet moved with a pressing urgency, motivated by more than just the desire to find shelter from the elements.

In her right hand, she fingered a strip of parchment she'd found on the pillow in her bedchamber. It was written in the same, bold script as similar notes she had received in the past. The last one had been two years before and had contained an almost identical message: *Meet me in the greenhouse. Fourth Watch.* There was no signature—there never was. But Meiran already knew who the author must be.

She couldn't wait to share her secret with him, the one she'd been waiting two long years to whisper in his ear.

Finding that note had filled her with a dizzying thrill of anticipation. Her stomach had been in knots all day. She hadn't been able to concentrate on the simplest task. She had walked around feeling giddy, catching herself daydreaming at the worst possible moments. She couldn't help it, even though it was no way for someone of her station to behave. She was, after all, the most powerful Grand Master in all of Aerysius.

She was also a woman in love.

Lightning strobed the sky, followed immediately by a peal of thunder that shook the air. The wind was at her back, pushing her forward with icy fingers that rippled her cloak out before her. Her dark hair spilled like a fan before her face, whipping at her skin.

She reached the end of the cloister and burst through a massive, iron-shod door. It was not more stone, or even cold marble, that greeted her feet. Instead, Meiran found herself on a narrow path within an old-growth forest.

There were many greenhouses in Aerysius. Most were used to grow food crops, some for herbs or even flowers. But the enormous structure she found herself within was the duplicate of a temperate rainforest. A miniature environment filled with ponds and streams, vegetation and animals.

Soft magelight glowed from behind stands of trees, filtered up from the ground, filling the forest with an ethereal glow. Overhead, rain beat distantly on the shutters drawn over the glass rooftop to protect it from the storm.

As she moved deeper into the forest, it became impossible to tell the environment was artificial. The air was warm and heavy with humidity. Meiran followed the trail around the edge of a pond to a small meadow aglow with magelight that moved like mist over the dark blades of grass. As she stepped onto the spongy lawn, Meiran halted with a sharp intake of breath.

He was there, at the far end of the meadow. Standing with his back to her.

Heart pounding, she crossed the meadow in quick, soft strides. She was so excited. It was hard not to giggle as she dashed through the swirling magelight on the grass. When she reached him, she laid her hand on the soft fabric of his shoulder, her touch hesitant. Slowly, he turned toward her.

She recoiled her hand in shock.

"Were you expecting someone else?" uttered a cold, malicious voice.

An intense feeling of horror overwhelmed her as Meiran shook her head in confused disbelief. She turned, wanting to run away, but froze instead. The lantern slipped from her fingers.

Twin shadows moved toward her over the grass. Not shadows. Something much, much worse. As they neared, the dark forms coalesced into shapes that were vaguely human but featureless, like demonic silhouettes.

Meiran tried to scream, but her throat constricted instead. An intense pang of dread spasmed her stomach. The feeling intensified, became choking, immaculate terror. She couldn't move. She couldn't breathe.

A shadowy hand rose toward her, dark fingers groping to touch her face.

Instinctively, she reached within. But the attempt was pointless. There was only silence inside. The constant rhythm of the magic field was absent, as if it had never existed at all. She was powerless against this enemy.

When the chill shadow of the necrator touched her, Meiran collapsed.

Chapter One
Acolyte of Aerysius

The Vale of Amberlie, The Rhen

Fog rolled in overhead, gray wisps groping with nebulous tendrils across the sky. Darien Lauchlin measured its progress against the jagged slopes of mountain peaks. The fog appeared to move at an impossible rate when viewed against the snowy ridges. It spread misty fingers across the face of the sun, lending a chill stillness to the air that made the early morning shadows grow even deeper.

It was a strange time of year for such a heavy fog. In Amberlie, late summer days usually dawned clear and bright, redolent with the fragrance of pine and honeysuckle. But this day a cold wind had greeted the graying east, and the air felt heavy with the promise of rain. Another storm was coming, Darien suspected. But what kind of storm, he couldn't guess. A peculiar storm, both out of place and out of season. He only hoped it wouldn't arrive today.

Today, he was coming home.

The only thing Darien heard was the sound of his own footsteps as he trudged up the dusty path. His worn-out boots made scuffing noises as he walked; he was too tired to pick up his feet. He squared his shoulders wearily and drew himself up under the weight of his pack. As he did, something inside it clanked as it rattled against the scabbard of the longsword he wore slung across his back. The sound grated on his nerves. Swords were not looked upon favorably under the shadow of Aerysius.

Ahead, he could see a crossroads. As he drew nearer, the noise of other travelers made it clear he wasn't the only person awake in the dim stillness of the morning. The trail topped a low rise, and then he saw them. They came from all directions, every day of the year, to converge at this place. They brought with them their troubles, their sick, their hopes, even their dead, and usually left with nothing. There were many more pilgrims than he remembered.

Darien stepped onto the road in a space between two groups of travelers. The people in front of him seemed one family. The man had the look of a farmer. He was flanked by two boys and a woman who carried a babe in her arms. The child's weak cries were heart-rending, as was the sight of the small, blue-tinged face. Darien felt a knot tighten in his stomach, but there was nothing he could do. Frustration was a feeling he had become all too familiar with. He directed his gaze back at the dirt of the road and tried to ignore the child's wheezing.

Ahead, the forest was thinning out. The sight fed him with hope, and he picked up his pace. Through a break in the trees, he caught sight of a ramp that stretched out over the riverbed.

Darien hurried forward and took the mother by the arm. "Come with me," he said, pulling her away from the rest of her family.

The mother's eyes widened in surprise as they took in the color of his cloak. She glanced back at her husband, who stood watching her go with a mixture of hope and fear in his eyes.

Determined, Darien pulled her along after him as he bored his way through the press of bodies gathered in front of the gatehouse.

The heavy pack lent him momentum, so they quickly reached the forefront of the throng. He glanced around, at last finding the gatekeeper seated behind a small desk by the gate. Trudging toward him, he insinuated himself at the front of the line, the sight of his cloak forestalling any complaints.

When the man behind the desk looked up at him, Darien was mildly surprised. He thought he knew every mage of Aeryslus. But the old man before him with thinning white hair and a face cobwebbed by wrinkles was unknown to him.

Then it dawned on him: the summons. All Masters had been recalled, including some who had never passed beneath the ancient arches since their Raising.

"Name and business," the old man grated in a monotonous tone. His mouth barely moved, as though he were unused to the most fundamental mechanisms of speech.

Darien took a deep breath, then supplied his name and title. "Darien Lauchlin, Acolyte of Aerysius."

As he spoke, he pulled back the fabric of his shirtsleeve, exposing the intricate markings that encircled his left wrist, forming what looked like a heavy metallic chain. The emblem was the mark of the Acolyte's Oath. It symbolized the first vow taken upon acceptance to the Assembly of the Hall. To serve the land and its people. With his life, if possible. If not, then by death.

The man took note of the markings and simply nodded. "You're late." He gestured at the ramp. "Get on your way, boy, and better pray that Emelda goes easy on you."

Darien suppressed a grimace. He'd gotten off to a late start after receiving the summons to return home.

"Let's go," he said to the woman, applying a slight pressure to her back. The mage who guarded the gate would have no knowledge of healing. Such study was reserved for specific orders, and no Sentinel or Querer would ever condescend to such a lackluster duty.

As Darien guided the woman and child through the gate, the crowd surged toward the opening. Immediately, guards stepped forward to press the throng back.

They had to step over a slight gap where the ramp ended, and a wood platform began. The people already gathered there were forced to shift back to make room. Darien ignored their stares, edging sideways to position himself against the platform's railing. He could feel the almost palpable tension of the people surrounding him, noticed how they backed away from the sight of his cloak.

The woman beside him dropped to her knees, gazing up at him with imploring eyes. Tears spilled down her cheeks, her mouth constricting in grief.

"Please," she begged, offering her child to him. "Help us. You can save him. Please. Oh, *please*."

Darien could only look down at her helplessly. She had mistaken him for a full Master because of the color of his cloak. It was not the first time the error had been made.

"I can't," he told her gently. "I'm just an acolyte. The only thing I can do is get you up there."

The woman collapsed over the small form in her arms. He knelt at her side, wanting to comfort her. Not knowing what else to do, Darien ran a hand over the tangled mats of her hair, clenching his jaw against a redoubled pang of frustration.

A shout rang up from below, signaling the guards to close the gate. Darien helped the woman regain her feet. He caught hold of the platform's railing and drew her against him.

The wood beneath them jolted. There was a sudden wave of panic as feet scrambled for better purchase. Then the entire platform seemed to take flight, surging backward and up. The gap between the gate and the ramp widened, exposing the swift waters of the river below.

He looked up and saw the ropes that held the platform aloft. Far below, many teams of horses labored in their traces to lift the platform up the cliff. The ground below drew farther away, the air taking on a slight chill.

Darien closed his eyes and reached out from within, tasting the flow of the magic field. Here, he had to be careful. A powerful vortex of magic surrounded Aerysius. Though he was only an acolyte, the wild cyclone of power was violent enough to hurt him if he let his mind stroke it the wrong way. For a full Master, such a mistake would be fatal—which was why the lift relied on horse power until it was well above the surging flux of magic.

There was a sharp jolt, and then the platform sped upward at a dizzying pace. They had passed into the calm eye of the vortex, and magic took over as the means of lifting them up the mountainside.

Darien noticed that the woman was hugging the child so hard, he was afraid she might crush it.

"May I hold him?" he asked.

The woman nodded, offering the child to him.

Darien received the small life softly into his arms, swaddling the babe in the folds of his cloak. He held him close against his chest, seeking to revive him with the warmth of his body. The wheezing babe stared up at him with soft brown eyes that made his heart ache.

The lift slipped silently into a bank of fog, so thick he couldn't see the child in his arms. Then, miraculously, the mist parted, and warm sunlight streamed from a brilliant blue sky, revealing the foundations of Aerysius above.

The city was carved from the side of the mountain, etched right into the vertical wall of granite. The spires of Aerysius seemed wrought from millions of glistening crystals, tendril-thin bridges arching between them thousands of feet above the Vale. To Darien, the sight was no less breathtaking than the first time he'd seen it, and this time there was added meaning.

He was finally home.

The platform slowed to a stop, halting beside an arching foundation. Above, a waterfall spilled down from the top of a soaring spire, birds diving in and out of the mist created by the spray.

But the sound of the woman sobbing beside him dampened any joy he might have felt over his homecoming. Looking down, Darien saw that the child in his arms lay completely limp, the soft eyes closed. He patted the small body with his hand, trying to prod any type of life out of it.

But the boy didn't stir.

He stood dazed as the woman removed the dead child from his grasp. The gate opened, and the crowd spilled past him off the platform. The woman fled after them, cradling the sad bundle in her arms.

Darien lingered behind on the lift, feeling numb as he stared down at his empty hands. He stood there for a while, his thoughts scattered like broken glass. It wasn't until the lift shifted under the weight of new passengers that he finally blinked, his mind snapping back into focus. He forced himself to move forward, turning sideways to forge a path through the oncoming crowd.

It took him long minutes of walking before he remembered where he was supposed to be going. He changed course, turning onto a side street that would take him into the heart of the lower terrace.

As he moved through the streets of Aerysius, Darien scarcely noticed people staring at him and moving out of his way. He didn't care. He wasn't in the mood to care and, besides, the same looks plagued him everywhere he went.

He was used to standing out in a crowd. The sight of a black-cloaked man bearing a sword on his back was a glaring contradiction that most people couldn't ignore. Masters of Aerysius swore the Oath of Harmony. They didn't walk about carrying weapons.

He climbed the wide steps in front of the Hall of the Watchers, passing beneath the ancient arches that stabbed upward into the sky like twisted spears. Inside, the circular hall was filled with a hazy amber light that filtered down from stained glass windows set high above. It was enormous, one of the largest structures ever built by man. Great pillars carved to resemble massive stone trees with spreading branches supported the weight of the domed ceiling. There were hundreds of them, row upon row.

He took a flight of steps that descended into the base of the hall. There, he found a woman seated behind a small desk, scribing something with a feathered quill. She continued to write, appearing completely engrossed in her task. Only when he stood across the desk from her did she slide her spectacles off her face, looking sideways up at him with an irritated expression.

"You're late."

Darien nodded. "I left a week after receiving the summons."

He wished he'd stopped at the Acolytes Residence to clean up a bit. The way the woman was staring at him made him conscious of every speck of dust from the road, of the week-old growth of stubble on his face. He saw her eyes come to rest on the hilt of the sword at his back. The woman's eyebrows flicked upward, her look incredulous. Not many people had the gall to come armed to an audience with the Prime Warden of Aerysius.

"I see you've grown too big for your britches, Darien Lauchlin," she said. "It might be wise to put off your Raising until you can remember you are yet an acolyte. You may be the Prime Warden's own son, but that does not excuse you. If anything, it means you must be seen as an example for others."

He didn't know whether she referred to his late arrival or the unsubtle insult of the sword. If she wanted him to remove the weapon, then she was mistaken. He had no intention of doing so. His mother would have to get used to the sight of it.

He waited as the woman merely stared at him. When it became obvious that he wasn't going to budge or offer apology, she shook her head and made a *tsk*ing sound with her tongue.

"Well, if you insist on acting like a child, so be it. Let your mother deal with you. Have no doubt, she will." She stood up, tossing her quill down with an air of finality.

"Come."

She turned her back on him, opening a door beside her desk. Darien followed her at a good distance as she led him down a hallway. He had been there before, many times. He really had no need to be shown the way. But his mother expected—or, rather, demanded—formality at all times.

The hallway ended at a white door. The woman opened it and gestured for him to wait. Darien paused just long enough to hear her announce him before brushing past her through the opening.

The room inside was filled with brilliant white light. The entire chamber was encased with windows that had scarcely a pane between them. The Prime Warden's solarium looked out from within the mountainside, the view an unspoiled panorama of the white-capped Craghorns and the Vale of Amberlie below.

Emelda Lauchlin was seated on a raised dais before the panoramic windows, her face impatiently expectant. Darien did not forget his manners. He went instantly to his knees, abasing himself until his black hair was spread out on the floor beside his face. He didn't dare move from that position until he was bid. So he waited, listening to the sound of his breath, the dead babe's face haunting his thoughts.

A long minute dragged by, followed by another. By the third, Darien had no doubt his mother was angry.

After five minutes, he knew she was livid.

"Arise."

He swallowed as he pushed himself off the floor. He felt the blood rush out of his head and, for a moment, he felt terribly dizzy. He saw that his mother had risen as well. She glared down at him imperiously from her position on the dais. She wore her ebony hair pulled back from her face, which only served to augment the stern set of her features.

For a long moment, they stood staring at each other across the distance between them. Then, more graceful than a queen, the Prime Warden of Aerysius descended the steps of the dais. She stopped before him, having to look up to meet his gaze. Her blue eyes burned fiercely, her lips pressed into a frown of barely controlled rage. Then, abruptly, she swept forward to embrace him.

Darien was taken aback. He moved awkwardly to return the gesture, which was made more difficult by the baldric he wore and the pack still slung from his shoulder. When they separated, he was surprised to see the anger on her face replaced by a warm smile of affection. Looks were not the only thing he had inherited from her; Emelda Lauchlin had a temperament just as unpredictable as his own.

"My son." She stared at him with wonder in her eyes. "You have changed a great deal."

Her gaze lowered to fix on the leather strap that crossed his chest. This was the critical moment, he knew. She would either accept him for what he was or reject him utterly, and it all hinged on whether or not she accepted the sword.

She chose to ignore it.

Taking him by the hand, she led him to a white chair and claimed the one beside it. Darien struggled out of his pack and leaned his sword against the chair's leather armrest.

He tried to gauge his mother's disposition by the way she held herself. She sat leaning forward slightly, arms open and resting on the cushions at her sides. It was a welcoming posture, one that invited him in instead of shutting him out. He took it for a good sign.

"Tell me," she pressed, "how fares the Front?"

It was time to make his case. Darien had rehearsed this speech all the way down from the Pass of Lor-Gamorth. But now, when the moment to deliver it was upon him, the carefully rehearsed phrases eluded him. Shaking his head, he decided honesty was the best thing he could offer her.

"We're dying," he said, staring down at a smear of mud on his knee.

As if sensing his struggle, his mother set a hand on his arm. The touch strengthened him enough to continue.

"The Enemy is massing in numbers never before seen. We don't have enough soldiers. We're facing a critical shortage of weapons and supplies. We're running out of ideas and, frankly, we're running out of hope. There's been precious little support from the South. The last group of men they shipped us was a pack of criminals up from Rothscard, and that's been months ago. We'll all be dead in another few months, either by the sword or by hunger, but it doesn't matter which. The fact is, you'll have Enemy hordes pouring down on top of you, and your only line of defense will be feeding the crows."

As he let the last words die, Darien felt an instant pang of regret. He hadn't meant to raise his voice. Silence followed while his mother only stared at him, her expression impossible to read. He felt drained, as though the flood of words he'd let pour from his mouth had sapped his strength.

"So, you are suggesting that the might of Aerysius should turn the tide of this war?"

Her words, though softly spoken, were deliberately chosen. His mother was trying to probe him to find out where he stood on the issue. It was a test, of sorts. Whether or not she approved his Raising might even depend on how he responded. But Darien didn't care. There was only one way he could answer her, and it was with the conviction of his beliefs.

"I'm suggesting there may not *be* an Aerysius if you don't Unbind the Sentinels," he said, the words sounding harsher than he meant. "The order exists to defend the Rhen against this very threat. I understand the need for the Oath of Harmony, but it has served its purpose. Times change, Mother. The time for the Oath has passed. If we don't Unbind the Sentinels, then there will be no hope. The Enemy will slaughter us."

Her eyes dropped to the leather-wrapped scabbard that leaned against his chair. Very carefully, she asked, "What then, Darien?"

Here was the crux of the test. Darien feared to step across this threshold. But he had already pressed too far to stop now.

"Let me receive the Transference from two Masters. Give me the strength to create a grand resonance. Then we can lure their forces southward and annihilate them."

His words were met by silence, as though they had fallen on empty space. Darien dropped his gaze and stared at the floor, knowing he'd gone too far.

It was long seconds before his mother spoke again.

"Tonight, you shall be Raised to the Order of Sentinels, as your father was before you." Her voice was cold, as icy as the mountain wind. "You will accept the Transference from Grand Master Ezras Nordric, who has decided to pass beyond and leave the trials of this war to the next generation. To you. You shall swear the Oath of Harmony in front of the full Assembly of the Hall. Before you do, you will take that thing at your side and cast it off the cliff. I will never hear the words 'grand resonance' out of your mouth again. Do I make myself clear, Darien?"

"Aye," he answered, feeling the last of his hopes dashed by his mother's resolve. Darien bowed his head, accepting defeat.

He would take the Oath, as she asked. Only, he didn't believe he could keep it. There was a harsh penalty for Oathbreakers. They would strip the power from him—a painful form of execution. Then they would hang his body from the arches as a warning, and also as a statement. The world needed to know that the justice of Aerysius was without mercy, even for its own. That was the price of betrayal, the price of Oathbreaking. Yet, if such an act could stop the war…

There was a text Darien had read once. It had been part of his curriculum: *The Mysteries of Aerysius* by Cedric Cromm. In it was a short biography of Grand Master Orien, who had stood on the crag now known infamously as Orien's Finger to bring the vast power of a vortex to bear against an invasion long ago.

Orien's desperate act had turned the tide of battle and driven the Enemy from the North. Then Orien had calmly knelt and surrendered himself to his punishment. Orien's face was among those of the Watchers in the Hall, his image carved severely in stone. He had been an Oathbreaker and had died a cruel death for his actions. Yet, he had also been a savior.

"You may go." His mother dismissed Darien curtly, waving a hand in the direction of the door. "Spend the rest of the day in solitude and reflection."

As he stood to leave, her voice stopped him.

"It's good to have you home. You remind me of your father so much. He would have been very proud to see the man you have become."

Darien nodded somberly as he gathered his things. His father had been a formidable Sentinel, and part of him was pleased at hearing his mother's words. But he also found them bitterly ironic. Gerald Lauchlin had despised the Mage's Oath yet had died preserving it. Darien had always aspired to follow the example set by his father, but he had no wish to meet such a similar, hypocritical end.

He strode back down the hallway, taking lengthy strides to put some distance between himself and his mother's solarium. He could hear his pulse pounding in his ears, almost as loud as the sound of his ringing footsteps. He mounted a flight of stairs that took him up, spiraling, into the Spire of the Hall.

He paused to catch his breath at a landing, cursing himself silently for the way he had mismanaged the interview. Heat rose to flush his cheeks as he clenched and unclenched his fists in anger. He stood still, taking slow, deep breaths until the throbbing of his pulse subsided in his ears. He started to move forward again, but a familiar voice stopped him short.

"So, the prodigal son finally returns."

Darien sucked in a sharp breath between clenched teeth. He closed his eyes, wondering just how many tests the gods would throw his way in one day. Then, opening his eyes, he slowly turned to face his only brother.

Aidan looked the same as Darien remembered. He stood leaning against the carved railing of the staircase, his black cloak flipped back over one shoulder in the manner he was accustomed to wearing it. It lent him a polished, aristocratic appearance. He stood with one hand tucked neatly behind his back, the other draped over the railing as though it were the armrest of a throne. He gazed upon Darien with eyes that were a perfect copy of their mother's.

"Still playing with your toys, I see? You should have abandoned them years ago." Aidan arched an eyebrow, strolling forward down the steps. He circled Darien slowly, eyeing the weapon on his back with an expression of distaste. "Or is it your intention to swear the Oath of Harmony upon that sword?"

Darien sighed, shaking his head. He'd hoped things would have changed over the two years of his absence. Meeting Aidan's gaze, he said, "I was thinking maybe we could just be brothers again. Perhaps it was too much to expect."

Aidan blinked, a gallant smile springing to his lips. "Not too much, I think. It was only a jest." He clapped Darien on the shoulder with a soft chuckle. The act was condescending, and the smile on his face seemed forced. "Really, Darien, you always take things much too seriously. Here, let me get that for you."

Aidan swept the pack off Darien's shoulder without waiting for a reply. He held the dusty leather away from his body, as though afraid some of the grime might smudge off and mar his appearance. He extended his hand in invitation.

As they climbed the stairs, Aidan made an attempt at conversation. "I trust your journey was safe?"

Darien nodded, thinking he didn't have the breath to waste on a reply as he considered the spiraling staircase still above them.

"Oh, I just remembered." Aidan turned to look back at him, smiling pleasantly. "I have a message for you from Grand Master Meiran. You do remember her, of course?"

Darien glared at his back. His brother was taunting him under the infuriating guise of politeness, just like he always had. Aidan knew all about the scandal that had hastened Darien's departure two years before. Everyone knew of it.

He had pursued Meiran for months, even though she was well above his station and he had no business being near her. There were no laws forbidding Masters and acolytes from associating in private, but the traditions of Aerysius were often more stringent than formal laws.

His mother had caught wind of the affair. She had Darien packed up and shipped off to the Front in all haste, without even a chance to say goodbye. Meiran had received a demerit, unheard of for a Grand Master of her status.

Aidan went on as though he were ignorant of the whole ordeal, "She sends her regards. Really, Darien, you must have made quite an impression before you left. It usually isn't considered proper for a Grand Master to be seen chasing around after acolytes."

"I won't be an acolyte much longer," Darien growled, fighting to control the anger his brother always had a way of provoking. He silently berated himself. He was feeding right into Aidan's ploy. Not wanting his brother to get the better of him, he added in a lighter tone, "Besides, I was the one who did all the chasing."

They arrived finally at a level high up in the Spire of the Hall. His brother led him down a well-lit hallway, stopping at a mahogany door about halfway down the passage. Aidan swept it open with a gallant swirl of his cloak, exposing the chambers within.

Darien stood in the doorway, surveying his new quarters with a feeling of trepidation. This was not the stark cell of an acolyte. The room was as large as his mother's solar, decorated lavishly enough to suit a nobleman. There was a fire already blazing in the hearth and a vase with cut flowers sitting on the dining table.

"Well, here you are," Aidan announced. "I trust you find your quarters adequate? I chose the location, but Mother made all the arrangements."

"It's far more than adequate," Darien muttered, feeling stunned and more than a little overwhelmed. He took a step inside, wondering if it would be possible to get used to so much space after spending the last two years freezing in the cramped cellar of Greystone Keep.

He collected himself enough to say, "My thanks, Aidan. It's wonderful."

His brother set his pack down by the door, hesitating as if uncertain whether he wanted the dirty thing to soil the floor tiles.

"I'll see you tonight, then," Aidan said. "Don't get too comfortable, now. You'll not want to miss your own Raising."

Darien barely heard the sound of the door closing as his brother took his leave. He stood gazing around the chamber, feeling too exhausted to think. Memories of the dead child kept creeping into his awareness, making him feel hollow.

Moving awkwardly, he leaned his sword against the wall beside his back. Then he slumped down into a heavily cushioned chair and found a goblet of wine already poured and waiting on the table beside him.

His hand trembled as he raised the goblet to his lips. He took the liquid into his mouth in thirsty gulps, trying to wash away the images in his head.

As he set the spent glass back on the table, his head suddenly felt too heavy to hold up any longer. He snuggled back into the soft cushions and gazed up at the painted ceiling, a soft ringing sound filling his ears.

The ceiling blurred, growing darker, the colors melting and running together.

He never remembered falling asleep. The drug in the wine acted swiftly.

Chapter Two
Two Goblets, Two Rites

Aerysius, The Rhen

The dark altar existed deep within the heart of the mountain. It was accessible only by someone with knowledge of the vast network of passages that had been formed by the natural action of running water and the hard labors of men thousands of years dead.

The man carrying Meiran's unconscious body had that knowledge, and other knowledge, besides. He had spent years of his life in preparation for this night, poring over forbidden manuscripts full of dark teachings and secrets purposefully forgotten. A perfect map of the entire cave system existed in his head, along with the methods of disarming the magical traps and devices rigged to prevent access. He had journeyed down these dark passages many times before. The ancient warren was his own personal sanctuary, the unholy shrine his private chapel.

The altar existed in a small chamber roughly hewn from the black rock of the mountain's heart. The walls wept the wet blood of the mountain down their coarse faces, glistening in the pale magelight he cast. Puddles collected on the floor, stagnant pools that splashed foul droplets up to soil the hem of his cloak as his boots disturbed their surfaces. He crossed the chamber to the far side, where he stooped to lay the woman upon the worn surface of the altar rock.

The altar was formed from a single slab of black stone with ancient, rusted chains set there to restrain a victim for sacrifice. It had been a common practice among the dark sects of ages past. He didn't bother with the chains, had even dismissed the necrators after they had served their initial purpose. The woman on the altar needed no restraint, either physical or ethereal. Meiran had been touched by hell's own shadow. She would never again awaken.

His nostrils sucked in the stale air of the chamber as he went about his business with meticulous efficiency. He removed the black cloak from Meiran's body, folding it carefully before placing it on the floor.

He then paused a moment, eyes drinking in the thin silk his action had exposed. His hand moved to caress the fabric's texture where it lay smooth against the firm curve of her hips. The touch stimulated him, inciting his heart to quicken its pace. In all his careful planning, he had never imagined this moment would be so irresistibly erotic.

With the back of his hand, he stroked aside a wayward lock of brown hair that had fallen over Meiran's pale, perfect face. He continued the motion, running his fingers down the side of her cheek, over her parted lips. He leaned down, brushing those lips with his own tender kiss.

When he bared the sword from its scabbard with a crisp ring of steel, he was pleased to find it just as sharp as he'd expected. In two quick motions, he laid open the skin of Meiran's wrists to the bone.

Stooping, he bent to catch the pulsing blood flow in a crystalline wine goblet. When it was full, he let Meiran's arm fall limply onto the surface of the altar.

He turned, then, toward the Well.

The Well of Tears stood in the center of the chamber, made of rough stone blocks and covered with a round slab of granite four inches thick. Around its rim were carved runes in an ancient, unholy script that looked like vicious slashes in the stone, as though made by the claws of a vile beast. The Well was a portal to the darkest depths of the Netherworld, a gateway that opened a conduit straight to the bowels of hell. Once opened, the Well would unleash the dark hosts of Chaos upon the world.

He would have the terror of the night at his command.

Kneeling beside the Well, he dipped a finger into the goblet of blood. The fluid dripped to the floor as he moved his hand to the first rune, tracing its form with the warm blood from Meiran's veins.

The blood took a moment to absorb into the porous stone. When it did, the marking began to glow with a pale green light. He moved around the rim to the next rune in the sequence, then another, dipping his finger into the goblet and repeating the act all around the rim. He moved carefully, taking his time, until all of the markings glowed with the same pale, sickening light.

But his work was not yet complete. The Well had to be unsealed from both sides. His action had unlocked the side of the gateway that existed in this world. But someone else would have to open it from the other side.

The lid was far too heavy to be shifted by the limited strength of a single man. So he reached within, aligning his mind with the rhythm of the magic field. As if pushed by the invisible hand of a giant, the cover of the Well of Tears lifted and slid aside, falling sharply to the floor with a resounding crash.

He turned back to Meiran.

Her blood was nearly spent, running in scarlet rivulets down the side of the altar and mixing with the pools of water on the floor. He moved to place two fingers on her neck, feeling for a pulse. It was still there, tremulous, and growing fainter. He stood over her, gazing down at her beautiful, ashen face until the tempo of her heart finally stalled in her veins.

He pressed his hands against her cheeks as she died, cupping her face as though with the tender embrace of a lover. There was a faint tingling sensation in his fingertips where they touched her soft skin, weak at first, then growing infinitely stronger. The flow of power swam up from within her, coursing into him, filling his body and mind with a shuddering ecstasy almost too great to stand.

He pulled himself on top of her, moving his hands behind her back to lift her body against his chest, hugging her fiercely as he absorbed the final spasms of current that flowed into him. When it was finished, he collapsed on top of her, spent and gasping.

He pushed himself off her, standing up. His breath still came in gasps, his body trembling from the deluge of energy from the Transference. With his newfound strength, he placed a finger on her forehead and uttered an enchantment that would have been completely beyond him only a few moments before. He pressed upon Meiran's soul a Word of Command, sending her spirit to the Netherworld with a task she would have no choice but to perform.

He lifted her body, carried the dead weight of her over to the Well. With one, smooth motion, he cast her in. The blue fabric of her dress rippled in the wind created by the speed of her fall. He watched as the sight of her was quickly lost, consumed by the shadows of the Well. He never heard her body hit the bottom. As far as he was aware, it never did.

Aidan Lauchlin knelt on the floor in the dim light of the Well's shining runes. He waited, wondering how long it would take her to complete the task he had Commanded of her soul.

Dark colors swam gradually into focus, hazing in and out across his vision. It took Darien long moments to realize it was the ceiling he was looking at and not some confused chiaroscuro that had taken on a life of its own.

Blinking, he sat up and gazed around the room in foggy bewilderment. He must have fallen asleep, though he didn't recall doing so. There was a throbbing ache in the back of his head. His mouth was dry, and his eyes ached when he rubbed them.

Beside his chair, the crystalline goblet sat empty. The bottle next to it was mostly full, completely untouched, save for the one glass that had been poured from it.

He wondered what time it was. It felt as though he'd been sleeping a long time. He struggled out of the chair, regretting the motion instantly. The throbbing in his head turned to a stabbing pain that lanced like hot irons into his eyes. Wincing, Darien squinted as dark blotches swam across his vision.

It took him a moment to recover enough to stagger across the room to the hearth. The fire had burned out, the coals gray and cold. That was the first thing he noticed. Frowning, he glanced toward the paned window. Through glass streaked with rain, he saw only consummate darkness. Panic seized him. It was late.

Then he noticed the clock on the wall with heavy iron counterweights. The position of the bronze hands on its face made the feeling of panic in his gut wrench into a wave of nausea. It was a quarter past the stroke of midnight. He was already late for the Rite of Transference in the temple.

"Bloody hell," he growled.

His mother was going to kill him.

Darien stood frozen, groping through the fog in his head to figure out what to do first. He had no time to clean up. His clothes were worn and travel-stained, his hair unwashed, his face unshaven. He'd taken no time to prepare himself mentally.

He sprang for the bedchamber, ignoring the stabbing pain in his head. His mother would have arranged for a wardrobe—she was never one to miss a detail. Yet he still exhaled a sigh of relief when he saw fresh clothing already laid out on the bed.

Stripping the filthy rags off his body, he donned the new black robes in a matter of seconds. One glance at the looking glass told him his face was a lost cause. He cupped his hands and filled them with water from the basin, splashing it over his cheeks. The towel he used to dry his face came away stained and filthy. He dragged his fingers through his hair, ripping through most of the snarls, then tied the long strands back with a strip of leather.

That was as good as it was going to get.

As he dashed out of the bedchamber, Darien suddenly remembered the sword his mother had ordered thrown off the cliff. He had absolutely no intention of doing so—the sword was a gift from Meiran.

But the weapon wasn't where he'd left it. Someone had removed it while he slept.

The curse Darien swore as he slammed the door shut would have chilled even his mother's cold blood.

He was well beyond fashionably late by the time he reached

the Temple of Athera in the upper reaches of the city. Being located on the sheer face of a mountain precipice, Aerysius was spread out more vertically than horizontally. Many of its streets were switchbacks, climbing steeply up the side of the cliff, that or granite stairs carved into the face of the mountain itself. Sky bridges linked the tops of towers at lower levels of the city with the bases of structures at higher elevations. Navigating the streets, particularly in the pouring rain, was difficult.

To Darien, the climb to the temple was a grueling punishment. His body ached at every joint, and the throbbing in his head refused to go away.

He was shaking and drenched by the time he topped the last flight of stairs. He thrust the temple door open, his long strides propelling him into a well-lit antechamber.

He stopped in the middle of the room and glanced about frantically, trying to figure out where to go. There were four doors to pick from, as well as two staircases to either side. He was about to just start trying doors when a cold voice from above halted him.

"I'm not certain who I should be more furious with: you, for arriving over an hour late, or your brother, for not bothering to present himself at all."

Darien slumped, shivering, not wanting to look up to face the wrath of his mother. She stood at the railing of the balcony, glaring down at him imperiously. At least she was alone; that was a small comfort. Darien wasn't sure he could stand the humiliation of another public dressing-down by her. He strode toward the staircase grudgingly.

His mother waited for him on the balcony. Fury radiated from her presence, sharpening her every movement. When Darien stopped in front of her, she grabbed his face, her fingers squeezing until they hurt. She jerked her hand away roughly.

"What is the matter with you?" she hissed between clenched teeth. "When I sent you away, you were ready for this. More than ready! But now I see you've come back to us with the manners of a swine and nothing but contempt for our ways."

Darien seethed with a silent rage that threatened to ignite.

Emelda was Prime Warden as well as his mother, but that was no excuse for the callous way she always treated him. She showed less respect for him than she did for the lowliest kitchen scullion. He didn't care that she held the keys to his Raising in her hand, didn't care that she had the authority to send him away again, perhaps this time forever. The anger inside burned fierce, impossible to contain.

"Then make your choice," Darien demanded. "Either let's do this, or tell me now, and I'll be on my way."

Emelda stared at him as if truly seeing him for the first time in her life. She blinked slowly before dropping her gaze. It was the only time in Darien's memory he had ever seen his mother back down.

The silence between them stretched. Finally, Emelda looked up to meet his gaze. An expression of regret had replaced the anger in her eyes. Darien almost didn't recognize the emotion, it looked so foreign on her features.

"I'm sorry," she said. "I've always held the highest expectations of you. Perhaps they have been too high. I suppose it's because, for the most part, you have always lived up to them."

It was Darien's turn to drop his gaze. Her soft words had extinguished the last spark of anger left within him. He stared at the floor, thoughts and feelings running through his head in a torrent, leaving him terribly confused. He didn't notice her hand moving until he felt the touch of her fingertips against his.

"It's time," she whispered. "Are you ready?"

Darien nodded but didn't speak. He felt incapable of trusting his voice. He allowed her to guide him toward a door off the balcony. He opened it for her and waited as his mother went through first, following silently in her wake.

What he found inside the chapel looked nothing like the formal ceremony he'd been expecting. What he saw, rather, appeared to be a gathering of old friends. The High Priest of Athera appeared to be gossiping with Grand Master Ezras, an ancient-looking man seated at the far end of the room. They seemed to be swapping old stories over drinks.

Beside them were a few other Masters he recognized, and even a Grand Master, all appearing to be just participating in friendly conversation. Yet, it was who he didn't see that struck Darien most deeply. His mother had already warned him Aidan would be absent. But he'd been hoping that Meiran would be there. It was more than just hope, really.

He needed her there.

Perhaps something urgent had come up. Or, more likely, she'd moved on to someone else. Whatever the reason, Meiran's absence quenched the last spark of anticipation Darien had left. He breathed out a sigh of resignation.

No one had prepared him for the ceremony, and he didn't know what to do. Everyone was staring at him, all conversation suddenly halted. A few people were shifting uncomfortably, some exchanging looks of irritation. He glanced at his mother, who nodded her head in the direction of Ezras.

Gathering his courage, Darien crossed the room in a carefully measured pace, to where the old man sat waiting for him expectantly. He tried not to look at any of the other faces in the room, not wanting to know what was written on them. Instead, he kept his gaze fixed on Ezras.

When he reached him, Darien dropped to his knees before the ancient Sentinel, bowing his head deeply. He wasn't sure if it was the proper thing to do, but it felt right. And now that he had chosen to make a place for himself at the Grand Master's feet, he was committed. By the unwritten rules of protocol, all he could do now was wait.

The waiting seemed to last a lifetime.

There was no sound in the room, not even a rustle of fabric or the tinkling of ice in a glass. Darien stared at the floor, his apprehension growing. He was beginning to get the feeling that there must be something else he should be doing, though he couldn't imagine what. The tension in the room was growing. The silence was stretching too long, even for the witnesses. He felt their eyes boring into his back. Feeling unnerved, he almost stood up.

Then he felt a pressure under his chin. The ancient Sentinel had reached down to take Darien's face in his hand, lifting his chin with gnarled fingers, directing his gaze upward and into his own.

Darien found himself looking into a pair of clear blue eyes that blazed with an acute flame of intelligence. There was no readable expression within them. There was only that single spark that burned intensely. Darien found himself transfixed by it, unable to break away. The old man's stare held him more securely than any iron shackle, even when he became aware that those penetrating blue eyes were doing much more than merely staring.

Ezras had been scrutinizing him the entire time.

Suddenly, Darien was filled with doubt. The old man before him was one of the most powerful mages in Aerysius and was also the most accomplished. Ezras had been a prevailing force in the effort that had turned back the Enemy at the Battle of Meridan almost twenty years before. He had later gone on to do the same at the Battle of Dobson Hollow. All accomplished while maintaining his Oath of Harmony. Darien wondered if he was worthy of accepting the Transference from this old man. He thought of his own professed opinions of the Oath and began to have doubts.

He doubted, but he did not look away.

Neither did Ezras. He sat staring Darien straight in the eyes as his cracked lips moved to form words.

"Did you know I was a friend of your father's?"

Darien blinked. His shock was as much due to hearing the sound of a voice after such a long silence as it was to the sentiment in the old man's tone. When he found his own voice again, it came out as a barely grated whisper:

"No, Grand Master. I did not."

Ezras nodded slightly. His ancient hand yet lingered on Darien's chin, while his intense blue eyes continued to assess his every reaction. After another long stretch of silence, the old man spoke again.

"You have his eyes. And I sense something else of him in you as well: you have his spirit. Gerald Lauchlin was an inspiring man and a loyal friend. You would do well to model yourself after him." Ezras frowned, pausing a moment in reflection. "Come to think of it, it seems you already have. He was late to his own Raising too. Well, perhaps not quite so late as yourself."

The high priest must have taken that moment as his cue. He stepped behind the chair Ezras occupied and leaned forward to ask him, "Are you ready, Grand Master?"

Ezras turned to look up at the priest with a warm smile devoid of any sign of regret. "Quite ready. This bag of bones some would call a body has stopped serving any useful purpose I can think of. Yes, I believe it's well past time. You may begin."

The priest nodded. He looked down at Darien, who was still kneeling at the Sentinel's feet.

The priest asked, "Darien Lauchlin, are you prepared to assume the chains of servitude that will bind you forever as a guardian of the Rhen and of its people?"

"I am, Your Eminence."

Darien was able to answer without hesitation, feeling himself bolstered by the old man's indomitable spirit.

"And are you also prepared to accept accountability for your every action, so that your decisions be always tempered by wisdom, compassion, and humility?"

"Aye, Your Eminence. I am."

The priest moved forward to stand beside Ezras. He placed a hand on the Sentinel's shoulder in a warm gesture that suggested an old friendship between the two men. He held his hand there as he stated formally, "Grand Master, may your journey to the Atrament be swift. Your time of service is at an end. Depart in peace, knowing that your service has not gone unnoticed nor unappreciated. Your name will be entered into the Book of Records, so that your works will be known until the end of time."

Ezras chuckled as the priest uttered the last line of the ancient ritual and removed his hand. "My thanks, Your Eminence. Most eloquently spoken. Though you should have omitted that last part about my works. I'm certain they're not worth the waste of parchment."

He looked down at Darien then, a warm and welcoming smile on his lips. "Come, young man. Take these old hands. All this pomp and ceremony is frankly getting on my nerves. I'd like to have an end to it."

"Aye, Grand Master," Darien whispered.

His heart beat furiously as a host of conflicting emotions warred within him. These were the last moments of the old man's life. Darien had never really known Ezras but realized he was quite fond of the man. The old Master's imminent passing filled him with a bitter sense of remorse.

At the same time, he also felt singularly responsible for the ending of that life. He knew his guilt was unjustified; the transfer of power from one generation of mages to the next was simply the way it had been since the beginning of time, the only way it could ever possibly be. Deciding to pass on his gift had been Ezras' choice alone. Still, Darien found it hard to shake the guilt, all the same.

There was also an acute sense of anticipation, knowing that the moment he had always waited for had finally arrived. That feeling of excitement was mixed with an intense pang of sadness that had been lingering at the back of his mind throughout the entire ritual.

He'd wanted so much for Meiran to be there.

But she was not.

So he did as the old man bid and took the mage's age-spotted and gnarled hands into his own, closing his eyes.

Almost immediately, he felt the stir of the conduit that Ezras established between them. He could feel the surge of it, the charge of power that flowed up his arms and into his chest, spreading out to fill his body with an overwhelming gush of exhilarating energy. It was as though every fiber within him had been suddenly awakened together at once. He could feel the magic field pulsing within him, throbbing, as brilliantly radiant as the sun. The feeling swelled, became encompassing, filling him entirely.

And then, abruptly, he felt the conduit slam closed.

When Darien opened his eyes, he found himself drained and weak. He gasped for breath as rivers of sweat streamed from his brow, his heart pounding like a stampede of horses in his chest. His cheeks were wet with spilt tears he didn't even remember shedding, and his whole body trembled.

The reality he awakened to was the same as before, and yet altogether different. It seemed more vivid, somehow, as though the world he'd known before was just a dim reflection that didn't quite do justice to the real thing. The hues of colors seemed more saturated, the shadows somehow less dense. All of his senses were overwhelmed, the experience surreal. He felt like a newborn just expelled from the womb, opening its eyes for the first time.

A shudder in the floor beneath him brought Darien's senses sharply back into focus. He pushed himself off the ground, rising to a crouch as a stab of fear lanced through him. Another tremor hit, this time big enough to rock the entire structure of the temple.

Everyone in the room surged toward the windows. Beyond the glass, the sky had taken on a pasty green hue.

Regaining his feet, he moved toward the others. As he neared the windows, Darien saw that the glow of light came from far below, from the square beside the Hall of the Watchers. A pillar of green energy had erupted from the center of the pavement, shooting straight upward into the sky.

"What is it?" he gasped.

It was his mother's voice that answered him, leaden and hollow sounding. "The Well of Tears has been opened. May the gods have mercy on us all."

Chapter Three
The Fallen

Aerysius, The Rhen

Aidan Lauchlin stared at the towering column of energy that thrust upward from the center of the square to stab the skies above Aerysius like a terrible, scintillating lance. The sight of the sickly green pillar filled him with a quivering sense of accomplishment.

The column of light stabbed into the sky, a potent signal that could be witnessed from as far away as the Black Lands. So vast was its power that the air around it shimmered. Lightning called forth from the clouds forked down to shatter against that terrible spire, wielding the might of the heavens against the vile power of the Netherworld. The very air was charged, the odor of it sickly sweet.

Aidan breathed in deeply, relishing the scent, savoring the sight of his creation with a feeling akin to rapture as he strode out into the luminous glow of the square. Against that glowing column, his form looked nothing more than a ghostly black shadow, though one with deadly purpose. His brother's sword rode at his back, still sheathed in Meiran's blood. He hadn't bothered to wipe the blade clean. He was yet hoping to give it back to its owner.

He walked toward the heart of the square, stopping yet fifty paces away from the brilliant spire of light. Aidan narrowed his eyes, finding it impossible to stare directly at the column. He waited almost casually, hands clasped behind his back, as lurid shadows danced behind him on the pavement. In the distance, the melancholy toll of a single bell rang out across the city. Aidan stared harder at the gateway, silently willing something to happen.

Eight shapes emerged from the glowing pillar, dark forms spreading out away from the gateway in a widening circle toward the eight points of the compass. Aidan squinted, trying to put features to the three figures approaching his own position. It was impossible at first; the shapes were only moving darkness eclipsed by the brilliant light.

Gradually, details began to emerge. As they neared, the figures resolved into human shapes that drew slowly out of shadow. The vague features yielded identity only slowly. It was not until the first was standing right in front of him that Aidan was able to put a name to the face no human alive had ever seen.

Zavier Renquist stopped only feet away, dark eyes considering him with sinister intensity. The tainted light of the gateway cast harsh shadows across the chiseled angles of his face. He wore his long brown hair pulled back in a manner that exaggerated the cruel effect of his narrow eyes and hawk-like nose. In life, Renquist had been the most distinguished Prime Warden to ever exist, his greatness tempered only by the greatness of his betrayal.

The histories all gave Renquist almost sole credit for the fall of Bryn Calazar, the ancient capital of Caladorn. It was Renquist's treachery that had precipitated the fall of Caladorn itself, propelling the northern empire into the darkening spiral that had eventually ended with the complete desecration of the land. In the years after, the name Caladorn had faded, only half-remembered by scholars and the wise. Most people now knew it only as the Black Lands.

But Zavier Renquist was a thousand years dead. The man now standing before Aidan was one of the Eight Servants of Xerys, God of Chaos and Lord of the Netherworld. In life, Renquist had allied himself with the forces of evil. Upon his death, he had become a true demon.

Other dark shapes drifted toward him. A man and a woman approached first. The man wore a felt hat and was garbed in a black long coat, though the fabric was tailored in a cut Aidan had never seen before.

The woman had dark skin and darker hair that flowed down her back to her waist. At her side paced two creatures that looked like enormous wolfhounds with glowing green eyes, their feet padding silently across the stone.

Aidan had no idea who the man was. Accounts of the Eight were often muddled and vague. But he knew the woman to be Myria Anassis, an ancient Querer who had sworn her allegiance to Xerys before the fall of Bryn Calazar. Her pets were not mere dogs. They were thanacrysts, creatures that fed solely on the life force of a mage. Aidan had always thought them but a figment of legend.

More dark shapes approached, moving silently around the turbulent green column. A bearded, red-haired man holding a silver morning star drew up to stand beside Renquist. Aidan took him to be Byron Connel, the Battlemage who had single-handedly destroyed Caladorn's resistance. The tall, dark-haired man with a red scar bisecting his face must be Cyrus Krane, an ancient Prime Warden of Aerysius who had turned rabid.

Another woman approached with platinum hair that glowed a pasty green in the light of the gateway, a demon-hound jogging at her side. Her wide, pale eyes lent her a sense of innocence that masked the viciousness of her nature. Aidan was not fooled; Arden Hannah had deceived the entire Assembly of Bryn Calazar, helping Renquist lead them to their doom. There were two others, a man and a woman in dark blue robes, who Aidan did not know. They halted to stand before him with the rest, silently contemplating him in the brilliant glow of the gateway.

It was Zavier Renquist who addressed him. "Your efforts have been met with gratitude by our Master. He is well-pleased. In exchange for unsealing the Well of Tears, Xerys commits to you the services of the Eight. We are yours to command, until the purpose of our summoning is fulfilled."

Aidan couldn't help the smile that formed on his lips. He was trembling with a pride and pleasure too great to be physically contained. But the distant sound of a tolling bell reminded him that he must not tarry long savoring his success. Time was running short. A greater work lay yet before him, and there was much to do.

"I command you to help me take Aerysius," he said.

Renquist simply nodded, as though the ancient Prime Warden had expected no less.

"The hour is late, and most of the Masters are asleep in the Spire of the Hall. They will only now be stirring from their beds and rushing to heed the warning bells. I need your assistance so I can use the Circle of Convergence. Hold the doors of the Hall so that my work may progress unimpeded."

Arden Hannah's eyes had been growing wider as Aidan revealed the perfection of his plans. He was certain she recognized the inspiration behind them; Aidan had derived most of his ideas from what he'd read of their own treachery.

"Then let us be about it," Zavier Renquist said, turning away. "Cyrus, I believe your friends might come in handy. Why don't you bring some along?"

Cyrus Krane grinned malevolently. Aidan felt an unnerving sensation grip the pit of his stomach. All around the square, pools of shadow emerged from the ground, melting upward to coalesce into black, nebulous shapes that vaguely resembled human forms. Aidan held his breath as he watched the dark forms solidify into a host of necrators akin to the first two he had raised. The terror they normally inspired didn't affect him at all; his bargain with darkness rendered him immune to their influence.

Most of the necrators glided soundlessly off into the night, slipping away into the shadows of the city. They would be about their own dark business, working their sinister purpose while he accomplished his own in the Hall of the Watchers.

Aidan made his way around the glowing pillar of light toward the Hall, the terror of the night gliding silently behind in the wake of his footfalls.

Darien could only stare at the green column of light that challenged the black dome of the heavens. Lightning crackled all around the pillar, stabbing at it from the sky as if all of the gods were assembled together in the clouds, marshaling their greatest might against it. From where he stood on the temple steps, he could see the Hall of the Watchers rising behind it in the square. Both the Hall and the arches in front of it were bathed in the same green light. A bell clanged in the distance, the sound of its toll a dire warning.

He was not alone on the temple steps. His mother stood beside him, staring at the towering atrocity in the sky. The other mages had gathered around them, all gaping upward.

The terrible urgency of the spear of light had driven them out into the darkness of the night, the clamor of the warning bells speeding their feet. Until they had halted on the temple steps, frozen by the dazzling abomination in the sky.

"By all the gods," someone whispered behind him.

But the gods had little to do with it. Someone had opened the Well of Tears, the ancient portal to the Netherworld that existed somewhere beneath the city—probably right under the square, judging by the location of the column.

How anyone could do that—*why* anyone would—was utterly beyond him. It had to have been a mage, one of their own number. Someone Darien probably knew. But a betrayal of such magnitude was unimaginable. He couldn't think of one person who could possibly harbor that degree of malice inside. It was unthinkable.

But if the Well of Tears had been unsealed, then the gateway to the Netherworld was open as well. It didn't matter who had accomplished the act. The forces of Chaos were now the impetus that drove that towering pillar of energy, thrusting it upward into the sky. The terror of the night would be unleashed into the heart of Aerysius. As the peal of the warning bells rang out across the darkness, Darien realized his home was under imminent attack.

"What do we do?" he asked, the sound of his voice lost somewhere in his throat. He was thinking of Meiran, wondering where she could possibly be.

"We must reach the circle." His mother's voice was shaking. "It's the only way. The Circle of Convergence was used once before to seal the Well of Tears. There must be a way to do it again."

"The last time the Well was sealed, it was open only in this world," said Master Finneus Corlan. "That's not the case this time. Before, we confronted but a mere seepage of the Netherworld's taint. The gateway now stands fully open before us. The Circle of Convergence is not the answer."

"Then what is?" the Prime Warden demanded.

"The Well must be sealed from both sides," insisted Master Lynnea. "We must split up. According to *A Treatise on the Well of Tears,* there is only one way to seal it completely: we must find the Well and deactivate the rune sequence. Then one of our Grand Masters must enter the gateway itself. It must be someone of at least fourth tier. The Well demands a sacrifice—"

"What are you saying?" Emelda snapped, cutting her off.

Master Lynnea blinked.

Finneus placed a soothing hand on the woman's shoulder. "What my esteemed colleague is trying to say, Prime Warden, is that in order to seal the Well of Tears, one of our two Grand Masters will have to enter the gateway. The mending of the seal in the Netherworld requires a sacrifice."

Darien glanced from one face to the other as his mother pondered her options. He had no desire to volunteer. He had experienced the wonder of Transference only minutes before. He'd not even had a chance to test his newfound strength.

His eyes found Grand Master Tyrius Flynn, who stood gazing up at the tall pillar of light. The man had years of experience working with magic and was vastly more prepared to face the challenges that might confront them. Darien felt his resolve solidify, knowing he should be the one to volunteer.

"I'll go down to the gateway," Tyrius announced into the night. "The only thing I ask is for a couple of good friends to come along and help me on my way." He turned to Darien. "But first I want to hear you swear the Oath of Harmony."

Darien found himself unable to look the Grand Master in the eyes. The old man had just saved his life, and knew it. What Tyrius was really asking was an easy settlement for any debt Darien might believe he owed him.

Thinking of it that way made saying the Oath an easy thing, despite his reservations. As Darien uttered the ancient phrases, they seemed to flow from his mouth of their own accord, requiring no conscious thought. He stared into Tyrius' eyes the whole while he spoke, silently admiring the old man's iron courage.

"I swear to live in harmony with all of creation,
To use my gift with temperance and wisdom;
Always to heal and never to harm,
Or my life will be rightfully forfeit."

Tyrius lay his hand on Darien's shoulder in a gesture of compassion. Then he departed, taking with him Masters Lynnea and Finneus.

The downpour had stopped. The night had become crisp and chill, but for the glowing column of energy and the lightning that licked against it. Everything around them had taken on its sickly hue, and the entire city looked otherworldly and empty. To Darien, Aerysius resembled what he imagined the Netherworld must look like: devoid of life, light, and color.

He followed in the wake of the small company that went down from the temple steps. They wound their way across a terrace and out over the narrow arch of a sky bridge that spanned the gap between the terrace and the tower of an adjacent building. As they crossed the bridge, Darien had an unimpeded view of the Hall of the Watchers, lustrous in the reflected light.

The bridge he stood on suddenly jolted as a tremor passed through the air. It was followed shortly by another. And another. The disturbances in the air were visible, coming at them in expanding, concentric rings with a focus far below in the Hall of the Watchers.

Darien didn't need anyone to explain to him what he was witnessing. Aerysius' Circle of Convergence was being put into play with malicious intent. The expanding rings of compressed air were the prelude to a structural resonance.

Darien felt his whole body shudder every time a wave of

energy passed through him. And the waves kept increasing, coming faster and harder, until it was all he could do to remain standing.

He had to get his mother off the bridge.

The other mages stood as if rooted, staring down at the disturbances coming from the Hall. Darien pushed his way through them and grabbed his mother by the arm, wrenching her into motion. He could feel the bridge shuddering beneath his feet, the rhythmic vibrations increasing in frequency.

As he neared the end of the bridge, the whole structure shivered and gave way beneath his feet. Darien threw himself forward, clenching his mother's arm in a two-handed grip.

The bridge crumbled and fell, Emelda and the others falling with it. Darien spilled onto the floor of a balcony, barely managing to retain his hold on his mother as her body slapped hard against the side of the building and hung swaying in his grasp.

Darien pulled, using all the strength he possessed to drag her up and over the edge. His mother lay there beside him, panting, her eyes staring vacantly up into the sky.

The resonance was still driving the air before it. Darien pushed himself to his feet, helping his mother up after him. The air itself seemed solidified. It jarred against him, knocking him with the force of breaking ocean waves.

He staggered, trying to keep his feet, while the building they stood on swayed with the rhythms of the merciless waves. Emelda almost fell, catching herself against him as Darien struggled to keep them both standing.

From far below, a loud noise rose from the Hall of the Watchers. The very stones of the ancient structure were starting to sing as they reached their breaking point. The tone quavered in the air like a grace note with each passing ripple of energy.

"Oh, by the gods, Darien," his mother moaned into his chest.

He held her, staggering, as below the note swelled to a wailing threnody. The Hall of the Watchers shuddered, the air filled with the nerve-grating noise of stone grinding against stone. And then, so very slowly, the spire of the Hall came crashing down.

The top caved in first with a gushing blast of dust and debris, the deafening roar of it ripping through the night, trembling the very mountain.

One wall of the Spire was left halfway standing, almost completely obscured by a swirling cloud of dust. Another tremor shook the structure, and the wall leaned over slowly. Then it crumbled, raining enormous chunks of rock down onto the roof of the dome. The Hall of the Watchers imploded violently. Pillars of dust were hurled into the gaping sky, illuminated by the lambent glow of the column of power.

Darien stared open-mouthed at the scene of devastation as though looking into the face of apocalypse. A chilling numbness overcame him, dampening his senses until even sound seemed to fade into obscurity. Timeless seconds crept by, and he was aware of none of them. The only thing he could do was stare out at the billowing clouds of dust as his mind grappled with the enormity of the devastation.

Aerysius was gone, though most of its structures yet remained standing. But the Hall of the Watchers was the heart of the city, and it had been ripped clean away, excised from the body. Darien didn't know how many of his brethren had died in the Hall, but he knew with a certainty that it must have been many. No one moved in the ruins of the square.

He remembered Masters Tyrius, Lynnea and Finneus, who had probably been down there somewhere. And the mages who had come with them in search of the Well were gone, their bodies fallen to the street many stories below. As far as he knew, his mother and himself could well be the only surviving mages left in all the world.

Meiran.

The thought ripped through him with the force of a death blow, the pain of it almost doubling him over. Darien's eyes scoured the ruins below until his vision blurred. But there was no movement in the scattered rubble, no sign of life. Only undulating clouds of dust swirled over the shattered remains of his home. The soaring structure of the Hall of the Watchers had been reduced to an enormous mass grave, the mounds of broken stone an immense burial cairn.

If Meiran had been there, then she was dead.

"Aidan."

The sound of his mother's trembling voice seemed to come from another world. Instantly, sound and substance came rushing back. Darien blinked as if waking from a nightmare, a cold sweat breaking out all over his body. The air was thick with rising dust, and his vision swam with tears he was too numb to shed. He wiped a hand across his eyes, restoring his sight. Then he turned to look at his mother's face.

Emelda stared at him with eyes wide with shock, shaking her head as her mouth stretched into a tight grimace of anguish. He took her into his arms, holding her against his chest as her body shook with spasms of grief.

Aidan had always been her favorite. Darien wondered why he could not summon even a fledgling tear over his brother's death. Perhaps he was past tears, past the ability to grieve.

With a last, long look at the ruins of the Hall, Darien forced himself to turn away from the sight. Delay now might cost them everything. They had to flee the city, but Darien doubted the wood platform would ever make the trip again to the valley floor.

"Mother," he whispered, gently pulling away. "We need to flee. Down the mountain. I know there's a way, but you've never told me. If it's some secret, I don't think it matters anymore."

Emelda blinked at him. Her face was a mess, all crusted in grime and smudged with tears. But deep within her eyes stirred a flicker of the strength he was used to. It was the same, innate strength that moved within himself.

"We must reach the Temple of Isap." Her gaze darted toward the southeastern part of the city, and Darien followed her stare. The sun would be rising eventually in that direction, but not for a while yet. There was definitely a chance the two of them could reach the temple if they kept low enough and made good speed.

But confusion continued to nettle him. It was another route he'd been considering. Placing his hands on his mother's shoulders, he pressed, "I don't understand. How can the priests of Death help us escape down the mountain?"

"The Catacombs," his mother whispered, shivering as if she had just revealed some dire secret. She probably had. "The Catacombs of Death exist partly in the Atrament. Distance and time have no meaning there. We can make use of the Catacombs to escape and go anywhere we like."

Darien frowned in disbelief. It seemed unimaginable that the Temple of Death could have harbored a secret of that magnitude for so long. If these Catacombs truly existed, then the priesthood of Death had found a wonder that would rival even the greatest works of the Hall.

"Then we must go," he agreed, feeling a pressing sense of urgency. He squeezed her shoulders. She was bleeding from cuts and scrapes she'd acquired during her fall from the bridge.

So Darien did what he had been trained to do all his life. He closed his eyes and reached within. Only, this time, it was different. Whenever he'd tried this same mental exercise in practice, there had always been just emptiness inside. But now his mind grasped something tangible. He could feel the song of the magic field as never before, soaring inside him like a symphony. He touched it, feeling it conform easily to his will, as though it were the most natural thing he had ever done in his life.

When he opened his eyes, he saw that his mother's injuries were healed. She looked renewed, invigorated. Her face was swept clean of grime, the torn fabric of her dress mended. She looked hale. And very much full of pride.

"Thank you," she said simply.

He took her by the hand and led her off the balcony into the shadows of the building. Emelda walked at his side down long flights of stairs and out into the empty street. They continued down and off the terrace, working their way eastward toward the bottom of the city. The night air was thick, filled with acrid smoke and choking dust.

The streets were littered with debris that had fallen from the heights. They often found themselves skirting a pile of rubble, as collapsed parts of buildings and bridges impeded almost every step. There were few people alive in the city. It was like walking in a world of the dead under the glow of that filthy green light. Every so often, the silence was pierced by distant screams.

They had been traveling for over an hour when Darien found himself confronted by an obstacle that looked impossible to cross or go around. An entire building had fallen across the road, cutting them off from the bridge on the other side.

They needed to reach that bridge. They were already at the lowest reaches of the city, at a split in the enormous rock face where the cliff bowed inward, creating a vertical crevice that cut deep into the sheer rock wall. The bridge that spanned the gap arched over a drop of thousands of feet. There was nothing but air below it, all the way down the sheer precipice to the valley floor.

A wolf howled, the sound eerie and mournful. The noise made Darien shiver with a feeling of dread; there were no wolves in all of Aerysius.

Something skirted the edge of his vision. It looked like a shadow moving on the far side of the road. But when he turned toward it, there was nothing there. Frowning, he rubbed his eyes as he pondered the situation. The only way to the bridge was up and over that wall of rubble.

So they climbed.

The going was slow, as the debris had a way of shifting underfoot. Darien let his mother go before him, picking out her own path as he trailed behind, steadying the blocks that threatened to slip out from under them with the force of his mind.

The more he exercised his power, the more he became accustomed to it. It was simply another extension of himself, just like his sword. He handled it expertly; he had trained for this all his life.

A block of rubble shifted overhead. Instantly, an avalanche of stone and marble started to slide down on top of them. Darien simply deflected the shower of debris, hardly sparing it a thought. He saw his mother turn to stare at him with respect in her eyes. Though Prime Warden, Emelda Lauchlin was still only first tier.

Darien knew why his mother had waited so long to arrange his Raising. She had been waiting for just the right time, when he could receive the Transference from an especially strong Grand Master. Ezras had contained five times the amount of power in his frail old body as Emelda was capable of wielding. It was possible she was allowing Darien to stabilize the larger pieces of rock by himself, to give him practice working with his newfound strength. Yet, he couldn't help admitting, it was also possible she couldn't do it herself.

They reached the top of the rubble and gradually worked their way down the other side. In the distance, another wolf-like cry broke the silence of the night. The sound chilled Darien's blood. He hurried his mother off the rubble and started toward the bridge.

A scraping sound from behind them made him stop. Whirling, Darien reached for the hilt of his sword and grasped only air.

A lone man was coming toward them from the other side of the street, black cloak rippling about him as he moved, face lost in shadow.

Darien released the breath he hadn't realized he'd been holding. He stood waiting for the man to approach. His mother stood at his side, looking at the newcomer with an expression of vibrant hope.

Darien was skeptical. At least there was someone else alive in the night besides themselves. He had the feeling that his mother was studying the shadows of the approaching face for traces of familiar features. She was hoping it was Aidan, he suspected, miraculously saved from the catastrophe of the Hall. Darien just hoped it was someone useful.

When the figure stepped out of shadow, his eyes widened in surprise. His mother drew in a sharp gasp and immediately started forward. Darien thrust out his hand and held her back.

She was right. It *was* Aidan.

But there was something very different about his brother.

Aidan Lauchlin halted in the middle of the street, regarding them with a narrow blue stare that somehow seemed more arrogant than usual, supremely more confident. Darien frowned, trying to put a finger on exactly what seemed so wrong. It was something subtle, something just not right. His mother pulled against his hold on her arm, struggling to free herself and rush toward the son she had thought was lost. But Darien tightened his grip, refusing her.

Then he saw it: Aidan was wearing his sword.

Darien could think of absolutely no good reason in the world why his brother would be carrying his own weapon. A few explanations drifted across his mind, but Darien rejected them all, until the only explanation left was one too terrible to consider.

But it fit. Horribly, it made a sinister kind of sense. Like Meiran, Aidan had also missed his Raising.

"What's the matter with you?" Emelda spat at him, tugging her arm in an effort to release his grip. Darien only held on more firmly.

"He opened the Well of Tears," he said, eyes only for Aidan as he searched the shadowy face before him for confirmation of his words. But there was no reaction on his brother's face. Aidan just continued to stare at him, eyes calm and arrogant.

Darien wished his brother would do something, anything. Shout in denial, rain him with curses, lash out with the scathing sarcasm Darien always found so infuriating. Anything but his silence.

His brother's complete lack of response confirmed Darien's worst fear.

A confident smile spread slowly on Aidan's lips. Darien reached within for the magic field, the action now almost a reflex. Then he stopped himself, recalling in horror his Oath to Tyrius Flynn. *Never to harm.* The words rang bitterly within the confines of his head, along with his plea to his mother: *Unbind the Sentinels.*

He was not Unbound.

He had uttered his Oath, the Oath he had already chosen not to keep. But something had changed in him. Darien didn't know if it was his experience with Grand Master Ezras or perhaps even Tyrius Flynn. Maybe it was the destruction of the home he had always taken for granted, or witnessing Aerysius's greatness being erased from the world.

Darien realized he would keep that Oath. Gerald Lauchlin had kept it to a bitter grave. His son could do no less.

Dimly, on the edge of his vision, he saw five dark shapes approaching. They looked like nebulous silhouettes of mist gliding toward him from out of the shadows of the street. A sickening horror rose inside him, a harrowing chill that was appalling. The air around him thickened until it was hard to even breathe.

Darien felt his mother's arm grow cold in his grasp. He knew what those black forms were, had read about them in texts, heard them named in the darkest tales and myths. He knew their only chance was to run. The touch of a necrator was not death; it was something very much worse.

Darien spun his mother around, propelling her toward the bridge. He started after her, but his foot caught in a crack in the street. He stumbled, thrusting his arms out as he fell to the ground. He caught himself with the heels of his hands and rolled, barely avoiding the necrator that melted up from the street in the exact place he'd landed.

Gaining his feet, Darien glanced behind to see his mother clearing the end of the bridge. It exploded behind her. Shards of broken stone flew toward him, and he flung his arms up to shield his face. He groped desperately for the power within, but there was nothing there.

Darien froze in the steel grip of the starkest terror he'd ever known in his life. It wrenched up from his stomach, clenching his throat, as all of the blood seemed to rush out of his head at once. He retained enough of himself to recognize the feeling for what it was: not a true emotion but, rather, the awful influence of the necrator that stood like a black wraith in front of him.

He forced his legs to move, backing away from it, stumbling over debris.

His brother walked casually toward him, a hand lifting the baldric that held Darien's sword over his head. Aidan flung the sword at him, scabbard and all. It slid toward him across the pavement, bumping along, coming to a rest at his feet. Darien reached down to retrieve it, never taking his eyes from the necrator. The other four were approaching as well. He gripped the scabbard in his right hand, the trembling fingers of his left hand closing around the hilt of the blade.

"Aren't you wondering who helped me unseal the Well of Tears?" Aidan asked, striding toward him. He stopped perhaps ten paces away, as though hesitant to come too close to the necrators.

Darien was too distracted to respond. The five dark shapes in front of him were pressing him slowly backward toward the edge of the cliff. And not just any cliff. He knew it wasn't just a simple fall to another terrace. His death wasn't going to be that clean.

Aidan took another step toward him. "I killed Meiran. It's her blood that stains your sword."

Darien looked down at the blade in its scabbard, not daring to bare the steel. It would only confirm what he already knew had to be true. Meiran had not been there at his Raising. That should have been enough to tell him something was horribly wrong.

The rage and pain that consumed him was overwhelming, a harrowing fury that swept aside every other emotion, burying him under a breaking tidal wave of wrath and grief. He almost lashed out with his mind, was on the brink of focusing his rage into a fiery spear of vengeance.

It wasn't his Oath that held him back.

It was the necrators. Three of them glided forward, their vile influence keeping his power in check.

"It won't hurt so very much," Aidan promised, moving toward him. "I've had much practice tonight. I'll even make it quick. Come, Brother."

Darien took a step back from him. And another. The necrators glided smoothly after him, maintaining their distance. Aidan strode between them as Darien looked around for anything he could use to defend himself.

There was nothing. His sword was useless against another mage, and the song of the magic field was silent inside him. There was only Aidan and the necrators, or the cliff. The choice was easy to make. Carrying out that decision, now...that was hard.

But knowing Meiran waited for him made it a little easier. He knew she would be there, somewhere in the distances that span eternity.

Darien had backed up as far as he could against the edge of the cliff. There was nowhere else to go. He held his gaze locked with his brother's eyes as he took one last step off the edge of the precipice.

Chapter Four
The Price of an Oath

Aerysius, The Rhen

Emelda Lauchlin landed roughly on the other side of the gaping chasm. Pushing herself up off the ground, she watched helplessly as her son surrendered himself to the mountain's sheer face.

There was nothing she could do.

She watched him go.

Emelda screamed Darien's name, reaching out with her mind across the distance between them—too little, too late. She collapsed forward, arms hugging her chest. A wail of mortal grief tore from the depths of her soul.

First Gerald, and now their son. It was too much to bear. And Aidan…Darien said it was Aidan who'd opened the Well of Tears. Emelda hadn't believed him at the time. Now, she did. Aidan was her child, her firstborn. He had opened the Well, destroyed the Hall of the Watchers, slain his only brother, and brought Aerysius to its knees. She couldn't understand, any more than she could stop the waves of anguish threatening to sweep her away in a harrowing current of despair.

And now he was coming for her.

Emelda watched through a blur of tears as delicate strands of energy twined across the yawning mouth of the crevice where the stone bridge had been only moments before. She gaped in shock at the span of solid light that formed, woven from silver filaments of magic. It was impossible. Such an act was well beyond the talents of even the mightiest Grand Master.

Emelda shuddered as her son mounted that glimmering span

and moved toward her, flanked by five living shadows that flowed soundlessly after him. Part of her wanted to run, but she couldn't summon the strength to do more than draw breath. A paralyzing fear crept up from her stomach, seizing the motion of her chest. The necrators moved past him, gliding swiftly toward her.

She took a trembling step backward and stumbled as Aidan stepped off the glowing bridge that shimmered out of existence just as quickly as it had appeared. She shuddered as his cold blue gaze fixed on her. There was nothing left of the son she knew in those terrible, piercing eyes. Fresh tears of horror ran down Emelda's cheeks as she shook her head in denial.

"Why?" she shrieked, backing away from the demon who used to be her son.

The malevolent sneer on his face was terrifying. He advanced toward her, shaking his head as if in disgust, then paused to consider her for a moment. In a voice she barely recognized, he said, "You're so pathetic, Mother."

The shock of the insult came as a hammer blow, driving the last bit of strength from her body. She moaned, covering her face with her hands and sobbing into them. That was all she could do. He advanced the last few steps toward her, reaching a hand up to caress her face.

She recoiled from the touch, backing away from him. "How *could* you? He was your *brother!*"

Aidan only chuckled. "You would be surprised at what I'm capable of."

Emelda whirled away from him, tears spraying from her cheeks as she sprinted in the direction of the ruined street. She didn't get far. Her body hit a solid wall of air and rebounded to the ground. She lay there, panting in the dust and dirt, staring up at the green-infected sky. Chest heaving, she saw him moving toward her again. Only, now, she knew there was nowhere to run. She was helpless. Her Oath prevented her from doing anything to protect herself. The dark presence of the necrators insured that she kept it.

She rolled onto her stomach, forcing herself to her knees and then to her feet. Fists balled at her sides, Emelda shrieked, "You destroyed the Hall! You killed *all of them!*"

Aidan shrugged offhandedly, turning his face toward the pillar of light and the ruins of the Hall of the Watchers. Ever so softly, he said, "They were weak. So was Darien…so are you."

His eyes locked on hers as he took a confident step toward her. "You've played at power nearly your entire life. Only, you have never truly understood its nature. I do.

"Always, you've taken me lightly. When it was time for my Raising, you chose a pitiful first-tier Master to initiate my Transference. You crippled me for life. But when it came time for my dear brother, you arranged it so he would receive the Transference from a strong Grand Master. Darien was a coward, and he was also a fool. He didn't lift a hand to save his own life—just see how he squandered that gift! I might have made use of that strength to create something truly meaningful. Instead, you chose to waste it on him. And just look what he accomplished with it."

"Darien kept his Oath!" Emelda shouted, filled with a sudden gush of pride tempered only by the grief she felt inside.

"Father kept his Oath as well," Aidan reminded her, "and see what came of it. My father *burned* because of your pathetic doctrine! He died *screaming,* tied to a stake. He begged you to Unbind the Sentinels before Meridan, but you denied him. Father's death was another meaningless waste. You've made a career out of sacrificing our family's blood in the name of righteousness."

He was lecturing *her* about sacrificing the blood of their family? Aidan blamed her for Gerald's death, but even that explanation didn't suffice. Nothing could come close to justifying the atrocities he had committed in that single, terrible night.

Darien's words came back to torment her: *Unbind the Sentinels.* Gerald's words. Uttered just before he had left her for Meridan by the Sea. Her husband had martyred himself to uphold a vow he didn't believe in, only because she had told him it was the right thing to do. Now their son had chosen to do the same. Could Aidan possibly be right? Was it really all her fault?

She knew that couldn't be true. She was not wrong. And that still didn't explain why Aidan had committed such heinous acts. He was deranged. There was no other explanation. And he was advancing toward her once again.

Emelda glanced at the cliff, knowing there was nowhere else to run. Darien had chosen to make an end on the rocks so far below. Perhaps she could do the same. It seemed fitting. The fall would be terrible, but at least death would come instantly.

Emelda dismissed the thought. She didn't have that kind of strength. Aidan was right; she was weak. The cliff was not an option.

He regarded her suspiciously. Predator-like, he stalked the short distance toward her, fixing her with the malevolent intensity of his gaze.

She allowed his approach. There was nothing left for her to do. But as he reached out for her, Emelda realized she was not yet ready to end her life. Tears of panic welled in her eyes as a shiver ran through her body. Aidan's hand froze an inch away from her cheek, a hungering smile on his lips.

She had wanted a cleaner death, something she could face with the dignity befitting a Prime Warden of Aerysius. But she was warden of nothing, and there was no dignity in this end. Emelda couldn't stop the tears that flowed down her cheeks, couldn't hide the despair and terror in her heart. The touch of Aidan's hand on her face was not comforting. It felt soiled, like a clod of dirt torn up from a grave. Emelda closed her eyes, knowing exactly what was coming.

A stabbing slap of air exploded between them.

Emelda flew backward as Aidan was hurtled in the opposite direction. Strong arms wrapped themselves around her and hauled her toward the street. She willed her legs into motion, stumbling after the black-cloaked man who had saved her life.

They ran through the crumbled streets of Aerysius, up a flight of broken stairs. The green light of the gateway was not enough to repel the shadows, and Emelda had no idea who it was she followed in that wild flight. It wasn't until he pulled her into the dim light of an archway that he turned around enough for her to catch a glimpse of his face.

At first, she'd imagined it was Darien, miraculously alive and hale enough to save her. But the features she encountered were completely familiar and yet utterly forgotten. Tyrius Flynn grabbed her shoulders and shook her until she regained her senses enough to realize she was still under the appalling influence of the necrators.

Emelda screamed. As she did, Tyrius clamped a hand over her mouth, muffling the sound. She kept screaming into his hand, over and over again, sucking breath in through her nostrils and wailing until there was only emptiness left inside. She collapsed into his arms, weeping helplessly.

"Emelda."

The sound of her name brought her back from the edge. She gazed up into the comforting brown depths of the Grand Master's eyes, knowing her old friend had now saved her twice.

"It—it was Aidan," she stammered. "He opened the Well of Tears. He killed Darien."

"I saw."

Tyrius' eyes were full of sympathy. She collapsed into his arms, pouring out her anguish into the soft folds of his cloak. Her body shook as he wrapped his arms around her, drawing her head against his chest.

"We cannot stay here, Emelda."

She didn't want to run anymore. She threw her head back, lips constricting against her teeth. But the scream she felt in her heart was stillborn; she knew he was right. Collecting herself, she pulled away from his embrace.

"Where are Lynnea and Finneus?"

Tyrius shook his head. "They're dead, the both of them. We came across a darkmage down by the Citadel. Emelda, Aidan is not alone. The Eight walk abroad again. There are vile beasts ranging all over the city and more necrators than I ever knew existed in the world."

"More must have come through the gateway. Tyrius, we were trying to reach the Temple of Isap. The Catacombs—"

"Yes," the Sentinel breathed, eyes widening. But then his brow furrowed, and he paused, considering. "The temple is only a short distance from here. But the journey will be perilous."

"Surely not more perilous than staying here," Emelda insisted. "And you're stronger now, besides. Lynnea and Finneus were both only Masters, but their combined legacies must have doubled your strength."

Tyrius shook his head, a pained look in his eyes. "I was afraid to do more than receive the Transference from Lynnea. I'd be fifth tier now, if such rankings mattered anymore. I deeply fear, however, that you and I are the only mages left alive in the world."

"Don't forget Aidan," she reminded him, shuddering. Emelda had no idea how much her son had managed to amplify his strength in the Hall of the Watchers. Judging by the bridge of power she had witnessed him create, Aidan was easily as strong as any two or three Grand Masters combined. Melding light into such a solid state, even in minuscule amounts, was one of the most difficult acts any mage could perform. It strained the boundaries of Natural Law too far.

"Oh, I'm not forgetting him," Tyrius growled. "If it weren't for my Oath, I'd have thrown a lot more than a ripple of air his way." The look on her face made him moderate his tone. "I'm sorry, Emelda. I know he's your child."

"He is not the child I bore." Emelda's voice trembled. "The son I birthed is dead. Both of my sons are dead." She could feel the tears trying to come back again.

Below her in the street, she saw a fleeting glimmer of light. Startled, Emelda glanced back to Tyrius. The gray-haired Sentinel took a step back, staring down at the ruined and empty street.

"What is it?" Emelda gasped.

Tyrius didn't answer. Another flicker rippled across the ground below them, disappearing almost instantly. Immediately, Tyrius was in motion, sprinting inside the partially collapsed building. Emelda followed as quickly as she could around shattered blocks and chunks of plaster that had fallen from the ceiling. It was dark within. Without a thought, she produced a soft glow of magelight that pushed away the shadows.

"Don't!" Tyrius growled.

She let the magelight collapse back into darkness, silently berating herself. Any use of the field sent ripples out into the surrounding pattern that could be detected even at a distance. She had given them away by her own stupidity. The necrators would be coming.

"We must flee!" Tyrius took her by the arm.

He led her down a littered hallway and around a corner. There, they were forced to pull up short. Before them, the walls and ceiling had collapsed entirely, blocking any chance of escape in that direction. Half a wooden staircase swayed overhead, the lower half ripped clean away. Part of the ceiling dangled precariously, looking like it could break off and fall at any time.

Growling like a caged bear, Tyrius swung her around with a steel grip, forcing her back into the hallway. He started forward, Emelda running to keep up with him. At last he halted, wrenching open a jammed door and ushering her out into the merciful light of daybreak.

She glanced around anxiously. They were in a courtyard bordered on both sides by solid rock walls. The rear of the courtyard was contained by a cliff that climbed upward to the next terrace. They were trapped.

Beside her, the old Sentinel closed his eyes and uttered a protracted sigh. Then he turned away from her, fixing his narrow gaze on the wall to their left.

"Get down," he said. He grasped her by the shoulders and pushed her to the ground.

Emelda covered her head as the wall erupted in an explosion of stone that rained down all around, littering the courtyard. When she looked up again, she saw that Tyrius had razed half the wall, the edges black and smoldering around the rupture.

"Well, if that doesn't point out right where we are, then I might as well send up a signal beacon." As he turned back toward the building behind them, Tyrius added, "I don't think a beacon will be necessary."

Behind them, a shadow fell across the threshold of the

doorway. Only, Emelda knew by the now-familiar sense of dread that it was no true shadow.

This time, she ran first. Toward the ruins of the wall, up and over the rubble, stumbling as her foot lodged between two blocks. Frantically, she tried to wrench her ankle free.

She fumbled through the terror in her mind, straining to hear the song of the magic field. But the necrator was too close, its dark influence too great. And it was gliding closer by the second. Emelda whimpered, tugging at her leg with both hands.

Then Tyrius was beside her, stooping down to pry at the stones with all his strength. One of the rocks shifted just a fraction. It was enough. Emelda jerked her foot clear and lurched to her feet as a lancing pain stabbed up her leg. She screamed.

Tyrius carried her, stumbling across another courtyard and into the building beyond as the necrators pursued. A flicker of light flowed behind them, writhing across the ground like a mass of glistening snakes.

Tyrius staggered, almost falling across the threshold of the next structure. He carried her up a winding staircase to the third level, only then pausing to set her down on the landing and catch his breath.

From below them came a strange scraping noise, like chains dragging on stone.

Emelda looked down at her ankle and choked back a groan. It was bleeding, her foot twisted at an unnatural angle. She couldn't heal it. She'd never learned and, besides, she didn't have the strength. But Tyrius pressed his hand against her foot, sending a wave of healing energy through her.

Emelda felt a sensation like a rush of cold water running up her leg. She watched her ankle straighten, the bone mending before her eyes. The pain vanished completely, as though it had never existed at all.

The scraping noises were louder, coming toward them up the stairs. Emelda pushed herself to her feet. Tyrius entwined his fingers with hers as he led her forward once more, up another two flights to a level high above the street. They followed a short hallway to an outside balcony, Tyrius leading her by the hand back out into the open air.

The balcony looked over the courtyard they had crossed five stories below. It jutted out from the building, extending to meet the mountain's stone face. An opening in the rail against the cliff led to a narrow stairway carved into the rock itself. The steps switchbacked up to the terrace above. Holding Tyrius' hand, Emelda mounted the narrow, treacherous steps.

There was no handrail to grasp, nothing to prevent a fall if she slipped. Her vision swam. She glanced down at the courtyard, which was a mistake. The palms of her hands broke out in sweat, the soles of her feet tingling. Tyrius steadied her, squeezing her hand reassuringly as he led her up the granite face.

Emelda turned just in time to see a bolt of fire lancing toward them from the ground. She winced as it impacted with the cliff above them, sending chips of stone raining down on their heads. She felt Tyrius' hand like an iron vice as another flaming spear shot toward them. Her eyes had only time to widen before it exploded in her face.

There was no heat, no impact. Emelda reached up and touched the skin of her cheek, amazed she was still alive.

Tyrius lowered his hand, and the brilliant shield he'd conjured in front of them disappeared. Emelda could only stare at him in open wonder. She was a Chancellor and had never been trained for anything like this. She kept forgetting Tyrius was a Sentinel and had seen the face of war many times in his life.

Below in the courtyard, a lone figure emerged from under the balcony. Emelda gasped. It was a woman. She was staring up at them, dark hair stirred by a breeze, her gown rippling about her. She was flanked by an enormous demon-hound with eyes that gleamed an unearthly light. The woman raised her arm, palm upward, and a small white flame appeared to dance in her hand. She smiled as she gazed upon it.

Tyrius raised his hand but then dropped it again. He jerked Emelda toward the last rise of steps, shouting, *"Run!"*

The flickering flame rose from the woman's hand and hovered for a moment in the air. Then it began spinning. It spun faster, swelling to a brilliant white sphere.

It shot toward them.

Tyrius hauled Emelda off her feet and pulled himself over the cliff's edge, lifting her bodily after him. Emelda got her legs over just in time as the spinning globe slammed into the side of the mountain beneath them. The ground heaved, and the air around them became like molten fire. Emelda covered her head, shoving her face against the dirt and holding her breath.

Beside her, through the fiery din, she could hear Tyrius screaming.

The screams ended abruptly, as though cut off short. Emelda was too afraid to open her eyes, too scared to move. She was still holding the Sentinel's hand, but the grip that had once felt like iron was now limp.

Slowly, the world stopped trembling. Emelda drew a ragged breath, choking on dirt and ashes and the very heat of the air that filled her lungs. She opened her eyes but saw nothing. Her vision swam, the world a disturbing haze.

A slight tingling sensation stirred within her hand, the hand that yet clasped Tyrius' limp fingers. The tingling grew, became a throbbing pressure that climbed up her arm and invaded her chest, spreading out to every fiber of her body.

Emelda gasped as recognition flooded into her, closing her eyes as she wheezed a moaning sigh. The warmth that flooded into her body was like ecstasy, but the sorrow that filled her heart made it seem more like anguish. She felt the conduit close, the last of Tyrius' sweet legacy absorbed into her shuddering body.

She rolled over and screamed. The power that raged within her was terrifying. Before, it had been like a flickering candle flame, glowing gently in the back of her mind. Now it blazed like a roaring firestorm. Emelda caught hold of it, finding herself almost swept away by the torrent of energy that raged within. She jerked her mind back, shuddering and faint.

Reluctantly, she turned to look at the body at her side. Tyrius was lying in a patch of dirt blackened to ash. Emelda covered her mouth with a clenched fist, choking back a strangled sob that still managed to escape anyway.

Tyrius was very much dead, although his flesh was still mostly intact. But his gaping mouth was charred, the sockets in his face empty. The boiling juice of his eyes ran down his blistered cheeks. By the look of it, he had been seared from the inside-out, probably when he had drawn in a mouthful of molten air to make that last, shuddering scream.

Emelda turned her head and vomited noisily in the dirt. When she thought she was done, her stomach spasmed again, and again, until there was only bile left to bring up. Wiping her face with the back of her hand, she rose, trembling, to her feet. She turned and stumbled away from the grotesque corpse, not wanting to ever, ever see it again.

Like Gerald and their son, Tyrius was now dead because of the Oath. The Oath she had told them all to keep.

Emelda wept silently as she picked her way through the empty streets. It seemed there was no one left in the ruined city but herself—no one alive, at any rate. Aerysius was now a city of the dead. Where had they all gone—the residents, the servants of the Hall? She crept around the still forms of fallen bodies, and once she stepped on a hand half-buried in a pile of debris.

There were fires up above on the heights. Thick, choking smoke billowed into the air. Aerysius was silent, the city bathed in a haunting light. And above, the green pillar yet spired, its wraithlike glow consuming even the dawn.

The Temple of Death was not far; Tyrius had been right. And it was intact, which was more than she'd dared hope. But Emelda gravely feared it would be as silent and empty as the rest of the city. She could think of no reason for the priests to have remained behind when they could have easily evacuated by way of the Catacombs. If they were already gone, then there was no hope. She was now sixth tier, but all of her dreadful strength would not help her navigate the Catacombs. For that, she would need the help of a priest. Or a very brave and clever priestess.

The temple door was shut and bolted from the inside. Emelda pounded on the heavy wood with both fists, then stepped back to gaze up at the walls. The temple was far from the largest building in the city. The followers of Death were not many. Most people usually honored the goddess only when they had to.

No one came, so Emelda picked up a brick and used it to bang even harder. She shouted up at the windows, calling for anyone who might hear her pleas.

At last, the temple door cracked open. A face looked out, but in the shadow of the doorway, Emelda couldn't see well enough to make out features. When the door opened a little wider, she realized she was looking into a face hidden behind a sheer veil of white, the trademark of a priestess of Death. The eyes looking at her through that translucent fabric were wide and dark, gently untroubled.

"Sanctuary!" Emelda cried, almost throwing herself into the arms of the priestess. The woman received her, ushering her across the threshold and bolting the door behind them. Emelda could hardly see through the tears of gratitude clouding her vision.

The interior of the temple was dim, lit only by a few tapers on tall iron candlesticks. There were only two windows above the door that admitted little light. But the shrine at the far end of the room was brilliantly lit by the combined flames of hundreds of glowing votive candles.

Emelda blinked, not understanding how there could possibly be so many. Then she realized: each candle represented a soul lost in the catastrophe that had destroyed Aerysius. Those candles had probably saved her life. The priestess had lingered behind instead of fleeing to safety, probably to offer those hundreds of tiny prayers. It was a valiant effort. Emelda turned back to the priestess with a new appreciation for the woman.

"I claim the right of Sanctuary," she announced, fighting to keep her voice steady. "I request passage through the Catacombs of Death, by right of the Temple's agreement with the Hall. I am Prime Warden Emelda Lauchlin. I demand my right of passage."

The woman blinked at her through the diaphanous white veil. She was striking, with dark auburn hair that flowed down her back. Her eyes gleamed with the bright spark of intelligence.

"That would explain why your candle refused to light," the priestess said, the sound of her voice soft and resonate. Emelda immediately recognized the lilting accent of Chamsbrey on her tongue.

"I am Naia Seleni, First Daughter of the Goddess Isap," the young woman informed her. "Perhaps you should sit a moment before we attempt the shadows of Death's Passage. The journey is not easy. I recommend we wait a bit."

Emelda doubted they had time to wait. But, too exhausted to argue, she allowed the priestess to guide her to a bench in front of the shrine. Emelda waited there as the woman retreated into the shadows of the temple.

As she sat, she allowed herself to consider the altar and its flickering flames. Looking at them, she wondered about the death each candle represented. How many had been lit for mages she had known and worked with all her life? Emelda stared harder, seeing each candle individually, allowing her gaze to drift gradually down one of the lines. She must not think of them collectively, she realized. Each candle added its own, distinctive light to the dance of flame, and each deserved singular consideration.

The priestess returned, carrying a chalice in her hands, the white gown she wore flowing behind her as she moved. The woman handed Emelda the chalice and waited while she drank deeply. The priestess accepted the empty cup, gazing at her from behind the glossy sheen of her veil.

"Would you care to offer a votive candle? I lit as many as I could, but I fear there are thousands more my prayers have neglected."

Emelda nodded, feeling the grief rise up again inside. She would light two candles: one for Darien and one for Tyrius. There were many more she would like to include in her prayers, but she knew the list would probably take days and fill many such shrines. She did not have that kind of time.

So she accepted a candle from the priestess and took a striker into her hand. Kneeling down before the shrine, Emelda decided the first prayer should be for Tyrius, who had died trying to save her life.

She depressed the striker, and the wick of the candle flared instantly to life: a bright golden flame that wavered gently.

Closing her eyes, Emelda whispered a soft, heartfelt prayer for the soul of her dear friend. Then she placed the votive candle on a shelf with the others, its single flame adding its light to the collective brilliance. A tear ran down Emelda's cheek as she withdrew her hand.

"Another?" the priestess offered.

Again, Emelda could only nod. She accepted Darien's candle, her fingers closing around the soft tallow. Her hand trembled as she depressed the striker. The first glowing spark missed the wick and floated to the floor, burning out long before it hit the stone. Emelda pursed her lips in concentration, desperately willing her hand to stop shaking. She squeezed the striker again.

This time the spark went right to the wick. A soft flame flared into being, glowing strongly. Then it immediately smoldered out.

Emelda sobbed in frustration. She tried again, but the candle refused to light. She started pumping the striker, producing spark after spark that rained down in a glowing shower to the stone floor of the shrine. She stopped only when she felt the woman's hand close around her own. Emelda looked up into the face behind the veil, her own eyes filled with tears.

"I don't understand," she cried, shaking her head. "Will the goddess not accept my prayers for my fallen son?"

The priestess looked down to regard the candle in her hand. "Try again."

Emelda squeezed the striker one last time. The spark wafted straight toward the wick of the small candle. The wick caught, the flame flickering only once before dying out again. The priestess nodded slightly, raising her gaze to look Emelda in the eye.

"The goddess accepts only prayers for the souls of the dead."

That meant nothing to Emelda. She shook her head again, weeping in frustration. In a voice quavering with suppressed grief, she whispered, "I don't understand."

The priestess' mouth turned upward in the faintest hint of a smile. In that comforting, resonate voice, she promised, "Your son's spirit yet lives."

Staring down at the unlit candle, Emelda almost choked in

disbelief. She looked up and searched the priestess' face, but she didn't see any sign that the woman was toying with her.

"How is that possible?" she whispered. "I saw him fall."

The priestess gently removed the candle from her grasp and, taking her by the hand, guided Emelda away from the shrine.

"The goddess never lies," she said in a soothing voice. "Place your trust in her."

Just then, the door to the temple jolted as something outside battered hard against it. Emelda whirled toward the sound and, to her horror, saw the temple door straining against the bar that held it.

"They're coming!" the priestess gasped.

She took Emelda by the arm and hurried her toward a staircase that led down into a dim basement below the altar. On the wall ahead were three doorways that opened to utter darkness. Emelda knew exactly where those passages led, and the thought of going into one made her shiver.

"Do you know the strictures?" the priestess gasped.

"I do!"

The sound of the temple door breaking open spurred Emelda forward. She bolted into the nearest doorway.

"Not that one!" the priestess cried, too late.

As her feet crossed the threshold, Emelda felt an unnatural shadow slip over her. The world lurched as though suddenly unstable, then quickly righted itself. She closed her eyes, fighting off a moment of panic. When she opened them again, Emelda found herself…somewhere else.

She was no longer in the temple.

A long, rock-encrusted passage lay ahead of her, lit by the soft glow of swirling magelight. She turned to look behind her for the priestess. Through a smoky screen of fog, she could see the temple basement. But it was empty.

The woman wasn't there.

Filled with trepidation, Emelda turned in a full circle, glancing about frantically.

"Prime Warden!"

The voice of the priestess echoed as though from a great

distance. There was an opening in the rock wall ahead. Another passage. Perhaps the priestess had entered the warrens through one of the other doors and was looking for her somewhere, wherever that passage led.

Emelda moved toward it, calling out, "Where are you?"

"Right here."

She turned around.

And froze.

The woman who had appeared behind her looked nothing like the priestess. She had platinum blonde hair and wore a chill, triumphant smile that was both beautiful and terrifying.

"You must be Prime Warden Emelda," she said, her smile deepening. "So nice to run into you."

Chapter Five
Sweet Lady Luck

Covendrey, The Rhen

Kyel Archer slouched, hands in his pockets, as he slogged with his head bowed through the muddy streets of Covendrey. His clothing was drenched, soaked through with rain, his hair plastered against his face. It had been storming for days with no sign of letting up. He'd almost forgotten what it felt like to be warm.

He missed the comfortable chair by his hearth back home. That chair had been lovingly shaped by his own hands. It fit him perfectly. He was not a craftsman by trade, though perhaps he should have been. He had a certain feel for wood. But he'd decided to keep his woodworking to a hobby, afraid of losing his love of the craft if he took to it for a living.

So he'd apprenticed himself to a merchant instead. He had a wagonload of trade goods to get all the way to Rothscard and back in a fortnight. In this weather, Kyel was skeptical he would be able to make that deadline.

The back door of the Dancing Boar Inn wasn't hard to find, even in the pouring rain. Kyel stamped the mud off his feet and let himself in. As he moved out of the rain into the comforting warmth of the inn's interior, he was surprised to find it nearly deserted. The Boar's common room was generally filled with patrons at any given time of day but, strangely, there were only two people sitting at a long table, another man squatting by the hearth, warming his hands over the flames.

Kyel knew everyone in Covendrey and recognized the men at the table as Aber Feldman and Dale Hodgens, the Boar's joint owners. The man by the fire was Traver Larsen, who ran a dye house on the other side of town. Kyel had grown up with Traver but knew Dale and Aber only socially.

He took another step, and a board beneath him groaned. The sound made all three men startle and turn toward him. Traver climbed to his feet, a slow grin forming on his wolfish face. He strode toward Kyel with his hand out, gesturing broadly.

"Well, look what the wind blew in!" he said with a laugh. "What are you doing, skulking around?"

"I came in the back way." Kyel directed his words to the two men sitting at the table. Both Dale and Aber stared at him with eyebrows raised, no doubt wondering if Traver's accusation of skulking had any grain of truth to it.

"Did I leave that damned door open again?" Aber said and rose from the bench, clunking his tankard down on the table.

"Next time use the front door," Dale admonished. "And don't just stand there, drippin' wet. Grab a towel and dry off next to that drunk of a friend of yours."

"You're drunk, Traver?" Kyel asked over his shoulder, heading to a neat stack of towels behind the counter.

"Cold sober," the man responded with a frown. "These good gentlemen won't even grant me a drop."

"And why should we, Larsen?" Dale asked. "You still haven't paid for all the crockery and chairs that were broken when you picked a fight with that fellow up from Southwark."

"Harlen Wood." Traver scowled, tossing his head against an unruly lock of hair that kept falling forward over his eyes. "He started the fight. I was just defending myself."

"Sure." Dale raised his tankard to his lips. "Just mind your manners, or you can find your way back out again. You know where the door is."

"Sure do," Traver said with a smirk that was almost a sneer. "You've thrown me out it enough times."

Kyel ran the towel over his face and scrubbed his hair with it. Sadly, there was nothing to do about his clothes. He tossed the towel into the rag bin then crossed the room to the river rock hearth, settling down by the fire next to Traver. The heat of the flames soaked quickly into his skin, a welcome relief.

"How are your boys?" he asked Traver, though he doubted the man had any idea.

"Oh, they're just fine. Getting to be real pains in the ass." He took a sip of water from the cup in his hand, his face skewing into a grimace. "How's your own get?"

"Just fine," Kyel muttered, the question provoking a sharp pang of homesickness. His son was little more than a baby. Kyel had never left home for so long. "I'm going to miss him," he sighed.

"Aye, I'll miss mine too."

Kyel glanced sideways at Traver. "Where are *you* going?"

Little bits and pieces of the conversation started tallying together in his mind, just like the long columns of numbers on the inventory sheets he worked with. What they added up to was certain trouble.

A broad grin broke out on Traver's face. He reached over and clapped Kyel on the shoulder. "Why, I'm going with you! I'm your driver. How's that for luck?"

Kyel reeled, feeling as though the bottom had just been yanked out of his stomach. What was the old man thinking, hiring *Traver* of all people? This run was too important for anything to go wrong. If Traver mucked it up…

He shook his head. "I don't understand. What about the dye house? What about Ellen and the boys?"

Traver waved his hand dismissively. "She gave me the boot weeks ago. I thought everyone in town knew."

The news made Kyel want to retch. The rest of the story totaled up, falling into place. So now Traver was looking for work, had no place to live, and no coin to pay for his habits. Somehow, he'd gotten snatched up by Kyel's own employer, who'd been looking for someone to make the Rothscard run.

And now Traver was his problem.

"I need a drink," Kyel said, standing up. He walked with shoulders slumped toward the back of the inn as images of drunken Traver disasters filled his mind.

Hunter's Home, The Rhen

The driver's seat beside Traver, Kyel still found himself wincing every time one of the wagon's wheels slipped into a rut in the road. Sometimes he wondered if Traver wasn't trying to bounce them around intentionally.

Even still, they were making good time, despite the bad weather. Kyel slept under the wagon most nights, afraid someone was going to plunder his goods or assault them at sword-point. There was rumor of deserters drifting down from the Front. He immediately regretted his decision not to hire a guard.

Kyel sagged in his seat, looking to the west. The sky was a brilliant orange, the sun sinking into a horizon green with pastures. The wilderness around them had started to wane a few leagues back, yielding to farmland: a sure sign they must be approaching a town up ahead.

They had left Dansbury three days before. There, they had stayed at a decent inn where Kyel had managed to get a good night's sleep between fits of Traver's snoring. Since then, they'd been sleeping under the wagon again. His back longed for a bed.

Almost every town they'd come across had offered some type of accommodations for travelers. The Great Northern Road was a major trade artery connecting many of the Rhen's kingdoms. Kyel just hoped the inn at Hunter's Home would be a civilized one and not like the seedy Scarlet Maiden in Weeping Springs or the Pig's Ear in Gentry.

The sun had already set by the time Traver drew the horses up in the yard of Hunter's Home's only inn. Kyel jumped down and stretched his legs for the first time in hours. There were not many people about, just two rough-looking men standing by the inn's door and a stable boy crossing the yard with a pail in hand. Kyel signaled the boy over, paying him a few coins for stabling the horses and locking the wagon up overnight.

The two men standing by the door glared at him as Kyel gathered his things and crossed the yard, their eyes tracking him the whole way. When he reached the door, the pair refused to move aside, forcing him to turn sideways to brush past them. He looked down, unable to meet their stares. He'd run into other men just like them on the road and didn't trust their type. Although unarmed, the two had the look of mercenaries—the kind not looking for legitimate work.

The interior of the inn was dim and rank with old smoke and bad liquor. Kyel crossed the greatroom toward a balding innkeeper who stood at the counter drying crockery with a cotton towel. He waited for the man to notice him, which took longer than it should.

"What can I do for you?" the innkeeper asked, not bothering to look up from his task.

"A room and a meal," Kyel responded.

The innkeeper flipped the towel over his shoulder and set the crock he was holding down on the counter. He extended his hand, palm upwards.

Kyel had to reach into his coin purse a few times before the man was finally satisfied, then he turned to see where Traver had gotten himself off to. He found his companion leaning against one of the log walls by the door, staring longingly at a pair of men in the corner intent on a quiet game of cards. Kyel blew out a sigh, crossing the room toward him.

"Come on," he urged, tugging at Traver's sleeve. "I've got us lodging for the night."

Traver glanced at him with a pleading expression. "Could I borrow some coin? I'll pay you back from my wages."

Kyel's first impulse was to tell him no. But Traver had been behaving himself rather well on the trip. It wasn't as though the Elk's Horn was a gambling den, and the two men seated in the corner seemed harmless enough. Reaching into his coin purse, Kyel dug out another few coppers and dropped them into Traver's hand. The way the man's face lit up made Kyel regret his generosity.

"You have a problem," he said, clapping Traver on the arm.

"It's never a problem if you're winning."

Shaking his head, Kyel swung his pack over his shoulder and

made his way toward the staircase, taking the stairs up to the second floor. He was going to wash up and enjoy a hot supper. After that, he was going to bed.

Traver grinned at the coppers in his hand as though they were gold pieces. Brushing a wayward lock of hair out of his eyes, he turned to assess the game in the corner. The men playing cards were probably regulars. Townsfolk, by the looks of them. The game they were playing was a quiet one. Too quiet, by Traver's standards. His coin probably wouldn't go very far with them, but he had to start somewhere.

He kissed the coppers in his hand, a little offering to his Lady of Luck, the goddess Dreia. Traver considered himself a special supplicant of hers, probably a favorite by now. She had blessed him many times before in the past—why not tonight? After all, he just wanted to take in enough winnings to buy himself a few rounds of drink. That shouldn't be too much to ask.

"Care if I join in?" he asked by way of introduction, hooking a chair over with his foot. He tossed a coin into the pot and plopped down, leaning forward with his head in his hands, elbows planted on the table.

That's how it started.

Three hours later, it was still going.

Lady Luck had never blessed him so well. He'd graduated from the corner table, moving up to a real game when a bawdy crowd of travelers wandered in. Since then, the Elk's Horn had turned into an entirely different sort of establishment. Word of his winning streak had gotten out, pulling people in from the street. Traver found himself the center of attention as a raucous crowd gathered around his table to watch him win hand after hand.

He'd had lost count of the number of pots he'd won in a row. He'd never even *heard* of a streak this hot. The cards in his hand were like a good woman. They knew when to stick, and they knew when to leave. People started buying him rounds. After the first few tankards, Traver stopped wondering who to thank. He just swished the ale around in his mouth, swallowed, and laid down another card.

He stared across the table at his current opponent, a merchant down from Rothscard who'd stopped in to buy a drink, then decided to try his luck. The cards in Traver's hand felt itchy, so he discarded the highest and decided to go low this time. That was the beauty of Knight's Cross, the game of the moment. Low cards stood as much of a chance as high, all depending upon how the hand was dealt. The merchant was dealing from three decks to prevent him from counting cards. Traver wasn't. But when he produced a perfect Cross for the second time in a row, the merchant folded and walked away.

Cheers went up all around the room. People clapped him on the back, while others beat on the tables. A woman leaned down to give him a kiss that started on the cheek but ended up with her falling into his lap with his tongue in her mouth. The kiss tasted like a salty twist of ale and wine, not unpleasant. Her breasts weren't bad either. Traver snaked a hand under her skirt to squeeze her thigh and was rewarded by a squeak of surprise. He winked at her and, settling her properly in his lap, looked around for another upstart who might want to try a challenge.

There didn't seem to be any takers.

But then one of the mercenaries he'd beaten earlier returned, probably wanting to win his coin back. Traver remembered the dirty, unshaven face well. The man had played a good game of cards. He must have managed to scrounge up more coin from somewhere.

The buxom girl in Traver's lap squirmed at the sight of the man. Traver draped a hand over her shoulder to steady her, although a certain part of him did appreciate her squirming.

He called a serving girl over with a wave of his hand, ordering another round. He patted the girl on the thigh then signaled his opponent to ante up.

Traver blinked, staring down at the gold piece the man pushed to the center of the table. He didn't have near enough to match that bet, even if he went all-in. He was going to have to walk.

Unless…

He lifted the girl by the hips and planted her firmly on the table. Standing, Traver excused himself and trudged across the room in the direction of the stairs.

He took the creaking staircase up to the inn's second floor. He knew which door was Kyel's as soon as he heard the snoring from the other side. He had those low, throaty sounds memorized. He opened the door and stooped to grope around in the darkness. As usual, Archer had stashed his coin purse under the bed.

Traver scooped up the purse and left. After all, he was riding the best winning streak of his life. That kind of luck just didn't happen every night. He swung the purse by its strap as he shuffled down the stairs and through the packed common room back to the table. Halfway there, he lost his balance and stumbled into a woman, jostling her drink. Ale spilled down the front of her dress, drizzling amber droplets down the gap of her cleavage.

The ringing slap that followed actually took him by surprise. Traver pressed a hand against his face. The woman had an arm like Harlen Wood. That one could try her hand at tavern brawling. She'd really be quite good at it.

He stumbled back toward the table, massaging his cheek and veering the whole way. It was almost time to call it a night. He was having a hard time focusing, and the sound of the room was becoming a muffled blur in his head. He hadn't bothered counting the number of rounds he'd put down, but he knew the total was up there. He just wanted to finish this one last hand then slip off to bed, preferably accompanied.

Traver almost sighed in relief when he saw the mercenary was still waiting for him at the table. The girl was gone, though, which was really too bad. He fell into his chair, thumbing the purse open enough to finger through the loose coins at the bottom. When he produced a fat gold piece, his rough-looking opponent raised an eyebrow in interest. Traver handed it over to the man, who put his teeth on it.

"A gold Silver Star," Traver boasted, slurring badly. "Can't go wrong with that."

The mercenary didn't reply. Come to think of it, he hadn't said anything all evening. But he did appear satisfied by the impressions his teeth made in the coin. He dealt, and Traver eagerly scooped his cards up off the table, trying to arrange them in his hand. He lost one in the process, groaning as it twirled downward to land on the table. He scooped it up as quickly as he could. Someone behind him laughed. Traver almost turned to say something, but then his eyes focused on the cards glaring up at him from his hand.

Another perfect Cross.

Traver threw his head back and howled, stamping his feet and throwing his cards down on the table. A cheer went up from the gathered crowd as he leaned forward to rake in his winnings. He couldn't believe it. He'd felt certain his Lady Luck had left him for another man.

He should have walked away then. But he didn't.

"How 'bout this," he slurred to his opponent. "Let's go another hand, and I'll give you a chance to win it back."

The sellsword shook his head. "Can't do it."

Traver screwed his face into a grimace. "Why not?"

"I got people I owe."

"You must have *something.*"

His opponent shrugged. "Just my horse."

Traver brightened. A horse was good. Archer could use a better horse. The nag he kept tied behind the wagon was a mean-tempered beast that was becoming nastier by the day. Traver put on his best game face, not wanting to appear too eager.

"Well, I'd have to see it," he allowed, trying his best to sound skeptical. He actually didn't care what the creature looked like, so long as it had four legs and a back to put a saddle on.

The mercenary looked over his shoulder and nodded at someone behind him. Traver's fingers itched for more cards to be dealt. He scooped his coins up from the table and downed the rest of his ale, waiting for the man to make his decision.

"Come on, then," his opponent said and scooted his chair back. "I don't have the bloody beast shoved down my pants, you know."

"Right." Traver stood up and caught himself on the table to keep from falling over.

He had to strain to keep the image of the man from becoming doubled as he followed him out of the inn and into the night. For some reason, his eyes kept trying to slide closed. How much ale had he put down? He knew his limit well, and he knew when he was well over it.

The mercenary led him into the dark stable. Traver scowled at the overwhelming stench of horse manure that assaulted his nose. Whoever the innkeeper was paying to muck out the stalls wasn't earning his keep. Soft nickers greeted them as they made their way down a dark aisle between rows of stalls. A soft nose brushed against Traver's arm, making him flinch.

The man opened the door to a stall, beckoning. Traver followed him in, stumbling over a pile of hay. It was dark inside, and his eyes hadn't adjusted yet. They weren't working well anyway.

He blinked, peering around at the shadows.

"Hey," he muttered, managing to slur even that one syllable. "I don't think there's a horse in here."

"He's a genius," said a voice from behind him.

Suddenly sober, Traver bent to reach for his boot knife. A steel-toed kick caught him in the side of the head before he could get his fingers around it.

Chapter Six
Dumb, Rotten Luck

Hunter's Home, The Rhen

The sound of the door banging open startled Kyel from sleep. Then hands were on him, hauling him out of bed and onto his feet. A group of men slammed him back against the wall, his head cracking against the wood. Someone twisted him around and snaked a muscled arm around his neck. He tried to struggle, but the man jerked his arm upward forcibly, holding it at an impossible angle.

Kyel groaned, feeling his tendons starting to give. He stopped moving, sagging as they bound his wrists behind his back with coarse rope. Then they wrestled him out the door. Kyel staggered down the hallway, two men guiding him firmly from behind.

When they reached the top of the stairs, he looked down to find the common room crowded with people. They were shouting and hollering, waving fists and brandishing weapons and tankards in the air. Kyel stared down at the crowd, his mind frozen by a numbing mixture of confusion and fear.

As he reached the bottom of the stairs, a young woman stepped forward and spat in his face. A blond-haired man took care of the spittle for him, tilting his tankard over Kyel's head and dumping the contents over him. He was propelled through the crowd as people screamed accusations in his face. He couldn't make out any of the words, didn't understand what they were shouting. It was all just a blurred, terrifying nightmare.

They hauled him out the door and into the night. The yard was full of people standing around, staring at another man who knelt in the dirt by the stable. A few men surrounded him holding lanterns and flaming torches, their faces glowing orange in the flickering light. Looking at the man kneeling on the ground, Kyel's confusion solidified into fury.

It was Traver.

Kyel felt his cheeks heat with a sudden flare of anger. What could the scoundrel have possibly done this time? By the looks of things, it must have been something far worse than just another rowdy tavern brawl.

Then he saw the body sprawled on the ground in the shadows of the yard.

The man holding him pushed him to his knees beside Traver. His companion looked even worse than usual, his head a bruised mess, his face caked with blood. He reeked a brutal combination of ale and horse manure. Traver's eyes were reddened and half-closed. Kyel couldn't tell if that was from the head injury or the drink, but it didn't matter. The facts were totaling themselves in his head. What they added up to was certain trouble.

"What did you *do?*" Kyel hissed at him.

Traver turned and regarded him with a dim expression, seeming to notice him for the first time. He grimaced and shook his head, looking baffled, as if it was all just dumb, rotten luck.

"I got jumped," Traver said. "But these lackwits who think they're the Emmery Deathwatch Guard keep saying I killed that man."

"What?" It was as bad as Kyel feared. Traver had stolen some coin from someone, gotten himself good and soused, then went and killed some poor fellow. "Oh, by the gods, Traver—"

A short but brawny fellow approached, waggling a finger at them. "Now, you just sit there quiet-like. Save your lip for the mayor. He's on his way, and when he gets here, you'll likely end up with your heads on a block."

"But I didn't *do* anything!" both Kyel and Traver exclaimed at the same time. Kyel turned his head and glared at his companion, who just shrugged sheepishly in his restraints.

"Well, I didn't."

They sat in silence after that, on their knees in the dirt of the yard. Kyel couldn't keep his gaze off the corpse sprawled only a few paces away. He thought he recognized the man, but it was hard to tell in the flickering light of the torches. The face had so much blood splattered all over it that the features were indeterminable.

He wondered if it was one of the men he'd seen in the yard when they'd first arrived. He hadn't liked the way they were staring at him. Kyel found himself wondering if Traver's story might have some grain of truth to it. It was possible they had seen the wagonload of goods and had marked Traver for an easy target.

Of course, that didn't explain how one of them had ended up dead.

Kyel made certain his voice was a dead whisper as he prodded his companion, "Why'd you get jumped? You don't have anything anyone would want to steal."

Traver hung his head. To Kyel, he looked like a mischievous boy who got caught by his mother. "I borrowed your coin purse."

"What?" Kyel couldn't believe it. He'd known that the man was a scoundrel—and a drunk, and a carouser, and a gambler—but stealing your own friend's coin was low. He wouldn't have thought even Traver's base morals were that appalling.

"It's a long story."

"I'll warrant it is! Everything with you is a long story. Your whole *life* is just one long, bloody tragedy."

"Actually, it might be a very short tragedy. Look."

Kyel looked. A small procession was headed their way up the street. The man who rode in front on a heavy draft horse still wore his nightclothes. Kyel took him for the town mayor. Behind him walked a mixed assortment of people, some holding torches, others wielding swords or farm implements.

He didn't like the looks of the man bringing up the rear. He was heavily bearded and carried the biggest half-moon axe Kyel had ever seen. The light of the torches reflected off the blade.

"Gods," Traver whispered beside him. "Wager that would smart a bit coming down."

Kyel couldn't take his eyes off that axe. He didn't understand. All he'd done was go to bed and, the next thing he knew, a group of townsmen wanted to take his head off. It wasn't fair. He thought of Amelia back at home and little baby Gil. He didn't want his son growing up without a father. He hung his head, wrenching his gaze away from the red glow of the half-moon blade.

Traver whispered, "You're a businessman, Archer. You talk us out of this."

Kyel let out a long, exasperated sigh. There was no hope. If only Traver truly would let him do the talking, there might be a chance. But Kyel knew there was no way the wretch beside him would keep his mouth shut.

The mayor dismounted a short distance away and tossed his horse's reins to one of his henchmen. He was a squat old man with salt-and-peppered whiskers on the sides of his face. He seemed like a good enough fellow, although anyone wearing his nightclothes couldn't seem too harmful. He leaned over the dead body, holding a spectacle up to one eye as another man handed him something that glinted in the torchlight.

Kyel frowned, staring at the object in the mayor's hand. "Isn't that your knife?"

Traver nodded. "What do you think our odds are? Three-to-one?"

"Is gambling all you ever think about?"

"Well, no, actually." Traver nodded in the direction of the headsman. "Right now, I'm thinking more about that axe. It doesn't look very sharp." He groaned. Tilting his head back, he worked his neck around stiffly. "Oh, gods, my head hurts."

Kyel turned back to the group of men still conversing over the body.

"We've scores of witnesses, Mayor," a man was saying. "Everyone saw the killer lose a heap of coin to this poor fellow. Not just coppers. Gold, mind you. Then everyone heard that bastard telling him to follow him to the stables. Seems he beat the poor chap senseless then knifed him real good. Then he passed out flat drunk. That's how we found him."

"Oh, is that the way of it?" Traver tossed his hair back from his face. "Then would you pray explain how I acquired this dent in my head? And if I knifed the 'poor chap' to get my coins back, then where are they?"

"We found this in the stable."

Kyel turned to see a tall and lanky man striding toward the mayor, carrying something in his hand. Kyel stared, trying to see what it was in the shadows of the yard. When the man stepped into the light, he almost groaned. It was his own coin purse. And, by the way the man was holding it, there was still a good amount of heft to it.

The mayor received the purse into his pudgy hands. He opened it, and Kyel could hear the sound of clinking coins as he sifted through the contents. The old man turned to Traver, shaking the purse as he walked toward him.

The mayor said, "So you're telling me there was a third party who knifed him, beat you senseless, and then didn't bother to abscond with the coin? That's a bit hard to swallow, don't you think?"

Traver shrugged. "That's the way of it."

"And what about me?" demanded Kyel. "I never left my room all night!"

The mayor looked over at the bearded fellow. The ugly brute stepped forward, gesturing toward Kyel with a wave of his hand. "We've two witnesses who say they saw him near the stable."

"I was sleeping!" Kyel shouted.

He was frustrated almost to the point of tears. He had no idea what had happened down in the stable. All he knew was that he had no part in any wrongdoing, and it should be perfectly obvious to anyone with half a brain.

He glanced across the yard, startled to find a mob pouring out the back door of the inn and moving in their direction. Kyel swallowed, looking again at the blade of the axe. His neck was starting to ache. He knew exactly where this was going.

"All right," the mayor grumbled, raising his hand to rub his balding head. "Give me a moment." He fingered Traver's boot knife, rotating it slowly. He glanced again at the corpse then held the small blade up to dangle in front of Traver's eyes. "Is this your knife?"

"Well, yes, but—"

Turning to Kyel, he hefted the coin purse. "And is this your money?"

"Yes, but—"

The mayor turned and walked away, by all appearances deep in thought. Kyel hoped he thought long and hard on it. The whole story didn't make any sense at all. But the mob gathered around them was growing impatient.

Kyel's stomach felt queasy. A town mayor was usually an elected official. The man would be thinking more about his endorsements than he would about true justice for the crime—which lowered their chances considerably. And, by the sound of the turbulent crowd, the people were demanding blood.

"I don't know, Halbert." One of the men who had ridden in with the mayor was shaking his head. "You can't execute two men on evidence this flimsy. Not a soul actually saw them do it."

The whole mob started shouting. Someone called out, "They murdered a man! Take their bleedin' heads off!"

There was a collective outcry of agreement. Some people shook their fists in the air as others began directing their wrath at the mayor. The poor man walked away, lumbering toward Kyel and Traver.

"Doesn't Rothscard send their convicts north to the Front?" the mayor asked one of his men.

"Aye, they do."

"Then we're in luck." He glanced back at his unruly constituents with a look of relief. "There's a group of Rothscard Bluecloaks in town. Perhaps they'll agree to take these two off our hands."

Kyel gaped. He shook his head and pleaded in a desperate voice, "I can't go to the Front! I've a wife and child at home! And a load of goods I'm supposed to haul out on the morrow!"

The mayor looked at him with pity in his eyes. His expression of sympathy seemed almost genuine. "Sorry, son. But if you really were in just the wrong place at the wrong time, then you're the unluckiest fellow I've ever met."

Kyel's head spun dizzily as the air in his lungs seemed to rush out all at once. "Damn you, Traver!"

Traver sighed. "Already am, Archer. Already am."

The bearded fellow chuckled, eyes sparkling with amusement in the glare of the torchlight.

"Your name's Archer?" he asked. "Hope you know how to use a bow."

Kyel glared at him vindictively.

Chapter Seven
The Bird Man

Vale of Amberlie, The Rhen

Darien was adrift in a sea of golden light that filtered downward in gentle rays. The light shimmered, shifting, and kept fading into darkness before coming back again. Hazy objects hovered overhead and all around. A soft breath of air stirred, making the shapes above him dance and spin. Gradually, the objects came into better focus. But even when he could make out the forms of the strange, fluttering shapes, they still didn't make any kind of sense. The whole image was surreal and utterly bizarre.

He found himself staring up at the forms of moving birds. Their wings were outstretched in the air overhead, though not in flight. Instead, the birds fluttered and spun on thin and almost transparent strings, dangling from a ceiling that sloped sharply overhead. There were dozens of them. Small sparrows and warblers, finches and jays. Hawks and eagles with great wingspans extended in a strange parody of flight. Above, mounted to a corner against the ceiling, a great horned owl regarded him somberly, eyes round and glassy, its expression perplexed.

Darien struggled to sit up, but the motion brought such a stunning pain in his head that he fell back again immediately. The light and the birds faded away, and it was a long time before they came back again.

When they did, he had no idea why they were still there. He had expected them to be gone, just another one of the strange dreams that had plagued his sleep. It took him a long time to come to the conclusion that this was no dream. It was just a very peculiar reality.

He was lying in a soft and comfortable bed. The birds continued spinning overhead, feathers stirring on a breeze admitted by an open window. Dim recollections were coming back to him, filling him more each minute with a tremendous sense of loss and foreboding. He remembered the disaster of the Hall, the column of light that pierced the night, his brother's cold, malevolent eyes. He remembered falling.

There was nothing after that until the birds.

He tried to sit up again, clenching his jaw against the pain and trying to fight back the queasiness in his stomach. He managed to get almost halfway up before the sound of a hoarse voice stopped him short.

"I wouldn't try that just yet."

He hadn't noticed the old man sitting on a stool in the corner of the room. The face was familiar, but Darien couldn't place it. He knew he had seen this man before, even recently, but couldn't remember where. The face that regarded him was quilted with wrinkles, age-stained and weathered. The nose was bird-like, resembling the beak of the golden eagle that dangled above his bed. The old man's puffy blue eyes were what made him realize that he was looking at the gatekeeper he had met the previous day in the Vale.

The old man stood stiffly, using his hands to push himself off the stool. With slow, shuffling steps, he moved toward the edge of the bed. He wheezed as he bent over, placing a hand on Darien's chest. He closed his eyes. As he did, Darien felt a rippling sensation pass through his body. The old man was another mage, and he was using his ability to probe his condition.

"The ways of healing are not well known to me," the old man said, removing his hand. "My specialties lie in other areas. I did what I could, but perhaps you can do a better job of it yourself when you are feeling a bit better."

Darien frowned as the import of the words sank in. Then his eyes widened. He'd forgotten that he was perfectly capable of healing himself now. He reached within and felt for the surge of the magic field inside. It was there, singing quietly in the back of his mind. Waiting to be used.

"Stop."

The urgency of the command made Darien force his mind back from the touch of the field. He opened his eyes, staring up at the old mage in confusion.

"Never attempt that again with a head injury," the man admonished, raising a finger. "You ought to know better, boy, especially this close to a vortex. But you're new, aren't you? Only yesterday, you passed my gate as an acolyte. Yet now I see a fresh set of markings on your wrist."

Darien lifted his hand and stared at the image of what looked like a heavy iron chain engraved into his flesh. The mark had not been there the previous day. The old man was right.

He had an identical emblem on his left wrist, which he'd acquired sixteen years before when he had spoken the Acolyte's Oath. Now, he bore a matching set of chains on both wrists, the symbol of a fully Bound mage. Darien rotated his arm, admiring the complexity of the pattern that wrapped all the way around his wrist, seamless and glimmering in the muted light.

"I suppose I should introduce myself," the old man said. "My apologies, but I'm unused to the ways of civilized manners anymore. My name is Edric Torrence, third-tier Master, if you must know."

Darien nodded weakly in acknowledgement. "Darien Lauchlin. Grand Master of the Fifth Tier." It felt incredibly odd to hear his lips utter his new title.

The old man blinked.

Such an elevated ranking was almost unheard of. Meiran was the only mage in all of Aerysius who would have been stronger than him. He had fallen in love with the only sixth-tier Grand Master in existence. But Meiran was dead. Along with all of the others.

"The city?" he whispered, though he really didn't want to hear the answer.

"Utterly destroyed."

Darien closed his eyes as a shiver passed over him. He had

guessed that would be the case. His last memory of Aerysius was a shattered, desolate tomb. He wondered if his mother had managed to escape. The explosion of the bridge may have offered her a chance to get away.

"Are there other survivors?"

The old man shook his head. "As far as I know, my friend, you and I are the only mages left alive in the entire world. And you are indeed lucky to be alive. Every person in the Vale was turned out this morning, witnessing the destruction on the mountain. Your fall from the cliff was marked by many. Including myself, for which you are most fortunate. I slowed your descent as best I could."

Darien winced, hearing that. He remembered nothing of the fall. The last thing he remembered was thinking of Meiran as he stepped off the cliff. It was well beyond fortunate that Master Edric had happened to look up at just the right time.

"You have my thanks," he whispered.

"I was actually rather shocked at finding you still alive," the old mage went on. "A few townsmen helped me haul you up from the river bottom. One of them recognized you. Apparently, you grew up down here. Ah, bother, I'm rambling, aren't I? You must forgive me. I'm no longer used to the company of people. My work is a solitary thing."

Darien didn't know what to say. Whatever the mage's work was, it was certainly an odd branch of magic, judging by the dozens of dead and yet undecayed birds spinning in the air above his bed. Perhaps something to do with flight, though Darien knew that was an impossibility. The magic field could support accomplishments that were true wonders, but human flight was not one of them. Yet, it did make him think. It was no simple feat the old man had performed, slowing his fall the way he had. Darien wasn't sure he could duplicate it.

The sound of a shout made him turn his head in the direction of the window. Now that he was listening, he realized he'd been hearing a constant murmur of voices for some time.

"What is that?" He wanted to sit up and look out the window, but he knew better. He had no wish to repeat the same mistake.

Master Edric frowned, his jowls sagging. "It seems that rumor travels swiftly. Folk have been gathering throughout the day. They know that Aerysius has fallen and that some dire evil exists on the mountainside above. The villagers fear for their lives. Many have come here, looking for hope. Looking for you, my young friend. Apparently, they all expect you to save them."

The explanation made Darien ill. He closed his eyes, feeling the same frustration he had experienced all his life: wanting desperately to help, yet incapable of doing anything meaningful. What was ironic was, now, he finally *did* have the power to make a difference. Only, he had spoken a vow to never use it, at least not in any way that would prove effective. Darien stared down at the markings on his wrist, suddenly resenting them.

"You know as well as I that there's nothing I can do," he muttered.

"I know absolutely nothing." Edric gazed wistfully up at the feathered ornaments twirling gently above his head. "But for my birds. That's the one thing I do know."

Edric's words provoked a memory Darien had almost forgotten. Back when he was a boy living in the Vale, there'd been rumor of a crazy old man who lived somewhere deep in the grove. Some folk called him the Bird Man. He stared up at Edric with renewed interest.

The aged Master reached down and patted him on the shoulder. "Rest now," he instructed. "When you awaken, I'll round you up something to eat."

Darien nodded and closed his eyes. It didn't take him a moment to fall back to sleep.

His rest was plagued by a relentless series of nightmares that repeated over and over again, one only ending to make way for the beginning of another. In his dreams, Darien watched Meiran die a thousand different deaths, each with its own twisted and often brutal variation. Sometimes he was there with her, holding her in his arms as the Hall of the Watchers collapsed on top of them. Other times, he witnessed her death only as an observer, watching as his brother took her life a hundred different ways.

In one especially vivid dream, he looked on helplessly as Aidan used his own sword to slit Meiran's wrists and held a crystalline goblet to collect her spilling blood. In the vision, Aidan smiled as he tilted his head back to drink deeply from that terrible cup.

In other nightmares, he was falling. He fell endlessly, over and over. Sometimes he felt his body shatter as he collided against a wall of rock. Other times, there was no end to his fall. He plunged downward into shadow, and there was nothing in the world around him but infinite darkness. Sometimes Meiran was falling with him, the fabric of her gown rippling in the wind.

Darien awoke in a cold sweat, clamping his mouth shut to contain the scream he was feeling inside. The nightmare he'd awakened from had been the most terrible of all. In it, he had seen Meiran kneeling before the Lord of Chaos. She looked over her shoulder and smiled at him, her eyes empty pools of filthy green light.

Darien lay panting, sweat streaming down his face. The nightmares had been too real, too vivid. He lay there trembling, trying to slow the pace of his heart, staring upward at the twirling birds. He tried to clear his mind of the image of Meiran with the green light of hell shining in her eyes.

His breathing finally calmed as the terror of the dreams subsided. He glanced around, finding Edric sitting on his stool, eyes poring over a text of some type. Seeing him awake, the old man closed the book and rose to his feet. He shuffled toward the bed in a stiff, arthritic stride.

"How long?" Darien asked.

"Two days," the old man said. "I was growing a bit concerned."

Darien felt shocked by the amount of time that had passed. No wonder the nightmares had seemed endless. At least his head felt better, only throbbing mildly as he raised himself into a sitting position. The room spun for a moment then slowly steadied itself. He felt weak. Probably from three days without anything to eat. But he felt mostly well, maybe even well enough to stand.

The old man smiled. "You can try healing yourself now."

Darien closed his eyes and took hold of the magic field, sending his thoughts probing deeply into his body. He quickly assessed the extent of his injuries, repairing everything amiss almost automatically. When he was done, he opened his eyes and moved his head, testing the feel of it. The pain was gone. The weakness, however, was still there. Hunger was not something that could be healed with magic.

"I have to admit, I'm envious," Edric said. "You could not imagine how difficult healing is for someone untrained to it."

Darien understood. As an acolyte, he had been allowed to choose the direction his studies would take. He had always aspired to be a Sentinel like his father. The charter of the order was to protect the people of the Rhen from the aggressions of the Enemy, all without the use of offensive techniques. He had spent many years studying under the guidance of skilled mentors. Knowledge of healing was a necessity on the field of battle, and one of the most difficult subjects to master.

Darien swung his legs over the edge of the bed, only then realizing he was naked. He looked around the small cottage and found his clothing piled on the floor, looking no better than tattered, filthy rags. Reaching down, he collected the formal robes his mother had given him and held them up. The black fabric was rigid with dried blood and crusted with grime. What had been a new and expensive garment now looked destroyed beyond repair.

Darien pictured how the robes had looked when he'd seen them new.

And, suddenly, they were.

In his hands, the garment had once again taken on a glossy black sheen, the cloth whole and unrent.

He slipped the robes on over his head then found his boots by the door, the same scuffed and dusty pair that had survived two years of soldiering in the Pass of Lor-Gamorth. Darien pulled them on and, as he did, his gaze was drawn to another object by the window.

His breath caught in his throat. He'd been holding the sword

Meiran had given him when he'd stepped off the cliff. It could have fallen anywhere. The chance that it had ended up here, in this room, was nothing short of miraculous.

He took the black scabbard into his hand, raising it before his eyes with a feeling of reverence. The leather-wrapped hilt of the sword gleamed in the cool morning light. He ran his hand over it lovingly, his gaze drawn to the jeweled crossguard.

"We found that by your side," Edric said. "I recalled you carrying it, so I brought it along." What he left unspoken was the air of disapproval remarked by his tone.

Darien nodded, resting the sword back against the wall. "It was a gift," he explained in a voice gruff with sentiment. "It's the only thing I have left of the person who gave it to me. You have my gratitude for saving it."

He managed to turn away from the blade. As he did, he caught a fleeting look of sympathy in the old man's eyes.

"I'm going outside," he said. "Have a look around."

As he moved past Edric, the old man caught his arm.

"Wait."

The old mage let go and went to a chest against the wall. There, he bent over, carefully removing an odd assortment of birds from the top of the chest, setting them gently on the floor. He lifted the lid and rummaged through the contents, finally producing a folded black parcel Darien recognized. It was a mage's cloak, complete with the Silver Star embroidered on the back, the symbol of Aerysius.

The old man pressed the cloak into Darien's hands. "Here, put this on."

"But it's yours," Darien protested, shaking his head in confusion. Why was the man giving him his own cloak?

"I have no need of it any longer. You, on the other hand, must keep up appearances."

Darien put the cloak on, fastening it with a silver brooch Edric handed him. Then he opened the door and stepped out into the brilliant light of morning.

And froze, rooted by shock.

There were scores of people gathered in the clearing before the little cottage.

Darien fought the sudden impulse to flee back inside and shut the door on that sea of anxious faces. But Edric moved up behind him, blocking the doorway and any hope of retreat. Noticing him, the people in the crowd turned and started shouting, jostling each other out of their way.

"I don't understand," Darien muttered, appalled. "What do they want from me?"

"Hope," Edric said.

Dismayed, Darien glanced at the old Master.

"I…I can't," he protested. "There's nothing I can do for them. And why me? Why not you?"

Master Edric only chuckled, a mischievous glint in his eyes. "Why, I'm just the crazy old Bird Man who lives in the wilderness up 'yonder. But you, on the other hand, are the last surviving Sentinel of Aerysius."

"I'm not," Darien objected. "I never had a chance to take an order."

The old man just looked at him sideways and scoffed. "You are the son of Gerald Lauchlin. Of course you're a Sentinel. What else would you be?"

Darien shivered, thinking of Aidan. He, too, was a son of Gerald Lauchlin. But his brother was just about the furthest thing from a Sentinel Darien could imagine.

He realized the crowd had stopped stirring. Silence consumed the glade before the Bird Man's cottage. All eyes were fixed on him, regarding him with a mixture of wonder and fear. There was an almost palpable sense of expectation in the air.

Then it came to him: they were all waiting for him to speak.

Darien froze.

All he could do was stare from one face to the next. He recognized many. One of the faces he knew well was Corban Henley who, in his youth, had been a gangly boy prone to misadventure. He'd been the leader of the local band of mischiefs Darien had belonged to himself. But he hadn't laid eyes on Corban in over a decade. The man standing before him now was still tall, but his lanky frame had filled out remarkably.

Unlike most of the people in the clearing, there was no trace of awe or anxiety in Corban's eyes.

"What will you do?" someone called from the back of the crowd.

Darien's nerves tensed. Everyone was looking at him as though they all expected him to call down lighting and save them from the terror in the sky. They had to know he couldn't do that. He was just one man—a man constrained by a vow to do no harm.

So, he did the only thing he could think of, the only thing that might make them understand. He pulled back his shirtsleeves, baring his wrists. He lifted his hands, the markings of the chains shimmering in the morning light.

"I've sworn the Oath of Harmony," he said in a raised voice. "There's nothing I can do against that." He glanced toward the thin pillar of light that shot straight up from the side of the mountain, visible even in the sunlight.

He'd hoped they would understand. But instead of accepting his words, the crowd in front of him devolved into chaos. People shouted curses at him. The cry of "Coward!" was raised by a group of men standing in the back.

Master Edric stepped forward, coming to his rescue.

"Now, wait a minute, all of you!" the old man bellowed.

The crowd went still as though stunned into silence. The only noise in the forest was the stir of air through the treetops.

Edric nodded, looking satisfied. He took a step back.

"Let the man speak."

Darien bowed his head, not wanting to confront the angry glares fixed solely on him. He could feel them pinning all their hopes and expectations on him and, for some reason, that made him angry. No matter what they thought, he was just one man.

He said just loud enough to be heard over the stirring of the crowd, "There's nothing I can do here. The battle was waged up on the mountainside, and it's over now. Aerysius is destroyed. I can't change that." He paused, taking a moment to gather himself. "But there's still a war going on in the North, and that's where I'll be headed. Perhaps, at the Front, I can make a difference."

His words were greeted by an uncomfortable silence. People exchanged glances, shifting uneasily.

One man called out, "Then you think the danger's passed?"

Darien shook his head. "If the Front fails to hold, there will be no place that's safe. If you wish to help fight this war, then you'll come with me. Otherwise, gather up your families and leave this place. The Vale of Amberlie is no longer safe."

"Why won't you protect us?" shouted a woman.

"That's your bleeding job, isn't it?" another man yelled.

"He's a bloody coward, that's what he is!"

"Stop it! All of you!"

Darien's gaze jerked to Corban Henley, who was making his way forward through the press of bodies in the crowd. "I've known Darien Lauchlin all my life. He's no coward." Corban stopped and looked at him. "You're going to the Front?"

Darien nodded. "I'm useless here. The Front is the only place I can make any difference."

Henley raised his voice to address the crowd. "What's wrong with you people? You're all standing here whining like a pack of helpless dogs. You all want something done, but instead of lifting a finger to help yourselves, you brand this man a coward because he won't do it all for you. Well, I see only one of him. And there sure as hell's a lot more of you." Looking at Darien, he said, "I'm no stranger to a blade. If you're going to the Front, then I'll come with you." He turned back to the crowd. "So, who's coming with us?"

No one spoke. Henley turned and spat on the ground. "Craven dogs."

A man stepped forward. "I'll go."

His voice was followed by a long gap of silence.

Then another man came forward, saying, "I don't have a family. I'll go with you."

Suddenly, the air was filled with offers of support. Darien let out a sigh. The critical moment had passed, thanks to Corban.

"I'll be heading out at first light," he told them. "I'll take any man who wants to come with me. The rest of you should go home and gather up your families. Leave everything behind. Make for Auberdale. That route would be your safest choice. We'll try to hold the North so that maybe, someday, you'll have a home to come back to."

There were no cheers; his words hadn't been meant to inspire. But the crowd dispersed, which was all Darien wanted to accomplish. Corban Henley gave him a nod as he turned away. Darien stood on the porch of the Bird Man's home and watched until the last stragglers disappeared into the forest.

"You need to work a bit on your delivery." Master Edric patted his shoulder then went back inside. Darien followed, having to duck under the outstretched form of a great heron hanging too low from the ceiling.

Once inside the cottage, Darien stopped. He stood gazing down at his wrist, rotating his arm.

"Don't stare at those chains too long," the Bird Man warned. "They'll begin to feel even heavier than they already are. Trust me. I know from experience."

Darien lowered his hand. "What will you do, Edric?"

"Me? I'm just an old man who loves his birds. I can't fight…the only thing I can do is fly." His voice trailed off. He stood gazing up at the birds slowly spinning on their strings.

The old Master shook his head sadly. "I know you think there's little you can do, but there, you're wrong. If you keep your wits about you, you'll find there are ways to win a battle without having to wash your hands in blood. Use your head. That's why I saved it for you. As for me…it's no good here anymore. My old friends have all flown away. Just listen."

Darien listened. Edric was right. Only the sound of silence greeted his ears. He hadn't noticed the complete absence of birdsong from the forest.

"Birds are smart." Edric smiled softly. "They always know when it's time to fly. As do I."

Darien wondered what Edric meant by that, but the aged Master didn't elaborate. Instead he left the cottage, closing the door behind him.

The Bird Man was used to waking frequently in the night to answer the urgings of a bladder that was just as old and tired as the rest of him. He crept out of bed, shuffling across the room under the spinning shadows of the birds that danced in the green light still piercing the sky above.

He knew what that light was. The gateway had filled his dreams, of late. Edric glanced at his birds, watching them dance in their endless pursuit of flight. He wanted to fly as well. He had always envied birds, envied them the freedom of their wings.

He relieved himself outside against the rough gray bark of a pine he had nurtured from a sapling. He turned to go back inside, but hesitated.

He wanted one last flight.

If anyone had actually been watching, all they would have seen was the form of an old man standing under the branches of a pine suddenly disappear into the shadows of the night. Their eyes would have entirely missed the small warbler that took wing from the place where the old man had just been standing.

The tiny bird fluttered, pumping upward and spiraling into the sky, its whistling queries the only sound in the still night air. The warbler fluttered across the disk of the rising moon, now diving, now soaring, finally backstroking to rest in the spot where it had first arisen.

If anyone had truly been watching, all they would have seen was a breathless old man shuffling out from under the shadow of an ancient pine, climbing stiffly back up the stairs to the door of his cottage.

Edric made his way back inside, but not to his own bed. Instead, he knelt beside the young man lying on a pallet on the floor. He waited, eyes studying the rhythmic rise and fall of the blankets, to make certain his young visitor was in the deepest stage of sleep.

Tenderly, he placed a trembling and rheumatic hand over Darien's chest, closing his tired old eyes. Above him, his silent friends whirled on a breeze, their feathers ruffling on outstretched wings.

The Bird Man filled his mind with the thrill of flight as he opened the conduit of Transference between them and offered up his ancient life.

Chapter Eight
Greystone Keep

Pass of Lor-Gamorth, The Front

Lightning streaked a sky filled with turbulent thunderheads, making the heavens blaze. As it faded, ice on the mountain peaks gleamed, a hellish afterglow soon devoured by consummate darkness. Winds ripped down from the mountain passes, brutally cold.

Kyel staggered as a gust of wind threatened to push him over, having to lean forward just to remain on his feet. The wind was so violent, it sucked the breath right out of his lungs. He'd lost the feeling in his hands a long time ago. His toes throbbed from the cold.

It should have been daylight.

When they'd started up into the Pass of Lor-Gamorth, the first hint of morning was warming the sky above the horizon. But as they'd climbed higher between the jagged black slopes, the light of day had slowly disintegrated.

Someone had warned him it would be like this. But no words could have prepared him for the horrifying reality of the Shadowspears. There was no sunlight, ever, in the mountains that bordered the Black Lands. There was only a death-dark sky filled with turbulent clouds that surged across the sky. The weather patterns here were an extension of the curse that had desecrated the lands to the north a thousand years ago, remaking them in hell's own image.

And Kyel knew he was walking straight toward those twisted lands, just one in a long file of exhausted men. He had known these men now for three weeks, the time it had taken them to journey from Rothscard across the grasslands of the North. They were convicts, one and all. Sentenced to death but delivered from that fate only to be conscripted into the war effort. It was still a death sentence, however commuted. There was no return from the Front. Everyone knew the only way out was to die.

Kyel had wept quietly every night the first week, facing the certainty that he would never see his wife or son ever again. He wasn't the only man who'd broken down. They all knew that every step of the long march carried them a little closer to the end.

Lightning flickered, and rolling thunder trembled the mountains. In that brief flash of light, Kyel made out the dark outline of a fortress built on a rocky outcrop. It was there for just an instant and then was gone, consumed by utter darkness.

The name Greystone Keep was legendary. The fortress at the edge of the Black Lands had existed for over five hundred years, holding the North against the incursions of the Enemy. Kyel had heard its name mentioned in stories, but had never imagined that he would actually see it with his own eyes.

As they climbed the slopes, the features of the keep became visible. A frayed banner whipped in the wind over a high turret, the only part of the fortress that looked intact. The crumbling walls were a lusterless gray, the stone infested with yellow growths of lichen. The ragged structure was supported by stone buttresses that appeared ineffective.

Kyel's legs were trembling by the time they reached the fortress. He followed the others through a large gate and into a circular room at the base of the tower. The wind ceased as soon as he crossed the threshold. Kyel sagged in relief. He felt weak and dizzy, his face stinging, his cheeks moistened by tears wrung from his eyes by the gale.

He wanted to stop there and rest. The air of the tower was warm, and he was exhausted. But the men who guarded them were merciless, forcing them forward through a doorway ahead.

The room they entered must have been the main hall of the keep at one time. But if there had ever been a ceiling, it had long since collapsed. The rear wall had also caved in, now just a heaping pile of rubble. There were no windows, only narrow slits that ringed the walls.

The guards ordered a halt, glaring at the prisoners with disdain. Kyel waited with a growing sense of unease as a soldier moved slowly down the line, unlocking their chains. Beside him, Traver leaned and almost fell over, earning a sharp look of reproach from the nearest guard.

Three men entered the room. They walked in crisp strides past the file of convicts, stopping halfway down the line. The man who stood in front had the look of a hardened soldier. He stood straight with his hands clasped behind his back, shoulders squared. He wore his long, graying hair tied back at the nape of his neck, his eyes cold and harsh like the black stone of the mountains. He turned to face them, running his gaze down the line.

"Welcome to the Front," he announced.

His voice resounded throughout the hall of the keep, echoing off the stark walls before falling off with a grim undertone of finality. There was a long pause as he surveyed the face of each man in line.

"Make no mistake, gentlemen. Every man of you is here to die. One and all, you've been convicted of crimes that warrant execution. That sentence yet stands—it has only been deferred. All of you will probably be dead in a year, much likely sooner. So, go ahead. Look around."

Kyel did as instructed, looking sideways at Traver, who returned his gaze with eyes widened by fear. Kyel glanced away, suddenly queasy, as he envisioned Traver lying dead on the black rocks of the pass.

"All those here are now your brothers," the soldier continued relentlessly. "How long you live and how well you die will depend exclusively on these men. So learn their faces well. They are all that stands between you and your grave.

"My name is Garret Proctor, Force Commander of the garrison here at Greystone Keep. The order that sends you to your death will come from my lips. I won't even think twice about it. There is no escape from the Front, so don't consider it.

Every crack and crevice of these mountains is guarded by experienced sentries. If you are ever found even ten steps away from your post, you will be slain. No questions. No one will care that you just stepped away to take a piss."

Kyel swallowed. He vowed silently that he'd never so much as scratch without permission.

The commander swept his gaze down the line of terrified men. When his stare fell on the man to Kyel's left, his eyes narrowed. "There is one of you here that won't heed my warning. It happens every time, without fail. Someone always thinks they can escape and will try to make a break for it in the night. I can promise you this, gentlemen: at least one of you will be dead come morning.

"On my right is Captain Devlin Craig. Half of you will be under his command. Captain Craig has been charged with holding the bottom of the pass, and he has kept that charge for over three years. On my left is Captain Sutton Royce. Captain Royce is charged with the defenses of Greystone Keep."

Captain Royce stepped forward. He was a robust man wearing a chain mail tunic covered by a tattered gray cloak. His brown eyes were just as stern as the commander's, though decisively more brutal. His face was covered by a thick growth of beard a shade darker than his hair.

"Greystone Keep holds the Pass of Lor-Gamorth," he rumbled. "If it should ever fall, then we will lose the pass. If we lose the pass, then we lose the North. And if the North should ever fall, the Enemy will sweep southward until every last city, town, and village of the Rhen looks just like that."

He pointed toward the back of the hall, where the entire wall of the keep had crumbled and fallen away. At first, Kyel could see only darkness broken by occasional flashes of a queer, muted light. But then a strong fork of lightning illuminated the land far below and, for just an instant, he could see a large expanse of scorched earth that stretched as far as the eye could see.

Kyel gasped as he realized he was staring down at the Black Lands. What was more shocking was the fact that they were actually, consummately black. Nothing could live there in that shattered waste. Nothing…but the Enemy.

Royce continued. "These walls have stood for over five hundred years. As you can see, they have been breached many times, but they have always held. It is my duty to make certain they continue to hold, and I will not hesitate to sacrifice as many lives as it takes to see that they do."

"So." The force commander stepped forward. "I will leave you with these final words: fight well and die well. And always remember that you are all that protects your homeland from the fate that befell Caladorn, the kingdom to the north you've probably only ever heard of as the Black Lands. If this keep should ever fall, everything you know will be desecrated by the Enemy, and everything you love will be destroyed."

With that, he turned and let his long strides carry him out of the hall, his gray wool cloak flapping behind him in his wake. Kyel supposed he should have felt relieved as the commander disappeared through the doorway. But, somehow, he felt that his situation had not improved. He almost wished the grim man would come back again. Kyel did not like the malicious glint in the eyes of Captain Royce.

It was Captain Craig that stepped forward then, surveying the line of convicts with a look of distaste. His arms were heavily gauntleted, his straw-gold hair disarrayed about his bearded face. He stood with his hands clenched behind his back in a somewhat casual facsimile of the commander's polished stance, an enormous sword in his hands.

As he waited, groups of soldiers entered the room, hefting between them four large sacks. They carried the sacks to the far corners of the hall and there dumped out the contents gracelessly on the floor. The clatter of falling metal echoed off the crumbled walls, ringing through the keep.

The soldiers began spreading out what looked like garbage across the floor in front of the fires. It took Kyel a moment to realize he was looking at piles of weapons, probably scavenged from the bodies of dead soldiers who had fought and died with those selfsame weapons in their hands.

Devlin Craig smiled as he saw the expressions on the men

before him. As though reading Kyel's own thoughts, he proclaimed, "You will now choose the weapon you will die holding. Whichever it is, be it sword, mace, bow, or spear, you shall eat with it, sleep with it, care for it like a child, and love it better than a wife. So, come forward. Choose your weapons well and then get back in line!"

Kyel walked toward the nearest assortment of arms. Unlike most of the boys he'd grown up with, he had never had the desire to wield a weapon. He watched Traver moving his hand over the collection, finally gripping the hilt of an enormous sword.

But Kyel had spent his entire adult life calculating totals and carving wood. He didn't think he would have the sheer brutality to drive such a blade home into living flesh. So he chose a longbow from the pile of scattered weapons, knowing well how the irony played on his surname. He didn't care; the smooth length of wood felt good as he closed his fingers around it.

He held the bow up, testing the weight of it in his hand. The wood looked to be cut from a single, long-grained stave of yew. There was no bowstring, just notches in the ends where a string could be anchored. The bow was slender and tapered, longer than he was tall.

The last man selected his weapon and filed back into line. Beside him, Traver was staring at the monstrous blade he had chosen, looking down at it with a perplexed expression on his face. If Traver had the strength to even swing that mass of steel, Kyel would be surprised.

They were divided then into groups, the men holding bows going to one corner of the hall while those holding swords and spears went their separate ways. Two soldiers walked toward Kyel's group of bowmen, their hands full of folded gray cloaks, which they threw on the floor. Kyel bent down, selecting one from the top of the pile.

They were then instructed to bed down right where they stood. There was to be no meal, no blanket. Just a rough wood floor and an open roof overhead. At least the fire behind him shed a little warmth.

Kyel donned the gray wool cloak and lay down, wrapping the

cloak tightly around his body. As he lay there shivering, he found himself thinking of his family. He closed his eyes and tried to pretend it was Amelia there beside him instead of a longbow. He hoped, in his dreams, she would be.

The sound of shouts woke him from sleep. Kyel sat up and looked around. It was late; the fires had burned low. There was a commotion going on all around, soldiers rushing to scale ladders up to a narrow ledge that ran all around the tops of the walls. There, men were positioned at regular intervals, peering out through narrow slits. A few raised longbows, nocking arrows to bowstrings and sighting out through the gaps.

Commander Proctor strode into the hall, barking a demand for a report. He was met by Royce and Craig.

"A large party approaches from the south," Craig reported, nodding his head in the direction of the tower.

Above, a flaming arrow shot over the open roof of the keep. It was followed shortly by another. A signal, though Kyel didn't know what it meant.

As he turned in the direction of the shattered rear wall, his eyes fell on a prone form laid out on the floor behind them. The man's back was pierced with three long arrows with the same type of fletching as those used by the archers on the walls. Kyel remembered the commander's promise that one of them would be dead come morning. Apparently, he'd been right.

Above, a third fiery shaft blazed across the midnight sky. A shout rang out from the pass below. Both Royce and Craig moved to a long, horizontal slit, staring down into the darkness below as the commander took up position in the back of the room.

Over the sound of the wind, Kyel could hear the echo of approaching footsteps. Whatever force was coming, it was no few. The bowmen on the walls swiveled as one, their shafts now aimed at the door to the hall.

Garret Proctor stood regarding the doorway with narrowed eyes. Royce and Craig drew up in front of him, one man to either side.

The door to the tower room opened, and suddenly a crowd of men was spilling in through the doorway. It took Kyel a moment to realize that the men congregating at the front of the hall were no threat. They were not soldiers. If anything, they looked to be farmers. Exhausted farmers, though some did appear to be armed.

The men staggered in shivering, swaying on their feet, their eyes widening as they noticed the bowmen on the walls with shafts directed at their chests. But they kept coming, pouring in through the open doorway, at least seventy of them. Possibly over a hundred. As the last man entered the hall, Kyel drew in a gasp.

This was no farmer.

The man was young with dark hair that spilled past his shoulders. There was an alarming intensity in his eyes that made Kyel want to draw away from him. He was clothed entirely in black and carried a longsword on his back.

He strode confidently forward, crossing the room toward where Proctor stood with his officers. As the man passed by, Kyel saw that his cloak was embroidered with the image of an eight-pointed star. He recognized the symbol and knew what it meant: the man before him was a mage of Aerysius.

Silence filled the hall as the man drew up before the officers. Commander Proctor made no move, just stood regarding the mage in front of him with critical eyes.

Then a slow smile formed on Craig's lips. All at once, he stepped forward and clasped the man's arm with both hands. "Darien! I didn't think we'd ever see you again. And by the looks of it, you've brought us a kingly gift. Praise be to the gods, man!"

To Kyel's astonishment, the two men embraced as if old friends. Royce eased his blade back into its scabbard, stepping forward to shake the mage's hand. Garret Proctor nodded a curt greeting, his expression no longer quite so harsh.

Kyel's gaze was drawn to the sword carried by the mage. That was strange. Masters of Aerysius were forbidden to bear weapons. Perhaps the man was merely an acolyte who hadn't sworn his oaths yet. That might explain the presence of the blade.

"What news have you?" the Force Commander asked.

The mage's face grew serious. In a tone grim with finality, he pronounced, "The Well of Tears has been opened. Aerysius has fallen."

Garret Proctor took a step backward, looking rocked. Kyel's own mind reeled as it struggled to make sense of the horrific tidings. He swept his gaze across the room, looking from face to face, and saw that every man in the keep was shaken by the mage's statement. Even the most hardened soldiers stood with their mouths open, eyes wide and full of dismay.

If Aerysius had truly fallen, then everything was lost. The Sentinels were the last, strongest line of defense the Rhen had. Without the Sentinels, there was no hope. The Enemy would flood down upon the vulnerable nations unchecked. There would be no repeat of the Battle of Meridan, where defensive magic had turned the tides of war.

It only took Proctor a moment to recover somewhat, though he was still visibly shaken. The sound of his voice carried only a whisper of its former strength as he asked, "What is left?"

The mage in the black cloak of dead Aerysius bowed his head. "To my knowledge, I'm the only survivor."

The force commander drew in a breath and turned away. Kyel couldn't see his face. But he knew the depths of despair that had to be written there, the same as on the face of every man in the hall.

Garret Proctor took a faltering step away, and then another. He walked stiffly toward a wooden chair, one of the few pieces of furniture in the room. Without hesitation, he cast himself down upon it.

Captain Royce lay a hand in sympathy on the mage's shoulder. But then he, too, turned away and moved to stand behind his commander.

The mage looked out across the hall. Kyel shivered when those unsettling eyes fell on him. Their stares locked for just an instant, but the man turned away, striding over to stand at the force commander's side.

Garret Proctor reached out and grasped the mage's arm. He slid back the dark fabric of his shirtsleeve, exposing a marking Kyel knew well.

He'd been wrong. The man standing before him was no acolyte. He was a fully Bound Master of Aerysius.

Garret Proctor looked relieved at the sight of the legendary symbol.

"Which order did you take?" he asked.

"I chose the Order of Sentinels."

Proctor nodded slightly. Then, much more directly, he asked, "How strong are you?"

The mage dropped his gaze, bowing his head as though ashamed. There was a moment's pause. Then, softly, he answered, "I am a Grand Master of the Eighth Tier."

There was a shocked murmur from all around the room. Soldiers groped for the comfort of their weapons. Even Craig and Royce took a step back away from the man. Kyel's own mind spun as he recalled something he'd read in *The Mysteries of Aerysius* by the famous historian Cedric Cromm. It was one of the few books his father had owned, so Kyel had read it enough times to have the passage memorized:

> *A mage passed beyond the sixth tier would be a vile abomination, creating chaos beyond imaginings. No mind of man is capable of withstanding the vastness of such power and should soon be broken down.*

Kyel's stomach clenched in dread. The man standing in front of them clothed in black was an abomination. By the authoritative expert on the subject, this Darien was already condemned, destined to be consumed by the unthinkable amount of power within him. It was only a matter of time.

But Garret Proctor did not seem to understand the dire corollary. He stared up at the man with eyes full of brimming hope.

"We have a chance, then," he uttered in a whispered breath.

"Yes. A chance."

Chapter Nine
The Last Sentinel

Pass of Lor-Gamorth, The Front

Darien slumped into a chair, taking in the circular room he found so familiar. Garret Proctor had made his home at the top of the tower of Greystone Keep for over fifteen years, yet in all that time, he had acquired few possessions. The dim chamber was as stark and barren as the man himself.

The only adornment was a large map that showed a rough image of the Shadowspears. The map ended at the northern extremity of the mountains. No one had ever managed to chart the Black Lands beyond the pass. No one who had made it back alive, at any rate.

There were a few pieces of furniture in the room: a small chest by the door and two decrepit chairs pushed up to a table that had been broken and mended so often that no two legs matched. The commander's bed was just a simple pallet, tucked up against the wall near the hearth.

Proctor took the chair opposite him as Royce fetched them earthenware cups. Miraculously, he produced a flagon of wine, hefting it proudly in his big hands before filling both cups. He placed one cup on the table before the commander and offered the other to Darien. The liquid inside was dark red, reminiscent of fresh blood. Darien swirled the wine around before tasting it, trying his best not to make a face.

"Don't you complain," Royce admonished. "That's all there is. A special present from the Queen of Emmery. You saw her latest shipment down in the hall. I'll wager she sent this wine along as a bribe to make sure we don't send that lot right back to her."

The Queen of Emmery was more gracious than other rulers. Infrequent shipments of prisoners and supplies was better than no reinforcements at all. Not a soul had been sent up from Auberdale in recent months, and Treshorne had stopped sending men to the pass years ago. The Southern nations had never aided Greystone Keep within living memory. Their kings had probably forgotten that the Front even existed. In the absence of a recent offensive, the nations of the Rhen had become complacent.

Proctor took a heavy drink from his cup. He closed his eyes as he swallowed the awful liquid, savoring it as though the wine were the most delicate vintage that had ever passed his lips.

"Tell me everything," he commanded.

Darien complied.

It was hard, reliving the memories. Harder still to see his own emotions mirrored in the eyes of the three men listening. When his words finally died, he felt emotionally exhausted. He sagged back in his chair, taking a long drink of the loathsome wine. After he swallowed that, he took another, tilting his head back and draining the cup.

For long moments, not a word was spoken.

Sutton Royce finally broke the silence. "Things haven't been much better here. Enemy soldiers are still massing in numbers unheard of. They're gathering just to the east, under the shadow of Orguleth. We've had raids almost nightly. They're probing us. Testing our fortifications and marking the locations of our sentries. Everything points toward a sizable offensive."

Darien nodded. The Enemy had been mobilizing even before he'd left the pass for Aerysius. His mother had known as well. That was the reason she had issued the summons, recalling every mage from the distant corners of the land. Aerysius had been gathering its might, preparing for open war. Bound as they were by the Mage's Oath, the Sentinels would have been meager defense against the size of the invasion that was surely coming.

And now he was the only mage left to wage that war.

Proctor must have been sensing the direction of his thoughts. The commander held Darien's eyes as he spoke with absolute conviction:

"You are the last surviving Sentinel of Aerysius. Your strength shall be our salvation."

Darien bowed his head, staring down at the empty cup in his hand. He set it down on the table, struggling with his emotions.

Garret Proctor had worked with the limitations of the Sentinels before, had calculated them into his tactics all throughout his long career. He had been at the Battle of Meridan. More than anyone, he should know better.

"I've spoken the Oath of Harmony," Darien reminded him, silently hoping the old soldier would understand.

It was Devlin Craig, his friend and brother in arms for two long years, who strode forward to challenge him on it. The huge man leaned forward with his hands on the edge of the table, staring across its length with a penetrating stare.

"I see you still carry your sword, Darien. Exactly what are your intentions? Are you going to keep your Oath? Or will you forsake it?"

Darien looked away, his eyes drawn toward the fire in the hearth. A log broke and rained sparks upward with a startling crack. He watched the them drift lazily, wafting on an updraft from the chimney.

"I thought to convince my mother to Unbind the Sentinels before Aerysius fell," he said, staring deeply into the fire so he wouldn't have to meet their eyes. "She refused me. I didn't understand at the time, but now I do."

He looked down at the symbol of the chain on his wrist, tracing it with a finger. "The Oath is all that separates me from the likes of Zavier Renquist and Byron Connel. Cyrus Krane, Arden Hannah…Myria Anassis. You must recognize those names. You know of whom I speak. It's a safeguard. An assurance that the power I wield does not corrupt me."

Garret Proctor waved a dismissive hand. "You speak of eight demons long dead and moldering in their graves. The fall of Bryn Calazar was a thousand years ago. You can't compare yourself to them."

The commander didn't understand. Just as Darien hadn't understood himself before he had been forced to decide between a cliff's sheer face or the shards of a broken vow.

He insisted, "The Oath is imperative, especially for me. Don't you understand? I *must* take it seriously. I am an *eighth-tier Sentinel.* There has never been a mage stronger than the sixth tier. Ever. In all of history. Do you understand why?"

Proctor's face was a study in grim resolve. "It doesn't matter. I've read Cromm's work. I can even quote you the very passage you're referring to. But that makes absolutely no difference to our present situation. Right here, right now, you can be a very effective weapon if you allow yourself to explore the full extent of your potential. Over time, you may even become a dangerous weapon. *But that is exactly what I need.*"

"I will not betray my Oath," Darien insisted.

Craig slammed his hand on the table, jolting Darien's cup. "Then why are you here? Tell me that! Aerysius is dead. Its traditions are dead! Why do you insist on holding to a vow you've always claimed you don't believe in?"

Darien started to push his chair back, but Proctor's raised hand kept him in his seat.

"There are other ways," Royce allowed. "The Sentinels who protected Meridan never broke Oath."

But Craig was having none of it. "Darien's father died at Meridan! And Lauchlin wasn't alone—twelve mages were lost within the first *hour* of battle!"

Proctor's eyes looked like smoldering, silvered coals. He said firmly, "We cannot use Darien the way the Sentinels were used at Meridan. If we put him in the thick of battle, he'll be a target for every Enemy spear in the Black Lands."

Darien had to nod in agreement. It was true. A black cloak was a target on any field of battle, a trophy prized by the Enemy above any other.

In an effort to appease, he assured them, "I still have my sword. The Oath doesn't prevent me from using it, just tradition. And I can heal any wound I take almost instantly."

Royce lurched around the table and grabbed a fistful of Darien's shirt.

"Can you heal yourself when an axe takes your head off?" he

growled. "Can you save yourself from the flames when you're beaten senseless? Your own father burned to death with those chains on his wrists! That's what the Enemy does to your kind. Is that how you wish to die? You're the last Sentinel left, Darien. You can't just throw your life away!"

"Or is that exactly what you mean to do?" Craig asked, his eyes filled with concern. "You've lost everything. Aerysius was destroyed by your own brother's hand. You've lost Meiran, and I know how dear she was to you. Tell me, Darien. Did you come back here just to die?"

Shaking in anger, Darien stood and firmly disengaged Royce's hand. The entire room reeled around him. Never in his life could he remember being so enraged at a friend. He clutched Royce's hand in a trembling fist as he glared his wrath into the man's face. Then he threw the soldier's arm away from him.

He growled between clenched teeth, *"I don't know what you expect from me."*

There was a long, gaping silence. Then:

"Stop."

The commander's word had the bite of an order. But neither Craig nor Royce backed down. Instead, they stood frozen in place, glaring.

Proctor said firmly, "Leave him be. He's been through enough."

There was a tense moment of hesitation before both soldiers finally relaxed. But Darien couldn't. He stood confronting the two men with shoulders tensed, quivering in fury.

Craig bowed his head, blowing out a heaving sigh. He took a moment to collect himself. Then he looked at Darien with sincere regret in his eyes.

"I'm sorry," he said, shaking his head. "And I'm sorry about Meiran. I'm sorry about everything. Gods, Darien." He turned and stalked away, a fist swiping out at the air in front of him.

Royce nodded. "Look. We're all tired. Let's get some sleep. We can hash this out in the morning." He looked over his shoulder and waited for Proctor to nod his permission before he left.

"You can bed down here in the tower," the commander said

to Darien, rising from his chair.

Darien took a deep breath and then nodded. He turned out his bedroll along the wall next to the hearth. Proctor took to his own pallet, fully dressed, as was his custom. Darien placed his sword on the floor next to him and eased himself down beside it, pulling his cloak tight about him as he lay his head back and stared up into the shadows of the rafters above.

He closed his eyes. He could still hear the throbbing of his pulse in his ears, a constant and irritating rhythm that seemed louder than the shriek of the wind that hissed in through the arrow slits. He measured the pace of his breathing, trying to calm his racing heart.

He lay there a long time, but sleep didn't come. After an hour, he pushed himself to his feet and crept across the floor. Moving as quietly as he could, he started down the steps and let the winding stairs carry him around and down to the tower's base.

The keep's massive oak door stood closed and barred, so he turned away from it. He would have liked to have gone outside, to stand looking out at the tall crags of the Shadowspears, as he'd done so often in the past. But instead, he walked toward the soft glow of light coming in through the door to the hall.

He picked his way quietly around the scattered bodies of slumbering men to the far corner. There, he stopped beside a fire that had burned low, now only a glow of dying coals, nodding at the two sentries who tended it.

Darien let his gaze wander across the floor, moving from one sleeping face to the next until he found the one he was looking for. Then he moved forward and knelt beside the slumbering man with curly blond hair and the face of an innocent.

Darien stared deeply into the man's face, taking in every smooth feature, his gaze traveling to the hand clasped limply around a longbow. He had noticed the man earlier, and something about him had drawn his curiosity.

He reached down, lifting the flaccid hand away from the smooth shaft of wood. He ran his fingers over the palm, tracing upward to stroke the pads of the fingertips. Beneath him, the young man stirred in his sleep, sensing the touch. Darien drew his hand away.

The skin he had felt was soft and smooth, but for a small buildup of callous at the base of the fingers. Those hands were used to the fine strokes of tools, not the steel grip of a weapon or the coarse handles of a plow. More intriguing was the small callous on the third finger of the right hand.

Darien turned his gaze to the bow at the man's side. It looked to be good wood. Gingerly, he drew it toward him, rising to his feet as he held the bow out before him, angling his gaze down the length of the shaft. There was no warp in the wood. It was an excellent bow, with a light draw weight, ideal for a beginner. He lowered it to his side, resting the bow on the floor like a staff. He turned, his foot scuffing against a metal hilt on the floor.

Darien raised his eyebrows as he took in the enormous bastard sword lying at the side of a slender man with tousled red hair. He appraised the man's delicate hands, scoffing silently. The man was a fool. He had selected a blade that was much too massive for him.

Darien picked the sword up off the floor and walked away.

Kyel awoke the next morning to find a full sheaf of arrows at his side, along with a new waxed bowstring. And Traver's sword had been replaced by another, this one much smaller and cleaner-looking. The blade was well-oiled, and someone had meticulously honed the dual cutting edges.

Traver had been irate. At least until he'd tested the edge of the blade with his thumb, wincing at the cut that appeared in his skin. After that, he stared down at his new weapon with growing appreciation.

It was still dark out, though the sun should have already risen. When he looked up through the open roof of the keep, Kyel saw the same black sky that had been there the night before, full of churning clouds and buffeting winds.

After a meager breakfast, they were assembled into lines and marched out to the practice yard. Fires lit all around the yard provided a good amount of light. A high wall on one side effectively blocked the wind. Kyel found himself separated from Traver and thrown in with a cluster of men holding longbows.

An old sergeant spent quite a bit of time modeling the proper grip to use and where to place the hand on the shaft. Kyel was already tired by the time he was finally allowed to nock an arrow to the bowstring. He gritted his teeth and pulled the bowstring back to his cheek. The action took every bit of strength he had.

He heard exclamations from the men up and down the line, which made him feel a little better. He trained his eyes down the arrow's shaft at the target, a man-size clump of hay with a circle painted on it. Exactly as he'd been instructed, he released his fingers as smoothly as he could manage.

The arrow flew wide of its mark. But that didn't matter. What mattered was what the bowstring did to his left wrist. Kyel yelped as the string slapped back against his skin, making him jump and almost drop his bow.

Behind him, he could hear the regular soldiers laughing. Kyel stared down at the red welt on his wrist in shock. That had really *hurt.* He glared back over his shoulder as he picked another arrow up off the ground.

This time, he held his wrist at more of an angle, away from the bowstring's recoil. Determined to get it right, he drew the waxed string back to his cheek. He took his time aiming, sighting down the shaft until the target slowly steadied. He was so afraid he was going to jerk at the last moment. With as much concentration as he could summon, he plucked his fingers away.

The bowstring hummed, and this time it didn't score his wrist. The shaft flew perfectly straight. It slapped into the clump of hay, hitting the mark just off-center. The farmer next to him laughed, grinning in approval. Another man clapped him on the back.

Kyel looked behind him, feeling no small amount of pride. He was the first man who had managed to hit the hay. The soldiers weren't laughing anymore. Feeling smug, Kyel almost said something. But then his eyes caught the shape of a dark form standing just to the right of the group of men.

Kyel's stomach lurched as he saw the look of satisfaction in the Sentinel's eyes, right before the mage turned and stalked away.

Chapter Ten
Legacy

Pass of Lor-Gamorth, The Front

Kyel felt a tap on his shoulder and looked up to find Sergeant Ulric, the dour old bowmaster he had worked with in the practice yard, hovering over him. Ulric motioned for him to follow then turned and walked away without waiting to see if the command was being obeyed. Kyel set down the plate of charred meat he had been half-heartedly picking at. As soon as the plate touch the floor, it was snatched up by one of the soldiers seated next to him, who brought the blackened morsel up to his lips with a grunt of thanks.

Kyel rose and fell in behind Ulric. The man led him wordlessly through the crowded hall and into the circular chamber at the base of the tower. There, the old soldier halted and ran a critical gaze over him, starting at Kyel's boots and working his way up to his face. Evidently satisfied with what he saw, Ulric started up the tower stairs.

Kyel had no idea who had sent for him or why he was being singled out. He wondered if it had something to do with his progress in the practice yard, which was the only thing he could think of that might set him apart from the other members of his company. He didn't know what to expect at the top of that turret.

Or who.

The air was cold and damp, moving in through arrow slits that followed the curve of the stairs up into the shadows of the rafters high above. The dim lights of torches cast a flickering, eerie dance along the wall. Overhead, Kyel could hear the flutter of bird or bat wings beating against the rafters.

He followed Ulric with a growing sense of unease. The spiraling staircase led to a room at the top of the high turret that smelled strongly of wood smoke and dust. The first thing he noticed was a wide hearth in front of him that had two neatly made pallets to either side. A blazing fire seemed to be doing a fair job of warming the place, despite the cold air coming in through the arrow slits. The chamber was conspicuously lacking almost any kind of fixture or decoration.

Gazing at the hearth, Kyel almost missed the shadowy figure standing against the wall to his right.

The darkly clad Sentinel stood with his back to them. He was tracing a finger along a contour in the map, giving no sign that he was even aware of their presence. But suddenly he paused, his hand dropping to his side.

A shiver ran down Kyel's spine as the man turned, fixing him with the same look of quiet appraisal he had worn in the practice yard. The mage nodded, dismissing Ulric without a word.

Kyel shuddered as he realized he was alone in the tower with an eighth-tier Sentinel of Aerysius.

The man extended his hand in a welcoming gesture. Kyel sat down at the table, leaning his bow against the wall behind him. The mage remained standing, watching him for a long moment before speaking.

"I saw you down in the yard," he said. "Have you ever held a bow before?"

Kyel shook his head. "No. That was my first time."

The mage nodded slightly then slid into the seat opposite Kyel. "My name is Darien Lauchlin," he said, extending his hand.

Kyel shook his hand, surprised that the man hadn't offered his long and imposing title. "Kyel Archer of Covendrey Township."

To Kyel's astonishment, he found the man grinning at him.

"Archer the archer," Darien said. "Now *that* will go over well with the men."

His smile was so honest and reassuring that Kyel found himself grinning too. The irony of his surname hadn't been lost on the members of his unit. The others had taken turns ribbing him about it all day.

The mage let his smile slip, but his eyes remained mild. "Do you mind telling me what you did for a trade back in Covendrey?"

"I was apprenticed to a merchant," Kyel answered, remembering to add the honorific "Great Master" only as an afterthought. His nerves tensed, hoping the mage wouldn't take offense at his hesitation.

The Sentinel waved his hand. "My friends call me Darien."

Kyel was struck speechless. A Grand Master of Aerysius had just labeled him a friend, whether he had meant to or not.

Of course he meant to, Kyel berated himself. Mages never did anything that wasn't deliberate. He wondered what the man was after.

"A merchant's apprentice," Darien said thoughtfully. "That would make you good with numbers. And you know your letters as well, I take it?"

Kyel nodded, admitting, "My father was an acolyte of Aerysius, but only for a time. He taught me my letters."

Darien's eyes widen at his words. Slowly, the man stood up from his chair and paced away, head bowed and hands clasped behind his back. He paused beside the hearth, staring pensively into the flames.

"I noticed you last night when I arrived," he admitted. "I hope you don't mind, but I've had my eye on you throughout the day."

Kyel fingered his bow absently. He produced the waxed and expertly tied bowstring from his pocket as a thought occurred to him. "You left this for me. And you switched out Traver's sword. Why?"

"I did him a favor. The blade he'd picked was too much of a weapon for him. The sword I gave him will serve him better."

Summoning his courage, Kyel asked, "Why have you been watching me?"

The Sentinel looked at him. "Have you ever been tested for Consideration?"

Kyel felt stunned. No wonder the man kept staring at him that way. Darien was hoping to find an apprentice, probably someone to follow after him. Kyel knew the gift was transferred upon death from one mage to the next in an unbroken line of inheritance. But not just anyone could receive it. The ability was rare, and Kyel knew for a fact he didn't have it. Darien was going to be disappointed.

Kyel said, "I've been tested. Twice. I never passed."

"Yet your father did."

"Aye," Kyel admitted. "But he didn't last long as an acolyte. Only two years. I don't understand. Are you thinking I could have the ability?"

"I can see the potential in you, but I've no idea how strong it is. Some people take longer to develop an affinity. If you were tested again, you might pass this time. It's possible, at least. I'd like to try."

"It's too late." Kyel sighed and shook his head. "I have a family…I did, at least."

Darien dropped his gaze. To Kyel, it seemed he was struggling with something that was difficult for him, like a dark secret he was afraid, or even ashamed, of admitting. When he looked back up, his eyes had lost most of their intensity.

"You heard what I said last night. Aerysius has been destroyed. I'm the only Sentinel left alive. I can scarcely provide an adequate defense for this keep, let alone the entire Rhen." He paused, shifting uncomfortably. "And I've another problem. There is too much of the gift in me. No one was ever meant to take on this much. Eventually, it's going to be more than I can live with. I need someone to pass on my gift to so that the legacy of Aerysius doesn't die with me."

Kyel looked away. He hardly knew this man, but for some reason, he felt moved by Darien's plight. He truly wanted to help him, but he wasn't a mage. And, even if he were, Kyel didn't think he had it in him to give what the man was asking.

"Wouldn't it just kill me too?"

"Not necessarily. If I can find another with the ability, I can divide the conduit between you. It's been done before. Then there would be two of you. And if you both go out and find two others within your lifetime…"

Kyel nodded, seeing where he was going with that line of

reasoning. Where there was now just one mage, in time there could be two…and then, eventually, as many as eight. But that's all there could ever be, no more.

Kyel frowned. "But all this hardly matters if I don't pass the test."

"That's right."

Kyel understood. He nodded slowly, drawing in a shuddering breath. He realized he was trembling as Darien stood and crossed the floor toward him. The mage lowered himself to a crouch in front of Kyel's chair, staring him keenly in the eye. Kyel cringed back, wanting to look away.

The last thing Kyel remembered was seeing the vast amount of grief that clouded the Sentinel's eyes.

And then the world around him dimmed to a distant point of light.

Garret Proctor looked out from the battlements at the top of Greystone's tower, Sutton Royce at his side. Softly, he asked, "Have you spoken with him again?"

The captain nodded, his hand clenching the baldric of the longsword strapped at his back. "He refuses to forsake the Oath. You know Darien. Once he's got his mind set, even a supreme act of the gods won't change his course."

It was Proctor's turn to nod. The man was just as stubborn as his father. It was that same arrogance that had gotten Gerald Lauchlin tied to a wooden stake.

Sometimes, in his nightmares, Proctor could still hear the sound of the man's dying screams.

Chapter Eleven
The Breaking Storm

Pass of Lor-Gamorth, The Front

The next two weeks went by in a blur of exhausting training sessions interspersed with tedious hours of boredom. Kyel found himself growing used to the routine, though he discovered he enjoyed the hours of practice with his bow far more than the time spent sitting around.

He remembered nothing of Darien Lauchlin's test. He only remembered wakening as if from sleep to find the mage backing away from him, head bowed. Kyel had felt horrible at the time. He knew how much the Sentinel had at stake.

"I'm sorry," he'd said.

But when Darien raised his head, his expression was one of wonder.

"No need to be," he said. "You passed the test."

The following days had gone by in a strange sort of haze. Darien had never approached him again, and Kyel made of point of trying to avoid him. Every day, he practiced with his bow until his arms were shaking.

Part of him still wanted to deny Darien's words. It all seemed so far from reality, it couldn't possibly be true. But when he left the practice yard, one look back at his target was enough to make him admit that perhaps the mage was right.

All of his arrows had hit the mark.

A vicious gust seized Darien's hair, playing it out behind him and tossing dark strands forward into his face. He felt ill at ease on the battlements at the top of Greystone's tower. He stood looking out through the opening of an embrasure, his hand resting on the wall.

Under the right conditions, he could sometimes see all the way down to the mouth of the pass, and even out across the distant wastes of the Black Lands beyond.

Tonight was such a night. The winds were violent, eliminating any chance that fog could gather to obscure the view. The Black Lands unfolded beneath him, revealed in their naked desecration, flowing out from the foothills like a dark sea to the gloom of the northern horizon.

He reached out from within to gain a sense of the swirling tides of the magic field. It felt different tonight, like slick rivulets of quicksilver draining off the slopes, rushing in unbridled currents toward the lowlands beyond. There was no good reason for the field to be surging so wild and unchecked.

Darien started thinking of the bad reasons. He felt certain there was a storm brewing. He could sense it in the air, just as he had the morning he'd arrived in the Vale. Only, this time, he didn't dismiss his intuition. He no longer had the luxury of mistrusting his own mind.

Turning away from the battlements, he climbed down the ladder back into the sheltered warmth of Proctor's quarters. He made his way over to the map on the wall, for the hundredth time tracing his finger over the faded markings. But still, nothing made sense.

Deep in thought, he tapped his finger absently on the yellowed chart, then traced a line across the map to the smudge that indicated the mouth of Lor-Gamorth. Then, slowly, he drew a line upward, about an inch, his finger pausing under the small letters that spelled the word *Orguleth.* As he figured the numbers in his mind, his finger traced out the path of his rough triangulation across a frayed fold in the map, out into the blank emptiness north of the mountain pass.

His hand paused then, the edge of his fingertip poised under the only mark in that entire void of uncharted area. It was an arrow, pointing toward the upper-right corner of the map.

Underneath the arrow were inscribed the words *'To Bryn Calazar.'*

Darien's finger tapped twice on the arrow. Then he spun away from the map and made for the stairs, scooping up his sword. He took the steps two at a time to the tower's base.

Kyel Archer was not hard to find. He stood out like a beacon of flame amidst the dim glow of the men around him. Darien crossed the hall toward him, men scrambling to move out of his way. Reaching him, he took Kyel by the shoulder and turned him around with the pressure of his fingers.

"Stay clear of the battle," he warned, then strode away toward the collapsed north wall of the keep.

Ignoring the stares aimed at him, Darien mounted a ladder to the catwalk at the top of the wall. He paid careful attention to his footing as he worked his way down the narrow ledge; heights had been bothering him ever since his fall.

Royce saw him approaching and turned, a look of concern on his face.

"Look to the east," Darien said. "They'll be coming from Orguleth at dawn." He watched Royce's eyes widen in surprise. It was sooner than they'd been expecting.

"Our plan won't work, then," Royce shouted at his back as Darien was already moving away.

Darien looked back at him. "No, it won't. But I've a better idea."

Kyel watched the Sentinel's black cloak vanish through the door of the hall.

"Smells like trouble," remarked Traver, who had been occupying his time by honing his blade with a small whetstone. He held up the oiled sword, turning it slowly in the dim light. Apparently, he found a place he wasn't quite satisfied with. He lay the blade back down and started going at it again.

A ringing cry echoed from below on the cliffs. Then a volley of fire arrows hissed across the open roof. There was a clatter of boots as the regular soldiers took to the walls, followed by a panicked commotion as the recruits reached for their weapons.

A shout from the doorway returned order to the keep. The men turned to stare at Commander Proctor, who stood with feet apart and hands folded over the pommel of a sword planted blade-down in front of him. He was flanked by his captains. Darien stood next to him, a chain mail tunic gleaming under his cloak.

It was actually happening.

Kyel felt a surge of sudden panic. There was going to be a battle. And, judging by the number of fire arrows that had flared across the sky, it was going to be big.

Kyel glanced over his shoulder at Traver, who stood cradling his sword, his chest rising and falling in shallow, rapid breaths. His eyes were wide, though not in fear, Kyel realized. The look on Traver's face was one of anticipation, perhaps even excitement.

The officers conferred quietly. When Kyel looked up, he saw Darien shake his head in response to a question. Then the group broke apart as the regular soldiers moved out into the crowded hall, making their way through the spaces between clusters of recruits.

Sergeant Ulric wound his way through the hall, pointing out specific individuals and signaling them to follow him. When he came near Kyel's group, his finger waved in the air as he selected only a few of the men around him.

"You, you and...*you.*"

Ulric's bony finger was pointing right at Kyel's chest. Kyel's legs felt weak as he collected his bow and fell in with Ulric's small group of hand-picked archers.

He followed the sergeant toward the front of the hall. When he looked up, he noticed the mage's eyes upon him again. Darien was frowning, obviously displeased. The mage turned and muttered something to Craig, who looked at Kyel and nodded.

"Ulric," the captain called. The sergeant sprinted over to him. The three men conferred quietly for a minute. When Ulric returned, he wore a look of frustration on his face.

"You're coming with us," he told Kyel, as if there had ever been a doubt. "But you're to stay clear of the fray and keep your head down. Orders from *above*."

By 'above,' Kyel assumed he meant Darien. He nodded, feeling a little disappointed. It wasn't as though he wanted to go out there and risk his neck, but he also didn't like being singled out. He shifted his gaze to the floor, heat rising to his cheeks.

They stood there for minutes doing nothing as the commotion continued around them in the hall. Then there was another shout from below followed by another fiery round of arrows.

A man whispered beside him, "This one's going to be bloody."

Ulric gathered them up and then gave the order to move out. Kyel followed the other bowmen through the keep's tall door and out into the frigid bleakness of night.

Traver was grinning, amazed he'd even been picked. This was going to be big—maybe one for the history books—and he was actually going to have the chance to take part in it. His hand fingered the cold steel of his sword as he waited his turn in the line of recruits waiting to be armored. He could use a stiff drink about now, though the thrill that filled him was practically just as good. Maybe even better.

He was almost glad for his luck; the Front was where he was meant to be. Not running some wretched dye-house back in Covendrey or driving a wagon along a dusty road with the constant reek of horseflesh in his face. The thrill of impending battle was far more intoxicating than any of his frequent binges. His hand quivered on the hilt of his sword, eager with anticipation.

Two soldiers pulled a tunic of quilted armor over him, cinching it tight. A hand clapped him on the back, sending him forward. On his way to the door, someone thrust a pair of gauntlets at him. Another man passed him a breastplate and helped him strap it on.

As he followed the line of foot soldiers across the threshold of the keep, Traver closed his eyes, whispering a soft prayer to the goddess Dreia, his sweet Lady of Luck.

⊛

Darien pulled back sharply on the gelding's reins, feeling the dark warhorse beneath him quivering, almost as though the animal could sense the coming storm. He looked out over the edge of a steep escarpment, down into the murky shadows of a canyon almost at the base of the Shadowspears.

From that vantage point, he could see the deep ravines and narrow rivulets that fed into the mouth of the pass. Behind him, he could hear the nervous shuffle of the men spread out along the rim of the escarpment, overlooking the canyon below. To his left across a narrow gap, he could see Devlin Craig mounted on his silver warhorse. Craig nodded slightly.

It was the signal he'd been waiting for.

Darien closed his eyes and reached out with his mind. It was no small feat of concentration, summoning the eddies of power that churned at the mouth of the pass. He groped outward, measuring the energy and friction of the wind.

With the will of his mind, he dominated the air currents, doubling the wind back on itself. At the bottom of the canyon, dozens of violent whirlwinds burst upward, churning the black dust of the river bottom and splitting into double-twisters that finally slowed and exhausted themselves against the slopes. The anger of the wind was gradually spent, fading into the stillness of an unearthly calm.

Silence replaced the din of the gale.

Below in the canyon, nothing moved. It was as though the entire motion of the world had frozen in place, the pulse of reality halted to a standstill. The distant trickle of a running stream was the only indication that time still moved forward at all.

Darien glanced back and saw that the ranks of soldiers flanking him were entirely still. The restless stir of armor and weapons had ceased, the men now staring out into the utter quiet that had swallowed the pass.

He raised his hand, spreading his fingers over the crystalline-black calm.

A fog rose in the canyon, spreading out from the river bottom, groping up the black slopes of the surrounding bluffs. The canyon was gradually devoured by swirling gray mists that clung to the rocks, rendering the view of the approaches impossible.

Darien looked for the outline of Devlin Craig, barely visible through the twisting tendrils of mist. Again, the captain nodded.

The sound of a distant thunder echoed up through the thick layers of fog. It seemed natural at first, like the rumble after a stab of lightning. But the noise was constant, growing. It increased in volume and proximity, swelling to a throbbing roar, escalating until it became clear there was nothing natural about it.

Darien glanced sideways at Craig. The captain was holding his hand in a fist above his head: the signal to hold. Darien could hear the ranks of the Enemy advancing under the cover of fog right below them.

The captain brought his arm down in a slashing motion.

Darien released his hold on the canyon. The fog abated instantly, revealing Enemy ranks spread out like dark waters across the river bottom. There were many more than he had expected. Cold fingers of dread traced upward from the small of his back, stealing down his arms to numb the touch of the reins in his fingers.

The gods had not listened to his prayers.

The advancing army below showed no trace of organization or discipline. But Darien knew better than to be fooled by the muddled appearance of those ranks. Somewhere in the choking desolation of the Black Lands, Chaos had transcended to devise an order of its own.

The ranks of archers behind him released their shafts with a throbbing hum of bowstrings. The first ranks of the Enemy dropped under the rain of gray-fletched arrows.

With a ferocious war cry, the black ranks of soldiers swept forward, storming up the side of the canyon under a hailing barrage of arrows. Armored forms dropped, littering the slope, to be consumed by the relentless flood that came behind, spilling over the lip of the canyon.

Craig drew his sword and spurred his mount forward. Volleys of arrows whistled over his head to drop in a deadly rain. To both sides, horse and infantry engaged with thundering force, pressing the Enemy back down the rise of the escarpment.

Darien grimaced as he saw a company of infantry rush forward, descending the slope in pursuit. He clenched his fist in frustration. The plan had been to hold the top of the slope, where they had the advantage, not follow the retreating Enemy back down into the gorge.

As he gazed out across that deadly sea, Darien felt the tension inside him ease, replaced by a numbing calm. He waited, watching as if through someone else's eyes as Craig ordered his horsemen over the slope to rescue the beleaguered foot soldiers.

The cavalry engaged the Enemy ranks. The sound of the battle resonated up the walls of the canyon, the ringing impacts of steel clanging against steel.

Darien opened his fist, sweeping his arm down to his side. With a cry that shook the air, hundreds of foot soldiers sprinted past him down the slope, feeding the frenzy of the battle. Beneath him, soldiers were flailing, rending, dying, breaking against the shield wall of the Enemy ranks.

He watched in frustration as his own men screamed and fell, their broken carcasses collecting in heaps upon the ground while he sat his horse out of range of the battle.

Darien looked to the north, toward the dark banks of a steep defile where he knew Kyel Archer was stationed. Sensing no threat to that position, he turned his attention back to the fight.

Traver brandished his sword as the first Enemy soldiers came crashing into the Greystone line of running infantry. He could feel his heart flailing wildly, the roar of blood in his ears dampening even the thunder of battle around him. Out of the corner of his eye, he saw the man beside him fall to his knees, a length of steel driven through his chest.

An Enemy swordsman kicked the man backward to free his blade. The eyes of the dying man glared up at Traver from the ground, a blood-washed hand clutching the gaping wound in his chest.

Traver tore his eyes away just in time to dodge a spear that hissed past him. At the same time, a sword slashed down from out of nowhere. He brought his own blade up just in time to block it, almost losing his grip when the jarring impact came.

He tried to recover, tried to get his sword back up as the Enemy blade swept around and came right back at his face. He dropped to the ground and thrust his own weapon up.

He felt the hilt wrenched out of his grasp as the Enemy warrior twisted above him. Something wet and soft splattered over his face. Traver brought his hand up to scoop whatever it was off, smearing it away. Rubbing what felt like slimy mud out of his eyes, he blinked and found himself staring down at the glistening wet ropes of entrails.

Devlin Craig wielded his sword like an extension of his arm as he wove through a sea of infantry, swinging his blade in great, hacking arcs. A rain of blood showered in his wake, bathing the flanks of his mount in a red, frothy sheen. Swatting a spear aside with a swipe of his blade, he continued the stroke downward to rip through the armor and bone of an Enemy swordsman.

Darien waited, the sounds of screaming horses and dying men assaulting his ears. The Enemy lines regrouped, the fragments of the Greystone troops wheeled and swept before them toward the mouth of the pass.

Darien sent his mind groping outward across the canyon, seizing a narrow wall of rock that sheltered the battlefield from a ravine on the other side. Wrenching the cliff, he watched the rock face tremble and then erupt with violence.

Scores of Greystone soldiers poured out through the gaping rent from the other side, taking up position where the cliff had just been. Archers knelt, firing volleys of arrows into the face of the Enemy charge. Bodies dropped to the canyon floor, showered with gray-fletched shafts.

The bowmen fell to the ground as ranks of cavalry leaped over their heads from the shadows of the ravine. Enemy soldiers turned and fled back toward Craig's charge of armored horse. As Darien watched, the Enemy ranks were cut down, wedged in a vice between two fronts of hurling death.

Kyel had been stationed with another bowman in a crevice far above the canyon. The sergeant had ordered him to wait there, keep his head down, and signal if he saw anything moving in the ravine below. But there had been nothing. And even if there had been, Kyel likely wouldn't have noticed.

His eyes were riveted on the clash of battle, watching in horrified fascination as magic and steel combined in a sinister combination that was brutally effective. Outnumbered and outmatched, the Greystone forces seemed to be prevailing against the crumbling Enemy resistance.

He was so fixated on the battle that he didn't notice the files of Enemy soldiers stealing up behind him in silence, far above on the ridge. He wasn't aware of their presence until a booming war cry issued from hundreds of throats.

Darien turned in his saddle, taken off guard by the appearance of a company of Enemy reinforcements across the canyon from him. Hundreds of armored men battered their swords against their shields and shook their spears.

Darien's breath caught as he realized Kyel Archer was stationed somewhere up on that slope, exactly in a position to be swept away by the Enemy charge.

Darien reached for the sword he carried strapped to his saddle. Sliding it from its scabbard, he brought the flat of the blade down against the dark hindquarters of his mount. The warhorse broke immediately into a gallop.

In a surge of wired muscle, the black beast gathered itself and took the edge of the escarpment in a powerful leap. The horse shuddered as its forelegs came down on the face of the slope, gaining momentum in long strides, descending the slope into the thick of battle and picking up speed as it went.

Darien raised his sword as the first Enemy soldier came at him. He swept out with his blade, deflecting a war axe. More soldiers disengaged from the fighting, surging toward him, drawn by the sight of his cloak.

Darien's sword rose to meet them, brushing blades aside and shattering spears as the heavy warhorse pounded through the thick of the fight.

Using the heels of his boots and the flat of his blade, he urged the gelding across the canyon in the direction of the cliffs. The horse took the ford of the river at speed, its flanks glistening as it surged up the slope on the far side.

Kyel glanced up at the stream of black-mailed warriors descending upon him. The bowman he'd been stationed with was dead, an arrow embedded in his chest.

Kyel angled his bow upward, sighting down the length of a shaft at the armored bodies spilling down the slope. He loosed his round, nocked another arrow, and drew. He watched the arrow plunk uselessly off a black breastplate. Cursing, he swept his hand back for another.

Something wrenched him backward and up. He didn't know what was happening as a powerful arm encircled his chest and heaved him face-first over the withers of an enormous horse.

Kyel managed to haul his leg over the animal's neck as Darien mounted behind him, kicking the charger forward. The animal broke into a run, struggling to stay ahead of the oncoming Enemy line.

Turning, Kyel saw soldiers breaking away from the front ranks in pursuit. Behind them, archers angled their bows and released their shafts. A cloud of arrows took to the sky, arcing toward them.

The arrows exploded in a shower of sparks that drifted lazily toward the ground. Incredulous, Kyel turned his head enough to gape into the face of the mysterious Sentinel who had just saved his life.

Kyel could see nothing of the kind but troubled man who had tested him in the tower. The eyes that met his were like voids of frigid dispassion. He turned back around, clutching his bow and closing his eyes, and prayed with all his might.

Traver looked up into the helm of the Enemy soldier that stood over him, the thought suddenly occurring to him to wonder why he was even there. He didn't know anything about battles or wars, blood and death. His Lady Luck had been with him for a while, her loving hand guiding his steel.

But now his luck had just run out.

He watched helplessly from the ground as the blade above him started its fall.

Devlin Craig swore an oath that would have made his mother bleed in her grave as he drew his mount up and disengaged from the fighting. His gaze followed the slope of the canyon toward the mouth of a ravine. There, hundreds of Enemy reinforcements surged down the slope like a raging flood. Before the swarming host raced an exhausted warhorse with two riders on its back.

As Craig looked on, the black gelding stumbled, almost went down, but gathered its legs beneath it and staggered forward. The Enemy host divided, the majority spilling into the canyon, while a smaller force broke off in pursuit of the flagging black horse.

Craig flexed his grip on his sword and kicked his heels into the flanks of his mount. Calling behind him at what was left of the men under his command, he abandoned the battle and set out at a gallop toward the Enemy charge.

Kyel knew they were going to die.

The thought didn't scare him all that much. It mostly made

him sad. He tried to think of Amelia but couldn't summon her image to mind. The only thing he could see was the end of the ridge in front of them and the cliff that dropped off sharply over a bend in the ravine.

Darien pulled back on the reins, jerking his horse's head around. The gelding's legs almost slid out from under it as the animal skidded sideways.

The Sentinel raised his blade, holding it swept back at a threatening angle as he turned the horse directly into the face of the Enemy charge.

It would be only a matter of seconds, now. Kyel closed his eyes but could not close his ears. The thunder of the oncoming charge swelled, became deafening.

The horse beneath him wheeled and broke toward the edge of the cliff, nearly throwing him off. Kyel felt the destrier gather the last of its strength and kick off with its hind legs, propelling them over the edge, throwing its full weight forward into the air.

Then they were falling.

His scream was cut short as the warhorse landed in the middle of the air, staggered, then gathered itself and surged forward, stumbling ahead. Incredulous, Kyel glanced down at a bridge of solid shadow that had been melded beneath them, arching across the gap of the chasm.

The horse leaped off the end of that dark, impossible span, coming down hard on solid ground and turning as it drew up.

Behind them, the bridge seemed to melt away, the shadows draining back into the dark recesses of the gap.

The Enemy force halted on the other side of the chasm, bellowing their rage across the cliffs, shaking spears and rattling shields. A few archers loosed their shafts, which simply slowed to a stop in midair and dropped, falling straight down.

An abrupt silence filled the gorge.

Kyel frowned, wondering why the Enemy force had suddenly stopped moving. He turned, looking behind them. He opened his mouth to gasp.

Just as he did, the air was sucked right out of his lungs as a gale of wind swept past them with a shrieking hiss, plastering his shirt against his back.

For seconds, he couldn't breathe. The scream of the wind was the eeriest sound he'd ever heard in his life.

And then the world exploded.

Kyel threw himself from the horse as the air turned to fire. He covered his face with his hands as a vast firestorm crackled by overhead, spreading quickly over the rim of the gorge. He held his breath against the roiling inferno. But then he let it out slowly when he realized the flames produced no heat.

The firestorm swept across the gorge toward the ranks of the Enemy. The lines broke in chaos, collapsing in disorganized retreat. The wall of fire paused, then gushed down the cliff into the canyon below, sweeping toward the main host.

Kyel couldn't believe he was still alive. Glancing up, he saw Darien still mounted on the back of the dark warhorse, face frozen in a look of dangerous intensity.

Traver watched helplessly as the Enemy blade started its fall, mesmerized by the black steel that hissed toward his chest.

The sword never impacted.

Another blade swept up to meet it, turning aside the stroke that should have killed him. Traver rolled away as a red-bearded swordsman stepped in front of him, driving the Enemy soldier back in a barrage of furious blows.

Traver's ears rang from the fury of the attack. The bearded swordsman feinted low then cut upward. As the dark blade fell to the earth, the Greystone swordsman cleaved his opponent's head off.

Traver looked away from the ghastly head that had somehow managed to stay helmed. He took a step back, turning to stare wide-eyed into the face of the man who had saved him. It was one of the farmers who had arrived with the mage. Corban Henley was his name.

But he didn't have time to thank the man. Henley was already moving away, cutting a path back into the thick of the battle.

Traver looked at the slope ahead, and his mouth dropped

open.

Hurling toward them was a fresh charge of Enemy reinforcements. Behind them swept a colossal firestorm driven by vicious winds of its own creation.

Traver closed his mouth, picked up his sword, and ran like hell the other way.

Devlin Craig pumped his straining horse with his spurs as he stole a glance back over his shoulder. What he saw was pure insanity. Enemy soldiers were fleeing an onrushing wall of flame, trampling the bodies of the fallen.

In the other direction, the Greystone ranks had reformed in a solid line along the edge of the canyon's wall. What was left couldn't possibly withstand the charging horde hurling toward them.

But then Craig glanced upward at the rim of the canyon. As he did, he almost lost his grip on the reins. There, lining the tops of the cliffs, were row upon row of foot soldiers and heavy horse, companies of bowmen and pikes. Banners rippled, even though there was no movement of air to stir them.

The charging Enemy soldiers saw it too. As one, the entire host wheeled, retreating toward the mouth of the pass. Greystone soldiers rallied as if in pursuit, screaming battle cries and shaking their weapons.

Before Craig's disbelieving eyes, the soldiers on the cliff walls seemed to ripple as one, flickered, then disappeared. His ears filled with ringing cries of victory.

Craig drew his horse up, glancing behind to see the firestorm swirling upward and collapsing in on itself, imploding into a brilliant ball high above the canyon.

In all his long years in the pass, that shining globe of fire was the closest thing to a sun Devlin Craig had ever seen.

For just a moment, the entire pass was lit as if it were high noon. Then the ball of fire exploded, showering the canyon with trails of sparks.

The cries of victory swelled, became a thunderous din.

Chapter Twelve
Grim Sense of Duty

Pass of Lor-Gamorth, The Front

Darien pressed his hand against the sweat-encrusted hair of his horse's neck, closing his eyes. He felt a shiver pass through the animal. The gelding staggered slightly then lowered itself to the ground, neck outstretched on the rocks as it lay down on its side. The black horse closed its eyes and nickered softly.

Kyel stared down at the animal with eyes full of concern. "Can't you heal it?" he asked.

"I already did." Darien lowered himself down beside the beast, running his hand over its wet and heaving side. "Now it only needs sleep to recover its strength."

Kyel nodded. Then his eyes widened. Reaching down, the young man fingered the torn black cloth of Darien's shirt, folding it back to expose a nasty-looking gash that had opened the top of his arm just below where the protective chains of ring mail ended.

"You're wounded," he gasped.

But Darien had already mended the injury before Kyel finished speaking. He stood up, trying not to look at the expression of wonder on the younger man's face. It made him feel uncomfortable.

Turning away, he started walking toward the bottom of the ravine, following the line of a dry stream bed back in the direction of the canyon. He could hear Kyel following him, the sound of his footsteps almost tentative.

"Where are you going?"

Darien didn't look back as he shrugged. He was too tired. The weight of the mail dragged at his shoulders. It was the same as it was with the horse. He could heal almost any injury with scarcely a thought. But there was nothing he could do to rid himself of the ache of exhaustion he felt down to his bones.

It was not just the battle that had taken the strength out of him. What he'd done that morning with his ability vastly outweighed any physical exhaustion he felt. As far as he knew, no mage in history had ever summoned the amount of raw power he had handled that morning without the aid of a Circle of Convergence. But it had taken its toll. As Darien trudged stiffly toward the canyon, he had to fight at each step just to stay on his feet.

Kyel must have noticed.

"We should rest a moment," he suggested.

But Darien forced himself to keep moving. He didn't have time to stop and rest. Not when he knew there were men up ahead dying.

Darien dreaded what waited for him in the canyon. It had always been the duty of the Sentinels after a battle to heal the injured. His duty, now.

He was not looking forward to it. It was hard enough, raising his hand and giving the order to send hundreds of men into battle. It would be much harder, looking into the eyes of those who had died by his command.

Darien remembered a time when he was a boy, when his father had come back from the Front and had stopped for a while in Amberlie to visit his sons before heading up the mountain. Darien remembered that visit well. His father had looked particularly haggard, and there had been a haunted look in his eyes. He had spoken of a battle, and of his grim duty afterward.

When his father had left, Darien remembered crying. Gerald Lauchlin had always been his hero. Darien had thought there was nothing that confident man couldn't handle with his usual, carefree tenacity. But his father had changed after that day. The shadows had never left his eyes. It was as though he'd taken a deep wound that all of his great strength could never heal.

Darien forced his feet to keep moving toward the mouth of the ravine. He tried not to think about what awaited him ahead. But at least he knew he didn't have to worry about his own eyes changing, shadowing, taking on the same haunted and battle-weary expression of his father.

He knew they already had.

He could see it in the face of every man that had the courage to meet his gaze. Even Craig and Royce, even Proctor. Even the young man following him now.

At last, they reached the place where the dry stream bed emptied into the canyon. There, Darien stopped, staring out across the carnage of the battlefield with growing dismay.

"Mother of the gods," Kyel whispered beside him.

Darien could only silently agree. He swept his gaze across the canyon floor, taking in the shocking sight of thousands of wasted human lives, literally piles of men fallen over each other, still limbs bent over fallen comrades, fingers limp and unmoving. Thin streams of blood flowed out from the heaps of Greystone corpses, running across the black soil in red rivers to mix with the blood of the Enemy.

He raised his right hand, staring down in contempt at the coldly glinting chain on his wrist. The piles of corpses were his fault. If it wasn't for his Oath, none of this would have happened. The fire he'd created could have burned hot more easily than cold. He could have immolated the Enemy ranks with a thought, melding flesh together with bone in a holocaust of will.

That was what Orien Oathbreaker had done. His one terrible act had driven the forces of the Enemy back into the Black Lands for over a hundred years. But Orien had also died a traitor's death, kneeling in shame to accept his punishment. Darien had always wondered why the man had surrendered himself so easily.

Now he understood. An Unbound mage was an abomination. That despised chain on his wrist was the only thing keeping him in check, saving him from himself. Corruption of the flesh was inevitable, a predestined fate meted out at the birth of every life. What Darien feared most was the corruption of his soul.

Sometimes, he could feel it already starting, an outgrowth of the vast amount of power he'd been forced to take in. The temptation to strip off that chain was growing harder to deny each day.

Especially now.

The sounds of the injured and dying accosted his ears. He forced himself to start forward, eyes scanning through the carnage for signs of movement, any trace of life. He quickly found an unconscious man with a gaping wound in his chest.

Bending over him, Darien placed his hand over the soldier's wound and closed his eyes. His head throbbed as he forced himself to grope through fatigue that was already almost unbearable. When Darien stood, he left behind a man slumbering in peaceful sleep, oblivious to the fact he had been scant moments from death.

Darien moved through piles of littered corpses, healing wounded as he went, working his way along the canyon wall while Kyel followed, trailing behind with his bow. The young man's expression was a mixture of horror, awe, and outright pity. Darien found himself consciously avoiding Kyel's gaze. He knew the pity was for himself, and he couldn't stand it. Shoulders shaking, he pushed himself up from the body of a man who his failing strength hadn't been able to save.

"Stop," Kyel begged. "You're exhausted. You need rest."

Darien shook his head, kneeling beside a man who lay groaning in agony, clutching his own dismembered arm as a steady pulse of blood pumped from the stump above his elbow.

There was nothing Darien could do about the arm. He willed the man into unconsciousness, his fingers gently loosening the soldier's grip on the gruesome appendage and casting it aside. He had to squeeze his eyes shut against the pain in his head as he staunched the flow of blood coming from the stump, forcing the flesh to fold and knit together over the white fragments of bone.

As he stood back up, a wave of dizziness made him stagger. He brought his hands up to his face, covering his eyes as he groped for balance. Kyel's hand caught his arm to steady him, an expression of concern clouding his face.

"Look." Kyel's voice was no longer pleading. "You can't keep this up. You can hardly stand on your feet."

Darien shrugged away from him. He could hear Kyel muttering under his breath, but he didn't care. He stumbled forward over torn limbs and shattered bodies, picking his way toward a motion on his left.

But as he knelt beside a dying soldier, he realized he'd made a mistake. He was staring down at the black helm of an Enemy swordsman. Darien started to push himself up, using his hand to wrench his weight off the ground.

As he did, a gloved hand snaked out and caught his arm, holding him down with an ironclad grip. He heard a low voice rattle in their vile tongue:

"We thought you dead, Battlemage. She'll be coming for you."

Darien ripped his arm away, staggering backward.

He could hear the man choking as he died. At least, it sounded like choking. Darien realized the soldier's death rattle was actually gurgling laughter. He could only stare in shock as the last breath wheezed from the gaping hole in the warrior's chest. After that, the man moved no more.

But that terrible laughter echoed on in his mind, along with the whispered promise: *She'll be coming for you.* He had no idea who *she* was, but the word sent a lance of dread stabbing through his heart.

He thought of the strange tides of the magic field, of the way the flows swirled and ebbed in ways completely different from normal. He thought of the map on the wall of Proctor's quarters, of his finger tapping the arrow that pointed toward the upper-right. The letters beneath the arrow that spelled out the words: *To Bryn Calazar.*

He thought of the gateway. What dark terrors had his brother unleashed? Closing his eyes, Darien drew in a trembling breath. There was only one kind of terror he could think of that went by the feminine pronoun 'she.' The mere thought was repulsive. Only, there was no other possible explanation.

Aidan had summoned the powers of the Netherworld to wield a deathblow to Aerysius. It made a terrifying kind of sense that his act had also liberated the Eight Servants of Xerys. And if either Myria Anassis or Arden Hannah were bending the lines of the magic field around Bryn Calazar, then he knew his life might very well be in grave danger.

The Eight had no chains on their wrists to Bind them, no Oath sworn to uphold. Only a dark compact with the Lord of Chaos. And if they were now aware of his presence, then the dead swordsman was probably right. *She* would be coming for him.

But there was nothing he could do about it.

Darien turned his back on the corpse and, stepping over the body of a decapitated bowman, looked for someone else, anyone else, whose life needed saving. He staggered forward, dropping down beside another man and forcing a flood of healing energy into his shattered frame. Then he went on to another, and another, until his head throbbed with the beat of every pulse and his vision blurred until he couldn't see.

Kyel Archer stumbled along beside him, holding him up and begging him to stop and rest. But his pleas fell on deaf ears. Darien forced himself to keep moving, keep healing, working across the canyon through jumbled piles of savaged bodies until he finally collapsed across the corpse of a Greystone soldier, overcome by sheer exhaustion.

That was how Devlin Craig found him.

Swearing an oath, the captain threw himself off his mount and trampled over the corpses of fallen comrades until he reached the young bowman who had flagged him down.

Dropping to his side, Craig glared his anger at him as he reached out and rolled Darien's unconscious body off the legs of a grisly cadaver. Craig pressed his ear against the mage's chest. Satisfied that his heart was still beating, he lashed out in anger at the boy.

"Why didn't you stop him?"

The young bowman opened his mouth, shaking his head. "I tried..."

Craig growled, heaving Darien's weight into his arms. He left the bowman there to fend for himself and heaved Darien over the back of his horse, swinging up behind him.

Kicking the stallion forward, he headed back up the pass toward Greystone Keep. He was angry. Angry at Proctor for underestimating the strength of the Enemy. Angry at Darien for insisting on holding to an Oath that was going to get him killed. And angry at himself for ever riding away from his side.

Sutton Royce was furious.

"What were you *thinking,* leaving him alone?"

Craig hung his head. "I suppose I wasn't."

"You're damned right, you weren't!" Royce paced away, slapping a pair of black leather gloves against the palm of his hand with a shocking *crack*. He took a deep breath, striving for composure.

"Tell me again about the boy." It was the first time Proctor had spoken since the conversation began.

"His name is Kyel Archer. I don't know much about him, other than he picked up the bow incredibly quick. Darien asked me to position him away from the fight."

"Has he returned yet?"

"No." Craig shook his head. The last he'd seen of Archer, he'd been standing in a heap of stiffening corpses looking completely petrified.

"Send a rider down to fetch him."

As he strode out of the room to comply, Craig chanced a glance at the pallet where Darien lay sleeping. There had been no marks on his body; Craig had checked him over for wounds. But other than the rise and fall of his chest, the man hadn't stirred in hours.

He relayed Proctor's order to a sentry then returned to the command chamber. When he entered the room, he found Proctor and Royce bending over one of the maps on the table.

"These same tactics aren't going to work for us again," Royce was saying. "The Enemy wasn't expecting a Sentinel, and even when they found out, they didn't know for sure whether or not he was Bound. But next time they'll know for certain. They'll see right through Darien's illusions."

Proctor nodded thoughtfully. His face looked more haggard than usual. Craig couldn't blame him; it had been a long day for them all.

"I must speak with this Archer," Proctor said. "If I'm right, then he is the key." His eyes looked suddenly hardened, as though he'd all along been battling some internal struggle that had finally, brutally, been resolved. It must have been a tough one. Proctor's face had gone almost gray.

"What do you mean?" Royce probed with a frown.

Proctor looked up to meet his captain's gaze, but he hesitated before speaking. "I can think of only one reason for Darien's interest in this Kyel Archer. The boy must have the potential. It is the sole explanation that fits."

Craig's mouth fell open. *Of course.*

The commander went on in a voice devoid of emotion, "Darien won't survive another battle. He's too impotent with those chains on his wrists, and he's too damn obstinate to keep out of harm's way. Have no doubt—we *will* lose him.

"Which leaves us with only one question that we must answer for ourselves: is there any way we can somehow turn this situation to our advantage?

"This is the way I see it." His eyes shifted to Craig, his stare hardening even more. "If we are going to lose one mage because he refuses to forswear his Oath, then the gods may have just delivered us another not so Bound. Perhaps we should expedite the opportunity."

Craig stared at him long and hard. Then he turned and left the room, his vision darkened by anger. He'd known Garret Proctor nearly his entire adult life. Craig had never had a problem with Proctor's cruel strategies—when they were directed against the Enemy.

He'd just never thought to see them employed against a friend.

Proctor still had Craig's loyalty; he owed him that much. But the man had just lost every last shard of Devlin Craig's respect.

Kyel saw two horses coming toward him down a steep embankment. There was only one rider on a brown horse, holding the reins of a chestnut mare that ran beside him. Kyel expected the man to gallop right by and was surprised when both horses drew up, the helmed soldier dropping down to the ground next to him. Lifting his visor, the man looked at Kyel sidelong, passing his eyes over him as if confused about something.

"Kyel Archer?" The words carried a heavy undercurrent of doubt.

Kyel nodded, wondering how the man could possibly know his name. But then it dawned on him. *Of course. Lauchlin.* The mage seemed to be taking no chances with his new acolyte. If that's truly what he was. Kyel had never been given the opportunity to turn him down.

"I have orders to fetch you back to the keep." The soldier's eyes were skeptical. "The force commander wants a word with you."

Kyel's brow furrowed. *Proctor?* That was peculiar. A cold prickle of doubt itched his skin. He climbed up on the spare horse as the soldier threw him the reins. He hung his bow over his shoulder and followed the man up the narrow trail.

When they reached the steps of the keep, Kyel passed the reins back and jumped down. He didn't know where they kept the horses. He hadn't seen a stable. But, then, he also hadn't seen but a small fraction of the men gathered in the pass that morning. Their numbers had come as a shock, albeit a good one. Kyel suspected there were camps spread throughout the Pass of Lor-Gamorth.

At least, there *had* been. He wondered just how many could possibly be left. The piles of corpses he had wandered through following Darien on his grisly undertaking made Kyel fear their forces had been decimated.

Entering the keep, Kyel wasn't sure at first where to go. He decided to just follow orders and head up the tower on his own.

As he passed by the hall door, he ran into the intimidating form of Devlin Craig. The man's eyes were even more hostile than Kyel remembered. The captain glared at him with an expression of distaste, his mouth curled in a snarl.

Kyel couldn't quell the growing feeling of trepidation swelling in his chest. Something had changed, and he didn't like it at all. He had the feeling something had gone terribly wrong. As his feet approached the opening to the tower room, Kyel found himself holding his breath. He didn't know what he was going to find up there, but he didn't think he was going to like it.

He stepped over the threshold into the barren, circular chamber and paused. He felt Proctor's eyes fall on him: that hardened, ruthless gaze that unnerved him completely. Kyel did his best not to waver under the weight of that stare.

The commander said, "You are to stand down from future battles. Your place is now here. Return your bow to the armory and collect your things."

Kyel's eyes drifted to his bow, the golden wood he had become so comfortable with. Since his first night in the fortress, that bow had never left his side. He didn't want to give it back. And he didn't want to leave his fellows. Most of all, he didn't want to spend his days as the constant companion of the daunting old warrior who stood glaring at him.

"No. Please, no. I mean—what I mean is…" Kyel forced himself to take a deep breath. "Please, no, Force Commander. With all due respect."

He stood trembling as the man circled him slowly like a hawk, hands clasped behind his back, gray cloak swaying in his wake. As the target of that predator-like stare, Kyel felt exceptionally like a mouse hiding in an open field, waiting for the raptor to descend.

His eyes fell on a black, narrow hilt protruding from the belt at the commander's waist. He'd never noticed it before, but the knife looked viciously intimidating, even more so than the sword at the man's side.

"Your place is now here." Proctor's tone brooked no argument.

"Please, Force Commander. Just let me keep my bow." Now, why had he said that? The stick at his side was the least of his worries. Maybe what he wanted was a weapon to defend himself against the man.

He glanced to where Darien lay by the hearth, his face more peaceful than Kyel had ever seen it. He would not be stirring for a while, Kyel thought, remembering the exhausted black warhorse they had left behind in the canyon.

"You're an acolyte mage," Proctor said. "What use have you for a weapon?"

The man knew.

Kyel felt drenched in cold, petrifying fear. He groped deep down inside, desperately trying to summon the last scrap of courage he could find. He still wanted to keep that bow.

"What use has Darien for his sword?" Kyel challenged, then quickly added, "Force Commander."

The harsh angles of Proctor's face softened just a bit. To Kyel, those stern blue eyes seemed to be almost smiling. A grim, satisfied smile that was more ominous than the man's outright glare.

"Keep the bow, then," he said softly, and strode past Kyel in the direction of the stairs.

"Wait," Kyel called after him.

Proctor stopped, turning slowly around.

"Tell me one thing," Kyel said. "Who are they? The Enemy?"

The force commander stared at him for a long moment without moving. Eventually, he said, "They were once the people of Caladorn. But they're not people anymore. They dwell in darkness and worship Xerys. For the last thousand years, they've made it their purpose to threaten us. To invade us. To destroy us. In the end, it doesn't matter who they are.

"That's why we just call them the Enemy. Because knowing what they call themselves isn't going to help us fight this war. We don't need to know anything about them. We just need to kill them."

With that, he turned and stalked down the stairs.

Chapter Thirteen
Two Vows

Pass of Lor-Gamorth, The Front

Kyel sat on a boulder protruding from an outcrop overlooking the Pass of Lor-Gamorth from the rear of the fortress. He'd wondered why no one had ever bothered to rebuild the keep's crumbled rear wall. Now he knew. There was nothing behind the structure but a small rock scarp and the sheer drop of a cliff. The mountainside was more of a defense than the rear wall of the keep had ever been. Incursion was impossible from that approach.

Kyel found it a good place to escape the stark chamber of Proctor's quarters. He didn't like being left alone with the force commander. Proctor reminded Kyel of a cleverly brilliant chess master who was ingenious enough to think six moves in advance, yet ruthless enough to sacrifice any given piece to gain an advantage. His eyes had taken on an emptiness just as barren as his chamber.

The sound of movement below startled Kyel from his thoughts. His hand dove for his bow, but he didn't nock an arrow to the string. The sentries were fewer in number, now, strung out at greater intervals along the length of the pass. But their eyes were now sharper than ever. No Enemy soldier could make it so far as the steps beneath Greystone Keep.

And he was right. The man who approached from below was no enemy. He might even be the only friend Kyel had left.

"It's a good view," Darien said, turning to glance over the lip of the outcrop. He didn't look like himself at all, wearing regular clothes, his hair falling in loose waves over his shoulders.

To Kyel, the different apparel seemed a drastic change. Darien looked shockingly less severe, shockingly *normal.* Even the chains on his wrists seemed to lose their emphasis.

He turned back toward Kyel, a smile on his face as he gestured at the boulder. "I see you found my rock."

"*Your* rock?" Kyel raised his eyebrows.

Darien nodded as he sat, bringing a knee up to his chest and leaning back. Kyel had to admit, he did look comfortable there.

"I come here often. It's a good place to sit, to think, if you've a mind to be alone."

Kyel winced. That was exactly what he'd been doing, though he didn't want to admit it.

"Have you given any more thought to my offer?" Darien asked.

Kyel opened his mouth but then closed it again, not knowing what to say. Other than his move to the top of the keep, there had been no mention of the test Darien had given him so many days ago. In fact, he hadn't brought it up once, not until now. Kyel had been starting to wonder if maybe the Sentinel had forgotten all about it.

Kyel shrugged. "I've been trying not to."

Darien seemed to accept his answer. He brought his hand up to the side of his face, stroking the stubble on his cheek as his eyes grew distant in thought. He sat there for a moment in silence as a breath of wind stirred his hair.

Summoning his courage, Kyel asked, "How was it for you when you became an acolyte?"

Darien's gaze remained inward as he replied, "It was different for me. Both my parents were mages. Aerysius was in my blood. When I passed Consideration, it came as no shock."

Kyel nodded. "What was it like, growing up there?"

"I've no idea," Darien replied. "I wasn't raised there. I lived my entire childhood in the Vale. My brother and I were fostered out to a widow who lived down the mountain in Amberlie."

To Kyel, that seemed strange. From what he knew from his father, it was not uncommon for mages to have families, even large ones.

As if sensing his question, Darien explained, "My father was a Sentinel, so he wasn't around much to raise us. And my mother was elected Prime Warden shortly after I was born, so she never had the time."

Kyel's eyes widened. Throughout history, the Prime Wardens of Aerysius had always been the highest authority in the Rhen. Even kings and queens knelt at their feet, though to the rest of the world they remained somewhat a mystery.

In an attempt to lighten the mood, Kyel asked, "So you've a brother?"

The sudden change that came over Darien's face was not what Kyel had been expecting. In the second before he averted his eyes, Kyel got a glimpse of the same, haunting shadows he had seen the night Darien had tested him. *Of course,* he thought stupidly. Darien's brother was doubtlessly dead, killed in the tragedy that had befallen Aerysius.

"I'm sorry," Kyel said. "I ought to have thought."

Darien bowed his head, dark strands of hair falling forward to shroud his face. In a tone as dead as the heritage of his home, he explained, "It was my brother Aidan who opened the Well of Tears."

Kyel could only stare straight ahead, struck utterly speechless. Now he knew the impetus that fueled the storm that raged behind the Sentinel's eyes. Darien had lost everything he'd ever known and ever loved, all at the hands of his own brother. What could anyone say to that?

He whispered, "What are you going to do?"

Darien looked up, the expression on his face so intense that Kyel drew back involuntarily. He answered quietly, "I'm going to kill him."

Kyel stared at him hard for a minute. "What about your Oath?"

Darien just shrugged. An awkward silence followed. Then, from out of nowhere, he managed a smile. "Want to go for a ride?"

The suggestion had come from out of nowhere, and Kyel had no idea what Darien's purpose might be. He was getting the impression he might know the Sentinel for a hundred years and still never understand the man.

"That sounds good," he agreed.

Darien's smile reassured him. For once, even the shadows seemed gone from his eyes.

Kyel waited at the steps of the keep while Darien went off to make arrangements. When the mage returned, Kyel was dismayed to see he was once again wearing his cloak and had strung the harness of his sword over it. He found himself feeling a little disappointed. He'd enjoyed the scant moments he'd spent with Darien dressed in the clothes of a normal man. The cloak had a power of its own, and Kyel found it distancing.

They walked together down to a paddock hidden in a bottleneck canyon below the keep and selected their mounts under the watchful eyes of the sentries. Kyel chose a light riding horse, unlike the black beast that trotted up to Darien when he slipped through the fence.

The last time he'd seen the charger, the animal had been stretched out in the ravine, looking little better off than dead. But when Darien had the gelding saddled and swung himself over its back, the horse picked its legs up smartly and tossed its head, making immediately for the gate without any prompting from its rider. Kyel mounted his own horse and followed after.

The path they travelled wound around the mountainside, following the curve of the slope. After about two leagues, the trail narrowed and then disappeared. Looking back, Kyel could barely make out the tower of Greystone Keep, a shadowy silhouette against the pale flickers of light in the clouds. The wind was starting to pick up. He pulled his cloak more tightly about himself.

They rode up into a narrow ravine between two great legs of the mountain. The farther they went, the deeper the shadows settled around them. Kyel found himself growing a little unsettled by the intense quiet of the place.

Darien brought his horse to a stop and glanced up to inspect the ridges surrounding them. At last, seeming satisfied, he let his mount move slowly forward.

Kyel didn't like this place. He was starting to wonder why

Darien had brought him there. Then a sudden, horrible feeling swept over him, like a terrible shiver of dread.

Kyel jerked back on the reins, eyes widening. He felt the skin on the back of his neck prickle. The feeling was like nothing he had ever experienced. It was as though something important had just been yanked away, as if a necessary and significant part of the world had been suddenly withdrawn. Only, he had no idea what had happened.

"You feel it," Darien said.

"Aye, I feel it. It's vile."

Kyel rubbed his arms, trying to scrub away the disturbing feeling. Darien didn't appear to be affected by the sensation. His gaze turned back to trace the folds of the mountain slopes. Without looking at him, he said flatly:

"Most men can't." He brought his hand up in a sweeping gesture, indicating the area around them. "This is a node. It's a place where the lines of the magic field come together in parallel direction but opposite in energy and cancel out. What you're feeling is the complete absence of the magic field in this place."

Kyel felt horrified as the impact of the mage's words sank in. "So, you're saying I've always been able to feel it, and this is what it's like when it's gone?"

Darien nodded. Kyel shivered; he didn't like it here and wanted to go back. But Darien urged his horse forward with the pressure of his legs, taking them deeper into the node. The feeling of dread intensified.

"You knew this was here," Kyel accused. "That's the reason why you brought me. You wanted me to feel this place." Suddenly, a new thought occurred to him, and the sensation of dread in his stomach took a nauseating, downward plunge. "You're powerless here."

Again Darien nodded, gaze sweeping upward to examine the slopes of the canyon. When he turned back, there was a small, sad smile on his face. "Like any other man."

Kyel reached for the comfort of his bow, caressing the soft wood. How could the mage just sit there on his horse, gripped in the terrible absence of the magic field, knowing how dangerous it was for him to even be in this place? But then he realized Darien was by no means as easy about it as he seemed. His gaze kept shifting back to the rocks as if scouring them. The shadows had once again returned to haunt his eyes.

"I want to go," Kyel urged. "This place is…foul."

Darien looked as though he agreed. Bringing his mount around, he turned it back in the direction they had come. As they started downward again, Kyel asked, "Why did you bring me here?"

"I think you know the answer. Consider it your first lesson."

Kyel had figured that. The mage had wanted him to get a taste of what he truly was. He'd never even known that he could sense the presence of the magic field, not until it had been utterly withdrawn. As they moved out from under the influence of the node, Kyel breathed a sigh of relief. The world felt abruptly…normal.

But now that he knew what it was and what it felt like, he could suddenly sense the magic field stirring, flowing around him like the currents of a river. There was nothing strange or foreign about the sensation. It was something he'd always known, all throughout his entire life. He had just simply never recognized it.

Darien stopped his horse and dismounted on the other side of the boundary. Kyel followed suit, letting his mount move away from him with its head to the ground, foraging for grass in the barren dirt. He followed as Darien wandered back in the direction of the node, then stood with his hand out, indicating that he wanted Kyel to walk back through the boundary one more time.

He didn't want to. But he did.

Again, Kyel felt that dreadful sensation of loss, as though part of the world had suddenly faded completely. This time, he was prepared for it, and the transition was not quite so shocking. It was as though there had been a quiet cadence in his mind, and now that rhythm was lost.

As he reemerged, he could feel the pulse coming back.

"Do you still deny your ability?"

Kyel cast a dispirited glance at the mage, wishing that he could. "No."

Darien had made his point all too well.

The Sentinel nodded, his expression enigmatic. He walked away a few paces toward the crest of the hill. His cloak played out behind him in the breeze as he stood gazing down at the pass, a black silhouette against the flickering sky.

Kyel found himself staring at the mage's profile, wondering if it would ever be possible for himself to cast such a similar, imposing portrait. He was a merchant by trade, a woodworker by choice, and now he was an archer in truth and not just in name. Where a mage's craft fit into that picture, Kyel could not begin to guess.

"I need an answer, Kyel."

Kyel rubbed his brow. He already knew what his answer was going to be, but it was not going to be easy, bringing that decision into reality by giving it a voice.

Darien was looking at him. Waiting.

He lowered his eyes. "All right, then. Yes."

Kyel kept his gaze lowered as he heard Darien's footsteps approaching. He was trembling, the bow in his hand quivering in his grip. The approaching footsteps stopped before him, and Kyel at last found the courage to look up.

"I need you to know what you're committing yourself to," Darien said. "You need to be certain of this decision. Your heart must be entirely in this, or I'm wasting my time."

Kyel found himself wanting more than anything to reject the man's offer. But he knew that was impossible. He had never been able to deny someone in need, and he couldn't think of another time in his life when he'd ever been needed more. He couldn't bring himself to look into Darien's eyes and tell the man no.

"I'm certain."

"Kyel." The way the Sentinel said his name made him shiver even harder. Holding his gaze firmly, Darien warned him, "You will not find me an easy master. There is a saying at the School of Arms in Auberdale I learned a long time ago: 'What hurts, teaches.' I find that applies to most lessons in life."

It was no more than Kyel had expected. His father had told him of the harsh burdens and constraints placed upon new acolytes. He didn't know if he would be up to Darien's demands, but he did know that he had it within himself to try.

"I understand," he said, forcing himself to look into the Sentinel's eyes.

Darien said, "I'm going to ask you to repeat the vow every acolyte of Aerysius swore before they were accepted into the Hall of the Watchers. The Hall doesn't exist anymore, but its ways are all I know."

When Kyel said nothing, Darien grasped his left wrist. His grip was firm, almost painful. Kyel could feel the circulation in his hand compromised by the pressure of it. As if in a dream, he found himself repeating every word the mage uttered, his lips moving slowly to form the syllables as their grim significance imprinted itself on his mind:

> *"I swear to exist only to serve the land and its people.*
> *With my life, if possible. If not, then by death."*

When he was finished, Darien removed his fingers from Kyel's wrist. Instantly, Kyel felt a flood of warmth moving back into his hand as the blood flow returned to it. He raised his arm, half expecting to find a red welt there from the pressure of the man's strong fingers.

But instead of a welt, Kyel found a glistening, metallic chain engraved into the flesh of his left wrist. He stared down at the ancient symbol, terrified by its implications.

Chapter Fourteen
Friends and Enemies

Pass of Lor-Gamorth, The Front

A shout from below woke Darien from sleep. He shot up out of his blankets and scooped up his sword. Taking the steps two at a time, he rushed down to the keep's main hall, where he found the men gathered around an injured scout who had been laid out on the floor. The man's chest was heaving for breath, his blood quickly spreading across the wood slats.

"The Enemy," he gasped. "Tens of thousands..."

Kyel flinched at the sound of Garret Proctor's fist smashing down on the oak table, jolting the entire piece of wood. But it was Sutton Royce who took up his argument for him, striding forward and raging into Darien's face:

"You have no choice!"

Darien glared back at him, fists clenched in rage. He growled at Royce, "What gives you the right—"

Proctor interrupted him. "He doesn't have the right. But I do."

Kyel had always thought the force commander was an imposing man with a daunting presence. But at the moment, he looked positively dangerous. The side of his face twitched as he rounded on Darien, lashing out at him in scathing tones, "Whatever else you might be, while you remain at my keep, you are subject to my authority."

"You have no authority over me," the Sentinel contradicted him coldly.

"You better believe I do."

Proctor glowered at him dangerously. "If I decide right now to have you dragged out to the yard and thrashed, there's not a damned thing you could do about it. Unless it's your intention to abuse your precious Oath?"

Darien stood regarding him silently for a moment then turned, stalking in the direction of the stairs. "Come, Kyel."

Kyel gathered his bow and shouldered his pack, then crossed the room to take his place at Darien's side.

Before Darien had a chance to take one step, Devlin Craig called out to stop him. "We number less than a thousand men!"

Darien glared back at him. "And I'm only *one man.* No one seems to understand that. Even if I did break my Oath, what do you expect me to do against *tens of thousands?"* To Proctor, he added, "You need an army, not a mage. Whatever happened to those birds you sent to Auberdale?"

The force commander's eyes narrowed even more than they already were. "Faukravar sends his regards, but regrets he has no men to spare us at this time."

"You're the only hope we have," Craig implored.

Darien hesitated only a moment. "Then there is no hope."

Darien's words still echoed in his ears as Kyel followed the Sentinel down the steps to the bottom of the tower. His emotions were so jumbled and confused that he didn't know which one dominated. He thought, perhaps, it was fear. He knew it ought to be.

Catching up to Darien, he asked, "Where are we going?"

Darien gestured with a nod of his head, off in the direction of the slopes below the keep. "The last place they'll think to look for us: the node. Royce is a good tracker, but I should have a few hours of peace to sort this out." He took a deep breath. "Round up some supplies. I'll fetch the horses."

Kyel moved to comply, wishing that Darien would have picked any other place in the whole world.

Royce stood atop the battlements of Greystone's tower, eyes tracking the two horses heading away from the keep, following the narrow trail that led to the river bottom. He kept his stare fixed on the black warhorse that walked in front, until it finally disappeared into the shadow of a ridge. He let his gaze drift heavenward. Above, thick clouds drifted across the sky, heavy with rain and sagging against the tall peaks of the Shadowspears.

Royce heard a soft rustling sound beside him as Garret Proctor shifted his weight. The commander's left hand was resting on an embrasure, his right hand fingering the hilt of the ebony knife he wore tucked in his belt. As Royce's gaze followed the path of the clouds, the force commander maintained a harsh scrutiny of the canyon below his fortress. Without looking up, he said in a half-whisper:

"You know what you have to do."

Royce bowed his head deeply.

Proctor's voice continued, cold and merciless as the mountains themselves. "Make certain the boy is touching him when he dies."

Rain began to fall. It came on slowly at first, just a damp, tentative mist that clung to Kyel's face and collected in glistening beads on the backs of his hands. Then light droplets started falling from the clouds, coming down erratically all around them. The raindrops grew heavier, fatter, until the clouds seemed to just open up and disgorge the weight of their water onto the thirsty flanks of the Shadowspears. A great rumble of thunder rolled expansively in the distance, dampened only by the whistle of the wind.

Eyes squinting, Kyel didn't know they were approaching the node until he felt the barrier come crashing down around him, stifling his perception of the magic field completely. The feeling was even worse, this time. He hadn't realized how much he'd come to depend on that comforting sense until he had started exercising it. When it was gone, the void it left behind was terrifying.

Confused and miserable, he slouched low in the saddle and tried not to think about it. He soon found even that impossible.

The thirst of his mind for the telltale pulse of the field was like a gnawing hunger that only grew stronger and wouldn't subside.

Ahead through the rain, he could see the shadow of the black horse pull up. Kyel dismounted and walked to where Darien was unloading the packs he had tied behind his saddle. Soon even the absence of the magic field was forgotten. At the mage's direction, Kyel found himself pounding stakes into the ground with the blunt end of a rock as Darien unrolled a large square of oiled cloth.

In short order, they had a lean-to constructed and a small fire glowing beneath it. But though all he wished was to throw himself down beside the comfort of the fire and warm his shivering body, Kyel didn't get the chance. At the mage's direction, he found himself set to work preparing breakfast.

It was not much of a meal. Darien had only given him scant time to gather provisions before ushering him out of the keep. He'd grabbed a few small bags from the stores without looking to see what was inside. So Kyel found himself cooking up a meal of half-rotten turnips and a few strips of salted beef that looked as if the rats had been at it first.

When he served up the sick mixture, Darien ate without complaint, staring out across the dreary landscape, his eyes studiously introspective. Throughout the meal, he never uttered a word. His gaze was directed outward at the recesses of the ravine. Or perhaps inward, withdrawn somewhere into the frothing turmoil that haunted his mind. Whatever the case, Kyel was left feeling alone, even lonely.

In an attempt to draw him out in conversation, he asked, "Why is your Oath so important to you?"

Darien blinked, lowering his head as his gaze slipped downward in thought. To Kyel, he appeared to be struggling for just the right words. When he finally spoke, his voice was almost wistful.

"The only reason I'm alive now is because I stepped off a cliff. I had no idea that the fall wouldn't kill me. It was only by blind luck that I survived. There was another mage below in the Vale who saw me falling and saved my life."

He paused a moment, rotating his hands so that his palms faced upward, his eyes contemplating the gleaming duel chains. "Sometimes I feel like I'm still up there on that cliff, only dangling from the edge by my fingertips. I can choose to keep holding on, hoping that somehow everything will turn out all right. Or I can choose to let go. Only this time, if I decide to fall, I know there'll be no one around to stop me."

Kyel felt hopelessly out of his depth. Try as he might, he couldn't understand what the man was trying to say. "So, you're afraid if you give up your Oath, you'll die?"

"No." The Sentinel shook his head. "When I was up on that cliff, it wasn't death that scared me. What scared me most was the fall itself."

"I don't understand," Kyel whispered.

"I hope you never have to."

Kyel looked to him for further explanation, but there was none forthcoming. Darien's stare had once again retreated inward, the shadows now storming violently across his eyes.

The day lingered, the rains tapering on and off. Kyel sat with his arms wrapped around him, shivering in silence. The horses foraged across the black dirt, necks stretched down in search of food. But there was none to be had. No blade of grass broke through the soil. In a land where sunlight simply didn't exist, no seed could ever take root.

A sound from down below broke the uneasy silence of the ravine. Kyel leaned forward, listening. Beside him, Darien sat sharply up and reached for his sword. Kyel saw his movement and went for his bow, feeling a sudden stab of fear. He glanced around at the surrounding slopes, seeking, but finding nothing.

Then, echoing up from below, he heard the rattle of tack and the plodding of hoofbeats. He stood, bringing his bow up and nocking an arrow to the string. Horses were approaching. He trained the shaft of the arrow on the chest of the first horse, a target far larger than its rider. But as he narrowed his eyes in concentration, he found himself releasing the tension on the bowstring.

To his relief, Kyel recognized the form of Sutton Royce,

flanked by a small number of mounted men. Darien had been right. Royce must be an excellent tracker, to have found them so quickly in the dark. The horses walked toward them up the slope, Royce out in front on his dark brown destrier.

Kyel lowered his bow as the captain and his entourage pulled up before them, perhaps twenty paces away from their makeshift camp. He felt heartened to see the man. Perhaps his presence meant there had been some resolution at the keep that would allow Darien to feel comfortable enough to return. Kyel longed for even the uneasy tension of Proctor's tower. At least the chamber was warm, and he could always escape if he had to.

Next to him, Darien let his blade slip fully back into its sheath. He stood still, watching warily as Royce climbed down from his horse.

"We need to talk, Darien," he said as he moved off to the side in the direction of a low hill to the north of their campsite.

Darien's eyes tracked Royce's gray cloak as he walked away with his back to them. Scabbard in hand, he moved out from under the lean-to and followed the soldier across the black soil toward the slope of the hill.

There, just out of earshot, the two men met and appeared to be speaking. Kyel had no idea what words were being exchanged. Darien seemed to be arguing heatedly, his expression irate, his motions brisk, though his voice was kept low enough that Kyel couldn't catch more than a few syllables. It was probably just a continuation of the argument in the tower, when Proctor had all but ordered Darien to forswear the Mage's Oath.

Darien turned sharply with a rippling length of his blue-black cloak, looking ready to stalk off and storm away. As he did, Royce's mailed fist came smashing down against the side of his head in a powerful strike that took him to the ground.

Kyel's mouth dropped open in disbelief. He grabbed for his bow but was immediately surrounded by Royce's men. They jumped down from their horses, caging him in with the bulk of their bodies, swords drawn and threatening. A man reached out and ripped the longbow right out of his fingers. Kyel started to fight for it, but the threat of a crossbow aimed at his face stopped him short. The grim soldier holding the weapon looked as if he had every intention of using it. The only thing Kyel could do was stand and watch the events unfolding on the hill, helpless to do anything.

Royce advanced, stalking toward Darien with his blade drawn and poised. His gaze was filled with cold fury, raging with a harrowing mixture of fire and ice. Kyel felt his eyes widen with a jarring slap of understanding.

Royce was acting under orders. He had to be. And, knowing the man those orders must have come from, Kyel feared the ruthless nature of their intent. Again, he thought of Proctor as a chess master, sitting in his dark tower day after day, brooding as his mind sifted through strategy in an attempt to find himself any desperate advantage within grasp.

Only, this time, Proctor was doing much more than sacrificing a mere pawn. Try as he might, Kyel couldn't think of any reason in the world *why*.

On the ground, Darien moved slowly, bringing an arm up to wipe a stream of blood from his eyes. Royce hovered over him, sword poised in the air. His lips moved, but Kyel couldn't hear his voice. In his hands, the blade of his sword trembled.

Royce bellowed, throwing his head back. The sound of his booming cry echoed off the walls of the ravine as he brought the sword up over his head in a double-fisted grip. The steel glinted white in a sudden flare of lightning. Then it was falling, streaking down.

Darien rolled out from under the blade as it cleaved deeply into the dirt. Somehow, he ended up on his feet, his own sword singing with a metallic ring as he drew his blade and flung the scabbard to the ground. He edged backward, holding the hilt with both hands as Royce advanced toward him.

Blood covered the side of Darien's face and ran down his neck. His eyes blazed with a molten fury that made even Royce's stare seem brittle in comparison.

The captain swept out with his blade, and Darien parried the strike. Then the mage advanced with a smooth series of cuts that made Royce's sword dance in the air to keep up with them. The soldier disengaged, swinging to the side as Darien dove after him, bringing his sword around to slice over his shoulder.

The blow was caught on the flat of Royce's blade. Steel shrieked as Darien's sword slid down the length of it.

They were both masters, Kyel realized, watching the graceful but deadly dance. Both men seemed equally matched, Darien's quick, confident movements making up for what he lacked of Royce's brutal strength.

They moved in a slow circle as their swords played in the air between them, first one man advancing and then the other, neither one losing an inch of ground. The soldiers surrounding Kyel were watching, also, attention riveted on the fight.

Royce pushed Darien away and thrust his sword out in a wicked undercut. But the mage dodged back, bringing his sword up to deflect the next hissing slice already coming at him.

Darien shifted into a two-handed grip as he pressed Royce backward down the hill with a quick succession of crisp, ringing blows. The captain was forced to retreat, his sword barely moving quick enough to deflect the attacks.

Royce's foot stumbled over a dent in the ground. He brought his blade up to shield his face as he fought to keep his balance.

But Darien didn't let up. He executed another precise sequence of attacks timed to exploit the opportunity and shatter Royce's defense. The captain was beaten steadily backward down the hill.

Darien lunged, letting his sword slide under the captain's blade. He caught Royce's crossguard with a twisting motion, then reached out with his hand and ripped the hilt out of his opponent's grasp.

Darien swept his blade back over his shoulder as Royce's sword fell from his hands. He stood there shaking, chest heaving, eyes burning with explosive rage.

A ringing peal of laughter echoed down from the ridge above them.

Thinking he was either dreaming or insane, Kyel glanced up the slope into the face of a pale and beautiful woman mounted on the back of a glistening white horse. Her platinum blonde hair spilled over her shoulders, stirring in the wind. The gown she wore was silver-blue silk, flowing luxuriously over the sides of her mount. Her youthful face was the picture of gentle innocence.

So in shock was he that Kyel almost didn't notice the line of Enemy soldiers spread out on both sides of the woman's horse, lining the walls of the ravine. All were archers, and every bow had an arrow nocked and drawn tight against a black-helmed head.

The woman's melodic voice rang out over the mountain slopes like sparkling silver bells of laughter. "To think I rode all the way from Bryn Calazar just to kill a wayward mage. Imagine my surprise at finding his own friends already doing my work for me."

She smiled, a playful glimmer in her eyes.

Kyel watched the woman's horse descend the slope toward them. She wasn't wearing a black cloak, but Kyel didn't need to see one to know the woman was another mage. An Enemy mage, despite her honey-innocent looks. She slid down from her palfrey's back, stepping lightly as she crossed the ravine toward them. Her eyes were wide and crystalline blue. On her lips, she wore a childish grin.

Three Enemy soldiers advanced at her side, sweeping forward with blades held at the ready. Together, they pressed Royce away from where he stood frozen under the threat of drawn bowstrings.

Enemy soldiers poured down the slope, surrounding the group of soldiers who had come with Royce. Two came forward and caught Kyel by the arms, hauling him over to stand with the other captives.

The woman gathered her skirts as she drew up at Darien's side. She reached a slender hand up to touch his face, caressing a finger down the side of his cheek.

"So, you're the Battlemage I've heard so much about," she said in that bell-like voice. "Do you have any idea what we do to your kind?"

The smile on her face radiated a thrill of anticipation as her pale eyes glistened in delight.

❂

Devlin Craig grimaced as he surveyed the sad collection of men going through the motions of practice in the yard. He had taken over their training for two days, and in that short amount of time had found himself growing more discouraged by the hour. After weeks of practice, the recruits had come a long way, but they were far too few, their talents still green and undeveloped. It took months to make a soldier, months these men simply didn't have. Not with the size of the Enemy host gathering on the other side of the two peaks to the north.

He stalked up to one of the recruits who was sweeping his practice sword around in a flowery dance of swirling arcs that looked impressive but were also grossly ineffective. Tearing the practice sword out of the man's hand, Craig hurled the wooden sword to the ground at his feet.

"If I wanted a dance master, I'd have sent to the Player's Guild," he growled, giving the recruit a sharp slap on the face. The frightened youth raised a hand to his cheek, mouth open wide.

"Get out of my sight," Craig growled, stepping forward menacingly and gesturing back toward the keep. "A few days of covering latrine pits might clear your head a bit. Now, *go!*"

The man whirled, ashen-faced in shame, and ran. Craig scowled, sweeping his gaze over the rest of the men who had paused in their practice to stare at him.

"Get back to work!" he bellowed, glaring as each man scrambled back into their stances.

Perhaps he'd been too hard on the boy, but Craig didn't care. He continued his survey of the men, strolling back down the line and examining each man's movements with a practiced eye.

Not one of them dared look up to meet his gaze as he walked by. They were all terrified of him, as well they should be. He was in a decisively bad mood.

The woman's breath stroked the skin of Darien's neck below his ear, the feel of it sending electric shivers down his nerves, spreading throughout his entire body. He turned his face away, refusing to look at her, as soft platinum curls brushed the side of his cheek. The scent of her filled his nostrils, a fresh yet subtle fragrance that reminded him of a field of blossoms. Her very presence exuded a frightening, seductive energy. She traced his lips with a soft caress.

"Do you know who I am?"

Darien shivered. There was only one person in the world she could possibly be, but that woman was a thousand years dead. He felt confident, though. She so perfectly matched the descriptions he'd read, it was uncanny. He decided to risk his guess.

"Arden Hannah."

The woman's eyes widened, a smile of appreciation blooming on her lips. "Oh, very good, my sweet. And you must be Darien Lauchlin, though I'm uncertain how that could possibly be. Your brother seemed quite convinced you were dead."

Darien's body stiffened. "How…?"

She pulled back enough to stare, smiling, into his face. Her hand moved to stroke the stubble on his cheek. She whispered in a low and breathless voice:

"You resemble your mother remarkably."

Darien flinched back from her touch. "You've never laid eyes on my mother."

The smile fell from her beautiful face, her lips pursing in an expression of profound sympathy. "But I have. I was staring right into her eyes the moment I killed her."

His vision reeled. Forgetting the threat of the bowmen, Darien staggered backward. His mind groped instantly for the field, but of course, there was nothing there. He cursed his own stupidity as his body shook in a furious mixture of revulsion and grief.

Arden smirked, her eyes wide and sparkling with amusement. She moved gracefully after him, the hem of her dress gliding across the black ground as she closed the distance between them. She was tall for a woman. As she drew up in front of him, her head came almost to the level of his eyes.

Darien clenched his jaw as she took his hand and pressed it into her own, running her soft fingers over his palm, stroking upward to trace the marks of the chain on his wrist. Closing his eyes, he suffered her touch as she leaned into him and whispered in his ear:

"Before you die, know this: a great host is gathering below Aerysius, waiting to sweep down through the Vale and flood into the North. A similar host is gathering here, in the shadows of Orguleth and Maidenclaw. In three weeks' time, when the sun rises between the Pointer Stones of Glen Farquist, those two forces will merge as one and topple the walls of Rothscard. This land you have sworn to protect will be desecrated, its people subjugated and destroyed."

As she spoke, a shuddering chill slithered over him, starting at his shoulders and working its way down the length of his arms, coiling in the pit of his stomach. He tried to pull away from her, but her arms wrapped around his back, drawing him close as she nestled her head against him, gazing into his eyes.

"But you won't need to worry about that," she soothed, smiling reassuringly. "Your worries end here today. My soldiers have brought plenty of wood. They know how much I delight in the sound of a man's dying screams."

Darien shoved her away from him forcefully, taking her by the shoulders and locking his arms to keep her at a distance. Arden stared at him as if wounded, her face darkening to a pout. But her eyes continued to gleam as she shrugged out of his hands and twisted away. She started to walk back in the direction she had come but then hesitated, turning back around as though she had forgotten something.

"By the way, your Meiran sends her love. I've seen her myself, kneeling at the feet of my Master in the Netherworld."

Darien collapsed to his knees as all the strength drained out of his body in a flood. He couldn't endure the vivid image that formed in his mind, provoked by the woman's malicious statement. It was the image from the dreams that plagued him almost every night, of Meiran staring up at him with the green light of hell in her eyes.

Above him, the sound of Arden's laughter echoed off the rock walls of the ravine.

The sound of hoofbeats made Craig turn. Frowning, he looked in confusion at the black warhorse loping up the trail toward him, empty stirrups bouncing at its sides. The Tarkendar halted in front of him, sides heaving, eyes rolling and showing the whites. Craig reached up and gathered the horse's reins, stepping back to let his gaze rove over the sweat-stained flanks of the gelding. There seemed nothing amiss with the animal, except for the alarming fact that it was absent its rider.

Instantly, Craig was in motion. Jumping on the horse's back, he wheeled the animal around and kicked his boots into its sides. Without hesitation, the warhorse broke into a gallop, angling back over the hill in the direction of the paddock.

Craig pulled the horse up next to the fence, his breath now coming in gasps from the grip of panic that seized him. He tore his eyes from horse to horse, dreading what he would find.

Just as he'd feared, Royce's dark stallion was absent from the herd.

"Darien," he whispered.

They had ripped the black cloak from his body, waving it in triumph like a captured banner. Then they had tied him to a stake. Darien hadn't even made an effort to struggle as he was bound tightly with sturdy rope. Then they had just left him there, lying on his side in the dirt.

He watched as Enemy soldiers hauled in armloads of wood, piling it in the center of the ravine. He didn't care. He was past the point of caring. The thought of the fire frightened him, numbing his body and chilling his mind. But that was all.

He feared the agony of the flames, but death itself would come as only a welcome release. He was tired of the nightmares. His passion for life had died with Meiran. Now, it seemed his very soul had been condemned to hell along with hers.

He watched as the logs of his pyre were mounded, dismissing the sight with acute indifference. His thoughts drifted to his father, wondering how that brave man had felt staring out at the same grisly scene. Darien found the thought strangely ironic yet comforting all the same. His mother had told him how alike he was to his father. Now, it seemed that parallel would be rendered complete.

Arden Hannah approached in a graceful sway of silk. Kneeling beside him, she whispered, "It's time. Are you ready to die?"

"I was ready a long time ago," he replied.

Black-armored soldiers stepped forward, seizing both ends of the stake. He was lifted and carried face-down toward the pile of wood in the center of the ravine. They laid him there beside it, angling the pole so that he had a clear, unobstructed view of what was coming.

As he watched, two more soldiers stepped forward, brandishing flaming torches that they threw onto the top of the pile. The dry kindling caught instantly, slithering ropes of flame racing over the thirsty fuel with a crackling, rushing hiss. Black smoke wafted upward, sparks drifting through the air like lazy snowflakes. The smell of it was chokingly thick. It stung his eyes as Darien tried to turn his face away from the intensity of the heat.

He felt soft fingers stroking the back of his head, running tenderly through his hair.

"Farewell, my sweet." Arden's delicate voice was barely audible over the crackling of the flames.

Then he was moving, the stake shifting as it was lifted upward into the air. He closed his eyes, holding his breath as the vicious heat of the smoke hit him square in the face.

He tried his best not to scream. He struggled desperately against his bonds as they braced the stake above the flames.

The heat was too much, too intense. He couldn't stand it, couldn't escape it. He felt his flesh starting to sear.

Darien writhed above the flames, howling in mindless agony.

Devlin Craig grimaced in dismay as he saw the column of smoke twisting upward in the distance, a black, roiling shadow against the flickering lights of the clouds. He knew instantly where the smoke was coming from and what its presence signified, realizing even before he veered his horse toward it that he was already too late.

He rode bareback, as did the rest of the men behind him. He hadn't wanted to waste the time it would take to saddle up and fetch his gear. He'd rounded up every man from the practice yard who could ride and put them on a horse.

But as he charged his gray stallion into the mouth of the ravine, he knew that his guess had been wrong. He'd feared Proctor had ordered Royce to slay Darien, trading the Sentinel's life for a new weapon, one potent enough to give him the slender chance he needed against the Enemy host.

Royce was Craig's friend, and Darien's, as well. But he was also a man enslaved by his commitment to duty. He would do anything Proctor asked of him, even if it meant sacrificing his soul along with the sum of his principles.

But the wafting column of smoke told Craig he'd been wrong. There was only one possible explanation for it. There simply wasn't enough wood in all the Shadowspears to kindle that kind of blaze. Only the Enemy could be responsible for such a fire, and there was only one reason they would have built it.

Craig resisted the impulse to close his eyes as his horse raced into the ravine. Darien Lauchlin had been the truest friend he'd ever had. Craig did not wish to look upon his burning remains.

The men behind him divided, spreading out, some angling their horses toward the slopes of the ridge, while those who remained formed a wedge behind him.

And then the fire was before him. He tried not to look at the charred body strapped to the stake, obscured by waves of heat coming off the blaze. Grimacing, Craig directed his mount toward the flames. He had no idea what the warhorse would do, presented with such a directive. But the gray stallion obeyed his command, charging faster as Enemy arrows whistled by him in the air.

The stallion bravely executed the maneuver taught to it by the horse masters of Southwark, reinforced by years of practice and training. The gray beast reared up as it dove into the fire, lashing out with its forelegs at the stake.

Craig dove off the horse, rolling away as he hit the ground. All around him, the sounds of fighting echoed through the ravine as his men engaged the Enemy. He forced himself into motion, blinking against the tears that stung his eyes. He ripped off his cloak and used it to beat the flames from Darien's body, then collapsed to the ground beside him, his ears assaulted by the screams of his dying horse.

Darien lay motionless, still tied to the smoldering stake. His clothes were nothing but ashes, his face blackened and blistered from the heat. Reaching for his knife, Craig sawed at the bonds with trembling hands.

He felt at Darien's neck for a pulse, detecting a flutter of heartbeat. But it was just one. That was all. Craig waited, but another didn't come. A tingling sensation stirred in the fingers of his hand, like a strange energy that seemed to want to slide up his wrist and into his arm. He almost withdrew his hand. But then he felt another flicker of pulse. The strange energy subsided, drawing back down into his fingertips.

Without thinking, Craig hefted the mage into his arms, stumbling as he surged forward with only one thought on his mind: he had to get Darien out of the node. He had no idea where the boundary was. Darien had only mentioned it to him once. Oblivious to the sounds of fighting around him, Craig staggered as fast as he could with the weight in his arms down the slope toward the mouth of the ravine. Once there, he collapsed in a heap over Darien's body.

He shook him as hard as he could, not caring that he touched scorched and blackened flesh. Charcoal-tatters of cloth came away with his hand. He raised a fist above his head, slamming it down into the mage's chest. Darien's head lolled to the side, blistered lips unmoving. Craig brought his fist down again with all his strength. Beneath him, the body jolted gruesomely.

He felt a hand on his shoulder and spun around, shocked to

find himself staring up into the face of the boy mage. Kyel Archer knelt beside him, shaking his head, eyes glistening with tears.

"Stop," he pleaded. "Please. Let him go in peace."

Craig bowed his head, averting his eyes from Darien's ruined face. It was wrong. So wrong. He deserved a better death than this. Craig tried to think of a prayer he could say, something to ease his friend's tortured spirit out of life. His mind groped for words. None came.

But then he realized he couldn't do that. He couldn't sit back and let his best friend go without a fight. With a growl, Craig grabbed Darien by the shoulders, shaking him without mercy.

"Breathe!"

He brought his fist down again.

"Come on, you bastard, breathe! *Heal yourself, damn you!*"

Below him, Darien's blistered lips moved as if to draw breath, but instead produced only a choking gurgle. Then the mage shuddered.

It was almost like a wave that started at the top of his head, passing over his body to his feet. As Craig stared down incredulously, the charred flesh beneath him whitened, the burnt cloth rewove and mended. Darien's chest spasmed with a sharp intake of breath, his head arching backward, eyes opening to stare vacantly at the sky. His eyelids dropped as the breath was released, but his chest rose again, assuming its normal rhythm.

Devlin Craig sat back on his haunches, throwing his head back in relief. At his side, Kyel Archer stared down at the renewed body of the sleeping mage, mouth open wide in disbelief.

The sounds of the battle unwound behind them. Craig wasn't sure, but he thought he saw a fleeting glimpse of blue silk disappearing over the ridge.

Chapter Fifteen
No Price Too High

Pass of Lor-Gamorth, The Front

The dark tower of Greystone Keep rose above a bank of mist like a lone island encased by a gray and swirling sea. The fog broke against its stark walls like ocean swells upon a shoreline, white-capped breakers licking against the gray embattlements before receding back again like a tide. The dark banner at its peak for once hung limp for lack of wind enough to stir it.

Devlin Craig reached his hand down to soothe the brown warhorse beneath him that had once belonged to Royce. The animal was nervous, unused to the strange weight and scent of its new master. Royce had raised the stallion from a colt. he'd been the only man to ever ride it. But Royce was dead. Craig had buried him with his own hands and piled the rocks atop his grave.

Ahead of him, Darien pulled his horse up and dismounted, leading the black gelding forward by the reins. Craig followed suit, as did the remainder of the men behind him. Corban Henley drew up beside him, and together the two of them flanked the Sentinel down the path that led across a dip in the ground between ridges. The thick curtain of mist parted before them to reveal the steep stair that led to the fortress above on the cliffs.

Craig was worried about his friend. Darien had scarcely spoken a word since he'd awakened late the previous night. There was something different about him, a subtle yet significant change. Craig had noticed it immediately, almost from the first moment the mage had opened his eyes. It was as though the shadows that always seemed to move behind his eyes had solidified into a tangible obscurity.

Craig didn't know what that meant, but he knew he didn't like it. The Darien that had emerged from the flames was not the same man he'd known. An acute sense of dispassion had fallen over him, shrouding his emotions like a pall. Craig was starting to wonder if part of him really had died in that fire, the part that mattered most.

Ahead of him, Darien's muffled footsteps slowed, coming to a stop. Glancing up, Craig saw the reason. It looked as if half the keep had turned out to greet their solemn homecoming, lining the cliffs and the steps, the fortress walls and the high turret. Only, it was not a welcome reception.

To his dismay, Craig saw that every soldier had a weapon in hand, every shaft and blade trained on their approaching party. Their path was barred by none other than the force commander himself, standing with shoulders squared and feet apart in the middle of the opening to the stairs. Proctor's face was set in harsh lines of anger mingled with disgust.

Darien raised Royce's bared sword before him like an offering, cradling it in his open palms at a level with his chest. He left his horse behind, crossing the distance between himself and Proctor at a slow and deliberate pace. Craig stayed where he was, transfixed by the scene. Darien stopped before the imposing form of the force commander and, closing his hand around the hilt, wielded the sword in a backwards grip.

With a sudden surge of force, the Sentinel bent his knees and brought the blade around, driving it point-first into the ground at Proctor's feet. The sword quivered there as Darien removed his hands from the hilt.

The force commander stared down at the shivering blade. Darien brushed past him, his shoulder grazing Proctor's arm roughly as he moved by, the boy mage scurrying after him. Bowmen along the cliffs tracked his movements with their shafts, tracking him as he ascended the rock-hewn steps and entered the keep.

Craig found himself left confronting his superior officer.

Garret Proctor brought his gaze up from Royce's quivering sword, fixing him with a look of molten fury.

"You betrayed my trust," Proctor accused.

Craig shook his head, feeling his anger mounting. "No. You betrayed mine. Royce is dead now because of it, and we came damned close to losing Lauchlin *and* Archer, both."

He frowned, sweeping his gaze over the man in front of him as if looking for a sign. "Do you even have a soul left, or did you sacrifice that too? Tell me, is there no price so high you're not willing to pay it?"

"No." Proctor's voice was cold as death. "The war we fight is the battle for existence itself. No price is too high, no sacrifice too great. I am willing to do anything it takes to survive. And I expect no less from any man who chooses to follow me."

Craig glared at him. Then he tossed his reins to Henley and followed Darien up the stairs. The archers slowly released the tension from their bowstrings, the soldiers lowering their blades.

He entered the fortress, the warmth flowing from the door of the hall a welcome relief. He yearned to go in and sit beside one of the hearths, to relax and ease the tension that gripped his shoulders like a vice. But instead, he let his feet take him up the winding stairs toward the top of the tower.

When he entered the circular chamber, he found Darien packing. The mage was squatting on the floor, tying up his bedroll. Kyel Archer stood behind him staring down at him with wide and fearful eyes. The Sentinel didn't look up as Craig walked toward him, but the boy glanced at him with a beseeching expression, as though begging him to do something, anything at all. He stopped a few feet away from Darien's back, watching him complete the knot he was working on with a sharp tug on the cord.

"You're leaving," Craig observed.

Darien just nodded, not pausing in what he was doing. Craig gazed down at him as the mage slapped his bedroll against his pack, securing it firmly with leather straps.

"Where will you go?"

Darien rose from the floor and, without looking at him, stalked across the room to the table and scooped up an old map.

"I'm going home," he said, still with his back to him.

Craig felt at a loss. He had no idea what to do. Darien couldn't be serious, but somehow Craig knew he was.

"Then I'll come with you."

"No." Darien shook his head. "This is my battle. You've your own war to fight."

With that, Darien slung his pack over his shoulder, gesturing for the boy to follow him. Craig moved forward, stopping him with a hand on his arm.

"Wait. Don't do this."

Darien finally brought his gaze up to regard him. "I don't have a choice."

He disengaged himself from Craig's grasp and started toward the opening of the stairs. But there he stopped, drawn up short by the form of a woman emerging from below, robed all in white with a sheer veil obscuring her features.

Craig's eyes widened in surprise. The woman seemed so utterly out of place against the stark confines of the chamber that her very presence seemed surreal. Distracted by her looks, he almost didn't realize the significance of the white veil and dress. When he did, the shock was like a blow in the face.

What was a priestess of Death doing here?

The woman swept her gaze across the faces of the three men in the chamber, her eyes finally coming to rest on Darien. She moved toward him, then swept to her knees at his feet, bowing forward and pressing her face against the floor. She remained there as the mage stared down at the top of her veiled head, frowning in consternation.

"Rise," he directed her finally.

Craig watched as the woman gracefully regained her feet, his mind spinning as he tried to make sense of the scene. It was not customary to abase oneself before any mage, even a Sentinel of Darien's status. Only the office of the Prime Warden had ever commanded such a humbling display of deference. He wondered what the woman was up to.

In a voice by no means gentle, Darien asked her, "What would the Temple of Death have of me?"

The woman dipped her head slightly, dark auburn curls spiraling out from under her veil. With an unruffled expression on her face, she stated formally, "Please allow me to introduce myself. My name is Naia Seleni, First Daughter of the Goddess Isap. I bear urgent tidings of your mother."

Darien glared at her, his jaw set in anger. "If you've come all the way here just to tell me she's dead, then you've wasted your time. I already know."

The woman blinked as if taken aback, her brow furrowing as she seemed to be reassessing the man before her. At last, she bowed her head. "I offer my most sincere condolences, Prime Warden."

"I am *not* Prime Warden," Darien corrected her. "Aerysius has fallen. The dead have no need of titles."

But the woman refused to yield. In a calm and yet adamant voice, she said, "You are the last surviving Master of Aerysius. Whether or not you acknowledge it, the office of the Prime Warden has fallen to you. And you are correct. The dead have no need of titles. However, the living still do."

Darien glared at her with a look that would have sent any other woman scurrying for the stairs. But the priestess held her ground and returned his gaze patiently.

"I have been sent to bring you back with me to the High Temple of Death at Glen Farquist, in the Valley of the Gods. There, your mother lies in state. The power of her gift has been transferred to a holding vessel and awaits you there to receive it."

Darien glowered at her. "Do you take me for a fool? A mage's legacy can be transferred only through physical contact."

The priestess gazed into his face through the screen of her veil. She said in a placid voice, "I apologize if I have distressed you. The vessel I am referring to is a relic of the Lyceum. It was placed in the keeping of Death's Priesthood before the fall of Bryn Calazar. I speak the truth, Prime Warden, this I swear."

"Don't call me that again."

The woman bowed her head, spreading her hands. "What

would you have me call you, then?"

To Craig's surprise, the mage simply shrugged as though defeated. "Call me Darien, like everyone else."

"As you wish. Darien." The way she said it made it sound like a taunt. "But though you deny your right to your title, I must urge you to never forget from where the name itself was derived. The words 'Prime Warden' were chosen because they mean, literally, 'first guardian.' Aerysius is no more, but that does not mean your responsibilities ended upon the death of your home."

"What exactly are you insinuating?" Darien asked.

"I could not help but overhear your conversation on my way up the stairs. Tell me, Darien. Do you truly believe the First Guardian of the Rhen would best serve his duty by wasting his life in a futile quest for vengeance? If you return to Aerysius, you will die. You have no chance against your brother's strength, nor the power of the gateway. Would not your life be better spent in service to the Rhen?"

Darien's eyes narrowed, seething. "You presume too much. You came here to take me to my mother. I suggest we go before she rots." He stalked past her out of the chamber, the sounds of his heavy footfalls echoing up from below.

Craig did not want to believe what he'd just heard. Once again, he had the gnawing feeling that something had shifted in the man, as though the part of him that had any feeling had simply just given up and died. He turned his head to find Kyel Archer staring at him, a look of questioning disbelief on his face. The priestess was regarding the opening of the stairs warily, mouth open and eyebrows raised.

Kyel followed Darien down the stairs, pausing only long enough to retrieve his bow and pack. He didn't want to go with Darien, but his place was at his side now. He'd found himself growing nervous around the mage. He was starting to wonder if the man had finally broken. There was, after all, only so much a person could take.

Downstairs, he found Darien standing on the last step,

confronting Garret Proctor. The mage's eyes were wide and wild, his hair falling in disarray. He stepped down onto the level of the floor, slowly circling the force commander with a glare of vicious contempt.

"Very soon, the Enemy will sweep down on you in numbers unimaginable." Darien leaned forward threateningly as he paced. *"You must fall back.* You'll have to harry them as much as you can and try to buy me time. I'll meet up with you at Orien's Finger at dawn on the morning of the Solstice. Draw the majority of their strength into the eye of the vortex, and I'll see to it you get your wish."

He started to turn away, but halted, stabbing a glare back at Proctor with hatred in his eyes. "I hope you're damn well satisfied. We're both going to burn in hell for this."

With that, he strode through the door of the hall as Proctor gazed after him in silence. Almost, Kyel thought there was the slightest hint of a smile on the commander's face.

Kyel moved as if through a haze into the hall, not really paying attention to anything but the panicked thoughts racing through his mind. So absorbed was he that he didn't notice Traver moving to intercept him.

"What's going on?" Traver asked, pulling him aside. Kyel looked at him in relief, comforted by the sight of his friend's familiar face.

"I think we're leaving."

Traver gawked. "You're going with *him?*"

He thumbed his hand over his shoulder in the direction of one of the hearths, where Darien was stuffing leavings from the evening meal into an oiled sack. Kyel hadn't told Traver about his commitment to the mage, fearing what his friend would say. Glumly, he reached down and folded back his shirtsleeve, exposing the markings on his wrist.

Traver's eyes went wide in alarm, his face paling. He grabbed Kyel's wrist, closing his fingers over the emblem, glancing quickly around as if making sure no one else had seen it.

He pulled Kyel after him by the wrist. Traver led him to a corner, where he pressed him back against the abrasive stone wall of the keep.

"What are you *thinking?*" he hissed. "That thing could get you killed!"

"Traver—"

But his friend continued right over him, "Look, if you were having problems, you should have come to me. I've lots of friends now that—"

Kyel shook his head. "Traver, it was my decision."

"Well, it sure was a bloody poor one!" the man shot back. "Perhaps it's not too late. Tell that darkmage you don't take well to responsibility. He'd have to believe you, because it's the plain truth. Tell him he'll have to find someone else."

"It's too late." Kyel shook his head miserably. "I've already spoken my first vow."

"Bloody hell, Archer! I always figured you were a little dense, but I didn't know you were downright stupid!"

Over Traver's shoulder, he saw Darien heading back toward the door of the hall. Kyel pressed his lips together, suddenly saddened. He didn't want to leave Traver behind. But the only other option was to talk Darien into bringing him along. He could only imagine how that would go over. Darien would put up with Traver for about as much time as it took the mage to toss him over the nearest cliff.

"Look, I have to go. Good luck to you, Traver. Try your best not to get killed, all right?"

"You're telling *me* not to get killed? With that damned thing on my wrist, I'd be a little more worried about my own hide! Do me a favor. If he tries to give you one of those bloody cloaks with the target on the back, just tell him black's not your color."

Kyel found himself grinning. "So long, Traver."

When he glanced back, he saw Traver slouching against the keep's cold wall, slowly shaking his head. Kyel left him there. He crossed the floor of the hall and, looking for Darien, walked out the gate into the cold, foggy night.

He strode down the stairs to where his horse was still saddled and waiting. Just as he drew up at the mage's side, Darien put his foot in the stirrup and swung himself over the back of his warhorse, sending it at a canter toward the path that led down and out of the pass. Kyel stared after the black gelding, not quite sure what to think.

Darien hadn't even looked at him, had just turned and ridden away. He felt wretchedly confused. Not knowing what else to do, he stood there by his horse and waited for the priestess.

It didn't take her long. The woman glided down the steps of the fortress with regal grace. She stopped beside him and regarded him with a questioning look. Her gaze slid slowly down his arm, and for a moment Kyel couldn't figure out what she was looking at. Her eyes widened as if she had just arrived at a startling revelation. When she looked up again, all trace of uncertainty had disappeared from her face.

It took him a moment to realize he'd forgotten to pull his sleeve back down after showing Traver the mark of the chain. Embarrassed, he tugged the fabric back over his hand. He was going to have to be more careful about that in the future. Traver was right. In the wrong places, that mark could get him killed. Even in the right places, it was not something he wanted generally known.

"Now, where did he run off to?" the woman muttered as she swung up onto the back of her mare.

Kyel nodded in the direction of the path.

"He certainly wastes no time," she muttered, kicking her mare forward.

They caught up to Darien about half a league down into the pass. He had slowed his horse to a walk and was riding with his head bowed. He didn't show any sign that he was aware of their presence until the woman's horse had drawn abreast of his own. Even then, he only glanced her way.

They rode in silence along the narrow path that carried them out of the mountains, winding along the steep slopes ever downward toward the Cerulean Plains. It was the same path Kyel had taken coming up, but he hardly remembered it. He hadn't been able to see much of anything and hadn't been in the mood to notice much, anyway.

But this was an entirely different journey. The wind was still, the lights of the clouds brighter. The sharp peaks of the Shadowspears thrust upward all around him, ranging away into the foggy distance. It was, he had to admit, the most beautiful night he had seen so far in the Pass of Lor-Gamorth.

The sound of Darien's voice actually startled him. "Where is the nearest entrance to the Catacombs?"

Kyel glanced toward the priestess, watching the frown that developed on her face beneath the obscurity of her veil. As if hesitant to answer, she took her time about forming a reply. "Death's Passage is no longer safe. Its secrets have been compromised. We must ride to Glen Farquist from here."

"Glen Farquist is a month's hard riding," Darien protested. "I can't afford that kind of time."

The priestess only shrugged, her motion disturbing the neat drape of her veil. "You must make the time. The Catacombs are not an option. They have become infested with dark creatures and fell shades. Also, the Eight are abroad and making use of them. Your own mother was murdered within."

Darien glowered. "The Enemy is preparing to mount the largest offensive we've seen in a thousand years. At Winter Solstice, two of their armies will sweep down through the North to merge at Orien's Finger. That's eighteen days from now."

The woman appeared startled. "How do you know this?"

"Arden Hannah told me."

The way he said it made it seem like the most natural thing in the world. But his statement made the priestess gasp. She yanked back on the reins, drawing her horse up. The look in her eyes was one of fear mixed with outright revulsion.

"You have actually spoken to one of the Eight?"

Darien nodded. "Right before she tried to kill me."

"You're quite a mystery, Darien Lauchlin," she said. "How exactly did you plan on returning to Aerysius to wreak vengeance upon your brother and still manage to make it to Orien's Finger by Solstice?"

Darien shrugged. "It's a week to Aerysius from here. And another week to Orien's Finger."

"And what do you intend to do once you arrive, Bound as you

are?"

"I hadn't the faintest idea until tonight." A strange smile formed on Darien's lips, the first Kyel had seen since his argument with Proctor in the tower. "But we must make use of the Catacombs. It's our only chance of buying enough time."

The woman shook her head. "No. I forbid it."

"Then our journey ends here." To Kyel's astonishment, Darien brought his horse around and turned it back the way they'd come. The woman stared after him with an exasperated look.

"You would give up your own mother's rare and precious gift merely to have a chance at slaying your brother?"

"That's right. When the battle is joined in truth, I can't afford to have Aidan at my back."

Kyel frowned. Perhaps the man was not insane, after all. What he said did seem to make sense. A desperate kind of sense.

The priestess relented with a sigh. "You would have made a formidable priest of Death."

"What I really need to be is a formidable mage," Darien snapped.

"Have no doubt. You are." The woman didn't appear pleased by that. "The nearest entrance to the Catacombs is at a shrine off the Great Northern Road, southwest of Wolden. We can make it there by tomorrow if we ride straight through the night."

The horses plodded along, picking their way down the narrow trail. Kyel found it hard to stay afraid when such extraordinary changes were taking place all around him. It happened so slowly that, at first, he didn't notice the transition. But gradually, the clouds were loosening their hold on the sky, and the dawn was becoming brighter.

Plants started to appear on the sides of the mountain slopes: sparse at first, then becoming denser the further they went, until the hills around them began taking on a hue of astonishing green.

And then a wondrous thing happened. The clouds parted overhead, and a ray of luminous sunlight fell across Kyel's face, far brighter than he ever remembered. He brought his hand up to shield his eyes, blinking as he stared up into a blue morning sky.

The sun had never felt so warm or so welcome. Below, the verdant foothills of the Shadowspears spilled down into a grassland so rich and green and exceptionally bright that Kyel found himself wanting to cry with joy. It had been almost two months since he had seen blue sky, or even so much as a single green leaf. The breeze stirring toward them from the grassland was warm with the sweet, rich smell of autumn.

"The Cerulean Plains," Darien stated. He lifted his arm, pointing toward a branch of the mountains that marched southward to their right.

"Orien's Finger lies in that direction. There's a Circle of Convergence at its peak, where Grand Master Orien made his stand against the Enemy four hundred years ago. The plains are covered by an enormous vortex that begins just north of the town of Wolden, which means we'll be passing through the outer margin of it."

Darien's eyes settled on Kyel's, fixing him with a significant look. "Don't try to get a sense of the field from this point on. Not till I tell you to. Without training, the field lines in a vortex can cause you pain if you stroke them the wrong way."

Kyel had read enough to know what a vortex was and what it meant. It was like a hurricane of power, a place where the lines of the magic field swirled and converged. He felt a shudder of foreboding as he stared down at the grasslands, which suddenly seemed to have diminished in their beauty.

Before, when he had trekked up this way, a vortex had meant nothing to him. But now that he'd started exercising his mind to consciously sense the magic field, reaching out toward it was becoming second-nature. Still, he didn't understand. He was not a Master, so how could the vortex possibly harm him?

But if Darien sensed his question, he didn't say anything. With one last admonishing glance, the Sentinel sent his horse forward at a lope down the mountainside. Kyel's mount wanted to break after it, but he held it to a walk with a firm hand on the reins. He looked over at the priestess and saw that she was staring at him.

"You never told me your name," she said.

Kyel felt a flush of embarrassment. Beside her, he felt so insignificant that he really hadn't thought it mattered to her, one way or the other.

"I, uh. Kyel Archer, that is. That's my name."

Beneath her veil, the woman's lips drew upward in a smile. Kyel couldn't believe he'd just fumbled over his own name.

"It is an honor to make your acquaintance, Kyel Archer." The priestess was still grinning in amusement. "You may call me Naia, if it pleases you."

He wasn't sure if it did please him. For the second time since coming to Lor-Gamorth, a person with an imposing title had asked him to use their given name. The first time, he'd earned himself a chain on his wrist. But at least the mark Darien had placed there was out in the open, where he could stare at it and consider its implications. There were many types of chains.

But the priestess seemed to be regarding him casually, a wistful expression on her face. "Is he a hard master?"

Kyel found himself thinking that question over for a minute, unsure of how to respond. The truth was, he really didn't know. His apprenticeship was only just beginning.

He shrugged, responding, "Darien is harder on himself than he is on anyone else."

Naia appeared to consider his words, glancing down at the place where Darien had drawn his horse up and was staring out across the plains.

Chapter Sixteen
Wolden

Wolden, The Rhen

Wolden was just as Darien remembered it: a large, ramshackle town that marked the end of the Great Northern Road. The very fact of its existence was something of a puzzle. Wolden had originally been established as a waypoint in the movement of supplies and soldiers to the Front, just an outpost of Greystone Keep. Yet, as trade to the pass had dwindled over the years, the town had continued to thrive and had even grown.

Other than Rothscard, Wolden was the most populated settlement in Emmery. And it was directly in the path an invading army would take, snug up against the foothills that climbed into the Pass of Lor-Gamorth.

Darien could not conscionably skirt the town without giving its people some type of warning. So he ignored the urgency that made him want to bypass the settlement.

The priestess was quick to figure out what he had in mind. She drew up beside him on her roan mare, adjusting her veil and saying in a lowered voice, "You must take great care in how you handle this. You'll not wish to create a panic."

Darien said, "I intend to find the mayor. I'll give him the information and let him figure out what he wants done about it."

The priestess nodded, though her eyes still looked troubled. He was starting to get the feeling he was in some odd sort of power struggle with the woman.

The trail they were following widened as they approached the town's north gate. Being situated so close to the Front, Wolden was fortified, ringed by a crenellated wall broken in places by guard towers. But Wolden had grown too big to be contained within the wall, and a good deal of the town had spread beyond it.

The first cottage they rode past looked dilapidated. A woman sat in a chair on the porch. Beside her was a basket of yarn and a small child that squatted next to it, intent on the basket's contents. The woman glanced up at the sound of their horses, a look of casual interest on her face. But then her expression crumbled, turning to a look of fear. She shot out of her chair, gathered the child into her arms, and bolted inside.

Darien frowned. What had prompted the woman to react that way? It was more than just the glimpse of his cloak. Most people of the Rhen were familiar enough with what that cloak represented not to be frightened whenever they saw one.

As they approached the gate, every person they came across seemed just as startled as the woman. They drew a broad variety of reactions, ranging from shock to dismay, even terror. Darien was used to people deferring to him, moving out of his way on the street, or staring at him when they thought he wasn't looking. But he had never experienced anything like this.

Even the guards stationed at the town gate gawked at them as they passed through, staring at him as though he were Zavier Renquist himself. They made no move to bar his way but edged away from him as far as they could. Darien turned to look over his shoulder, watching as a man with a crossbow abandoned his post and fled down a side street.

Darien cursed himself. He had been a fool not to consider the swift wings of rumor. No doubt word of Aerysius' fall must have preceded their arrival in Wolden. If the people of this town thought every last mage was dead, then he could imagine their shock at seeing him riding in with a priestess of Death.

Their party was quickly surrounded by mounted guardsmen. And even though their weapons were sheathed, Darien didn't like the looks in the eyes of the guards who ringed them. They were afraid. Frightened men could be desperate men. And he was powerless within the perimeter of Orien's Vortex.

A guard with graying hair approached them on his horse. He looked Darien up and down, dipping his chin in a stiff greeting. "Your pardon, Great Master, but the mayor would like a word with you. You are advised to come with us."

Darien ran his gaze over the tight circle of men, then nodded. The guard leaned forward and caught his reins. Immediately, two more guardsmen drew their mounts around to flank him. Another kicked his horse forward, insinuating his mount between Naia's and his own. Together, they led Darien's horse forward, encircling him like a hostile escort.

The mayor's house was not far from the gate. It was not a house at all, really, but rather a small palace. In the North, elected offices turned over about as often as Southern kingdoms changed dynasties. The mayor of Wolden had probably enjoyed his position for decades.

The guardsmen guided them through an iron gate to a path that wound through a garden of symmetrical flower beds. The whole affair reminded Darien of the Queen's palace in Rothscard, only on a miniature scale.

The guards ordered them to dismount before a flight of marble steps. Darien climbed down from his horse, studying the guards warily as he waited for the priestess and Kyel. His new acolyte looked a little unsure about what to do with his bow. Darien shook his head at him, indicating with his eyes that he ought to leave it behind with the horse. Kyel reached up and hung the bow from his saddle.

The guards led them up the steps and through a large door. A foyer spanned the entire front of the mansion, with a white staircase that curved upward to a balcony on the second floor. The room was elegantly furnished, every piece of furniture a work of fine craftsmanship. Letting his gaze wander, Darien discovered what looked like a priceless collection of oil paintings mounted high up on the walls. One in particular, a nude of a woman sitting alongside a bath, had the unmistakable broad strokes and bold contrasts of a Gabrizi. Darien swallowed, wondering how in the world he was going to convince the owner of this collection to leave it all behind.

They were led down a short hallway and into a snug room with a large table entirely too big for the space, leaving scant room for anything else. A man was already seated behind the table, his hands folded neatly on its polished surface. He made no move to stand, instead just gestured with his hand at two chairs across the table from him.

"Please, have a seat."

Darien paused before making a move toward one of the chairs, taking a quick survey of the man in front of him. He assumed it was the mayor he was looking at, although the man was younger than he had expected, with short brown hair and a plumpish face. He wore a simple tan jacket, though the cut looked well-tailored and expensive.

"Mayor Blake Pratson." The man nodded by way of introduction as Darien removed his sword and took the seat across from him.

By the rules of etiquette or even common courtesy, the mayor should have risen to greet his guests. Naia's presence alone should have been enough to demand it. But the mayor of Wolden just sat back in his chair and waited until Darien and Naia were seated, Kyel lingering awkwardly on his feet. The priestess looked furious, her dark eyes glaring through her veil. Kyel appeared to be making a conspicuous study of the wood of the tabletop.

Darien thought about demanding an explanation for the treatment they had received but decided against it. He needed this man's cooperation. Instead, he leaned forward, extending his arm toward the man across the table and supplied his name, leaving off his title. Pratson looked down at his offered hand with a look of disdain. At last, he reached out and clasped it in a tentative grip.

Darien said, "May I introduce First Daughter Naia Seleni of the Temple of Isap. And this is my acolyte, Kyel Archer."

He let go of the mayor's hand, noting the clammy feel of the man's skin. Like the guards, Blake Pratson was afraid of him, which made no sense. As mayor of Wolden, the man should know that Darien was powerless here within the turbulence of the vortex. The entire town of Wolden was effectively mage-proof. Yet, if the feel of his hand betrayed his apprehension, the mayor's face was a study in unruffled self-assurance. Sitting back in his chair, Pratson folded his arms across his chest and regarded Darien with a skeptical expression.

"You'll have to forgive my shock, Master Lauchlin," he said. "You see, I've had word from the Queen of Emmery that Aerysius has been completely destroyed. Begging your pardon but, by all reports, you're supposed to be dead."

Darien nodded thoughtfully, thinking that, while such news might give the man pause, it still didn't explain Pratson's anxiety or the outright fear on the faces of so many of Wolden's citizens. There was something else going on here, but the man was being slow to let on about it.

"The report is accurate. To my knowledge, I'm the only survivor."

Outwardly, Pratson's face conveyed a look of polite interest. Only the slightest narrowing of his eyes gave away his doubts.

The priestess shifted in her seat, her fingers stroking the back of Darien's hand under the table in warning. Glancing up, he saw that another man had moved into the room behind him. He had come in so quietly that Darien hadn't noticed his presence. Which was alarming. His ear was trained to pick up on such noises. Either he had slipped in his vigilance, or this newcomer was not an ordinary guard.

Something about the man reminded him of the blademaster he had studied under in his youth. It wasn't a physical resemblance, more in the way the man held himself and the air of casual confidence he projected. Unless Darien missed his guess, the man was a Guild blademaster.

He found himself liking this situation less and less. Pratson was openly studying him now, analyzing his reaction. Darien could no longer pretend to ignore the insult of the guards. Striving to keep his voice as even as possible, he said to the mayor, "Why don't you tell me what this is all about."

Pratson shook his head. "First, you tell me what brings you to Wolden."

"As you wish," Darien allowed softly, folding his hands on the table. "I bear ill tidings from Greystone Keep."

He described the size of the Enemy host waiting on the other side of the pass while the man listened blandly. As he spoke, he had the growing feeling that not one word of his account was being taken seriously. Pratson just sat there, leaning back in his chair and looking almost bored. When he was finished, the mayor reached a hand up and rubbed his temple.

"Do you have a shred of proof that this army does, in fact, exist?"

The statement sent Naia bolt upright in her seat, hands gripping the edge of the table as she gasped in disbelief, "You dare question the word of a Sentinel?"

Pratson shrugged. "I fear I'm left with little choice." Turning to Darien, he said bluntly, "Your very presence here is a mystery to me. I find almost everything about you troubling. For one, I've always heard that mages were forbidden to bear weapons, and yet you come to me carrying steel at your back. What do you think, Broden? Is that sword just the fancy decoration it looks?"

"No." The tall guardsman shook his head. "He's had Guild training."

Darien's eyes narrowed as he turned to look at the man behind him. Broden hadn't been with the other guardsmen who had escorted them through town. In fact, Darien hadn't seen him at all, not until he had so silently entered the room.

"Broden's good," the mayor said with a wry grin. "Give him a few more minutes, and he could probably name the blademaster you studied under."

It was scarcely a secret anymore. "Nigel Swain was captain of Aerysius' guard. He taught me the art of the blade."

Broden nodded warily, sucking in a cheek. "I remember Swain." He glanced at Pratson. "He left the Guild for Aerysius some years ago, just as he says. You know him, too. He's captain of the Queen's guard now."

But the mayor still didn't appear convinced. Slowly, he said, "And then there's also the mystery of your name."

His words caught Darien by surprise. "What of it?"

"Everyone knows Emelda Lauchlin was Prime Warden. Are you claiming to be a relation?"

"I am her son."

Pratson's eyes ticked toward Broden. Instantly, the man was in motion. Darien rose halfway out of his seat, hand reaching for his hilt. But he was taken by surprise, his reaction too slow. The cutting edge of Broden's sword was already frozen at his neck. Slowly, Darien retracted his hand, keeping his eyes fixed on Broden. Beside him, Naia was on her feet, glaring at Pratson in outrage.

The mayor explained, "In her note to me, Queen Romana mentioned that the downfall of Aerysius was brought about through the betrayal of the Prime Warden's own son."

Darien blinked in shock. That explained everything. They had mistaken him for Aidan. He felt a sickening nausea in his stomach at the thought of it. No wonder the people had stared at him that way on the street.

Beside him, the priestess addressed Pratson in a near-whisper of threat, "In most territories, it is considered a capital offense to detain a Master against his will."

But the mayor simply dismissed her words with a wave of his hand, smiling confidently. "The town of Wolden is well within the protective margins of Orien's Vortex. A black cloak means nothing here."

Naia looked down, her long veil brushing the surface of the table. Darien watched her from the corner of his eye, his gaze still locked on Broden. Slowly, the priestess raised her head, folding her hands neatly in front of her.

"What if we can offer the proof you require?"

Pratson shrugged. "Then, by all means, please do so."

Darien couldn't imagine what Naia was talking about. He listened to her as he stared into Broden's eyes, watching for any subtle change. Usually, where the eyes moved, the blade followed.

Naia explained in a patient, almost lecturing tone, "Prime Warden Emelda had two sons. It was Darien's brother Aidan who sacrificed his Oath of Harmony in order to bring about the destruction of his home. As you can imagine, if Darien had committed such an act, he would no longer bear the chains of the Oath upon his wrist."

Pratson pursed his lips, turning to Darien with eyebrows raised expectantly. Darien sighed, feeling disgusted. It always came back to his Oath. Always. Glaring at Broden as if daring him to strike, he raised both hands and shook back his sleeves, the material falling away to expose the hated markings there.

Darien shuddered as he looked at those twin chains. He found just the sight of them repulsive. He had to force himself to keep his arms raised as Pratson sidled out from behind the table, walking around Naia to take Darien's right arm into his hand. The mayor's palm was even clammier than before. Darien closed his eyes in loathing as the man raised his wrist up almost under his nose, inspecting the emblem closely.

He wanted to strangle Naia.

The mayor released his arm. As he did, Darien heard the guard's blade sliding back home into its scabbard.

"You have my most humble apologies," Pratson told him, drawing away. "And my most sincere condolences."

"Thank you," Darien muttered, falling heavily back into his seat. The priestess regained her own chair beside him, placing a comforting hand on his arm. When he looked over at her, he saw Naia's eyes were full of regret.

Pratson remained standing, bringing a hand up to rub his brow wearily. "One week, did you say?"

Darien nodded, feeling drained. "If that. Proctor has less than a thousand men under his command. It all depends on how well he can make use of tactics to slow them down."

The mayor looked as if he simply didn't understand. That, or he just flat-out refused to believe. "Surely, Greystone Keep can hold its own in a siege far longer than you give them credit for."

"There will be no siege," Darien insisted. "If Proctor allows himself to be surrounded, his entire force will be destroyed."

Pratson paced away toward the fireplace, raking a hand through his hair. With his back to Darien, he asked, "And if this Enemy host is not stopped in the pass, what makes you think our people will be safe even in Rothscard?"

"Your people will be far safer in a fortified city with its own standing army than they ever will be in Wolden."

The mayor nodded, turning back with a look of resignation. His face was pale and glistening with a sheen of sweat. Shoving his hand into the pocket of his jacket, he retrieved a white kerchief, using it to dab at his forehead. "Then I suppose I ought to thank you, Master Lauchlin, for the warning. Is there anything further you require?"

On impulse, Darien pushed his chair back and rose from his seat. "I'd ask you to leave something behind for the soldiers passing through in your wake."

Pratson frowned at him. "What do you have in mind?"

"Anything you can think of that might be of use to a retreating army. Food. Remounts. Medicinals. Weapons, if you have any to spare. Arrows, especially, would be critical. An army on the run doesn't have time to stop and retrieve spent shafts."

"Greystone archers have always favored the longbow, have they not?"

Darien nodded.

Pratson raised his hands helplessly. "Out here on the plains, we've little use for them. I'm afraid I am simply not equipped to supply an army with arrows for bows we don't use."

But Darien was not about to let the man off that easily. "What sort of bows do you have?"

"The local nomads use horn bows to defend their grazing territories. I've supplied my own guardsmen with them."

Horn bows. As the mayor had suggested, arrows meant for the horn bow would be of no use to the Greystone archers. And yet…he had seen one of these horn bows on a guard at the gate. It was much smaller than the longbow yet had the look of an effective weapon.

Such a bow could be used from horseback. Longbows could not, at least not without enormous difficulty. The only chance of success Proctor had would be to strike and fall back, as fast as he could, as often as he could. If his bowmen were mounted and supplied with horn bows, their chances would be greatly improved.

Darien asked, “How many bows might you be able to lay your hands on in the span of a week?”

“While trying to organize an evacuation? You ask too much.”

“What I’m asking for is the means of defending your homeland,” Darien reminded him. “If you provide the Greystone archers with horn bows and remounts, they could make use of them to harry the Enemy and slow their advance.”

Pratson stared at him with raised eyebrows. “I can try. But I make no promises.”

“Do your best. For every Enemy soldier that falls along the way, that’s one less to threaten the walls of Rothscard.” He released his grip on the mayor’s arm.

Pratson scowled at the floor. “Now I remember why I’ve never liked dealings with your kind. No good news ever comes on the wings of a black cloak.”

He reached out and clasped Darien’s hand in parting. Naia rose, gathering her white skirts and dipping her chin as she moved past Darien out the door. Kyel followed in her wake, looking a bit pale.

Darien almost smiled as he watched his young acolyte leave, thinking the meeting had been a good lesson for him. Then he frowned, remembering the next lesson he had planned. It was almost time to implement it.

Chapter Seventeen
Follow the Field

The Cerulean Plains, The Rhen

Wolden disappeared behind them, swallowed up by the rolling folds of the prairie. Kyel closed his eyes and slouched in his saddle, moving with the steady rhythm of his horse's gait. It felt good to feel the sun on his face. He tilted his head back, luxuriating in the warmth of the breeze that caressed his cheeks and ruffled his hair.

He paid little attention to where they were headed, happy just to watch the scenery go by. It wasn't until the priestess angled her horse off the road and guided it westward that Kyel began to wonder where they might be headed. Every once in a while, a small tree broke the monotony of the grass. Otherwise, the prairie was like a sprawling ocean, stretching out in infinite tides to the distant horizon.

"Where are we going?" Kyel asked, contemplating the enormity of the view that surrounded them. It made him feel extraordinarily small and insignificant, yet hale and fortunate at the same time.

Naia glanced back and smiled. "There is a shrine of the goddess a few leagues west of here," she said, her veil fluttering about her face.

Staring out into the vast emptiness before them, Kyel wondered aloud, "Why would anyone want to build a shrine all the way out here?"

The priestess slowed her mount, pulling back on the reins until she was riding abreast of him. "Death is a universal human experience, Kyel. It doesn't happen just in towns and cities. Also, the governorship of this province strictly forbade us from building a temple in Wolden."

Kyel found that strange. "Why?"

"Oh, for political reasons," Naia said as her mare twitched its tail into Kyel's leg.

"I fail to see how a temple has much to do with politics."

Darien glanced back over his shoulder and exchanged an amused grin with the priestess. Kyel frowned, feeling like the butt of some joke he didn't understand.

But when Darien turned his smile on him, Kyel realized there was nothing scornful about it. Rather, the mage's expression seemed almost fatherly. He said, "Once you become a bit more traveled, I think you'll find the temples have more authority than most people would guess."

Kyel nodded, thinking it strange a man only scant years older than himself could make him feel so much like a child. He figured it was because Darien's range of experiences was so vastly different from his own. Kyel had lived in the same remote township all his life, learning what he could about the world from what he could glean from the few books that passed his way.

Darien, on the other hand, had actually been to many of the places Kyel had only ever read about. More than that, a critical part of his training had been the study of the Rhen and its various peoples. It created a broad gap between the two of them, making Darien seem far older than he actually was.

Kyel realized he didn't even know the man's true age. When he'd first met Darien, he remembered thinking how young he looked for a full Master. Kyel frowned. That had only been two months ago. Yet, in those two months, the Sentinel seemed to have aged.

He thought back to the night Darien had tested him, when the mage had shared his fear about the amount of raw power he'd taken in. Kyel couldn't help wondering if that had something to do with it. Darien no longer resembled the quiet, gentle man Kyel remembered meeting that night in the tower. There was nothing quiet or gentle about him any longer. Darien reminded him of a banked fire burning low, awaiting only the smallest draft of air to ignite.

The sun was starting to sink toward the horizon when Darien drew his horse up and announced it was time to make camp for the night.

Naia objected, "If we press on ahead, we could make it to the shrine before full dark. It's not much farther."

But Darien was already unloading his horse's saddlebags. "Not tonight. I've something for Kyel to do first."

Kyel waited for him to elaborate, but the man didn't say another word. Finished with unloading the last of his bags, Darien hobbled his horse and turned it loose to graze.

Kyel decided he'd better stop watching and offer to help. Soon, he found himself set to the task of wading through the tall grass in search of wood while Darien and the priestess finished setting up their campsite.

Finding enough wood for a fire in the middle of a prairie was not as easy as it seemed, Kyel soon discovered. He tromped through the grass over uneven footing, his boots sinking through the topsoil into burrows abandoned by whatever animal had originally dug them. He spread his hands out at his sides, letting the blades of grass trail against his palms as he moved through it.

At last, he found a small, dead tree hidden completely in the grass. He wouldn't have seen it if he hadn't tripped over it first. The wood was decayed and brittle, so it wasn't hard to snap off enough branches to make a few armloads of wood, which he hauled back to the campsite.

As soon as he had the wood brought in, he found himself set to clearing a space for the fire and then cooking supper, as well. After which, he got to clean everything up while the priestess lounged on a bed of grass and Darien occupied himself by sliding a whetstone along the edges of his blade in long, slow strokes.

By the time Kyel had cleaned out the last pan and stuffed it back into his pack, he'd had just about enough. He'd half a mind to tell Darien exactly where he could shove this whole acolyte business. It was starting to feel more like servitude than any apprenticeship he'd ever heard of.

He was just about to cast his tired body down beside the fire when the Sentinel finally sheathed his blade and rose to his feet. He walked away from the camp, beckoning for Kyel to follow.

Kyel didn't bother suppressing his groan as he trudged after him. Darien led him up the rise of a low hill, where he stopped and turned, waiting for Kyel to shuffle up the slope. The moon was rising over the mountains in the east, its disk a murky yellow-orange.

"It's time for your next lesson."

Kyel felt a shiver of dread caress his skin. There was something in Darien's tone he didn't like.

"The first step is learning how to sense the presence of the magic field," Darien said. "You managed that quickly. Let's see how well you do with the second step: learning how to read its strength and direction."

Kyel was taken aback, especially after Darien's warning to him earlier that day. "Can you do that? I thought you said this was a vortex."

Darien shook his head. "I can't. But for you, this vortex provides a great opportunity for learning."

"If you say so." Kyel still didn't like the sound of it. He also didn't like the way Darien seemed to be deliberately avoiding his gaze. Instead, he appeared to be looking out at the moonrise, as if studying it for some portent or sign.

Darien said, "You'll need to reach out from deep inside your mind and get a sense of the magnitude and direction of the field. In a vortex, the field lines run almost parallel and become compressed together till they overlap. It's called superposition. The strength of the field increases the further you go in.

"There's a trick about it. You'll have to ease your mind along the direction of the current. If you go against it, you'll know right off."

Kyel swallowed. "That doesn't sound very reassuring."

"It's not meant to be."

Kyel could only nod. Taking a deep breath, he did what Darien told him, opening his mind and tentatively reaching out toward the magic field. Immediately, he felt a stabbing jolt in his head that crackled down the fibers of his nerves like a slap of lightning.

With a cry, he brought his hands up and hugged his head. The pain was gone, but the memory of it still jolted through his body.

"That bloody *hurts!*"

Darien shook his head, folding his arms. "Then you went about it the wrong way. Try again."

Kyel brought his hands down and stared up at him incredulously. "You're not serious. I can't do that again!"

"You'll do it till you get it right. Now. Try again."

Kyel couldn't believe what he was hearing. Darien stared down at him, arms folded against his chest. There was no hint of sympathy or even compassion in his face. He just stood there, waiting expectantly.

Feeling at a complete loss, Kyel tried to do what the man wanted. This time, he used a slightly different approach, using the most delicate touch he could manage. He actually felt the field for an instant, a tremendous, wild energy that seized his control and wrenched it sharply away.

This time, the pain was exquisite.

Kyel screamed, doubling over. Clutching his head, he fell to the grass and flopped onto his back, gasping. The pain took longer to go away. His head throbbed with the pulse of every heartbeat, and his body shook in quivering spasms.

At last, the grip of the pressure in his head eased enough for him to relax back into the soft grass. He lay there, trembling, staring up at the stars as the Sentinel lowered himself down beside him and placed a steadying hand on his arm.

"Try again."

Kyel shook his head. He couldn't do that again. He blinked back tears as he stared up into Darien's face. *"Why are you doing this to me?"*

The look in Darien's eyes was as hard and desolate as the black slopes of the mountains behind them. He rose to his feet, turning his back. Then he walked away.

Kyel watched him go, feeling hurt and more than a little

betrayed. He could still sense the weight of Darien's disappointment lingering in the air long after the man was gone.

He had no desire to return to their camp. He didn't want to get up. His joints ached, and it wasn't just from the ride. So he lay there in the soft and scratchy grass, looking up through the tall blades at the wash of stars above in the heavens. The stars were so many, their lights seemed to combine and run together.

He lay there for perhaps an hour. Maybe longer. He had no way to be sure. Around him, the night was cooling steadily, and the ground was growing hard. There was a rock digging into his back that he hadn't noticed before. Kyel sat up, yawning, and used his hands to push himself to his feet.

Looking around, he tried to remember the way back to their camp. The fire had burned out; he couldn't see the glow of the coals. But at last he made out the form of his horse grazing in the distance.

He trudged back down the slope of the hill toward the shadows of their campsite. But when he reached it, Kyel looked down in dismay.

Both Darien and the priestess were gone.

Kyel's pack and bedroll were still there next to the ashes of the fire that had been smothered with dirt. But Darien, the priestess, and their belongings had disappeared as surely as if the prairie had just opened up and swallowed them.

Angry, Kyel tossed himself down on his bedroll. Had Darien decided to abandon him, just because he hadn't been able to handle the test of the vortex? Or was it because he'd given up after only trying twice? Whatever the reason, it hardly mattered. He was alone.

Kyel's hand went to a foot-long piece of wood lying next to him on his blanket. He picked it up, wanting to throw something. He moved his arm back to toss it. Just as he did, he noticed words carved into the bark. Blinking, he held it up before his face, staring down at the letters that had been scratched there, then rubbed over with charcoal to darken them.

Follow the field.

Kyel almost choked on the sudden anger that flooded through

him. He howled in rage as he threw the piece of wood with all his strength. His horse looked up from its grazing, snorting as if offended by his action.

He couldn't believe Darien was doing this to him. The man had said he wouldn't go easy on him, but this was downright cruel. He should just pile his things on his horse and ride back to Wolden. From there, he could follow the Great Northern Road all the way back to Covendrey, back to home. He'd been doing the man a favor when he'd agreed to accept Darien's offer. If this was the way he was going to be treated, it wasn't worth it.

He surged to his feet and went to his horse. The moon was full and bright, so it wasn't hard to see as he saddled the animal and loaded it up. He swung his leg over the horse's back and, with one last, contemptuous glance at the campsite, set his mount heading east, back across the prairie toward the road.

"You did it to yourself, Darien," he muttered.

He'd gone perhaps half a league before he pulled back on the reins. Cursing the mage silently, he wheeled the animal around and sent it at a gallop back to the campsite, where he climbed down and led the beast forward.

He had made the Sentinel a promise, and the mark it left on his wrist was a visible reminder that was going to haunt him to his grave. Kyel had never gone back on his word in his life. He wasn't about to start now.

He thought about just heading west, the direction the priestess had been leading them. Naia had said the shrine was only a short distance away. Maybe he could find it on his own, without having to open his mind to the fierce energy of the vortex.

Or maybe he would get turned around in the dark and find himself hopelessly lost. Grudgingly, he decided that strategy wasn't going to work.

Closing his eyes, he tried to brace himself for the pain. Then he groped outward with his mind.

The lightning-like strike in his head was immediate and intense. It almost took him to his knees. In his mind, he could hear Darien's voice coming back to torment him:

Try again.

"No," Kyel groaned, shaking his head even as he forced his will out again into the torrent of the field. This time, he actually got a sense of the direction of the current, right before the searing backlash of power drove into his mind like a molten dagger.

Sobbing outright, Kyel staggered forward, clenching the reins of his horse in one hand, his other hand clutched around the back of his head, gripping his hair in a fist. His vision was so streaked with tears that he could hardly see. He felt his way ahead with his feet, stumbling as he tripped over something in the grass.

He groped again for the field, taking just a tentative sample before flinching back away from it. He waited for the slap of pain. It took a moment to realize that it hadn't come. Startled, Kyel blinked the tears out of his eyes.

He'd done something different. Something right. Only, he wasn't sure what it was. He tried to remember, but it wasn't something he'd consciously thought about. He just hoped he could repeat it again when he had to.

But now he knew where he was going, at least.

The currents of the vortex were raging in a south-westerly direction, sweeping across the rolling swells of grass. It was a good thing he hadn't just started walking, hoping to blindly run into them. The flow of the field was slightly different from the direction they had taken in from the road. He would have ended up hopelessly lost.

Kyel put his foot in the stirrup and pulled himself into the saddle. He was too tired to walk, so he let the animal carry him over the open grassland, pausing after a while to check his bearing against the field lines. Again, he felt that sharp, searing jolt, though not as painful this time. So he refocused his mind and cringed in the saddle as he tried yet again.

This time it worked, and he knew now what he'd done differently. Instead of just casting his will out across the flow of the field, he had felt along it, going with the current instead of cutting across.

He almost laughed. It was so easy. He couldn't believe what

he'd been putting himself through just to figure out this trick. He kicked his horse to a lope across the grass, not even bothering to draw back on the reins the next time he reached out and stroked the power of the vortex.

He rode for perhaps an hour, following the lines of magic as they bent gradually further toward the south. By the time the figures of two horses appeared on the horizon in front of him, Kyel had become adept enough at gauging the field that he no longer had to continue groping out to reach it. Instead, he just left his mind open to it, keeping it in a state of constant awareness.

When he reached them, Kyel saw that both Darien and the priestess were sound asleep, their horses grazing a short distance away. Kyel dismounted, making no effort to be quiet as he slung his pack down on the ground beside the sleeping figures and turned his horse loose to graze.

Darien didn't stir, even while Kyel rummaged through his pack and rolled out his bed. It made him so angry. While he'd been back there, all alone and sobbing in pain, Darien had been making himself a cozy little camp and falling blissfully asleep.

Kyel had almost come to think of the mage as a friend. How utterly foolish he had been.

When he woke, Kyel found the sun had risen well above the mountains. The camp was pretty much broken down around him. Darien was just fixing the last bag to his saddle.

Naia smiled a warm greeting Kyel's way as she broke off a bite of biscuit. He pushed himself up into a sitting position, rubbing the sleep out of his eyes.

His back was sore, his joints stiff, and he was still very tired. He'd had little sleep the previous night and none at all the night before. He felt as if he could have just gone on sleeping throughout the entire day.

Darien turned and, noticing him awake, started toward him. Kyel looked down, not trusting himself to keep the anger he felt from infecting his eyes. Darien stopped and knelt beside him in the grass.

"I'm not going to apologize for what I did," he said. "And I don't expect your forgiveness. You made it here. That's all that matters."

Kyel felt his stomach sink like a lead weight. The man had no remorse, harbored no feelings of guilt or shame. More and more, Darien was starting to remind him of Garret Proctor.

He seemed to be waiting for Kyel to say something. When he didn't, the mage stood and dusted off his clothes. As he started walking away, Kyel heard him mutter, "It took me half a year to learn what you did in two hours last night."

Kyel had a stinging retort ready on his lips but decided to leave it alone. Darien's mentor probably hadn't dumped him down in the middle of a vortex and left him all alone with a galling message to follow the field lines.

Chapter Eighteen
The Catacombs

The Cerulean Plains, The Rhen

They rode with their backs to the sunrise as the day grew warm around them. In the distance, a small structure rose from the sea of prairie. It looked so forlorn, only a square patch of brightness in a vast expanse of unrelieved green. Darien knew it must be the shrine. He'd seen others like it before, scattered in various places throughout the land. This one looked even smaller than most.

There were no paths leading to or from the shrine. The sea of grass just stopped at the threshold. Inside, marble tiles took over where the prairie ended.

They dismounted in front of the doorway and, to Darien's surprise, the priestess led her horse inside. Its hooves made a sharp clatter on the tiles, slipping a bit as they fought for purchase.

Darien had never much cared for the temples of Death, although this was the first time he'd actually been under the roof of a satellite shrine of the goddess. His mother had often compelled him to go with her to Aerysius' temple to offer prayers for the soul of his father. Those trips had always disturbed him, and he'd always left with the feeling that the Atrament must be a cold and dismal place.

The shrine was just like a temple, but on a much smaller scale, complete with all the typical trappings. Stationed at the far corners of the room, long tapers held by tall candlesticks burned with lively flames. Darien wondered who tended the shrine. Someone had to keep the tapers lit and sweep out the floor occasionally. But there was no one within, and certainly no space where anyone could possibly be living.

He led his horse into the shrine, bringing it up alongside the priestess' mare. The black gelding tossed its head as its hooves encountered the unfamiliar surface. The space inside was barely large enough to contain the three horses. The priestess walked forward to a ledge that supported three votive candles. She gazed down reverently at the tiny flames, then closed her eyes as if offering a prayer.

Darien felt drawn toward the candles himself. Each of those fragile lights represented a prayer for a departed soul. It had been a long time since he had offered such a prayer.

Compelled by a whim, he moved to stand beside Naia and picked up one of the candles from the ledge. The priestess' eyes followed the motion of his hand, but she said nothing as Darien held the small votive candle before him, contemplating it in silence.

He found a striker on the ledge. The flint was old, and it took him a few tries to create a spark. The wick of the candle flared up immediately, producing a strong, healthy glow as he set the candle down on the ledge with the others.

But then something happened that was entirely unexpected. The glowing yellow flame darkened as if a shadow had passed over it. The light dimmed, becoming pale. Then the candle's flame flared up brilliantly, as if seized by a sudden draft of wind, before turning a filthy shade of green.

Darien couldn't take his eyes from it, filled with horrified recognition. It was the same color as the pillar of energy he had seen in the sky above Aerysius. The putrid, ethereal glow of the Netherworld.

Naia hissed like a feral cat. Her hand swiped out, knocking the candle off the shelf and casting it to the floor, where she stomped on it with her feet until it was reduced to nothing more than a crumbled pile of tallow.

The violence of her reaction appalled Darien almost as much as the sight of that terrible green flame. With one last kick of her slipper, Naia sent the whole pile scattering across the dark tiles of the floor.

Then she rounded on him, shrieking, *"How dare you* desecrate the altar of the goddess with that abomination! Whose spirit was that candle meant for? *How do you even know a soul so vile?"*

Darien took a step back away from her, struggling to control the sorrow that threatened to overwhelm him. But the priestess was relentless. She advanced on him, eyes flaring in anger and revulsion.

"Tell me who that candle was for!"

Darien twisted away from her. He hung his head, scrubbing his hands through his hair as he fought for the strength he needed to give voice to what had once been his most terrible fear, now twice confirmed.

He whispered, "Her name was Meiran Withersby."

"Who *is* that?" Naia demanded, her eyes narrowing in confusion. "It takes hideous acts to condemn a soul to the Netherworld!"

Darien couldn't bear to meet the priestess' eyes. Staring at the floor, he admitted, "She was the woman I loved. My brother killed her with my sword, then committed her soul to Xerys to unseal the Well of Tears."

Naia's mouth fell open, the anger draining away from her face to be replaced by a look of horrified disbelief. She shook her head, sagging visibly.

"Gods' mercy, Darien."

A terrible anger suffused him at her choice of words, eclipsing even the pain of his grief.

"The gods have no mercy." He spun away from her, footsteps echoing loudly as he crossed the floor of the shrine to the doorway.

There he stopped, staring out into the cool autumn sunlight, choking back the threat of tears. It was a truly beautiful day. He tried to take comfort in it but found he could not. There was only one thing he could think of that would ever bring him peace.

Darien closed his eyes, envisioning what it would feel like to drive his blade hilt-deep into his brother's chest.

He lingered there in the entrance, leaning against a marble

column that supported the roof. Behind him, he could hear the priestess and Kyel conferring in voices too soft for him to make out the words. But he didn't need to hear to know what they must be saying.

At last, the murmured conversation ended. The sound of footsteps moved toward him across the tile. Darien turned as Kyel came to stand beside him. His young acolyte had been silently seething at him all morning, but now there was only a look of troubled kindness in his eyes.

"Naia says we need to go." Kyel reached up to place a tentative hand on his arm. "Are you all right?"

Darien nodded, swallowing. He closed his thoughts to his grief, walling it away in the back of his mind and sealing it there with the mortar of his will. He was surprised, actually, by Kyel's concern. After what he had put the young man through, Darien wouldn't have blamed him for holding fast to his resentment.

"Thank you," he whispered.

He turned and walked back into the shrine, away from the warm glow of morning. Inside, he found Naia occupied with lighting the tapers of a candelabra set into a niche in the wall. Darien looked on as the priestess moved to touch the wick of each taper with the glowing end of a slender wooden splint, working in no apparent order, until the last candle was lit. Then she reached out and extinguished the splint between her thumb and index finger.

Darien frowned, wondering what the purpose of the candle-lighting had been, watching as the woman moved back into the center of the room and took up the reins of her mare. She glanced toward him, a frown of concern on her face.

"The horses may not like this part," she warned.

Darien took her point. Moving to the head of his own horse, he grasped its bridle under the gelding's chin, staring down at the crumbled tallow that was all that remained of Meiran's candle.

It was such a simple thing, a votive candle. Simple, and yet amazingly profound. That was all he'd wanted: just one heartfelt prayer. Yet, even that was denied him. The remains of his good intentions were strewn across the floor under his feet like so much scattered dust.

He tried to avert his eyes from the sight, but it was impossible. His gaze kept slipping back to the remnants of the candle despite every effort of his will.

As he stared down at the crumbled tallow on the floor, he realized that it was vibrating, shimmying as the floor itself trembled beneath his feet.

Startled, Darien glanced up at the priestess. Her smile of reassurance calmed him, but he didn't like the way the floor seemed suddenly unstable. A terrible screeching groan, like the rake of metal against rusted metal, shrieked through the chamber.

Then the floor was moving, jolting downward.

His horse screamed, trying to rear, as Darien clung to its bridle and almost lost his footing. His stomach took a plunge as the floor lurched sharply out from under him and then settled, lowering almost smoothly. He glanced up, amazed, as the walls of the chamber seemed to stretch above them.

"If you wanted to scare me, it's working," Kyel said, staring upward with frightened eyes. All around them, the walls of the room seemed to be lengthening, the ledge where the candles yet glowed rising ever higher above their heads.

"Kyel, sense the field for me here," Darien said, feeling wretchedly ill at ease. The currents of the vortex were lethal to him, but he was only asking his acolyte to practice the same technique he'd learned the night before. He watched Kyel's face, pleased to see that the young man showed no sign of effort or fear of pain.

"It's not so intense," Kyel reported after a moment.

Darien took comfort in that. It meant he could soon take a sample of the field himself. Not just yet; he wasn't a fool. But he had been strangled for two days by the barrier he'd been forced to erect in his mind against the vortex. He was grateful to know that at least that strain was almost done with.

But the darkening of the chamber quickly quenched any relief he might have felt. The floor jolted again, coming to a rest as the light suddenly seemed to leech away as if sucked into the shadows of the walls. A crack appeared along the floor in front of them, yawning wider until it was an opening that shed a soft amber glow into the darkness.

Naia led her mare through the doorway, then waited for them to join her.

Darien led his own horse forward over the tiles. He found himself in a dim, cavernous hall. The source of the light came from huge urn-shaped braziers spaced at intervals along the walls. The ceiling was high, supported by massive stone columns that marched down the entire length of the room. The walls were carved in bas-relief, depicting various images from the Book of the Dead.

"What is this place?" Kyel wondered, openly gawking as he brought his horse forward into the space between columns.

"It is called the Inner Sanctum." Naia's voice echoed through the room. "Our temple has many holy mysteries, and halls such as this are one. Knowledge of its purpose is reserved only for initiates of Death's priesthood. Of course, should you wish to learn more, you could always join," she added with a smile.

"He's spoken for," Darien assured her.

Kyel winced, looking a bit pale, but nodded adamantly as his eyes continued to roam over the dark grandeur of the place.

They led their horses up the center aisle. The sounds of the animals' hooves echoed off the walls and ceiling, the noises magnified by the marble surfaces. As they approached the far end of the room, Darien noticed that there were two dark passages ahead, opening out of opposing walls. He could see nothing within, not even an inch beyond the openings. It was as if the dim light of the chamber just stopped at the thresholds, prevented from spreading further.

Naia stopped her horse and reached into her saddlebag, fishing out three silk scarves. She took one for herself, tossing the other two to Darien, who frowned down at them before handing one to Kyel.

The priestess took her scarf and began wrapping it around her mare's head, covering its eyes. Darien moved to his own mount and did the same, winding the fine material like a bandage around the Tarkendar's black face.

"These doorways mark the entrance to Death's Passage," Naia said as she watched him tying off the scarf.

When Kyel was done, she led them toward the black, gaping hole on the right. There, she drew up and turned toward them, a look of warning in her veiled eyes.

"Before we enter, know this: the Catacombs exist partly in the Atrament. There are many mysteries within, which you will doubtlessly find troubling. And there are dangers, as well. Especially now that Death's secret has been compromised. We must exercise great care yet proceed as quickly as we can. Fortunately, the way is not long.

"And I must warn you: the living are expressly forbidden to communicate with the dead. You *must* ignore any shade that tries to distract you. If you do not, then you will be guilty of breaking the Strictures of Death, and you will not be allowed to return again to the world of life."

She fixed her gaze on Darien. "I gravely fear what manner of shades you might draw to yourself."

Darien felt a spark of anger. "Meiran's not there, remember?"

But Naia shook her head, a regretful smile on her face. "I would love to meet your Meiran," she assured him softly, "but I was not referring to her. I was thinking, rather, of the troubling fact that nearly every person you've ever known has died. Remember the Stricture. No matter what you see, you mustn't interact with the dead in any way."

"I'll do my best."

Naia nodded and turned away toward the dark passage. She paused a moment, bowing her head in prayer, then stepped within. As she passed across the threshold, a shadow fell upon her. Her image flickered once and then was gone, lost completely in the darkness that moved to consume her horse as well.

"Are you sure you don't want to ride to Glen Farquist?" Kyel said as he stared at the dark passage ahead. He looked pale as he sucked in a deep breath and, holding it, stepped through the doorway.

Darien watched, fascinated, as his acolyte's image flickered before disappearing altogether, just as Naia's had. He was starting to get the sense that there was much more magic involved here than in just the trip down. Death's mysteries seemed to be fairly riddled with the workings of magecraft.

Which suggested a partnership that must have existed, at least at one time, between the priesthood of Isap and Aerysius itself. He could easily imagine such a trade-off. It would have been well worth the effort for the ancient Masters to assist in the construction of the Catacombs if, in exchange, they were allowed uninhibited access to them.

Shrugging off his thoughts, Darien whispered a soft word of comfort to his horse, then led the animal forward.

As he crossed the threshold of the doorway, it seemed as if the world wavered for an instant when the shadow fell over his eyes. He experienced a momentary surge of vertigo, as if the framework of reality had suddenly shifted. But then the shadow parted, and the motion of the world steadied. Blinking, he stepped out of the darkness into a dim stone corridor.

Death's Passage

The priestess and Kyel were there ahead, waiting for him. The corridor was more like a cave than a hallway, crudely hewn from granite rock. A soft light glowed along the walls and clung to the ceiling, a misty silver luminescence. Magelight, Darien realized, staring in open wonder. He had never seen its like outside of Aerysius itself.

"Welcome to the Catacombs," the priestess said in a lowered voice.

They walked forward, following the slope of the corridor, the horses picking their way carefully. The air was frigid, and there was a stale odor to the place. The churning magelight cast lurid shadows across the walls. A thick fog clung to the floor, stirred by their footsteps.

Darien didn't like the feel of the air. It seemed thin, almost stretched. Even sound seemed to carry differently through it. The plod of the horses' hooves sounded stifled and hesitant.

There was a peculiar reverberation to the noise, like a muffled echo.

After a few hundred paces, the passage took a sharp turn and then opened up into an immense chamber. Darien let his eyes wander up the far wall and found himself having to crane his neck to get a glimpse of the ceiling high above.

This was no mere cavern. The chamber they were in could have engulfed the Hall of the Watchers several times over.

And the walls were not solid.

Darien studied them, attempting to figure out the architecture that lent the walls a honeycombed appearance. Then it dawned on him: the holes in the rock were vaults.

Thousands of them, each vault containing white-shrouded human remains.

The entire chamber was an enormous tomb. It even smelled like one. His nose was accosted with the commingled stench of myrrh and decay. In front of him, he heard Kyel make a gagging noise.

The priestess seemed completely unaffected. This was, after all, her profession. Darien found himself darkly speculating how many corpses Naia had washed and blessed before she had become so immune to the stench of death.

He gazed at the priestess, wondering what had possessed the woman to choose such a grim occupation in the first place. She was young, and elegantly lovely. Naia would have had suitors lined up at her door if she were a common maid. But, he had to admit, there was nothing common about her.

Naia carried herself with an air of confidence that was compelling, and her dark eyes behind her veil shone with intelligence and wisdom far beyond her age. He had to force himself to avert his gaze. Despite himself, he found the priestess intriguing. More intriguing than he would have liked.

His eyes lingered on her back as Naia led them into the middle of the vast chamber. They walked through the cavern, past rows of sarcophagi carved with the likenesses of the dead they contained. Darien found himself confronted by the marble faces of men, women, and even children.

"Who are these people?" Kyel asked, flinching back from the outstretched hand of a statue.

"Nobility, for the most part," Naia said. "Whoever can afford to pay for such treatment. Such a burial does not come without a price."

Darien found himself staring harder at the macabre faces, wondering if he might find one he recognized. They were moving through what amounted to a maze of marble, winding around statues and sarcophagi, even mausoleums with family names etched into their stony exteriors. Magelight glowed from the walls, pushing back the shadows only a fraction. The air grew even colder, the stench of decay more robust. Darien shivered, seeing his own breath turn to mist before his face.

"Stop," the priestess commanded.

She was staring at him with a frown of puzzlement on her face. Darien didn't like the look in her eyes.

"What is it?"

"You have an aura," she said, forming the words slowly.

Darien glanced down at himself. A faint green nimbus surrounded him. The glow was so pale, it was difficult to see. But the aura was there undeniably.

"What does it mean?" He spread his arms out and studied the unsettling hue that crept up his sleeves and surrounded his hands. He didn't like the color. It reminded him of Meiran's candle. A whispered breath of apprehension shivered down his spine. He looked at the priestess in alarm.

"I have no idea what it means," Naia said, her face slack with concern. "But I gravely fear the implications."

Darien stared at her, waiting for the priestess to elaborate. But she merely turned away and led her horse forward. Darien started after her, looking down at himself in trepidation, then followed the woman through the strange city of the dead.

As he passed by a statue of a girl with disquieting stone eyes, he thought he could hear the sound of distant laughter, soft, like the echo of a memory. He turned to study the statue, noticing the eyes had taken on a mischievous glint. Perhaps the expression had always been there. But he couldn't suppress the nagging feeling that, somehow, the statue's face had changed.

He started forward and heard the sound again, this time from behind. He turned to see a softly glowing shade, the hazy reflection of a small girl with a playful gleam in her eyes. The wight disappeared almost instantly. He backed away, filled with a mixture of wonder and sadness.

He found Naia watching him, a soft smile on her lips. "Death does not discriminate. It takes the very old and the very young, alike."

Darien nodded, glancing back again at the weathered granite statue. Strangely, he found himself mourning a child he'd never met and would never have the chance to come to know. But he found himself powerfully moved by the chance encounter with her shade.

The priestess led them into a marble mausoleum. It turned out to be the entrance to a passage that opened out of the floor, sloping downward. It was paved with glistening black marble, and the horses had to struggle to keep their footing. The air grew slightly warmer again, though the magelight barely sufficed to light their way. Darien thought of casting a misty light of his own, but decided against it, not fully trusting the magic field in this place.

The corridor leveled out, curving slightly. The passage ended at a bridge that spanned a drop of hundreds of feet over a slowly-moving river of black water.

A chill breath of stale air stirred his cloak as Darien led his horse out onto the bridge. The walls of this chamber were vaults, just as the last had been. Only, this time, there seemed no end to their height, the ceiling lost somewhere deep in shadow. The dark waters below churned and bubbled, releasing a foul miasma like a festering swamp ripe with decay.

Stiffly, Darien asked, "How much longer?"

"The exit is not far."

They moved off the bridge and into a stone passage that cut between rows of sarcophagi. The scent of death was much stronger here, so much so that Darien had to hold his cloak up over his face.

From behind came a soft but nerve-grating noise, like the scraping of metal against stone. The noise slowly faded. But then it grew louder again, a shrill, raking sound, much closer this time.

"What is that?" Kyel demanded.

Darien spun around, eyes scanning the shadows of the passage behind them. He'd never heard anything like that in his life. Almost, it reminded him of the sound of dragging chains.

The noise faded and was gone.

Swallowing against a cold lump of dread, Darien decided it was time to try the magic field. He reached out with his mind and sampled the energy of the current, relieved to find it biddable. He opened his mind to the field, holding it at ready, just in case.

The noise was back. Louder. Right behind them.

Darien whirled, hand reaching for his sword. Slithering through the fog behind them swirled a glimmering mass of sparkling light. The glowing tendrils writhed toward them like a thousand squirming snakes.

Darien forced his mind back from the magic field, too late. The flickering threads angled toward him with sinister purpose.

"Naia!" he gasped, tugging on the reins of his horse.

The priestess glanced back, terror on her face. Then she was running, pulling her mare behind her as Kyel sprinted forward.

Darien's horse reared, breaking free and bolting away. With a curse, he started after it. Then he skidded to a stop, flinching back.

Out of a doorway appeared a creature that resembled a massive wolfhound, head lowered, eyes glowing green. It growled low in its throat, the crusted fur of its hackles rising. Darien backed away from the beast. His hand rose to his shoulder, baring his sword.

Behind him, one of the writhing tendrils of light groped toward him.

Darien threw himself sideways even as the demon-hound leaped for his throat. He spilled over the top of a sarcophagus, slipping to the ground on the other side. There, he lay on his back, panting, frantically looking for an escape.

The thanacryst appeared over the lid of the sarcophagus,

snarling down at him. From its jowls dribbled fetid globules of slobber.

Darien rolled to his feet. He stumbled backward as the beast sprang after him. Whirling, he made for the shadow of a doorway. He slid around the corner, pressing his body close against the wall, his breath coming in shallow gasps.

From the other side of the doorway came a low, menacing growl.

Darien raised his blade, drawing it back and holding it there with trembling hands. He held his ground and waited for the beast to come.

The thanacryst's muzzle edged around the corner. The nose quivered, scenting the air. Its glowing eyes trained on him.

Darien brought the blade down with all his strength. The steel connected, but he didn't pause to see the results of the strike.

Spinning, he threw himself through a doorway.

A loud *thud* echoed behind him. Shocked, Darien stared at the marble door that had slid shut, cutting him off from the passage behind. He groped frantically at the smooth door, gripped in numbing shackles of fear. He backed away from it, blade held in a double-fisted grip.

He glanced around. He was standing in a broad corridor with passageways leading off at intervals to either side. His eyes swept from one doorway to the next, scouring the shadows beyond.

Hesitant, he edged forward. As he passed the first dark opening, another door slid closed with a resounding *thud.*

Darien stopped, staring at the door in disbelief.

He crept forward again, only to find his way immediately blocked by another closing door, this one cutting him off from the main passage, as another door swept open on his left.

Darien stared at the new opening warily. He was beginning to get the sense he was being herded, steered purposefully by some unseen hand. He didn't want to go in the direction that hand was leading. But there was no alternative. Every other way had been sealed.

Lowering his blade, he moved through the opening into another lightless corridor. There was no magelight here to see by, and he was reluctant to make his own. Another door slid closed beside him, then he found himself confronted by a solid wall ahead.

Darien sheathed his sword, using his palms to grope his way along the walls. He could see nothing except for the soft green aura that surrounded his hands. The terrible absence of light sharpened his fear. Anything could be stalking silently behind him. Anything.

The walls steered him into another passage just as dark and terrible as the last. He felt his way along, hands exploring. Up ahead, a soft light beckoned him forward.

Taking heart in the glow, Darien moved toward it. Another door slid closed, the sound a jarring *thud* that shuddered through his every nerve.

He stopped, glancing around at a chamber suffused with amber light. The room was completely empty, just four high walls climbing upward to a vaulted ceiling. Suspended by a chain high above hung an enormous wrought-iron chandelier that shed a muted, wavering light. Only, the glow did not come from the light of tapers. It came from six golden orbs that hovered above the chandelier itself.

Darien stood gazing up at the orbs, hands spread out at his sides. His eyes moved to the walls, desperately seeking a way out.

The light wavered, then slowly dimmed. Above him, the orbs began to rotate, their pale light fading out smoothly into darkness. Shadows lengthened, closing in and drawing over him.

An icy sweat broke out on his forehead. He edged backward, pressing his back against the cold marble door. Hardly daring to breathe, he gazed out into the blackness ahead.

Then, from out of the darkness, a faint azure glow appeared.

It seemed to bleed right out of the shadows, moving silently toward him. Darien gasped as he realized he was gazing upon the pale glimmer of a wight. Another appeared, this time on his right. Then another.

Soon there were dozens of shades ringing the walls of the chamber. The gleam of the wights illuminated the hall, casting back the shadows with their ethereal blue glow. More appeared behind, pushing the others forward.

With a terrified sense of awe, Darien found himself surrounded by shades, each hazy form vaguely familiar. His eyes leaped from face to face, startled recognition flooding into him.

They advanced slowly, emerging from the walls to creep silently toward him through the darkness. Darien wanted to draw back away from them, but there was nothing he could do. There were too many. The marble door at his back was hard and unyielding.

Terror in his heart, he stood his ground and faced the dead of fallen Aerysius.

They were all here, every Master and Grand Master he'd ever known. Tyrius Flynn, Grand Master Ezras, Lynnea, Finneus, Master Harrison. So many others. Scores of them, a host of familiar faces, as well as strangers he'd never met. They moved toward him, crowding him, gazing at him with unreadable expressions.

The shade of a man reached out an arm toward him. Startled, Darien found himself cringing away from the gnarled fingers of Edric Torrence, the strange Bird Man who had saved his life.

As Darien looked on, a lone wraith parted itself off from the host, moving toward him, stopping within reaching distance. Darien shook his head, knowing this was the one thing in the world he couldn't take. He wanted to turn away, wanted to deny the image that confronted him. But it was impossible. He could do nothing but helplessly stare at the face in front of him with features so achingly familiar.

His father looked just as Darien remembered him, the last time he ever saw him alive.

"My son," Gerald Lauchlin whispered. "You've come home."

A ghostly hand reached toward him.

Darien couldn't help himself. Impelled by nearly two decades of sorrow and remorse, he moved toward the comfort of his father's embrace.

Kyel clutched his horse's reins in a white-knuckled grip, his other hand shaking as he fought to control the wildly flailing beast that reared up over his head. The Tarkendar lashed out with its forelegs as Kyel jumped away from the animal's hooves.

"Get control of it!" Naia shouted.

"I can't!"

The priestess strode forward, raising a hand before her face. She reached out toward the black gelding's head, taking the horse firmly by the bridle. The animal settled back to four legs, its withers quivering and glistening with a slick sheen of sweat.

Kyel glanced back the way they had come. The corridor was dark and empty. There was no sign of the slithering lights. And there was also no sign of Darien. Realizing the mage was gone, Kyel jerked his gaze back to the priestess.

"We have to go back," Naia gasped.

Kyel knew she was right. He'd just assumed Darien was following them.

"You don't think…" he started to say but was unable to complete the thought.

The priestess blinked as if waking from a trance, eyes flicking toward him wide with fear. "We must hurry! Without my guidance, the halls will assume he is a wandering shade and seek to take his spirit back into their keeping."

Kyel frowned, troubled by her words. He didn't want to go back, afraid of what they might find.

Darien reached toward the glowing form of his father. He felt just as he had as a boy of eight, when he'd run bounding down the path from the widow's home in Amberlie Grove to greet his father returning from the war. The tall Sentinel in his black cloak had swept him up in his arms, spinning him around twice before clasping him against his chest in a strong embrace.

The joy of his father's homecoming had been tempered only by the look of resentment on Aidan's face when he discovered his little brother had beaten him, winning the race to be the first scooped up in their father's arms.

But Aidan wasn't here now, and the proud smile on the

glimmering face before him was just as warm and genuine as Darien remembered it. He moved forward, filled with a numbing euphoria.

Another wight swept forward, reaching out to bar his way.

"Stop," commanded the shade of Grand Master Ezras, turning to glance back over his shoulder. "Gerald, don't touch him."

As Darien looked on in confusion, the smile drained from his father's face. The glimmering blue aura around him wavered. "He is my son. He has come home to us."

But the shade of Ezras was adamant. "No. He does not belong here. He is not destined for this place."

Ezras reached his ghostly hands out, clasping Darien's father by the shoulders and turning him gently but firmly away. Aghast, Darien watched as the glowing wraiths turned away from him as one, receding, departing back into the shadows of the walls from whence they came.

His father looked back to cast an imploring glance his way before he, too, faded and was gone. Complete darkness settled in, descending on the chamber like a moonless winter night. Darien took a step toward the center of the room, eyes groping desperately through the shadows.

"Father…"

He sank slowly to his knees, bowing his head in shame. There had been tears in his father's eyes. Never in life had he seen that proud man cry.

Kyel followed Naia down the passage, back toward the chamber of vaults. The strange flickering creature didn't seem to be there. But neither was Darien. Except for its macabre stone furnishings, the wide corridor was empty.

The priestess stopped in an alley between two rows of sarcophagi, gaping around as if lost. Kyel felt a moment of panic, clinging fiercely to the reins of the two horses.

"What do we do?"

"There is only one place to look," she said. "The walls would take him for a lost spirit and direct him to the Hall of the Masters.

Fortunately, the way is not far."

Kyel nodded. He followed the priestess back through the maze of stone monuments, winding her way through dark alleys toward a broad doorway. As he came around the corner, Kyel stopped as she knelt over a dark stain on the floor.

"What—?" he began, then noticed the trail of paw prints leading off down the corridor. The sight chilled him.

"Blood," Naia said softly, standing up.

"Darien?"

"No." The priestess shook her head. "Demon blood. A thanacryst, by the prints. We must hurry."

She led him onward, sliding open stone doors with a gesture of her hand. She led them into a passage far too narrow for the horses to walk side by side. Kyel had to tie the Tarkendar's reins to the saddle of his own mount, leading the horses single-file into the shadows ahead.

"This is it," Naia whispered. Her words echoed in the darkness.

The priestess' tone was tense with worry.

At last, another door slid open ahead of them. Kyel heard the sound of it, even if he couldn't see anything. There was the clop of hoofbeats as Naia's horse moved forward. He followed cautiously, a cold feeling of dread tingling his skin.

"Darien?" the priestess called.

The air was distinctly cooler here, and there was a slight draft. Kyel sensed they were entering some type of chamber.

Then he saw it: the soft glow of the aura that surrounded Darien's body.

The mage was sitting alone in the black emptiness, knees drawn up against his chest. Kyel gaped at the sight of him. He'd almost taken him for a shade. Darien's head was bowed, arms wrapped around his legs.

"Darien," Naia said again.

The Sentinel looked up, gazing at them with haunted eyes.

"We must go." Naia lowered herself at his side, placing a hand on his shoulder.

Darien nodded. He looked dazed. Naia took him by the arm,

helping him to his feet and guiding him back toward the door. But as he approached the opening, Darien stopped and turned back.

"He said I don't belong here," he whispered. "He said I'm destined for another place. What did he mean?"

"You spoke with a shade?" the priestess gasped.

"No. He spoke to me. What did he mean?"

"I don't know," Naia whispered.

Kyel thought perhaps she did know. Darien seemed to accept her words, moving forward to claim his horse. He still looked shaken, more so than Kyel had ever seen him.

Naia led them back through the labyrinth of passages, stopping at a large, dark opening in the wall. There, she paused, her eyes once again fearful as she turned to look back over her shoulder.

"This is the exit to Glen Farquist." Her words carried a heavy undercurrent of fear. To Darien, she said, "This is where we find out if what you did broke the Strictures of Death. If everything is fine, you will arrive at a shrine in the High Temple."

"And if it's not?"

"Then you will find out what that shade you met was trying to tell you."

Darien nodded. Moving past her, he led his horse forward. He didn't hesitate as he stepped into the opening. His image flickered once then was gone, consumed by the shadows on the other side.

Chapter Nineteen
The Temple of Death

Glen Farquist, The Rhen

Kyel stepped out of Death's Passage into a sudden gush of brilliant light. He gazed around, trying to get his bearings. They were in a shrine made entirely of brown marble. Light streamed down in thick rays from the ceiling, washing over them.

Ahead, Darien turned to look at him. His mouth was slack, his eyes dark and weary. He looked dazed, but mercifully alive. Kyel led his horse forward to stand beside him. He found his gaze drawn past his master to the life-size statue of a woman situated in an alcove.

The marble face was serene, yet remarkably powerful. One of her long, elegant arms was swept back behind her, the other extended forward, palm upward with fingers slightly curled. It was as if she expected him to press an object into her waiting hand. The face seemed to be considering him with a pensive expression. He had the feeling he was being scrutinized by those daunting marble eyes.

Behind him, he heard a voice and turned. A young man had joined them in the chamber and was speaking quietly to Naia off to one side. The man was dressed in white robes with a white stole draped over his shoulders. He turned and regarded the entrance to Death's Passage uneasily, then took the reins of Naia's mare. He led the horse forward, walking toward Kyel.

"May I take your reins?" the young priest asked as he reached out and removed the scarf from the gelding's head. Kyel watched as the man tied all three horses together in line and then led them away.

When he was gone, Naia approached Darien. The mage still lingered at the base of the statue, gazing at the compelling marble figure. The priestess placed a hand on his shoulder.

"Who is she?" Darien asked, not taking his eyes from the statue.

"The Goddess of the Eternal Requiem."

At her response, Darien's study of the marble woman became much more intense. The priestess' mouth drew into the slightest frown. Kyel sensed something more had just passed between the two of them, something to do with the statue. The priestess did not seem to care for Darien's interest in it one bit.

"I'll show you to the guest rooms," she said, striding away a few paces before stopping to wait for them.

Darien shook his head wearily. "We've come all this way. I wish to see my mother now."

Naia's frown became a look of concern. "Perhaps it should wait until after you've had a chance to rest."

"I'm fine," Darien insisted. "I'd just like to see her, please."

The priestess nodded.

"I'll wait here," Kyel said, uncomfortable with the idea of viewing a dead woman he'd never met. Especially since this particular woman had been dead for some time now.

"I think you need to come too, Kyel," Naia said, glancing at Darien for confirmation. The mage nodded slightly.

Kyel didn't understand why. If it had been his own mother, he would have wanted to spend his last moments with her in private. But he did as they asked and followed the priestess through a doorway.

They climbed a flight of stairs to a wide corridor with windows on one side that looked out upon a large garden courtyard. Kyel was impressed. This particular temple was different from anything he had ever seen. He'd almost forgotten where he was, at Glen Farquist in the Valley of the Gods, where the largest and most magnificent temples existed, and where all the governing bodies of the various religious sects dwelt. This was the High Temple of Isap, a palace in its own right.

And it was spectacular. Looking across the courtyard, Kyel saw the main sanctuary, a majestic domed structure. Row upon row of stained glass windows graced its sides. Its tall dome was clad in bronze that had weathered to verdigris over time.

Kyel fixed his eyes on the sway of Darien's cloak. The mage was walking with his head lowered, shoulders slumped in weariness. Naia muttered something in his ear, earning herself a sharp glare of reproach. Kyel had never seen him look so haggard, as if all the recent events were just now catching up with him.

Naia bristled at his glare, dark eyes flashing even through her veil. Kyel wondered what she'd said. Darien's stride had shifted until he was almost stalking, fists clenched in anger. He didn't look at the woman again, keeping his gaze trained on the floor.

Under his breath, Kyel heard him mutter, "It's my right."

"I cannot bar you from the shrine, Darien," Naia said. "But I must urge you to reconsider and think very carefully about what I told you the night we met."

"And do what?" Darien asked. "Stand down and allow Aidan to admit a second Enemy host through the Vale?"

"There are other ways."

"No. Even if I could convince Faukravar to hand over his entire northern army, it would hardly be enough. This war will be won or lost by magic, not military strength."

"So instead, you intend to set yourself against your brother *and* the Enemy, alone?" Naia flung her arms out in exasperation. "I'm sorry, Darien, but as strong as you might be, you are only one man."

"Orien was just one man," the mage reminded her. "Yet he was able to turn back the entire Third Invasion by himself."

"Orien was a martyr."

"He was an *effective* martyr."

"The people of this land don't need another Orien," Naia snapped. "What they need is you, alive."

Darien stopped, turning to regard the priestess wearily. "I don't see any other way. And I don't believe you do, either. I appreciate your intentions, Naia. I truly do. But don't make this harder on me than it already is."

The priestess closed her eyes, drawing a deep, steadying breath. After a moment, she looked back up at him. "Very well. I'll leave it in the hands of the goddess. I just pray she finds your purpose unjustified."

"Unjustified?" echoed Darien, face flushed in anger. "Can you honestly think of one person in the last thousand years who's had better reason to kneel at that statue's feet than myself?"

"No, I honestly can't," the priestess replied. "That is exactly why your decision worries me so much."

The Sentinel looked as though he wanted to say something more. His hand rose from his side toward her. But then he let his arm drop and turned away, striding down the corridor as Naia stared after him with a stricken look on her face.

Kyel waited until the priestess moved to follow him before he fell in behind, confused by what he'd just witnessed. He had no idea what their words had meant, but the content didn't seem to matter all that much. More important had been the look in Darien's eyes right before he'd turned away.

The corridor ended at a door that opened into a transept of the main sanctuary. Naia swept open the door, admitting them into the hall. Kyel followed behind Darien, noting the way the mage so carefully avoided Naia's eyes as he brushed past her.

"This way," she said in a lowered voice, leading them across the white tiles of the transept.

Kyel found himself surprised by the simplicity of the sanctuary that seemed almost at odds with the temple's ornate exterior. The walls were faced with limestone blocks that glowed in the colored light that spilled through the stained-glass windows. The sanctuary was simply an enormous space decorated with nothing other than a wondrous kaleidoscope of dazzling light. The effect was stirring, like moving through a soothing, dream-like haze.

Naia led them to the center of the room, where the transept merged with the main hall. There, on a raised dais surrounded by layers of white roses, Emelda Lauchlin lay in repose.

Kyel stopped, feeling a sudden pang of trepidation. The Prime Warden lay in a shimmering blanket of light that filtered down from above. Her pale skin seemed to glow, suffused with a radiance that created an almost natural flush of life. She was covered by a transparent shroud set with thousands of tiny, shimmering crystals that scattered the light into glittering rainbows of color.

Kyel took a few steps closer as he gazed at the woman's body in wonder. The Prime Warden looked remarkably alive, even hale, as if in the embrace of a deep and gentle sleep.

And she was beautiful. Her hair was dark and rich, spilling down around her face in soft, gleaming strands. She looked no older than Darien, her face untroubled by the years. She looked so much like her son, it would have been impossible to mistake the relationship.

Darien moved forward into the wash of brilliant light and knelt at his mother's side.

Kyel resisted the urge to turn away, feeling his presence there an invasion on the fragile privacy of the moment.

But Darien wanted him there. So Kyel forced himself to watch as the mage leaned forward and pressed a tender kiss against his mother's forehead. Then he turned to Naia and asked softly, "How did she die?"

The priestess moved to stand beside Darien, placing a hand on his shoulder.

"A demon followed us into the Catacombs. Your mother was injured, and she died here a week later." Naia paused, allowing her gaze to slip down to the body of the Prime Warden. "I'm so sorry, Darien."

The mage nodded, looking thoughtful. He whispered, "Arden Hannah."

Naia's glance darted back to his face at the mention of that evil name. But she made no effort to either confirm or deny it. Instead, she squeezed his hand and rose gracefully from his side, leaving him there alone. She walked over to Kyel and took him by the arm, guiding him back toward a wall of the transept.

Kyel whispered, "She's been dead all this time? How…?"

Naia smiled sadly as she released his arm, stopping to lean with her back against the limestone wall. "The methods of preservation are another of our temple secrets. For funerals of state, it is customary that the deceased be available for public viewing anywhere from one to six months. The truth is, a body so preserved is protected for many, many years."

Kyel shook his head in wonder, marveling, "She seems alive."

"Thank you."

Kyel frowned. He started to say something, but the sound of another voice startled him. He turned to discover that a white-robed figure had drawn up silently beside him.

"The First Daughter's talents are sought after throughout the land," an old man wearing the stole of a priest of Death assured him. "In some circles, her work is considered an art form."

Kyel gaped at Naia, amazed. So the body of Darien's mother had been her work, every meticulous detail arranged by her own hands before she had departed on her journey to find Darien. Naia smiled with a trace of self-conscious pride at his reaction. Turning to the priest, she said:

"Your Eminence, may I present to you the acolyte, Kyel Archer. Kyel, this is His Eminence, the High Priest of Death, Luther Penthos."

Kyel gawked openly at the bald man who was smiling at him genially. Minus the white robes and the stole, Luther Penthos would look like someone's aged grandfather. His blue eyes were crystal-clear as he reached out a hand and clasped Kyel's arm in a warm gesture of greeting.

"It is a pleasure to meet you."

"Your Eminence," Kyel said. The man's grip on his forearm was strong. When he released it, Kyel had to resist the urge to rub his skin.

A motion behind the priest caught his eye, and he glanced up to find Darien walking over to join them. The mage looked even more haggard than before.

"Your Eminence, I would also like to present the new Prime Warden, Darien Lauchlin, Grand Master of the Fifth Tier."

"Eighth Tier," Kyel corrected her absently.

Naia visibly blanched as she turned to stare at Darien in shock. The high priest blinked, but his smile returned as he reached out and clasped Darien's arm.

The old man shook his head in wonder. "Eighth tier. I'm not certain if I've ever heard of such a ranking."

"It's not meant to exist," Darien confirmed darkly. "I fear I'd be considered something of an abomination."

"You don't look like an abomination to me. Although, I must say, you do look like a man who could use some rest."

"We all could," the Sentinel agreed.

"I should let you retire to the guest wing, then. But before I forget, I have something that is yours by rights."

The old man fished in a pocket of his robe, drawing out a wide, silver collar. It was attached to a medallion set with what looked like an enormous red jewel. The stone glowed a brilliant shade of crimson, the light coming from deep within its facets. It seemed to have a life of its own, pulsing like a heartbeat. The high priest pressed the medallion into Darien's hand, squeezing the mage's fingers closed around it.

"What's this?" Darien stared down at the gem's radiance, which moved over his palm like webs of light reflected off a pool of water.

Luther Penthos took a step back as if trying to distance himself from the object. "The medallion is called the Soulstone. It is a storage vessel that contains your mother's gift. For someone to accept the Transference, they must simply put it on. I must, however, caution you against its other aspects."

Darien fingered the medallion in his hand, studying it intensely. He traced his thumb over the gleaming band of the collar, then glanced up with an expression of concern.

"How is it that an object such as this came to be in the possession of the Temple of Death? Forgive me, Your Eminence, but Aerysius has always laid claim to such heirlooms of power."

Luther Penthos nodded sagely, crossing his arms over the white fabric of his stole. "A thousand years ago, this medallion was the property of the Lyceum of Bryn Calazar. It was placed into our keeping before the fall of Caladorn, with the one restriction that knowledge of its existence should never be allowed to pass to the mages of Aerysius.

"However, since Aerysius is no more, I have decided to place the Soulstone into your hands. I have never felt comfortable holding such a thing, even in my deepest vaults."

He went on, "You've spoken lightly of abomination today, Prime Warden, but that object you are holding is a true abomination, if ever there was one. I am more than glad to have it out of my possession than you could possibly know."

"Why is that?"

"Because it was with this very medallion that Zavier Renquist struck the first killing blow that precipitated the overthrow of the Lyceum. The Soulstone is far more than just a storage device, you see. When it is full with a mage's gift, the stone glows with an inner light, just as you see it now. But when it is empty, the stone is black and lifeless.

"If it is placed in that condition around the neck of a living mage, the gem has the effect of ripping the ability from that person. Such a death would be particularly cruel. So have great care with that medallion, Prime Warden. Should it fall into the wrong hands, it might be sorely used against you."

Darien stared down at the medallion in his hand. A play of emotions ranged over his face, as if a truly inspirational notion had just occurred to him. He raised the Soulstone to clutch it tightly against his chest. A wistful smile appeared on his lips, growing until it spread to touch his eyes.

"Thank you, Your Eminence," he breathed. There was no mistaking the ominous excitement in his voice.

The high priest didn't seem to miss it, either. The old man's face hardened into a frown, and he stabbed an anxious glance sideways at the priestess. Naia regarded Darien with a look of startled indignation. Kyel felt his own stomach wrench. He found it easy to follow the mage's train of thought. Darien wanted to use that medallion on his brother, and the desire for it was strong enough to make his eyes shimmer with the thrill of anticipation. The look on his face was frightening.

In a carefully controlled voice, Luther Penthos said, "You have my condolences on the passing of your mother. I knew Emelda

Lauchlin well, just as I also knew your esteemed father. And I can assure you, Prime Warden, that neither one of your parents would condone what is so obviously passing through your mind."

Darien blinked, torn away from his dark thoughts by the old man's blunt words. He shot the high priest a look of resentment, tightening his grip on the medallion until the hand that contained it was trembling.

"Before you presume to judge me, why don't you go stare for a while at the shades of my brethren in your Catacombs. While you're at it, go look upon the ruins of Aerysius and the unholy light of hell that corrupts the skies above it. Then, if you still can, come back and tell me the man responsible for those atrocities doesn't deserve to die a traitor's death in pain."

"He is your brother," Naia protested before the high priest could wave her into silence.

"The gods abhor fratricide, regardless of intent or reason," Luther Penthos said. "Such an act would condemn your soul to the Netherworld for all eternity."

Darien shrugged indifferently as he stuffed the medallion into a pocket of his cloak. "Then at least I'll be at peace."

Kyel heard Naia make a strangled sound as Darien strode away. Turning to the high priest, she explained rapidly, "He wants to offer himself before the Goddess of the Eternal Requiem. I tried to convince him otherwise, but he's obsessed with the notion."

Luther Penthos stared at Darien's back until the mage disappeared through the doorway.

"If you cannot dissuade him, then I'll try. But there is nothing we can do to stop him. It is forbidden to deny the petition of a supplicant."

Kyel moved forward, inserting himself between them as he turned to Naia.

"What are you saying? What exactly is he trying to do?"

The priestess looked up at him. "Darien intends to disavow his Oath of Harmony and commit himself instead to the Goddess of Death in an ancient rite called a Bloodquest."

Chapter Twenty
Goddess of the Eternal Requiem

Glen Farquist, The Rhen

The corridor was dark and silent, the echo of his boots the only sound, the azure glow at his feet the only source of light. There was no one in the halls but himself, no one to question him about where he was going and why. He had already made his decision. Now, all he wanted to do was get it over with.

Darien descended the stairs and pushed open the door of the shrine, letting the magelight spill ahead of him into the room. He fed the light with a trickle of power and looked on as it spread out toward the four corners of the room, illuminating the shrine in an otherworldly glow.

Darien turned his gaze to the nearest torch and watched it sputter into flame. He looked around the room. Fire erupted along the walls, each individual torch blazing to life in quick succession. Then he let go of the magelight, allowing it to recede into the shadows of the floor.

Pacing forward, Darien looked up into the marble face of the goddess. A shiver of apprehension stole down his back, inspired by the statue's serene but critical eyes. He stopped, his chest at a level with the goddess' outstretched hand.

Darien stared at the bent fingers as he contemplated the curious significance of the gesture. Then he dropped to his knees, bowing forward and pressing his hands against the cold stone of the floor. He closed his eyes, emptying his mind of all thoughts save one.

Sitting back, he raised his hand over his shoulder, his fingers closing around the hilt of his sword. He drew the blade slowly forth, wielding it before his face as he grasped the hilt in both hands. He lowered the weapon carefully, taking it by the flat of the blade.

"Goddess have mercy on me," Darien whispered as he stood. He offered the sword into the statue's outstretched hand. The hilt fit easily within the marble cradle of her palm, fixing itself perfectly in the clasp of her bent fingers. He stepped back, releasing his grip and staring in wonder at the sight of the goddess wielding his own sword, the point leveled at his racing heart.

A thin line of sweat streaked down his brow as he knelt on the floor, abasing himself before the statue. His breath came in gasps, heart pounding in his ears. Unbidden thoughts flooded his mind like a drowning river, churning images and twisted feelings of violence and tragedy, betrayal and grief.

Before the discerning eyes of the statue, Darien bared his innermost soul, ashamed by the bleakness of it.

He knelt there on the chill floor of the shrine, staring up into the face of the goddess as slow degrees of exhaustion stole over him. Sometime in the darkest hours of night, the torches winked out one by one.

When the last flame finally guttered and died, Darien did nothing to restore the loss of light. Instead, he lay back across the hard tiles. When sleep finally took him, his dreams were plagued by the shades that haunted the desolate vaults of the Catacombs, calling out to him across time and eternity. It was impossible to tell whether those pleas were cries for vengeance or urgent appeals to abandon his perilous course.

Drenched in a cold sweat, Darien writhed in his sleep on the stone floor of the shrine, completely oblivious to the changes taking place above him in the darkness.

He awoke to bright, saturating light. Squinting, Darien pushed himself up off the floor, for a moment disoriented as he sat there blinking, trying to make sense of his surroundings. Dim memories of the night crept slowly back to him, and with them came a shiver of foreboding. He looked up at the statue, his eyes tracing the silken flow of the goddess' robes upward to her face. As he gazed up into her stone visage, a silver glint above her caught his eye.

It was his sword, held aloft by a slender arm that was now extended over the statue's head. The blade was poised in the air at a threatening angle. Darien froze, feeling a heart-numbing sense of dread. He brought a hand up to rub his eyes, an effort to deny what he saw. But when he looked back up, the blade was still there, wielded firmly in the goddess' stone grasp.

Darien pushed himself the rest of the way off the floor, rising stiffly to his feet. As he did, a soft rustling sound behind him made him turn. Startled, he saw Naia sitting behind him on a step. He wanted to turn away from her, anxious to avoid her grief-stricken face. But for some reason, he found he couldn't take his eyes off her.

Sitting there in her white gown, hunched over with her arms wrapped around herself, the priestess looked nothing more than a frail child, scared and alone. The look in her eyes was imploring. Part of him wanted to go to her and catch her up in his arms, to offer her what comfort he could.

But she was a priestess of Death, the white veil that stood between them an outward symbol of her vow of chastity.

And then there was Meiran, not yet even two months dead.

Darien bowed his head, ripping his gaze away from her and turning back to the statue of the goddess with fresh resolve. He took a step toward it.

"Don't."

The urgency in her voice stopped him, but he couldn't bring himself to look at her. Instead, he stood in the middle of the room as if frozen. He could feel her eyes on his back. Darien stared at the statue, praying for the goddess to give him the strength he needed to finish what he had started.

"Please don't do this."

Her words made it seem possible that he had a choice. It would be so easy just to turn and leave the shrine, to abandon his sword and simply walk away. The temptation was sweet. With one decisive act, he could preserve his integrity, his dignity, even the tattered remnants of his humanity.

But at what price? And who could he ask to pay it?

"I must," Darien said. He didn't know if the response was intended more for her, or rather for himself. There was scant conviction in his tone.

He heard the stir of her gown against the tile, the whisper of her slippered feet as they crossed the floor toward him. Her hand touched his cheek, directing his face toward hers with gentle pressure. He stared through her veil into her deep brown eyes, desiring nothing more than to drown himself in them and forget everything else in the world.

"No one's making you do this," she insisted. "No one has the right to expect this of you."

It took every shred of courage he had to turn away. "I don't have a choice."

"Have you even paused to consider the repercussions that might arise from this? Or the ethical considerations?"

"Of course I have." Darien backed away from her toward the statue. "This is war, Naia. I'll leave the question of ethics to the clerics of Om. Let them stew over it for the next hundred years. I don't have the time."

But she was relentless, moving forward until she had him cornered against the statue's base. "And what of you, Darien? Are you prepared to accept the personal costs?"

"What do you mean?" He frowned at her.

"Simply put, you don't seem like the sort of man capable of genocide. Yet, if you use your strength to turn back these armies, you will have the blood of thousands on your hands. And not all those deaths will be Enemy casualties, unless you intend to strike down each soldier individually, one by one. Are you certain you could live with that guilt?"

He bowed his head, knowing she was right. But he also knew it made no difference. This was the plate the gods had served him. Without meeting her eyes, he said, "I'm not certain of anything, at the moment. In truth, I've done my best to avoid thinking about the sort of questions you're asking."

"Then perhaps that means something, Darien. Perhaps you should give yourself more time to come to terms with this decision before rushing into a commitment that could destroy you."

"No." What she was asking was impossible. If he paused even a day, there was a chance he would lose his resolve. "I don't have time. If Arden Hannah's right, then both armies are already on the move. Everything else she told me has so far proven true. As we speak, men under Proctor's command are likely engaging the Enemy. Greystone Keep might have already fallen. I have but a fortnight to travel all the way to Orien's Finger, or Rothscard will be next. And then Auberdale.

"Don't you understand? I don't have the *right* to stand here debating ethics with you while the North falls around me. Once I thought I had that luxury, but I don't anymore. There are no simple answers to your questions. I could still be standing here struggling with them as the South falls, as well."

As he spoke, a change crept over Naia's face. The feverish intensity dissolved, replaced by an expression of uncertainty. And there was something else there as well, reflected back at him from the depths of her eyes. He wanted to deny it, but there was no mistaking the tender compassion in her gaze.

"Then I'm coming with you."

"What? Naia, you're a priestess. Your place is here, not on a field of battle. I don't understand what purpose you think you could even serve."

She shrugged as a sad smile formed on her lips. "Someone is going to need to keep you human."

Darien just stared at her. What did she think, that he was going to turn himself into the next Zavier Renquist? His mind reeled, suddenly plagued by doubt. That was exactly what he had been afraid of, all the times he'd argued so passionately about his Oath. But that had been before Royce's betrayal, before the fire. Before Arden Hannah had touched him, caressing his face the same way Naia just had. But Arden's touch had been poison, a slow-acting venom that was rotting his soul.

Naia said, "Take me with you. That is my one condition for

helping you, if you insist on going through with this."

Darien sighed, shaking his head. "You'll do nothing but slow me down."

"And Kyel won't? I'm a far better rider than your acolyte."

"Kyel is not coming with me."

"You're turning him loose?" she gasped. "By the gods, Darien, the boy's not nearly ready!"

"I need him to do a few tasks for me. And he'll be much safer in Rothscard."

At that, Naia choked out an incredulous laugh. "You're sending that boy to the *Queen of Emmery?* Oh, I pity poor Kyel."

Darien couldn't help but smile. It had been one of the better notions he'd conceived late in the night. He had no doubt Kyel would find himself in over his head, but that was exactly the position he wanted him in. "It will be a good learning experience for him. A true lesson in diplomacy."

"You're a harsh master, Darien Lauchlin." Naia smiled.

"I try."

Her smile was so infectious he found himself grinning back. "So what do you think His Eminence will say about me stealing you away from him?"

Naia's gaze took on a positively devious glint. "I'm quite certain he won't stop me. Especially if I neglect to tell him I'm leaving."

"I hope Kyel isn't taking lessons in obedience from you." He let his smile fade, his thoughts returning to the issue at hand. Behind him, the goddess still stood with his sword held aloft in a warding stance. "So how do we do this?"

The priestess sighed, looking upward to the statue. "I need to make a few arrangements. Why don't you go clean up a bit, or the goddess still might find it in her heart to reject you."

Her words brought a vivid image to mind of the night of his Raising.

"What?" Naia sounded concerned.

Darien blinked, retreating from his thoughts. "Oh, it's nothing. This just reminds me a bit too much of the last rite I participated in. I only hope this one has a better outcome."

She stared at him with a look of incomprehension. "I hope so, too."

Frowning up at his sword firmly wielded in the goddess' hand, he asked, "If the gods abhor even the notion of fratricide, then why was my petition accepted?"

"It would seem, in this case, that an exception has been made."

Then she left him, departing in a shimmering sway of silk. Darien watched her go, following her movements with his eyes. When she was gone, he turned and glanced back up at his sword, seeking there for solace. But it was the wrong thing to do. The blade reminded him too much of Meiran.

As did Naia.

He found Kyel still asleep, wool blankets piled over him, his head resting on a mound of goose-down pillows. Darien sat on the edge of the bed, reaching his hand into the pocket of his cloak. He withdrew the silver medallion, running his fingers over the facets of the pulsating gem.

Kyel stirred, rubbing the sleep out of his eyes. He squinted upward, eyes fixing on the Soulstone in Darien's hand. His brow creased as he pushed himself upright.

"This is for you," Darien told him, offering the medallion to Kyel. The young man reached for it hesitantly, lifting it by the silver band of the collar. He held it, swaying, before his face.

"I want you to keep this on you at all times and never let it out of your sight. But don't put it around your neck just yet. You'll have to wait till I say the time is right. Do you understand?"

"Aye. I do." Kyel let his hand drop to the covers.

Darien studied the young man's face, trying to read his expression. So many of the plans Darien had made in the quiet darkness of the shrine depended on his young acolyte. He decided not to dilute his expectations; Kyel could only refuse him. And if he did, then it would be better to find out now, when he still had a chance to reformulate his strategy.

"I'll be leaving you for a time," Darien said as he studied Kyel's face intently. "While I'm gone, I have two favors to ask of you."

"You're sending me away."

The boy was perceptive. He was also not happy about the notion. Darien decided to admit the truth. Or, rather, a version of it. "In part. I can't risk us both. If something happens to me, I'll need you to carry on in my stead."

"I'm not certain I could do that." Kyel frowned up at him.

"Then let's hope you're not put in that position. But if you are, I trust you'll make whichever decisions are best."

Kyel nodded, looking sullen as he turned the medallion over in his fingers. "So where is it you're sending me?"

Darien stood up, reaching down to pluck the Soulstone out of Kyel's hands. He wanted the young man's full attention. Kyel finally looked up at him, silently fuming.

"First, I need you to ride to the Temple of Wisdom, which is just across the valley. Present yourself to the clerics there and tell them you represent the Prime Warden."

"I thought you didn't care for that title."

Darien shrugged. "It does seem to have its uses. In war, we must find whatever weapons we can, and use them however we can manage."

"So now you're going to war against the clerics of Om?"

Darien shook his head. "No. You are."

Kyel's look of shock was mildly satisfying.

He went on to explain, "I must find a way to seal the Well of Tears. I've no idea how to accomplish that. If anyone does know, it will be Om's clerics. Have them take you down to their vaults but insist they provide you with someone to help you with the research. If you don't, they'll just let you muck about down there till you die of old age having never found a single thing. It's one of their common ploys."

Kyel frowned up at him. "Why would they not wish to help me?"

"Because the clerics of Om are intensely jealous of their pearls of wisdom. Information is power, Kyel, and no one gives away power easily or freely."

Comprehension dawned in Kyel's eyes, yet doubt lingered there, as well. "You said you had two favors. What's the second?"

"You'll have only three days to search for information in the vaults. Then I'll need you to journey to Rothscard and meet with the Queen of Emmery. Again, tell her you are my representative, and I've given you full authority to treat with her."

"I suppose I can do that," Kyel responded skeptically. "But what exactly am I supposed to say to her?"

Darien allowed himself a smug grin. "You're to tell her that by order of the Prime Warden, she is to yield over command of her army to me. If she refuses, inform her politely that she's out of a throne."

Kyel's face drained to an ashen color. "You're not serious! You want me to threaten a *queen?!*"

"Believe me, Romana Norengail can use a good threat," Darien assured him. "If she attempts to argue—which she will—tell her *politely* that the new Prime Warden has forsworn his Oath of Harmony. That ought to convince her nicely. By the way, if she offers you wine, it would behoove you to refuse her. *Politely.*"

"Sometimes you scare me," Kyel muttered.

"Good. Perhaps if you emulate me, you can scare Romana out of her army. The Queen's general is a man named Blandford. Inform him he'll need to arrive at Orien's Finger by dawn on the morning of the Solstice, not an hour later. If he's late, then he needn't bother showing up at all. I'll meet him there if everything goes right."

"And if it doesn't?"

"Then you'd better learn how to command that army."

Darien let the door swing closed on Kyel's wide-eyed stare, smiling to himself as he strode down the hallway. The boy would do well. What he had said to Naia earlier was true. This would be an invaluable learning experience for him.

He found the door to his own room, where he had stuffed his pack the day before. It was still there, the bed undisturbed. A fresh pitcher of water had been left by the washstand, along with a tray of food that had sat there all night. Darien bypassed the tray, going instead to his pack and sliding out what was left of the sack of jerky he'd brought down with him from the pass.

He unfastened the silver brooch that held his cloak, drawing the dark fabric off his shoulders with one hand as he stuffed a strip of dried meat into his mouth. He went through the motions of chewing, not even tasting the food as he swallowed it, undressing at the same time. Darien pulled a fresh shirt and breeches out of his pack and put them on, dismayed by the fit. He was losing weight.

He walked to the looking glass that hung on the wall over the washstand, stunned by the image that gazed back at him. He scarcely recognized himself. He stared into the mirror, transfixed by his reflection as he reached up and drew his fingers over the dark stubble that covered his face, a face that looked ten years older than the last time he'd seen it. What amazed him most about the image that regarded him were the eyes. They were his father's eyes, exactingly recreated in his own face, complete in every detail, every haunted shadow. Darien shuddered, turning away from the mirror.

As he did, a wave of energy swept over him with violent, raking fingers. The reflection of his back in the looking glass wavered for a moment in a flare of indigo light that rose up from the floor to surround him. Tendrils of power crawled over him, groping at the fabric of his clothes, ripping through his hair, clawing at the skin of his face. The energy receded only slowly, drawing downward to the floor and then flickering out altogether.

Darien gazed somberly down at the garments he wore that suddenly fit his lean body perfectly. It was remarkable, what he could do with his power, without sparing scarcely a thought to the act. He didn't have to look back at the mirror behind him. The reflection would only confirm what he already knew. His face was clean-shaven, the grime and dust erased from his skin. Even his hair smelled clean as he raised his hands to draw it behind his shoulders, catching it up and tying it back. He went over to sit on the bed, finding his cloak where he'd tossed it down on top of the covers.

He couldn't put that cloak back on. At least, not as it was. Not if he was going to truly embrace the title Naia kept insisting he use. He would need the kind of authority that only the office of the Prime Warden could lend him if he was to accomplish the tasks he'd set out for himself.

As he looked down at the blue-black fabric of the cloak, Darien willed it to change. And it did. He stood up, drawing a cloak of gleaming white over his shoulders and fixing it in place. By all appearances, it could have been his mother's cloak, the defining emblem of the Prime Warden of Aerysius. The fabric felt strange. It felt heavier, although he knew his act had done nothing to the material but remove the pigment.

He passed the strap of his baldric across his shoulder. The leather scabbard hung empty at his back. He opened the door and strode out into the hallway, determined to return to the shrine and reclaim his sword from the goddess' hand. He knew the price would be the chains on his wrists, but he was willing to pay it. The conviction that had held him to his Oath had been the first thing rotted away by the poison feel of Arden's touch.

He descended the stairs, working his way through the warren of halls and corridors to the shrine. White-robed priests and veiled priestesses glanced up with startled expressions before ducking their heads in deference to the cloak. Darien did nothing to acknowledge the looks, barely noticing the men and women that moved around him in the halls. His mind was intent on his purpose, to the point that everything else around him seemed irrelevant and remote.

Lost in thought, he almost didn't notice the high priest who stood in shadow, blocking the entrance to the shrine. Darien stopped in the middle of the stairs, one hand poised on the handrail. Luther Penthos regarded him with a careworn expression, eyes narrowing as they pondered the significance of the cloak.

"You must know I'm opposed to this," the old man said. "The goddess has made her choice, so there is nothing I can do to stop you. But nothing prevents me from stating my opinion. I believe you are making a disastrous mistake that will have far-reaching consequences. If you go through with this, know that you do so not only against my better judgment, but also against my will. From this moment forward, I will hold you in the utmost contempt."

Darien glared down at him. "Stand aside." Though spoken softly, his tone conveyed a dangerous insinuation of threat.

The high priest bowed his head. Darien swept down the stairs, brushing past him as he thrust open the door to the shrine. He stepped down the last tiled step into the brilliant light within, slamming the door shut behind him.

He let his eyes wander over the statue of the goddess as he fought to collect himself. His encounter with the old man had left him shaking.

A streak of white from the corner of his eye was the only warning he had as a sword swiped down in front of his face. Darien winced away from it, but a hand caught him by the hair, wrenching his head back sharply as the edge of the blade kissed the flesh of his throat. A strong jerk on his hair forced him to his knees as the blade followed his movement, its honed edge biting wickedly into his neck.

Darien stared up into the veiled face that hovered over him, appalled. The ruthless intent written in Naia's eyes was without compassion, her face terrifying in its authority. The woman he knew was gone, replaced by a sinister angel that threatened him with his own sword.

"There are three faces of the goddess," the priestess said. "The face of Mercy, the face of Sacrifice, and the face of Vengeance. They are three, as they also are one, each inseparable from the other. To gaze upon one is to gaze upon them all. To commit to one is to commit to all three. You have come here to pledge your life to the service of the goddess, to become her leveling hand of Vengeance. She has determined your cause just and worthy. Do you foreswear all prior oaths and dedicate your life to seek the blood of another?"

The press of the blade at his neck bit dangerously as Darien swallowed, his throat moving against it. "Aye, I do," he whispered.

Her hand coiled around in his hair, tightening its grip. "Hold out your hands."

He did as she asked. The sword swept down from his neck and

parted the flesh of both wrists at the same time, laying open the skin across the twin markings of the chains. Blood welled from the deep gashes, beading to the floor in fat, crimson droplets. The priestess knelt beside him, setting his sword down on the floor and lifting a bronze chalice in its stead.

"You are now pledged to the service of the goddess, your duty consummated only when Aidan Lauchlin is destroyed, bereft of body and heart, mind and spirit." As she spoke, Naia took his right wrist in her hand, catching his blood in the chalice, and then lifted it to his lips.

"Come. You must now drink from hatred's bitter cup and taste of the blood you swear to mete."

She tilted the chalice, spilling the warm liquid into his mouth. Darien gagged, unable to bring himself to swallow.

"Drink!" the priestess hissed.

He squeezed his eyes shut as he forced himself to gulp down the mouthful of blood. A spasm of nausea clenched his stomach, but the priestess had him by the hair again. She lifted the chalice again to his lips and forced the remainder of its contents down his throat.

Then she withdrew her hand. Darien collapsed forward, clutching his arms against his chest. Pain flared from the gashes in his wrists, as if a white-hot iron were being pressed into his flesh to cauterize the wounds.

He moaned, writhing with his head pressed against the floor, trembling in agony. Rolling onto his side, he brought his arms up in front of his face and gasped at the sight that confronted him.

The wounds were healed, though the pain was still there, still wretchedly intense. But where the chains had been was now only a set of fresh, angry scars. Darien sat up, consumed by a sudden, terrible feeling of loss.

"What have I done?" he whispered.

He couldn't stop trembling as the priestess wrapped her arms around him, drawing him close. He collapsed into Naia's embrace, clutching her against him desperately.

Chapter Twenty-One Glen Farquist

Glen Farquist, The Rhen

Kyel set the breakfast tray down on the edge of the bed, staring at it wistfully. The scattered crumbs were all that remained of the second real meal he could remember eating in months. Had it only been that long? It somehow seemed like years. He tried picturing the face of his wife, but for some reason her image in his mind was vague and indistinct. Kyel finally gave up, feeling unsettled. He hadn't given thought to Amelia in days. And baby Gil. His son was two years old, now. Kyel had missed his birthday.

He looked out the window. Covendrey was not very far from here. Little more than a fortnight's travel. He was closer to home than he had been since the start of his journey.

Kyel lifted his arm, pushing back the fabric of his sleeve and staring down at the marking of the chain. He wished he could get rid of it, tear it right off his skin and simply go back to his family. He wished he'd never let Darien talk him into any of this.

But then, where would he be? Certainly, no closer to going home. He would still be back in the pass with an army coming down at him.

Sighing, Kyel turned and left the room. He knew he really didn't have time to waste, not if he was to accomplish any of the tasks set out for him.

He found the door to Darien's room open. But the mage was already gone, if he'd ever been there at all. The bed looked undisturbed, and there was an untouched tray of food sitting by it. Kyel frowned down at the tray, thinking of the two meals he'd eaten since arriving at the temple. Obviously, Darien hadn't been in his room all night.

And there was only one other place he would have gone.

Kyel felt saddened by the thought. He remembered asking Darien once why the Oath was so important to him. The mage had given him some vague story about falling off a cliff. Kyel hadn't understood a word of it at the time. Now he did.

I can choose to let go. But this time, I know if I decide to fall, there will be no one around to stop me. To Kyel, the meaning of those words now seemed as clear as a pane of glass looking out on a stormy sea.

Darien had chosen to take that fall.

Kyel knew there was a good reason why every Master of Aerysius was required to swear the Mage's Oath. The tradition had been instituted after the betrayal of the mages of Bryn Calazar, to prevent such a thing from ever happening again. The Oath of Harmony was a safeguard.

In his desire to seek revenge upon his brother, Darien was at great risk of becoming just like him. Kyel knew he had already seen it in him, the bitter poison of that hatred. It was spreading in him. Kyel feared it would eventually consume him, if it hadn't already.

"Excuse me…Kyel Archer?"

He turned to find the same young priest who had taken their horses the day before. The man was lingering in the doorway, holding a parcel wrapped in folds of white silk. He offered it to Kyel with a peculiar look on his face.

Kyel received the package uncertainly. As he did, he realized the priest was even younger than he'd previously thought, barely older than a boy.

"The First Daughter requested this be made for you," the young man said.

Kyel stared down at the parcel in his hands. His fingers felt numb as he fumbled at the knotted strip of ribbon. When he had it undone, what the parting silk revealed made him wince.

Kyel lifted the black cloak up before his face, holding it with a feeling of revulsion mixed with reverence. The Silver Star seemed to glitter in the candlelight. Every stitch was perfectly even, tapering toward the eight points of the rays. Kyel stared at it, wondering how such careful embroidery could have been accomplished in just one night.

"My thanks." Kyel had the urge to take the cloak to his room and stuff it down as far as he could in his pack. But he knew he couldn't do that. Such an act would hardly be fit repayment for the gift. These people had been considerate hosts, and he owed it to them to show appreciation for their generosity.

So it was that Kyel found himself removing the tattered gray wool he had worn every day since his arrival in the pass and donned in its place the ill-omened badge of dead Aerysius.

From the doorway, the young priest said, "His Eminence requires a word with you."

Kyel turned to find the man looking at him with open wonder in his eyes.

"Just let me get my things." Kyel ducked his head, feeling self-conscious.

The new black cloak fluttered behind him as he walked back down the hall to his own room. There, he collected his longbow and shouldered his pack. He turned to leave. With a flare of panic, he suddenly remembered the Soulstone. The medallion was still lying on the stand beside the bed where Darien had set it. Relieved, he strode over and picked it up, stuffing the heirloom into the pocket of his new cloak.

Kyel followed the priest down the stairs and through a maze of hallways. He waited as the young man held a door open for him. He nodded his thanks then moved into a dimly lit study.

Luther Penthos was already there, seated at a desk that held three tidy stacks of parchment. The priest extended a hand, inviting him to take the seat opposite. Kyel removed his pack, setting it down awkwardly beside the chair along with his bow and quiver.

"Your Eminence," Kyel said.

The man scowled at the cloak. Then lifted his stare to confront Kyel.

"I want to know where your master is going. And why he took

my daughter without my permission."

Kyel felt as if someone had just poured a goblet of cold water over his head. "Naia is your daughter? Your…*child…?*"

The old man nodded, his blue eyes narrowing dangerously. "And someday she may even be high priestess, unless your master corrupts her first."

"Darien would never touch your daughter."

But even as the words passed his lips, Kyel knew he had doubts. The interplay he'd witnessed between the two of them the day before made him wonder. For just a moment, Darien had looked like he'd been on the verge of embracing the priestess. Kyel had even felt comforted by the sight. It was a wonderful thing to see him display such a simple, tender emotion. But Darien also hadn't known what Kyel did now.

He had no idea what kind of fire he was playing with.

Leaning forward, the old man demanded, "Why else would Naia run off without even asking me? Without telling me where she was going? She left with *him!*"

He punctuated the last word with a jarring slap on the desk that made Kyel flinch.

He found himself wondering what Darien had done to merit such ire from the old man. There was more going on here than just Naia's disappearance. Something must have happened between the high priest and Darien that had set the man against him.

"I don't know what his plans are," Kyel admitted. "He didn't tell me. The only thing I know is that he'll be at Orien's Finger on the morning of the Solstice."

"Orien's Finger," Penthos echoed. His face went slack. "Are you quite certain?"

"Yes. Why? Whatever is the problem?"

The high priest leaned back in his chair as his eyes wandered up the wall behind Kyel. "In ancient times, there were eight Circles of Convergence. Two were lost to us when Caladorn fell. Three more have been either destroyed or lost through the years. There are only three circles remaining that we know of. One is on the Isle of Titherry. Another existed in Aerysius, but by all reports that circle now lies entombed beneath the ruins of the Hall of the Watchers. The only other Circle of Convergence in existence is on the summit of Orien's Finger."

Kyel wanted to kick himself for not seeing sooner what had been staring him in the face all this time. The numbers suddenly totaled themselves in his mind. The circle. The Soulstone. The Bloodquest. Naia. The cliff's edge. And, on top of it all, Darien had deliberately left him behind.

He'd wondered at the time if the mage hadn't simply devised those errands as a means of getting him out of the way. He'd figured Darien was planning something particularly dangerous. But now Kyel feared it was something much more sinister than he'd previously imagined.

Kyel whispered, "He said two Enemy armies are going to be merging there."

"So he intends to use Orien's Circle to turn them back." The priest's voice was chill, like a breath of air from a grave. "Your master is an eighth-tier Sentinel, and Orien's is a lesser circle. It was never designed to focus the vast amount of power he is capable of drawing."

Kyel groaned.

"Go," the high priest ordered. "If you ever see your master again, tell him that he's a contemptible fool. *And tell him I want my daughter back."*

Kyel fled the high priest's study in a rush. Before he knew what was happening, he found himself being escorted out of the temple by two white-robed priests. As soon as he was outside, the reins of his horse were thrust into his hand and the temple door slammed shut behind him.

Kyel stood on the temple steps, slowly blinking in confusion. The chestnut gelding whinnied, shoving its muzzle into his chest. Kyel stroked its neck absently, looking back over his shoulder at the verdigris dome of the sanctuary. Everything was already starting to go wrong. And he hadn't even begun yet. He mounted his horse and kicked it forward, away from the temple out across the flat floor of the Valley of the Gods.

As he rode, Kyel marveled at the soft pastel hues of the desert around him. If Darien had wanted him to become better-traveled, then he was certainly getting his wish. The cliffs ahead were growing steadily larger, rising from the red soil of the valley floor. He thought he could make out something set in the sheer wall of rock ahead, like shadowy lines traced into the face of the cliff.

As the gelding approached the valley wall, Kyel felt compelled to draw back on the reins. The image ahead resolved into an enormous temple carved into the face of the cliff itself. Great stone pillars rose from a terrace, supporting an overhang that projected outward from the cliff.

The whole structure was bordered by two enormous images of bearded men engraved in bas-relief, their laureled heads encircled by halos of sunbeams. Kyel had seen such representations before.

He knew he had reached the High Temple of Wisdom.

The passage was narrow and dark, the ceiling so low that Kyel had to duck his head as he followed his hooded guide through a vast expanse of solid rock. The path ahead angled sharply downward. Kyel trailed his hands over the rough stone walls to either side.

The cleric was not the same man he'd met at the temple's entrance. He had waited by the door until a guide was summoned to lead him through the dark warren of tunnels within the cliff. From there, Kyel had been handed off from one guide to another, each leading him a little deeper into the labyrinth.

Kyel had thought the Temple of Wisdom looked massive from the outside, especially when he'd stood dwarfed beneath the carved rock pillars. But his journey through the dark passages had begun over an hour ago, and they had yet to reach their destination. The entire plateau must be hollow, to contain the enormity that was Om's temple.

The sloping passage seemed to go on forever, straight ahead and always down. The brown-robed cleric held a flaming torch that provided a globe of wavering light immediately surrounding them, but the passage both ahead and behind fell quickly into darkness. Kyel was starting to feel a slight sense of panic, as if the walls and ceiling were pressing in on him. He knew it was all in his mind, but he could not escape the feeling he was being buried alive.

It would have been some comfort if his guides had made any attempt at conversation. But he'd been passed along from one cleric to another without one word ever spoken.

The passage opened into a broad cavern dripping with natural embellishments. Their path wound through a maze of tawny spikes that hung from the ceiling and shot upward out of the floor. Kyel stood amazed, staring around at the jagged cave decorations. Their path led them through columns that erupted from the floor and past stony waterfalls frozen in time.

His guide led him through a dark opening in the wall ahead. Kyel stepped into yet another narrow passage even colder than the last. He wondered how far underground they had come, and how much farther they had yet to go.

They came to a place where the passage was cleaved by a broad corridor, then turned onto a main thoroughfare. Kyel found himself surrounded by scores of brown-robed clerics who passed by in silent swarms, as often as not laden with armloads of scrolls and manuscripts.

What was even stranger was the sound of this bustling underground boulevard. Other than the soft sounds of footsteps and the rustle of robes, the corridor was completely silent.

At the next intersection, Kyel was passed off to yet another guide, this one a young man with the cowl of his robe pulled up over his head. With only a gesture of his hand, the man directed Kyel down a narrow hallway that ended at a door.

That door was the first piece of wood Kyel had seen since entering the temple. His guide rapped once with his knuckles before opening it, then stood back to admit him into the room.

Kyel stopped as soon as his feet crossed the door's threshold.

Seated on an uncomfortable wooden stool was a man dressed in the clothes of a commoner. He looked to be roughly middle-aged and plump, with thinning brown hair parted over a high widow's peak. He wore a kindly expression in his red and watery eyes. There was even the hint of a smile on his lips as he nodded a cursory greeting.

But it was the man next to him who drew Kyel's attention. This man was very old, his white hair streaked with gray. A wiry beard groped down his chest, ending in a point. He sat with fingers steepled on the table in front of him.

Kyel squared his shoulders, thinking of how Darien would have conducted himself in a similar situation. *Emulate me,* the mage had said. But that was easier said than done. Kyel had nothing of Darien's innate self-assurance, though the black fabric of his cloak lent him a small amount of confidence.

"Your Eminence," Kyel said, bowing his head. He had no doubt in his mind that the old man was the High Priest of Wisdom. He felt a warm flush of satisfaction when the priest acknowledged him with the slightest nod.

Buoyed by this success, he took a step forward into the room. "My name is Kyel Archer. I'm an acolyte of the new Prime Warden, Darien Lauchlin."

The high priest raised his eyebrows and glanced at the man beside him, who returned his look with a frown. The two of them stared silently at one another for a long moment. Finally, the plainly-clothed man leaned forward on his stool.

"Greetings, Acolyte Kyel. You must forgive him but, as all of Om's clerics, His Eminence has sworn a vow of silence."

That explained a lot, Kyel thought, while at the same time thinking how awkward such a vow would be, especially to men whose lives' work was the recording of information.

"My name is Cadmus," the man said. "I serve as the Voice of His Eminence. Why don't you have a seat?"

Kyel sat, shifting nervously. The two men looked as though they were mired in some sort of silent conversation, fixing their eyes on each other intently. After a few uncomfortable minutes, Cadmus turned back to him.

"His Eminence wishes to see your left wrist."

The unexpected request made Kyel wince. The chain was a private matter, not something he felt comfortable exposing to strangers. He felt deeply offended by the request.

But he found himself complying anyway. It was a small price to pay if he wanted access to their vaults. Lifting his left arm, Kyel pushed back his shirtsleeve. Exposed, the metallic marking on his wrist glimmered in the candlelight. Both men stared at the mark, stared at him, then turned back to each other, their eyes silently conferring as Kyel lowered his arm.

"His Eminence wishes to know how you came by such a marking."

Kyel didn't know what to say, or rather how much to say. Fumbling for words, he told them, "Darien—I mean the Prime Warden—he had me speak a vow…"

"Do you remember this vow?" pressed Cadmus, leaning forward.

"Aye." Kyel swallowed. "I do."

"Would you mind repeating it?"

Kyel took a deep breath, feeling a stir of tension as he recalled the words of the Acolyte's Oath. It wasn't difficult. They had been impressed deeply into his mind the day Darien had held his wrist and made him repeat them.

Even before he was finished, the clerics turned away, gazing at each other with shocked expressions. Kyel watched the silent conversation passing between the two as a play of emotions progressed over each man's face.

At last, Cadmus turned back to him. "His Eminence is confused," he said. "Darien Lauchlin died during the destruction that befell Aerysius. This fact is known and has been confirmed. His name has been added to the List."

Kyel wasn't sure what list the man was referring to. He assumed Cadmus meant some list of casualties, though the emphasis on the word made him wonder. But they didn't know everything, these clerics of Om. For the Temple of Wisdom, they'd certainly gotten some bad information.

"No." Kyel shook his head. "He's alive. I mean…"

Plainly, they didn't believe him. He closed his mouth, striving to think how he might convince them. He needed these clerics to believe that Darien was alive, was in fact Prime Warden, or he had no leverage to gain access to their information.

"You could ask the high priest at the Temple of Isap," Kyel suggested at last. It wasn't much, but it was the only proof he had to offer. "Darien was just there this morning."

The old man frowned at his words.

Cadmus said, "His Eminence wishes to know why your master was at the temple."

Kyel opened his mouth to tell them about Darien's mother but then decided against it. That line of conversation would inevitably lead to the Soulstone. Only, there was just one other explanation he could offer.

Forced to choose between the two accounts, Kyel chose the one he thought was the least damaging. It would scarcely be a secret much longer if Darien followed through with his plan.

"He swore a Bloodquest," Kyel admitted grudgingly.

The high priest's eyes widened, his cheeks flushing with color. He gestured angrily as he glared at Cadmus. Kyel wondered if he'd made a mistake. Whatever silent conversation was passing between the two men, it was hostile. They seemed to be arguing heatedly with their eyes. At last, Cadmus sat stiff on his stool, turning back to Kyel.

"His Eminence asks that you retire with him to his chambers, where he can speak with you at greater length."

"No."

Kyel was startled by the fierceness of his response. He hadn't meant it to come out that way. But he didn't have the time nor desire to be drawn into a lengthy explanation. He had too much work to do.

The Temple of Wisdom traded in knowledge, and that's what they were doing: pumping him for information. He'd already played into their manipulations and told them more than he ever should have. *Knowledge is power,* Darien had said. If that was true, then he had the upper hand. Kyel had been apprenticed to a merchant, and he damned well knew how to barter.

"That's not why I'm here," he said firmly. "I need access to your vaults. And I require someone to help me with my research."

After only the briefest pause, Cadmus asked, "His Eminence wishes to know what information it is you seek."

Kyel nodded. It was a fair trade, and necessary. If he wanted someone to help him with the research, then that someone would have to know the topic of his search eventually. He took a deep breath.

"I need to find a way to seal the Well of Tears."

Both men's eyes widened simultaneously, and they turned to stare harshly at each other. After long seconds, the high priest finally nodded.

"Your Prime Warden charts a highly dangerous course," Cadmus said, turning back to Kyel. "His Eminence agrees to allow you access to the vaults and will provide you with the assistance of a cleric to help you with your research during the hours of daylight. But in return, he requests that you join him in the evenings to share with him your story."

It was a fair trade, at least one that Kyel thought he could live with, if he watched himself and doled the facts out sparingly.

"That I can do," he said.

The high priest nodded.

"Very well." Cadmus stood up and offered Kyel his hand.

Kyel rose to his feet and took the plump man's hand in his own, feeling quite proud of himself as he sealed the agreement.

Chapter Twenty-Two
Fortress in the Eye of the Storm

Pass of Lor-Gamorth, The Front

Lightning traced the sky over Greystone Keep as a gust of wind ripped at the black pennant that clung tenuously to its staff at the top of the tower. The frayed banner crackled as a single fiery arrow arched above the stone walls of the fortress. Two more shafts whistled by overhead, followed by a volley. The pennant fluttered, wafting once more before it finally swayed to a rest.

Devlin Craig stared at the banner with a sense of foreboding confirmed by the hiss of the signal arrows arcing up from the bottom of the pass. He'd been expecting this for some time. But now that the threat was upon them, he couldn't help but feel that all the preparations they'd made in the past five days were merely an exercise in futility.

The reports coming in from Maidenclaw grew more dismal by the day, even by the hour. The most recent calculations placed the Enemy strength at somewhere around forty thousand, an estimate that was still growing.

His own men numbered less than one thousand.

Craig turned away from the battlements and strode toward the ladder, climbing down into the relative warmth of Proctor's chamber. Stamping his feet on the floor, Craig tried to work some feeling back into his legs. Autumn had faded sometime in the last week, and winter in the pass was always a harrowing affair. By the chill feel of the wind, Craig feared the first winter storm was already on its way.

At least there was some comfort in knowing he wouldn't have

to spend another winter in the Pass of Lor-Gamorth.

For once, Proctor was not at his map. Instead, Craig found him staring out through the narrow opening of an arrow slit. The force commander had one hand raised, pressed against the wall by his face. The other hand fingered the hilt of the narrow dagger he always wore tucked into the belt at his waist. It was seldom visible, usually covered by the folds of his cloak.

Craig always found the sight of that dagger unsettling. It was called a misery knife, a traditional weapon worn by soldiers of the Enemy to give a final stroke of mercy to those fatally injured in battle. Proctor had received the dagger as a gift some years ago and had worn it at his side ever since. He even slept with it.

Craig walked stiffly across the circular chamber to stand behind his superior officer.

"It's happening," he said, and waited for the man to respond. But Proctor was silent, not showing any sign that he'd even heard.

Craig felt a stabbing slap of fury. After all the ruthless plots Garret Proctor had hatched, the man seemed suddenly indifferent, now that the end was at hand.

"If you hadn't driven Lauchlin away, we might've stood a chance," Craig accused. Then he stiffened, seeing the force commander's hand slide slowly down the ebony hilt of his knife, knuckles whitening as he gripped it.

"Is that what you think?"

Craig sensed that he was treading on very dangerous ground, but he continued all the same.

"Am I wrong?"

Proctor turned to fix him with an icy glare. He uttered in frigid, barren tones, "I did what had to be done. Before, we stood no chance. Not against a host this size."

Craig was still doubtful. "And you think we're better off now?"

Proctor raised an eyebrow as if challenging Craig to press him further. He appeared to be waiting, perhaps even patiently. But Craig knew better. He had an entirely different end in mind for himself than the blade of that wicked knife.

"I'm not accustomed to being questioned by the men under

my command," Proctor snapped with narrowed eyes. "For over fifteen years, I've held the Front with little more than my nerve, my wits, and my audacity. I've never asked for accolades or even gratitude from the nations I protect, and I've never had either. The one thing I've ever demanded is the respect of my own men."

Craig lowered his eyes. Garret Proctor was arguably one of the best military strategists in all of history. Once, not even that long ago, Craig had felt an immeasurable swell of pride to have the privilege of soldiering under such a commander. He could remember nights when he would sit back at the table in awe, watching Proctor's eyes wandering over his map, struggling just to visualize the layered calculations and subtle inferences melding together within the man's head.

But his respect for Garret Proctor had been dealt a sobering blow. In his mind, the image of the man who had once been his hero was now irrevocably tarnished.

Into the interval left by Craig's silence, Proctor uttered, "Select a small contingent of volunteers to fire the keep and buy our escape with their lives. Then get every man you can on a horse."

Craig stared at him, stunned, unable to believe what he'd just heard. "You'll let them take the keep?"

"We fall back," Proctor confirmed, the threat in his eyes cautioning the captain not to question him again.

Craig took the warning to heart and turned away without another word. He left the command chamber, letting his boots carry him down the winding steps of the tower. He trudged into the open hall of the keep and crossed the floor in long strides.

Men who had already seen the signal arrows now drew forward to assemble by the shattered remains of the north wall, inferring the nature of the threat that confronted them from the look on his face. Silence fell over the hall as the soldiers gathered to hear him speak.

"We abandon the keep," Craig announced.

The reaction produced by his words was swift. Cries of protest rang from the walls as the men surged forward as one, shouting and brandishing fists, even weapons, in the air. Craig jumped onto a large pile of tumbled blocks, trying to elevate himself above the press of bodies. The upturned faces that glared at him were dangerous in their hostility.

"That's the order."

Craig stood and waited for silence. It came slowly, but eventually even the rustle of bodies ceased. When he was sure he had their full attention, he took a deep breath and summoned the courage to continue.

"I'm asking for volunteers: men who'll be willing to stay behind to offer resistance while the rest of us retreat down the pass. If you decide to remain, know that your death will buy the rest of us a fighting chance. I can promise you that your sacrifice will not go unremarked. Or unavenged."

The faces before him darkened, and he could almost feel their righteous skepticism. They knew well, just as he did, how hollow that promise was. The scouts who'd brought back reports from the mouth of the pass had not been ordered to silence. Every man in the keep knew the numbers of the Enemy host that confronted them.

The scornful faces before him reduced his words to the shameful collection of lies that they were. He knew he couldn't blame them if not a man stepped forward to volunteer.

They deserved better.

They deserved to know the truth: that every last one of them was going to die, and no good account would come from their ends. The vast strength of the Enemy would be like a raging tempest, and they would be simply swept away by that storm. But he couldn't bring himself to tell them that. In the end, it seemed, he was craven after all. Devlin Craig bowed his head and waited, but no one moved.

At last, a lone man stepped forward from the back of the crowd, winding his way through the press of bodies toward the front. Craig raised his eyebrows, frowning when he recognized Corban Henley's red-bearded face. The burly man had one hand clutched on the hilt of the sword that rode at his side, his face as impassive as a cold chunk of stone.

A murmur ran through the gathered men as they parted to let

him pass. When he reached the front of the crowd, Henley stopped and simply stood. He didn't look at Craig, but stared beyond him, down into the blackness visible through the rift in the wall.

He was not the man Craig would have picked. Henley was a good soldier, far too good to be wasted in such a futile endeavor. But no one else was coming forward. Craig scanned the crowd, but their hostility was still almost palpable. Even Henley's example had not been enough to inspire, and it should have been.

Finally, another man drew forward. When Craig saw who it was, he almost gasped in disbelief. Traver Larsen had come to him as a scoundrel, an insubordinate rogue who Craig had felt certain wouldn't last a fortnight before getting himself killed, probably by his own comrades in arms. From the beginning, Craig had determined that the best use of the man would be to make a harsh example of him. But Larsen had never given him the opportunity.

Instead, the man had changed. From almost the moment he'd picked up a sword, Traver Larsen had transformed into one of the hardest-working recruits Craig had ever trained. And now he stood at Henley's side, just the two of them, alone.

But then the crowd shifted.

At first Craig didn't understand what was happening; the change was subtle. It took him a moment to realize that Henley and Larsen were no longer alone at the front of the crowd. The entire mass of men had moved forward collectively as one. He stared down at the group of soldiers, abashed by their courage.

Craig found himself in the grim position of having to choose his volunteers.

He limited his choice to a dozen, selecting mostly archers. He didn't pick either Henley or Larsen. He wanted both men by his side, not wasted on a hopeless venture.

When it was done, he looked up to find Garret Proctor standing in the doorway. The force commander stepped forward and addressed the hall in a booming voice:

"Take only what is necessary. We ride within the hour. *Now,*

MOVE!"

Craig watched as men scurried in every direction. He lingered on the mound of blocks for another moment before turning away. As he scaled the ladder to the catwalk at the top of the walls, he could feel Proctor's eyes on him.

He paused and stared out through the opening of an arrow slit. At first, he thought he could see movement far below, somewhere down in the bottom of the pass. But it was just roiling ground fog, nothing more. The Enemy was not yet upon them.

He traced his hand over the stone blocks that rimmed the opening. These stark walls had stood for hundreds of years, protecting the nations of the Rhen. In his mind, he could hear Royce's voice as a distant, haunting refrain, that same speech the man had delivered to every batch of new recruits: *Greystone Keep holds the Pass of Lor-Gamorth. If it should ever fall, then we will lose the pass. If we lose the pass, then we lose the North. And if the North should ever fall, the Enemy will sweep southward like a storm.*

It had always been Royce's duty to hold the fortress. But Royce was dead, and now the walls he'd sworn to protect were simply being abandoned. In a way, Craig was glad his old friend was not alive to see this day. The fall of Greystone Keep would certainly have broken him.

Craig rode in silence beside his commander at the head of the long column that descended the dark cliffs, heading southward into the heart of the pass. Above and behind him, the fortress was visible as never before, aglow with the light of dozens of fires.

Proctor had turned Greystone Keep into a death trap. Nothing had been left behind for the Enemy. Nothing, with the exception of a half-dozen bowmen whose arrows hissed down from the high walls as the fortress burned beneath their feet.

Craig heard a distant crash and turned to see the roof of the tower caving in, consumed by the fierce glow of ravaging flames. Sparks shot upward, wafting high into the sky. He turned away from the sight, fixing his gaze on the black dirt of the path before him.

He almost brought his hands up to cover his ears as the sound of distant screams drifted toward him, carried by the still night air. The whistling hiss of arrows ceased, and a sad, eerie silence lingered over the remote crackling of flames.

Then another sound rose behind him, soft at first, then growing to a thunderous, echoing roar. Craig did cover his ears then, closing his eyes as well, against the deafening cry of victory pealed from thousands of Enemy throats.

Devlin Craig didn't have to look behind him to know that the fortress that had guarded the Pass of Lor-Gamorth for over five hundred years stood no more.

Chapter Twenty-Three
Unveiled

Northern Chamsbrey, The Rhen

Darien stared ahead at the sheer white train of Naia's veil, fascinated by the way it was played out at her side, rippled by the gentle current of a zephyr. He wondered at the veil's significance. It was reminiscent in some ways of a bridal scarf, a badge of goodness and purity. In other ways, it reminded him of his mother's funeral shroud, elegant even as it was isolating.

The veil fluttered upward, and for the briefest moment he had an unobscured view of her face. It was as if the clouds had parted, admitting a fragile, transitory ray of sunlight into his dark and winterish world. Then the skies closed again as the breeze ebbed, and the veil fell back into place. It had been but a chance gesture of the wind, nothing more. But to Darien, that brief glimpse of Naia's face had the magnitude of a sobering epiphany.

He realized that he loved her. And he damned himself for it.

They rode in silence into the bleak grayness that preceded the dawn, their horses climbing out of the desert into the green foothills of the mountains. The path they followed was the one that had led them out of the Valley of the Gods two days before, now rising into the rolling hills that marked the beginning of the Craghorns.

To the north, Darien could see the sharp peaks of snow-clad mountains in the distance, evocatively familiar. The sight of the Craghorns beckoned him, drawing him like a child intrigued by the candle's tempting flame. Aerysius was there, somewhere, high up on the vertical face of one of those white summits.

But instead of taking the northern fork, Darien turned his horse southward. He glanced over his shoulder for one last view of the mountains as he guided his mount toward the center of the path.

"You're going to Auberdale?" Naia gazed at him with a perplexed expression.

"I need Faukravar's northern army."

The confusion on her face turned to a look of comprehension. "So that's why you sent Kyel to Rothscard. To beg Romana for her army."

"Begging was not what I had in mind."

Naia pursed her lips thoughtfully. "I still fail to see how you plan to accomplish all that you intend to do in less than a fortnight. Travel alone will scarcely take us to Aerysius and back to Orien's Finger in that amount of time, and that doesn't include a stop in Auberdale."

"That's true," Darien agreed. "There's not enough time. Aidan will have to wait."

Naia looked concerned by his answer. Which confused him. That was the part of his plan he'd expected her to like most.

She said, "You told me you feared to have Aidan at your back. I wondered about that at the time. Your brother has done little but sit like a spider in his web ever since he gained control of Aerysius. Do you expect him to move against you now?"

Darien shook his head. "Aidan has not been idle, I assure you. For one, there are no passes above Aerysius to admit a force through that corridor. Aidan has been hard at work creating some sort of passage through the Craghorns. And the Eight are under his command, and they haven't been idle at all. Arden Hannah told me she came from Bryn Calazar. That stinks of a union between Aidan and whatever dark terror governs the Enemy."

This time, the dawn of comprehension on her face was overshadowed by the worried lines of fear he'd been expecting.

"An alliance?" She looked appalled. "So all of this has been Aidan's scheme—to use the combined might of the Enemy and the Netherworld to conquer the Rhen for himself?"

"My family has always had an ambitious streak."

Naia shook her head. "To think, all of these horrors wrought by just one man. But you still didn't answer my question. What is the danger if you put off confronting your brother until after the battle?"

Darien shrugged. "Aidan commands Renquist. I'm going to have a hard enough time minding the Enemy without having to worry about being attacked by eight demons and their pets at the same time."

Naia's face went pale. "What will you do, Darien?"

"I'll have a few things on my side," he said, trying to reassure her with a smile he simply didn't feel. "I'll have two good-sized armies behind me. And Orien's Vortex will give me some protection. If he wants to take me, Renquist will need to move his mages in close, into the eye of the vortex itself. As I figure it, the battle will be won or lost depending on who gains Orien's Circle first. Whoever controls the vortex will control the field of battle."

"But, Darien, what if they're there already? The Eight? Even Aidan?"

Darien shook his head. "They're not expecting me. I'm certain Renquist thinks I'm dead, or at least Arden ought to. That's my greatest advantage: the element of surprise is on my side."

Naia looked as if she wanted to believe him, but her eyes beneath the veil were full of doubt. It was the best strategy he'd been able to come up with. Using Orien's Circle, at least he had a chance. But there were so many things that could still go wrong. His first big challenge lay just ahead over the hills.

And he couldn't afford to spend much time in Auberdale. Faukravar was known for stalling, miring his opponents in tangles of intrigue. The King of Chamsbrey had given Darien's mother headaches on more than one occasion, and Emelda had been a strong Prime Warden.

Darien didn't kid himself. He'd never had the patience for politics. In Auberdale, he was going to be very much out of his element.

⊛

They followed the road to the south for the remainder of the day. The landscape changed around them, the scattered trees thickening into a densely forested woodland. The sky gave way to a canopy clad in orange and burnished gold. Leaves rained down on the road as the branches stirred above them in the breeze. Winter was approaching swiftly. Already the air carried with it a sharp chill.

Naia had been silent for most of the day, her eyes either remote in thought or cast downward in a meditative study of the road. Darien thought he knew the reason. Her mood had turned after their conversation that morning. By the time the sunset arrived, he found himself missing her company.

He guided his horse off the road, looking for a place to set up camp for the night. They could have reached Auberdale easily by pressing on after dark. But Naia's silence bothered him, and it made him reluctant to enter the city with her in such a somber mood.

Determined to do something to cheer her up, he selected a spot on the rise of a hill, a patch of green grass in the midst of a stand of trees. The far side of the hill provided a sweeping view of the lowlands below, with the walls of Auberdale visible in the distance against the southern horizon.

To his disappointment, Naia seemed unaffected by the view, merely glancing once over the rim of the hill as she went routinely about the process of helping him set up the campsite. Darien felt dismayed, wondering what it would take to bring the smile back to her face.

When he saw her digging through her pack for the dried food stores they'd carried with them from Glen Farquist, it gave him an idea. Leaving her by the fire, he strode off alone into the thicket, eyes scanning the ground and the trees for any sign of movement.

It took him a little while of searching, but at last he found a hare. Yet, even as he did, he was unsure of quite what to do with it. If Kyel had been there, he would have borrowed his acolyte's bow to bring the animal down. But Kyel wasn't there, and all Darien had was his sword. And his ability.

With the slightest wrench of his mind, the hare collapsed on the spot. There was no writhing or squirming. The animal simply dropped and was dead.

Darien felt himself shiver involuntarily as he walked toward the fallen hare. He knelt over it, staring bleakly down at the limp carcass. He had never before used his ability to take a life, even a small one. It was a new experience, and unsettling. What disturbed him most was how effortless the act had been. It had taken almost no thought whatsoever to transfer what he already knew from his study of healing and adapt it into a killing strike. He had taken the wondrous gift of life and had corrupted it into its converse: the ignoble gift of death.

As Darien grasped the limp animal by its hind legs, he felt wretchedly soiled. This was not the use his gift had ever been intended for. He thought of Grand Master Ezras, the mage who'd surrendered his life to pass on his ability to him. What he had just done seemed to slight that great man's noble sacrifice. Ezras had held fiercely to his Oath his entire life, even in the most dire of circumstances. The man would have gladly yielded his own life before slaying so much as a simple hare with the use of his gift.

Feeling sickened, Darien took out his knife and slit the animal's plump belly, scraping its guts out with trembling fingers. He skinned the carcass and drove it through with a branch sharpened into a spit, then knelt to wash up in the crisp water of a brook. By the time he returned to their campsite, his hands had finally stopped shaking.

Naia looked up as he sat down on the other side of the fire from her, bracing the spit hare at an angle over the flames. Her eyebrows raised in appreciation at the smell of cooking meat. Darien tried his best to smile, but his heart wasn't in it.

"Thank you," she said simply.

Darien just nodded. His entire motive for killing the hare had been to cheer her up. But now that his efforts seemed to have worked, at least a little bit, he found it was he who needed cheering. He leaned forward to turn the meat, but the motion was just a way of avoiding her eyes.

"What's wrong?"

She had seen through him anyway. It was an uncanny knack she had. No matter how well he tried to hide his feelings from her, she always knew them. Before her, every wall he threw up crumbled to sand and ashes. Darien leaned forward, folding his arms across his legs as he struggled to think of how to put his emotions to words.

"I've never killed anything with my gift before," he admitted finally. He felt ashamed. It had been only a stupid, tiny hare. Whether it had died in a trap or by the force of his mind shouldn't have mattered.

But it did.

The priestess seemed to sense it, too. A look of sympathy formed on her face. The expression made him angry. He didn't want her pity. Of all the range of emotions he wished he could elicit from her, that was the one thing he simply couldn't take. He stared down at the campfire's flickering flames as if drawn to them, mesmerized by the fire's orange-yellow glow.

"I care for you, Naia."

The look of stunned shock on her face hurt more than her pity. Darien pushed himself up, not knowing where he was going as he stumbled toward the edge of the hill. He stopped there, surrounded by the whispering branches of the forest. In the distance, he could see the lights of Auberdale, a dim glow on the dark line of the horizon.

He considered the lights, or tried to. But all he could think about was Naia. Why had he said that to her? He couldn't imagine what he'd been thinking. Without intending to, he'd been cruelly unfair to her. He hadn't even considered the decision he was forcing upon her, asking her to choose between his selfish desires and her life's work and ambitions. He had no right to put her in such a position. He was a fool.

He watched the lights twinkling below, wishing he could be anyone else in the entire world.

The crack of a twig snapping made him turn. She was standing not a foot away from him, her gaze intent upon his face. Darien squeezed his eyes shut against the torture of her presence.

As she moved into his arms, he grimaced against the anguish of knowing he was doing her a terrible wrong. At the same time, he felt such a thrill of exhilaration that everything else in the world seemed remote and trivial.

He drew her against him, pressing his face into the silken softness of her veil. Her hands slid behind his back, stroking his hair as he closed his eyes and immersed himself in the tender compassion of her touch.

When she finally drew back, he found himself staring into her eyes, overwhelmed. His hand rose to the sleek transparency of her veil. With reverence, he lifted the fabric and drew it from her head. He let his arm fall to his side, still holding Naia's veil as he traced a finger over her cheek. When he felt her lips press against his, he could almost imagine what it felt like to be alive.

Auberdale, The Rhen

Godfrey Faukravar was the rightful King of Chamsbrey. But the man known infamously as the Vile Prince had earned his epithet long before the crown was ever placed upon his head. Faukravar was notorious for his brutal handling of the Crofter Rebellion, which had ended in the cold-blooded massacre of over three hundred commoners: men, women and children, alike. Another feather in Faukravar's cap was the War of Five Days, when he had used the combined might of both his armies to squash the small but embittered province of Glaster that had risen up against him. Godfrey Faukravar was renowned for both his cunning political intrigues and his ruthless nature, a potent combination.

Darien was not looking forward to meeting the man. In his opinion, the King of Chamsbrey was undeserving of the title. If he could be assured his action wouldn't spark a civil war, Darien would have considered removing the man bodily from the throne. But there were simply too many hounds lurking under the King's table, waiting to snap up the scraps their monarch threw at them from time to time. If a vacuity of power ever existed on the throne of Chamsbrey, every dog of the pack would fight tooth and claw over it.

Within, Darien heard the herald announce them:

"The First Daughter Naia Seleni, Priestess of Isap…and her escort."

Darien had not provided his name. He hadn't seen the necessity; the white cloak of the Prime Warden that fell down his back would be enough for Faukravar to identify him. If not, then the threat of his sword ought to give the man pause. Darien had donned a pair of leather gloves just for the occasion, to cover the glaring absence of the chains on his wrists.

He stepped forward, following the sweep of Naia's gown through the door to the throne room. His eyes moved over the priestess' slender figure as she walked before him. Naia seemed very much in her element. Having been on the receiving end of her political graces, Darien appreciated having her there. He watched as she dropped into an elegant curtsey before the throne.

Darien lifted his eyes to regard the King. He made no move to kneel. By rights, Faukravar should be the one on his knees. The white cloak worn by Darien outshone the splendor of any crown.

But the man on the throne appeared not to notice it. If he did, then he was certainly not ready to acknowledge the emblem of the Prime Warden that had inserted itself unannounced into his throne room.

The King of Chamsbrey was older than Darien had expected, a man somewhere in his late fifties. His silver hair was streaked with strands of faded brown, worn in perfect, shoulder-length curls under the golden circlet of the crown on his head. He was dressed in opulent layers of black and violet robes, with an ermine-trimmed cape covering the whole affair.

Faukravar stared unblinking into his eyes. When it became clear Darien had no intention of kneeling, the King's lips compressed to a narrow line. One of four men who surrounded the throne stepped forward, a hand resting on the pommel of the sword at his side.

"One is expected to bend knee in the presence of a King."

Darien kept his eyes trained on Faukravar. Behind him, he heard soft rustling sounds as the guards by the door tried to figure out what to do. A soft ringing noise scraped down his nerves as a blade was slowly bared. An uneasy tension spread through the room, growing as long moments dragged by. Darien simply waited and did nothing, while Naia remained frozen in the depths of her curtsey.

On the throne, the Vile Prince blinked.

"An interesting companionship," he said finally, leaning back and raising a hand to finger his wiry goatee. "A white-cloaked mage, by all appearances, and a priestess of Death. Tell me, First Daughter, how might we be of service to the temple?"

Naia rose to glide forward with a swirl of her gown. "Thank you for the favor of this audience, Your Grace," she said in a clear and ringing voice. "But I am not here at the bequest of my temple. Instead, I have come to present to you the new Prime Warden, Darien Lauchlin."

The King glanced back at Darien, raising a skeptical eyebrow. "*Another* Lauchlin?" He sounded bored. "My, but that name does seem to be coming up rather often of late, and not always mentioned in the best of contexts. We are intrigued. But we are also mystified. By what right do you claim the office of Prime Warden?"

"I elected myself," Darien responded dryly.

Naia elaborated, "Darien Lauchlin is the son of Prime Warden Emelda."

The King's lips twitched into a smirk. "Aidan Lauchlin is also her son. Does that make him Prime Warden, as well?"

The silence that followed was broken by the sound of nervous chuckles. Darien waited.

At his side, Naia gestured expansively. "If I may, Your Grace? Aidan Lauchlin destroyed the Hall of the Watchers and ordered his own mother slain. Is that the kind of Prime Warden you would wish to replace her?"

Faukravar dismissed her argument with a wave of his hand. "It doesn't matter what we wish. The title itself is empty. Aerysius is fallen. A king without a nation is not a king. And the last soldier left standing is not a general."

Darien watched him a moment longer, then slowly shook his head. He'd known better than to let the man maneuver him into a corner, which was exactly what Faukravar was attempting to do. If he hadn't, in fact, already succeeded. Taking a step forward, he addressed the King in a carefully controlled voice:

"I'll not be questioned over my right to my title. Whether you like it or not, I'm the last mage left alive who hasn't sold his soul to Xerys."

By the look on Faukravar's face, the King couldn't have cared less if he had. "Then why *are* you here?"

"I came to ask you to lend me your northern army," Darien said, infusing all the confidence he could muster into his tone. "As we speak, two great Enemy hosts are swarming down from the Black Lands. They'll be close enough to threaten your walls in one month's time. If I hope to stand a chance of turning them back, I'll have need of your northern forces."

This time, the laughter that filled the chamber was much louder. Even Faukravar allowed himself a grin. "You expect me to just *give* you one of my armies? How incredibly impetuous."

Darien waited as the cold wash of anger drained slowly out of him, until there was only emptiness remaining in its place. Dredged up from the depths of the emotional void that consumed him, his tone was frigid.

"I need your army, Your Grace, and I'll not be leaving Chamsbrey without it. I thought to ask first, out of courtesy. You have until sunset tomorrow to make your decision."

"And should I refuse?" the King baited.

"Then I'll take it from you outright."

Gasps of indignation filled the chamber. All around the room, Darien could hear the shiver of a forest of steel being bared, the sounds of footsteps as the guards distanced themselves from the walls, preparing for a fight. He could have removed his gloves. That would have given them something to think about. But he didn't.

Instead, Darien turned and walked calmly toward the door,

pausing only as two guards with swords bared stepped forward to block him.

He gazed at both men with the slightest dare of a smile on his lips, waiting for them to decide whether they were ready to die for their King.

It was Faukravar who decided for them, sparing their lives.

"Let him go."

"Well, he's certainly arrogant enough to be a Lauchlin."

Faukravar glanced sideways at Chadwick Cummings as the rest of his ministers snickered at the man's comment. The King himself sat clenching the arms of his throne, gripped in a cold rage provoked by the man who had just insulted his honor and his sovereignty. He couldn't recall ever being treated with such cavalier insolence.

"He's the very image of Emelda, in face as well as temperament," Clement Landry pronounced.

The King nodded, for once in full agreement with his Minister of State. He had met with the late Prime Warden on enough occasions to have recognized her looks glaring out at him from the face of her impudent son. It seemed the man had inherited a full measure of Emelda's overconfidence without a grain of her subtlety.

"Opinions?"

Cummings spoke first, his voice raised above the drone of the others. "His threat is empty, Sire. Even if he truly is a mage, he is Bound by the Oath of Harmony."

But Faukravar remained skeptical. There was something about the man that made him wonder. "Did any of you note the emblem of the chains?"

To his disappointment, all four of his ministers stood shaking their heads. He was furious at them, almost as furious as he was with himself for not thinking of the chains when the man was in front of him. He had allowed Lauchlin to unbalance him.

Lance Treaton, his Minister of the Treasury, bowed his head sadly. "I tried to mark them, my liege, but he was wearing gloves."

"I abhor riddles," the King grumbled.

"What of this Enemy host?" asked Landry. "Is there a reason to suspect it might actually exist?"

Cummings spoke up. "In his last letter, Garret Proctor mentioned he was facing a serious threat with a critical shortage of men and supplies."

"Proctor whines more than a tavern wench, and louder," proclaimed Treaton.

But the King was not troubled by Lauchlin's mention of the Enemy. It was the man's other threats, especially the veiled ones, that worried him more. "That doesn't concern me. To reach Auberdale, any force would have to cut all the way through Emmery and lay siege to Rothscard along the way. Let Romana deal with them, if such a host exists."

"What should we do about Lauchlin?"

"Nothing, until we know more about him." The King tapped his fingers on the armrest of his throne, frowning in thought. After a moment, he beckoned his guard captain forward.

As the man crossed the floor, Faukravar commanded him, "Find out where he's staying. I want men positioned around him at all times, watching every move he makes. I want to know whether or not he wears the marks of the chains. And find out more about that sword he carries, what significance it implies. Also, I want to know the nature of his relationship to that priestess."

"Maybe he's just fucking her," said Landry.

"Perhaps. If so, find out."

Cummings moved forward. "Your Grace, I must urge you to treat this mage with the utmost caution. He is, after all, the brother of the very man who brought Aerysius to its knees. It is conceivable they're in league. How else did this Darien manage to survive when all else fell?"

The King raised an eyebrow. "An interesting notion. Find out about that, too."

Another Lauchlin. He was already sick to death of the name.

Darien gazed down at Auberdale through the paned-glass window of the room he had taken at an inn. The size of the city never ceased to amaze him. It sprawled along the banks of the River Nerium, a mottled collection of disparate structures and haphazard streets ambling off in every direction. The dark towers of Glassenburgh Castle rose over the slow waters of the Nerium, the sharp teeth of its fortifications visible even at a distance.

Turning from the window, his gaze traveled across the floor to where Naia lay spread out across the covers of the room's only bed. He wanted nothing more than to collapse into bed with her and drown his troubles in her arms. But he couldn't do that.

Last night, it had taken every ounce of will he possessed to restrain himself when she'd crawled under his blanket. He'd fallen asleep with Naia in his arms, trying to ignore the desperate ache inspired by her closeness.

She looked up at him and smiled, her face unobscured by the fabric of her veil. Darien moved away from the window and sat down beside her on the bed. As he did, Naia touched the back of his hand, stroking his skin with her fingertips.

"You were magnificent today," she said. "I must admit, I had a few doubts."

He'd had more than just a few, going in. "No." He shook his head. "You're the one who was magnificent. You must have been a courtier before you ever became a priestess."

She batted her hand at him with a look of feigned outrage. Darien tried to get up, but she caught him by the arm and drew him back down beside her.

He closed his eyes as her lips wandered over his cheek, trailing upward to his forehead. Again, he was filled with longing as he let his mouth explore the graceful curve of her neck. When he felt Naia's hands slip under his shirt, he wanted to groan.

But instead, he took her hands in his own and, removing them gently but firmly, rolled away from her onto his back. He stared up at the beams of the ceiling, fighting against a raging desire that made his breath ragged in his throat.

He wanted her, wanted all of her, with a need that was almost savage. The game they were playing was just too dangerous. Every time they touched, he found himself facing a losing battle. He felt besieged, his walls quickly caving in. Eventually, the struggle inside was going to defeat him. And when it did, Naia would be the one to suffer.

"What is it?"

She frowned down at him as she propped herself up with an elbow on the bed. Her auburn hair burned almost scarlet in the light streaming in from the window. It draped down to spread across the covers beside his face.

Darien shook his head. "I can't do this. It's not fair to you."

His words seemed to infuriate her. She rolled off the bed and wrenched herself up, stalking away from him as he watched in confusion.

"Perhaps you should have thought about that last night."

"I did, but…"

"But?" she spat, plucking her veil off the floor. "But then you led me to believe you have feelings for me, when it's obvious you don't."

Darien sat up and looked at her in amazement. "What would you have of me?"

Naia flung the veil at his face, but it only fluttered down to land softly beside him on the bed. "I want you to make up your mind, Darien. Do you really care for me as you say you do? Or are you just infatuated with the idea of me? You need to think about it. I can be your lover, or I can be a priestess, but I can't be both. You decide."

With that, she grabbed up her veil and stormed to where her gown lay folded on a chair, pulling it on over her shift.

And then she was gone, the door slamming shut in her wake.

Chapter Twenty-Four
The Pursuit of Wisdom

Glen Farquist, The Rhen

The vaults of Om's temple were not what Kyel had expected. He'd thought they would be like the libraries of Aerysius his father had often spoken of, well-lit rooms with shelf upon polished shelf of ordered manuscripts and well-tended documents. But the vaults of Wisdom were nothing like a library. They reminded Kyel more of Death's Catacombs.

The chambers where Om's clerics stored their vast accumulation of knowledge were a warren of man-made caves existing well below the level of the high priest's chambers. Indeed, they were so far beneath the earth Kyel could almost feel the weight of the soil overhead crushing down on him.

After three days of research, he still couldn't pretend to understand the system used by the clerics to catalog it all. Had he not managed to secure himself an assistant to help search for the references he needed, Kyel figured he could have spent years down there in the bowels of the earth without finding anything remotely related to his topic.

As it was, progress was tediously slow. The silent cleric assigned to him had found him a small table with an oil lamp as its sole adornment. Since then, the cleric simply came and went at long intervals, depositing odd assortments of manuscripts, maps, codices, and scrolls of parchment. By the third day, Kyel found himself encased by stacks of books he hadn't even had a chance to thumb through yet.

He had no idea how the man did it, but the brown-robed cleric was much quicker at locating information in the maze of vaults than Kyel was at searching through the man's findings. He was starting to grow desperate. As he stared down at the piles around him, he wondered if the priests weren't trying to throw him off his search by overwhelming him with information.

Most of which was completely useless. Kyel stared down at a dusty leather tome in dismay before carefully closing the ancient cover. After three days, it seemed he was no closer than when he'd first begun. Oh, he'd learned a lot of interesting facts he hadn't known before, but scarcely any of it pertained to the elusive subject of the Well of Tears. Kyel was beginning to consider himself an expert on the history and traditions of Aerysius and was even growing confident in other, darker, areas as well.

His hand moved to a copy of *The Mysteries of Aerysius,* which had been one of the first treasures the cleric had unearthed for him. Before now, that text had been his only source of written knowledge on the subject, and he had refused his assistant when the man had come to take it away. But Cromm's work, like almost everything else, yielded nothing pertinent.

In all his browsing, he'd found the Well of Tears mentioned only three times. The first instance had been almost as an aside, just a vague reference to its link with the gateway. It was mentioned again on a fragment of parchment. It told of how the Well of Tears had been opened once by a rogue mage, who had sought to augment his own strength with the power of the Netherworld. The Well had been successfully resealed that time only with the aid of Aerysius' Circle of Convergence. But then again, it had not been fully open.

The scrap was not very helpful. Kyel was starting to come to the conclusion that Darien had set him to the task of chasing his own tail.

He found the third mention of the Well of Tears in an account of the fall of the Lyceum of Bryn Calazar. The text referred to the subject of the Well frequently throughout its ancient pages. Kyel found himself scanning the book avidly, fascinated by its contents. He hadn't known that the evil which had consumed Caladorn had actually started in Aerysius itself—or, rather, beneath it. Apparently, in the cliffs that supported Aerysius, there was a network of passageways used by the founders of the city. But after hundreds of years, the network had fallen into disuse and was eventually abandoned.

It was discovered again some centuries later by the forbidden cult of Xerys. The followers of Chaos sequestered themselves down there in the dark, using the forgotten halls and chambers as places to convene secret meetings and dark masses, even ritual sacrifices. It was the malevolent priesthood of Xerys that created the Well of Tears in the first place.

According to the text, the gateway to the Netherworld had been established so that the powers of Chaos could be harnessed and used in the war against Caladorn. The Prime Warden of Aerysius, Cyrus Krane, had conspired with Zavier Renquist to establish a link with the Netherworld that would tilt the balance of power in favor of the darkmages. The Well was eventually resealed, but the damage had already been done.

In the end, Bryn Calazar fell and the rest of Caladorn was consumed by the Netherworld's taint. It was a war that had never really been won. The same battle was yet ongoing, the reason why Greystone Keep had been erected to defend the Pass of Lor-Gamorth from the Black Lands in the first place. Renquist had aspired to remake the world in hell's dark image, and the sinister machinations he had fostered in life had lived far beyond his span of mortal years.

The text was fascinating, and even though Kyel knew he shouldn't be spending his precious time reading it, he simply couldn't help himself. The book even contained a map of the vast cave network beneath Aerysius on a half-rotten page.

He wasn't able to resist the temptation. The page was already loose and falling out. So Kyel waited until he was sure the cleric would be away for some time.

Then he quickly pulled the map the rest of the way out, folded it up, and shoved it into the pocket of his cloak alongside the weight of the Soulstone. He felt awful after doing it, sorry to have desecrated the ancient text. Heart pounding, he kept glancing around to see if anyone had noticed his abuse of the book as he continued with his foraging.

By the dim light of the oil lamp, he scanned over the faded letters on a crumbling scroll of parchment, rolled it back up, then stuffed it into the pile collecting at his feet. He reached for the next book on the top of the pile and read the gilt title, *Diplomatic Etiquette.*

Kyel scowled down at the text, wondering what could have possibly been running through his assistant's mind when he'd pulled that one down from the shelf. Surely, there would be no mention of the Well of Tears in such a work. Still, Kyel found himself intrigued. He would have need of such knowledge for his meeting with the Queen of Emmery.

With a shrug, Kyel set the text aside, thinking he would take it with him to read later that night. The next book in the stack was a spectacularly illustrated manuscript with the title *Sieges and Scrimmages: A Compellation of Modern Warfare Tactics and Strategy.* Noticing the date on the cover, Kyel shook his head. The tactics described by the manuscript couldn't possibly be very modern. According to the date on the cover, the book was over three hundred years old.

He took a quick peek at some of the hand-rendered illustrations, then set the manuscript down at his side. Again, he had to wonder why the cleric would have brought him such a thing.

The man returned again, heaping another armload of books onto the top of the tall column already growing by his chair. Kyel nodded his thanks as he reached for the first book on top.

He almost dropped the thin text when he caught sight of the title. *The Family Lauchlin* was inscribed on the leather cover, the first cover he had seen unsullied by years of layered dust.

Kyel's mouth went dry as he flipped open the book and, thumbing past the first pages, considered the flowing script of the author's hand. To Kyel's amazement, he found that the first chapter was an encapsulated overview of Darien's family history.

> *Since the first recorded mention of a Lauchlin in the annals of Aerysius (circa 1266), the name has figured*

prominently in the histories and governance of the Assembly of the Hall. To date, Lauchlin has been the surname of ~~six~~ seven renowned Sentinels and ~~two~~ three Prime Wardens…

Kyel skimmed the rest of the page, amazed, and flipped quickly to the back of the book. But, strangely, he discovered that almost half of the pages were blank. Thumbing forward again, he found the last entry at the end of the written portion of the text:

> **Darien Lauchlin, Grand Master** *(1718 – ~~1747~~): Mage of the Order of Sentinels[(?)]. Son of Grand Master Gerald Lauchlin and Prime Warden Emelda Clemley Lauchlin. Confirmed Acolyte in 1730 at 12 years of age. Mentored by Master Lynnea Nelle, Master Harrison Geary, Master Cedric Fisk, and Grand Master Roland Blentley. Commendations for Meritorious Achievement (6), Dedicated Service (9), and Distinguished Scholar (12). Demerits for Violating Curfew Restrictions (17), Insubordination (4), Willful Defiance (2), Unauthorized Research (3), Trespassing in Restricted Areas (3), and Gross Misconduct (1). Subject of Expulsion Inquiry (1745); suspended from active mentorship and exiled to Greystone Keep (1745–1747). Received fifth tier Transference from Grand Master Ezras Nordric in 1747 at 29 years of age. ~~A casualty of the destruction of Aerysius in 1747~~. The only known survivor of the destruction of Aerysius and self-declared Prime Warden. Foreswore the Oath of Harmony in 1747. Possible second Transference of third tier magnitude, source unknown; report unconfirmed. Father of Gerald Withersby (1746 – 1747).*

Shaken, Kyel read the last line again.

He closed the book's cover. Meiran had given Darien a son, and he didn't even know about it. And, Kyel silently swore to himself, he never would.

Not if he had anything to do with it.

It was going on early evening when he finally broke off his research with a feeling of failure and headed back up the long stairs to the living quarters. His brown-robed assistant led him back to his cell, where Kyel collapsed on the small, hard cot, thoroughly exhausted.

His time had run out, and he still had no idea how to go about sealing the Well of Tears. Darien had given him only three days. Even if it had been three months, Kyel doubted he could have come any closer.

It was almost time for supper, and His Eminence would be expecting him again. Kyel had promised the man three nights of his company, and this was to be their last meeting. Already, he had been forced to yield more information than he had originally planned on. The voiceless old man seemed to know when he was trying to be vague, and Cadmus was exceptionally talented at digging for details and prying facts out of him.

Brushing the lint off his black cloak, Kyel left his small cell and began the journey again, hopefully for the last time. Wandering through underground hallways and large subterranean avenues, he passed a large water clock, pausing as he looked up at it.

He was late.

He hastened past scores of clerics moving by him with distant expressions on their faces. It was a strange life these men led, living down in the dark with only the smell of dusty manuscripts to keep them company and no words ever heard. It seemed such a lonely existence. He couldn't imagine why anyone would want to commit themselves to such a way of life.

Kyel arrived at the door of the high priest's chambers. He found himself confronted by a beaming Cadmus, who beckoned him inside with a wave of his hand. The smell of supper made his mouth water as he crossed the foyer to the dining room.

There, he was amazed to find a bountiful feast spread out across the long table, with more courses than he could possibly eat. Kyel resisted the impulse to throw himself down in his chair and dive in. His stomach had been growling ever since he had made the decision to skip his mid-day meal and work through it instead.

But he hesitated, looking at the high priest seated at the head of the table. Suspicious, Kyel doubted the spread of food was simply a parting gift. He had worked in trade long enough to know when someone wanted something from him. Kyel took his seat across from His Eminence. As he did, he saw that Cadmus' smile suddenly seemed forced. What was going on that he didn't know about?

As Cadmus took the seat opposite him, Kyel sat back and waited nervously for his host to serve him the first course, as was the courtesy even in Covendrey. The old man took Kyel's plate and spooned on the helpings solicitously, even ceremoniously, before offering it back to him.

But as Kyel stared down at the food on his plate, he found himself losing his appetite. Even Cadmus had not spoken a word, and an uneasy silence lingered over the room in the absence of conversation.

"Do you mind telling me what's going on?" Kyel looked at Cadmus instead of the high priest. He regretted the words almost instantly, knowing he was overstepping the bounds of courtesy.

Cadmus shared a long, silent look with His Eminence, then set his fork down carefully across his plate. Standing up, he walked around the edge of the table, having to twist sideways to squeeze his portly frame around the corner of a bureau. From a drawer, he produced an elegantly bound text, which he held tucked against his chest so that Kyel couldn't see the title.

"We have something for you," Cadmus said as he moved back to his seat.

He handed the book across the table to Kyel. The black leather cover was imprinted with the words:

A Treatise on the Well of Tears

by

Master Devrim Remzi

Kyel felt his jaw drop as he folded back the dusty cover, trying not to crack the ancient binding. He quickly scanned the first few pages, realizing the text was exactly what he'd been searching for, exactly what he needed. He couldn't believe it. But instead of feeling appreciative, the text in his hand filled him with ire.

"You've known about this all along," he accused. "Why did you have me waste my time down there for three days?"

He closed the book with a snap that tossed a small cloud of dust up into his face, making his nose itch. The high priest and Cadmus looked at him silently, their expressions blank. What had they been doing, just feeding him rubbish while he could have been halfway to Emmery by now? Delaying him while they milked him for information at night?

"Was it truly a complete waste of your time?" asked Cadmus.

"Yes," Kyel insisted.

But then he thought about it. His research in the vaults had given him a much deeper perspective on the situation they faced, even some revelations.

"No," he admitted grudgingly.

The high priest nodded. At his motion, Cadmus reached into his shirt pocket and withdrew a folded piece of parchment, which he held up between two fingers. Kyel stared at it, at the words inscribed with heavy strokes of black ink: *His Eminence, the High Priest of Wisdom.*

Handing the letter across to Kyel, Cadmus informed him, "We received this note from your master shortly after your arrival."

Unfolding the crisp parchment, Kyel felt fury rising like angry heat to his cheeks. He traced his eyes over it, noting the careful script that seemed almost pressed with force into the page. A strange tingling sensation filled him the moment he started reading.

His Eminence, the High Priest of Wisdom,

Thank you for receiving my acolyte, Kyel Archer. Please provide him with a text which I require, A Treatise on the Well of Tears. If you would kindly allow my acolyte to borrow the original text, I will take great pains to assure that it is returned to you promptly. I regret that I must also beg a favor: please withhold knowledge of the text's existence from my acolyte until after he has spent three days' study in your vaults. I sent Kyel to you under the pretense that he is to be searching for information on the Well of Tears. However, it is my wish that he be provided with the following listed materials so as to progress further in his training. If you can think of any other resources that might be helpful to him, please include them in his course of study. I would be much appreciative, as Kyel does not have the benefit of Aerysius' libraries to broaden his knowledge. Thank you for your time and assistance.

Yours in the Pursuit of Wisdom,

Darien Lauchlin

Prime Warden of Aerysius
Distinguished Order of Sentinels
Grand Master of the Eighth Tier

Below the last line appeared to be an almost comprehensive listing of the books Kyel had been searching through for the past three days. *The Mysteries of Aerysius* was listed first, followed by *The Fall of Bryn Calazar.* The list of titles and authors continued even onto the back of the page. As he scanned down the rough columns, Kyel saw that he recognized most of the works.

But nowhere was there a mention of a book entitled *The Family Lauchlin.* That must have been an addition of the high priest's, probably falling under Darien's request for 'other resources that might be helpful.'

It had been helpful, all right. Kyel just wished he could get the name Gerald Withersby out of his head. It provoked too many images of his own son. He couldn't imagine the horror of seeing Gil's name and death date scrawled on such an entry.

"So this was all just some damned trick?" He crumbled Darien's letter in his hand, shoving it into his pocket. It was just as his trial with the vortex, one of Darien's callous lessons. Kyel was damned near fed up with them.

"You furthered your education, didn't you?" said Cadmus. "And you learned much more than if we had just given you a stack of books and asked you to sit and read. Knowledge is, after all, the First Pillar of Wisdom. Truly, your Prime Warden is as insightful as he is brash."

Insufferable is more like it, Kyel thought, fuming. Lifting *Treatise on the Well* in his hand, he stood up from the table and turned to the high priest.

"Thank you for your hospitality. I'll just be on my way."

But the old man shook his head.

Kyel sank back down in his chair. He set the text in his lap and held his head in his hands, propping his elbows on the table. Beneath him, his plate of food looked as cold as it was ever going to get.

"What is it you wish to discuss this time?" he asked dismally.

"His Eminence desires to know only one last detail before you leave our hospitality. He wishes to know, to what dark use does your master intend to put the Circle of Convergence on Orien's Finger?"

Chapter Twenty-Five
Dangerous Audacity

Auberdale, The Rhen

"He's staying at an inn called the Four Quarrels in Southarbour, Sire. And it appears that Landry was right in his guess. They're sharing a room together, and a bed."

Faukravar nodded, absently stroking his goatee. He had figured as much. It was the only explanation that fit. Temple priestesses simply did not go flitting about in the company of vigorous young men, alone and unescorted.

"Excellent," the king said, feeling his mood lighten. "What else?"

Chadwick Cummings cleared his throat noisily. "I'm sorry, Sire, but he's kept to his room all day. Only the priestess has emerged. Apparently, they must have gotten into some sort of row; she left the inn this morning in quite a heat."

"I can't imagine, with his charm," the king muttered. The comment sparked a round of polite chortles from his entourage.

"Let me think!" He glared them all into silence. He still knew next to nothing about Lauchlin. He felt certain the man was who he claimed, but there were too many inconsistencies about him. The mage's sword bothered him the most.

"So we still don't know for certain whether or not this mage is tame. I don't like it. I don't like it at all." His grip intensified on the arms of his throne. Every puzzle had a solution, even this one. If he could just see it. Then he realized that the solution had already presented itself. A sinister smile formed on his lips.

"You had the priestess followed?"

"Of course, my liege."

The king nodded graciously. "Good. Have her escorted to the North Tower. Should diplomacy fail, we will use her as security."

Cummings stepped forward, a frown on his plump face. "Sire, do you truly think it's wise to provoke him?"

"Why not? He provoked me, didn't he? Let's just see if he can maintain his cloak of arrogance when he finds out we have his whore locked up in chains."

The shadows of the city were lengthening by the time Darien turned away from the window. He had been there often on and off throughout the day, staring out through the rippled glass at the busy streets below. He was growing weary of the constant bustle of people that moved beneath his window like a solemn and anonymous procession.

He had lost track of the number of white dresses he'd seen gliding by, yet none had brought Naia back to him. It was as if the priestess had been simply swept away by the tides of people flowing through the city streets. The hour was growing late, and he had no idea where she could possibly be.

If something had happened to her, it was his fault. Vaguely, he wondered if Naia's disappearance was some sort of punishment for his transgressions. Perhaps the vengeful goddess he'd sold his soul to was exacting atonement for his sins.

Darien realized now the magnitude of the injury he'd committed when he had chosen to lift Naia's veil. He hadn't thought the decision through. He had let his emotions rule him in a moment of vulnerability, and now he was paying the price.

At least he could give her the answer she wanted. He'd told Kyel once that sometimes it felt as though he were still falling from the cliff. He thought he had finally found someone to pull him back from the edge, another miracle like the Bird Man. He knew better, now.

What had happened last night had been the wrong place, the wrong time. The wrong person. He couldn't expect Naia to save him from the cliff's edge. He couldn't risk the real possibility he might pull her over with him.

He loved her too much for that.

Again, he was reminded of the ancient Bird Man who had saved his life. *Birds are smart*, the old man had said. *They always know when it's time to fly.*

It was Naia's time to fly. Perhaps she had flown already. If not, then he would somehow find the strength to open the door of the cage he had so selfishly placed around her. Then he would say goodbye, stand back, and watch her go.

A soft pattering noise tapped on the window. Looking up, he saw it was starting to rain. Once, he had loved the sound of the rain. He could remember many nights, lying awake late at night with Meiran in his arms, listening to the sound of the rain splattering against the window in her bedchamber.

Meiran was another woman he'd simply had no business being with. Why was he always drawn to the very things he shouldn't have? The only two women he had ever loved were forbidden him. Meiran was dead now, her soul condemned to hell because he had ignored tradition and chosen to take her anyway.

And now Naia was missing.

The parallel was too complete, too decisive. The more he thought about it, the more it filled him with dread.

Naia had left her pack, and her horse was still in the stable. She hadn't flown. Her coat was still folded neatly on the chair. Outside, there was a downpour. Naia would not be caught out in such weather without her coat. Even if she was furious with him, she was also sensible. She would have returned by now.

There was only one explanation left, and it made perfect sense. Darien cursed himself. He should have seen this coming. His mother had warned him about the King of Chamsbrey. And, if he were Faukravar, Darien figured he probably would have done the same.

The King had taken Naia to use as leverage against him. The only question that remained was what he was going to do about it.

It was really no question at all. One woman he loved had already been sacrificed simply because she'd made the mistake of loving him back. He would be damned if he was going to let that happen a second time.

Darien paused only long enough to test his blade before slapping the baldric on over his shoulder. He stuffed the white cloak into his pack and started to reach for his gloves. But he drew his hand back instead.

By taking Naia, the King had made an open declaration of war. And if Faukravar wanted a war, then that was exactly what he was going to get.

It was It was well past dark by the time he arrived back at Glassenburgh Castle. The rain had finally stopped, but his clothes were soaked through to the skin. It was bitterly cold. Darien shivered as he let go of the wall and dropped to the ground on the other side. It took only the slightest ripple of shadow to elude the watchful eyes of the guards as he walked toward the moat.

He gathered in the web of shadow that surrounded him and crossed the drawbridge. Once inside the bailey, he pressed himself against the wall and loosened the web. The shadows melted away, dissipating back into the night.

He removed his pack and sword, setting them down. Drawing out the white cloak, he pulled it on over his shoulders, fixing it in place. When he stepped away from the wall, his clothes were once more fully dry. He reached for the hilt of his sword, checking to make sure that the blade was loose in its scabbard. Then he stalked across the yard toward the castle's entrance.

This time, the guards saw him coming. That was the last thing they saw.

Drawing his blade, Darien sliced out with four quick, successive strokes. As he stepped through the castle's doorway, he left behind only dead men on the steps. He slammed his blade home, not bothering to wipe the wet sheen of blood from the steel.

Inside, he found the castle lit for an occasion, the sound of music and ringing laughter coming from a hall to his left. Darien followed the noise of distant applause as he strode down the empty hallway beneath a glowing spread of chandeliers. He moved as if in a dream, eyes loosely focused on the hallway ahead, the sounds of the castle muted and indistinct.

He turned a corner and vaguely noted the hazy shapes of people spilling in and out of a doorway as if moving through a mist. They were dressed formally, the women in long gowns of silk and velvet, the men in capes and embroidered vests.

Darien was hardly aware of the press of people around him as he inserted himself into the crowd. He didn't notice the frowns of the men who stepped back away from him. He couldn't feel the eyes of the women running over him as he moved through the doorway.

The fog that glazed his senses abruptly fell away, shattered by the sound of a woman's scream immediately followed by a ringing shriek of steel.

Someone had noticed the sword at his back. Or the star. Whichever. It made no difference.

The music stopped playing as people turned toward the sound of the commotion. All movement in the ballroom ceased as every face turned, fixing solely on him.

He had walked into a gala.

At the far end of the hall, a quartet of musicians slowly lowered their instruments as the motion of crossbows being raised drew his attention upward to the gallery.

Over the heads of the guests, he could see the King seated on a raised dais at the far end, flanked by his lackeys. Faukravar's eyes were dark and coldly seething.

The cruel look on the King's face washed away any doubt Darien had left. Provoked to a rage of fury, he stepped forward as the crowd parted before him, opening a clear path between himself and the King.

He trembled as he strode between the ranks of guests, the cold anger that filled him inflamed by the taunting promise in the King's malicious glare. He crossed the length of the room, ignoring the threat of the guards coming toward him. He didn't pause, even as the first man stepped forward to take him.

The crowd surged back as Darien slid his sword out and drew

it downward, parting the flesh of the man all the way from his neck to his crotch.

He brought his sword around, sliding the steel under the next man's guard. He kicked the dead man off his blade, watching the body crumble to the floor. Darien stepped over the corpse as the mob surged back from him.

He closed on the dais as the rest of the guards fell back to protect their King.

The sound of wails and desperate weeping seemed strangely distant in his ears, as if the crowd behind him was very far away or in another world entirely.

Eyes only for Faukravar, Darien reached out with his mind and flung the guards away from him, throwing the men backward against the walls with a gust of solid air.

On the throne, the King glowered down at him as Darien sheathed his sword and mounted the steps to the dais.

He didn't slow his pace. Shaking in rage, Darien advanced on Faukravar and backhanded the man across the face.

The King's head whiplashed around as the golden circlet of his crown tumbled to the floor and rolled off the dais. Bracing his hand on the back of the throne, Darien clutched the man's collar and hauled him bodily out of his seat.

"Where is she?"

Dumping him back down, Darien simply waited. The King slowly brought a hand up and touched it to the red mark on his cheek, eyes glaring defiance.

"I thought it expedient to have her detained. If anything happens to me, your lover will suffer the same fate."

Darien shook his head. "No. I have neither the time nor the patience to play that game. Have Naia brought to me here, now, or I swear by the gods I'll kill you with a thought."

His words provoked a stir of movement in the gallery as the crossbows trained at his back adjusted their aim. Faukravar spared a glance at his recovering guards.

"Your threats grow just as tiring as they are empty. Since you've done no real harm here tonight except by the common steel of your blade, I must assume you've sworn the Oath of

Harmony. There is nothing you can do to touch me with your power."

Darien scowled as he raked his sleeve back to expose the angry red scars on his right wrist. He held his arm up before Faukravar's face, watching the King's eyes slowly widen. He reached out from within, caressing the man's mind with the honed edge of his wrath.

A change came over the King's face. His cheeks went white, jaw clenching in pain. Trembling, his hands clutched the arms of the throne as he threw his head back, gasping a long and shuddering breath.

"Release her!" Darien commanded, wrenching Faukravar's mind.

The King slumped forward, moaning.

Darien waited as Faukravar recovered enough to draw himself up again. The defiance in his eyes was gone, replaced by a look of terror.

Faukravar raised a shaking hand, signaling his men.

Darien stood back, sweeping his eyes over the diminished crowd. Two men ran out even as more guards spilled into the back of the room. The guests who remained were few and seemed frozen in place, staring with looks of horror in their eyes.

He stood quietly, arms clasped behind his back, as long minutes dragged by. Gradually, the pulsing careen of his heart returned to normal, the rage that consumed him slowly dissipating.

He stabbed a glance over his shoulder at the King. "If she's suffered any harm, you truly will wish it was my brother here instead of me."

Faukravar lowered his eyes, either too frightened or too repulsed to meet his gaze.

Darien's breath caught as a small contingent of guards swarmed into the ballroom, Naia in their midst. The priestess' white dress was rumpled, her veil disarrayed. But Naia moved with a stately grace as she seemed to flow toward him through the parted crowd of onlookers.

Then she saw him.

A look of dismay formed on her face as she took in his blood-splattered clothes, saw the bodies of the fallen guards that impeded her path. The ashen face of the King, crownless, on his throne.

Naia stopped in her tracks, her skin paling to a shade just darker than her snowy gown. Darien felt his heart sicken as Naia's expression defeated him as surely as he had just defeated the King.

Darien slid the blood-stained cloak from his shoulders, shoving it back into his pack in a crumbled heap. He was exhausted, his head aching as he moved over to a bowl of water on the table. He dipped his hands into it and scrubbed them together violently, the water in the bowl turning a murky shade of red. He shook his hands dry, then walked back to where he'd slung his baldric over the back of a chair. As he reached for it, he felt Naia's hand on his arm.

"This morning, I asked you to make a decision."

It was the first time she'd spoken since they had left the castle. He drew the baldric on and lifted his pack over his shoulder.

He said, "In two days, I leave for Orien's Finger with the King's army. You won't be coming with me."

She blinked, staring up at him with an injured look. "Why not?"

There were too many reasons to name. He chose the one that mattered most. "In the past few months, I've lost everything I've ever cared for. You are the one thing I have left that matters to me at all. I don't think I could stand it if I lost you, too."

She raised her hand toward him, reaching up to stroke his face. Darien turned his head away from her touch, drawing back. Then, thinking better of it, he bent and pressed a kiss against her forehead, trailing his hand down the sheer fabric of her veil.

Solemnly, he whispered, "Goodbye, Naia. Fly free."

He moved out into the dim light of the hallway, shutting the door quietly behind him as he left.

Chapter Twenty-Six
Desperate Measures

Pass of Lor-Gamorth, The Front

The Pass of Lor-Gamorth was obscured by swells of fog that clung to the flanks of the Shadowspears. From his perch on a ridge overlooking the gorge, Traver could see nothing but the few men that shivered at his side, clustered together for warmth. It was as though the world more than ten paces away didn't exist. Even the light in the clouds seemed muted to a wraith-like glow.

With a trembling hand, Traver raised his limp waterskin to his lips, tilting his head back. When nothing came out, he shook the tanned goat's stomach next to his ear. All he heard was rattling ice. He tossed the waterskin down by his side.

He could feel Henley's body shivering, pressed up against him. The Valeman coughed, a wet and rasping noise that made Traver glance sideways at him in concern.

It was the third day since they had abandoned the keep. Traver wished they were out of the pass. Already, they could have been down from the mountains and out into the light and warmth of the plains below.

But Garret Proctor had ordered them to do anything they could to slow the Enemy advance. So that's what they were doing—or trying to do. Traver wondered how much longer they could keep it up. They had already lost a quarter of their number, as much to the relentless cold as to the whispering, black-fletched shafts that fell out of the sky.

Henley coughed again, and this time Traver could feel the Valeman's whole body spasm against him.

The sound of a birdcall drifted out of the stillness of the pass, a low and hollow-sounding *whooo-oo*. The noise made Traver start, his hand going to the hilt of his sword.

Men staggered to their feet, eyes darting as they scanned the haze of mist. Traver patted Henley on the back in a gesture of comfort as the Valeman pushed himself to his feet with a grimace. Trudging forward, Traver moved to stand at the edge of the ridge, looking down at the swirling ocean of fog that obscured the approaches.

Nothing happened for minutes. He started to hope that maybe the birdcall had been a mistake. The appalling silence that choked the Shadowspears remained undisturbed, as complete as the eternal night.

Then he heard it, softly at first, like the drone of a distant waterfall. As the sound built gradually, Traver could make out the deliberate cadence of it. The noise swelled, became a rumbling quake that shuddered the mountains as it drew ever nearer. Thousands of shod feet moved beneath them.

Henley's barked order spurred them into motion.

Traver crouched beside the pile of boulders at his side and shoved one forward with all his might. The rock's sharp surface raked against his numb fingers, but he felt no pain as the boulder rolled off the edge of the ridge, tumbling down into the line of advancing infantry below.

The sounds of commotion and screams echoed above the clamor of Enemy drums as a rain of stone hailed down all along the ridgeline. Bowstrings hummed, and a cloud of arrows parted the mist, arcing into the pass. Volley after volley hissed over the edge.

Traver gritted his teeth as the numbness in his hands turned into a throbbing ache. But he kept moving, shoving stone after stone down the slope, while the rest of his company labored to do the same. Then another noise rose over the cries of death and panicked screams, drowning out even the sound of the war drums.

"Fall back!"

Traver ignored the command long enough to heave one last

rock over the slope, then turned and sprinted away, just as a wave of black-armored warriors spilled over the ridge behind him.

He leaned forward, arms pumping at his sides as he tried to catch up to the men fleeing ahead of him. Whispering death hissed by all around as black-fletched arrows found their marks. In front of him, men were dropped in mid-stride, slumping forward with dark shafts bristling their backs. Traver sprinted for all he was worth.

It wasn't fast enough.

A lance stabbed downward, grazing the side of his cheek. Grabbing for his sword, Traver staggered as a warhorse wheeled back around in front of him. He could see the shadow of a face beneath the rider's helm. The lance dropped and angled at his chest, the dark warrior kicking his mount forward to charge again. Traver glanced desperately for any means of escape, but all he could see was the flooding tide of infantry behind him.

Turning back to the charging horse, he brought his sword up and swept it back over his shoulder. Then he brought the blade down with every last ounce of strength he possessed.

His arms shuddered from the impact as his sword sheared through the armor on the animal's neck. The horse went down, tumbling. One of its hooves clipped him in the leg and he fell with it, losing his grip on his sword. The blade flew from his grasp, spinning away as Traver fell to the dirt.

He started to get up, but for some reason his legs wouldn't work. He struggled, desperately clawing at the black earth with his hands, but his lower half simply wouldn't budge. With a frustrated scream, he wrenched his head back far enough to see the twisted form of the dead horse collapsed across his legs.

He did the only thing he could think of and squirmed up against the belly of the dead animal, tucking his head into the gap between the spread forelegs. Closing his eyes, he prayed to his sweet Lady Luck as the storm broke over him.

"We can't take another day of this," Craig warned, surveying their tattered campsite nestled in the cleft of a ravine. There were no fires, just a few scattered tents, and nothing but scores of men huddled together in tight clusters, shivering against the icy chill of the wind.

The force commander nodded, his cold eyes looking out at the campsite and seeing none of it. Instead, his eyes were loosely focused on something in the air right in front of him. There was nothing there; there never was. Ever since they'd abandoned the fortress, his gaze was drawn often to something Craig simply couldn't see. His eyes would wander, sometimes for minutes on end, tracing the empty air in front of his face.

"We go down tomorrow," Proctor announced.

Chapter Twenty-Seven
The Field of Tol-Ranier

The Field of Tol-Ranier, The Rhen

The first pale streaks of dawn were just beginning to gray the horizon as Darien looked down on the ancient battle site known as the Field of Tol-Ranier. There, the camp of the King's northern army lay spread out before him in orderly rows of black tents that stood out against the glistening white sheen of winter's first snowfall.

The sight of the encampment bothered him. It had been two days since he'd ordered Faukravar to prepare his army for the march, and yet it seemed that no measures had been taken to arrange for such an expedition. As Darien considered the silent encampment below, a slow anger filled him.

It was still very early. Yet, there should have been more movement than he could see among the tents. Soldiers should have been about stoking cook fires, honing their weapons, and preparing for the routines of the day. But instead, the encampment of Faukravar's army looked nearly deserted, just a token few men left behind to give the suggestion that there might be more.

He kicked his heels into the Tarkendar's sides, sending the horse forward down the hill at a springing trot. Darien reached down, feeling at his side for the comfort of the sword fixed to his saddle. He wrapped his fingers around it, the leather laced around the hilt rough and soothing to his skin.

He was glad he had lingered in the city as long as he had, shadowing Naia until she had finally slipped out in the falling snow, not knowing that her departure was remarked by a silent observer looking down from the city walls. Darien had feared Faukravar would move against her again, but now he knew why the King hadn't. The Vile Prince had been making other, more sinister, plans.

The camp ahead was a trap. He could sense it. A trap rigged to spring if he stepped his foot into it. But even with that knowledge, Darien felt no fear. There was little they could do if he was prepared.

And so he was. He had spent a lot of time in thought over the last two days, summoning the strength he would need to face the trials that awaited him in the days ahead. Laying new plans, altering old ones. Taking what he knew from his training and adapting it to new, more deadly, applications.

Naia's departure had helped, more than she could ever know. She had taken with her his heart, leaving him with only a festering wound in its place. Which was good. The emptiness that now filled him knew no compassion. Without compassion, there could be no pain, no mercy, no remorse.

With those feelings set aside, he was free to transform into what it was necessary he become: a weapon melded together with purpose. Tempered by Arden's fire, quenched by Naia's love. Forged on the anvil of Proctor's cruel cunning, dedicated in the font of Meiran's spilt blood.

There was nothing they could do to touch him. For the first time ever, he was truly Unbound.

The few men left behind in the encampment looked up as he rode through their midst. There was no surprise on their faces, no shock at the sight of his cloak. But there was fear.

Darien could almost smell it as he rode past them: a sickening, rank odor that disgusted him. He rode through the camp, past long lines of tents and doused fires. All the while, he was followed by the nauseating stench of their fear. He couldn't ignore it. He couldn't make it go away. It infected him.

Reaching out from within, Darien tasted the magic field. It was a delicate, throbbing pulse that flowed through him, following the contours of the surrounding landscape. It moved in a north-westerly direction, pointing like a compass arrow directly toward

Orien's Vortex. The rhythm of the field was peaceful, like a slow and stately dance.

He kept his mind open to it as he directed the warhorse up a snow-covered hill, the animal's hooves making crunching noises in the loose white powder. At the summit, he drew back on the reins as the gelding sidestepped with a nervous snort.

Faukravar's army waited at the base of the slope in front of him. The soldiers were formed into divisions, with light cavalry in the front flanked by ranks of infantry, perhaps twelve thousand strong. Archers stood ready, bows raised skyward with arrows already nocked. And behind him, Darien could hear the empty encampment stirring.

The trap had sprung.

Glancing behind, he saw soldiers pouring out of the tents, hundreds of them, running through the snow with weapons drawn. At the same time, the archers in front of him released their bowstrings, hurling a thick cloud of arrows that seemed to choke the very sky. Darien watched the arrows arc upward, waited until they curved overhead and began their plunging descent. Smiling grimly, he drew deeply on the currents of the magic field.

The air around him shivered, then lashed out at the cloud of arrows like the crack of a thousand whips with a thousand angry tails. The arrows shattered, splinters of pulverized shafts drifting through the air. There was a sound almost like falling hail as broadheads rained down from the sky, splashing harmlessly to the snow.

Darien signaled his horse with the pressure of his legs. The gelding swept forward along the crest of the hill, moving quickly up to speed, sprinting with all its great heart to deliver him from the jaws of the closing vice.

On his right, the soldiers spilling from the encampment were almost on top of him. And on his left, a thundering wedge of cavalry was hurling up the hill.

The two jaws of the vise snapped closed behind him. The gelding reared on its hind legs, spinning around as a twisting rope of flame snaked across the ground, blooming instantly into a crackling wall of fire that thrust upward into the sky. Horses screamed, striving to break their momentum. The acute intensity of the heat forced the soldiers pursuing him to fall back.

Darien gazed upon his creation with a feeling of pride. The roar of the fire drowned out all other noise, waves of heat roiling in the air above licking tongues of flame. There was no smoke; nothing was burning. The fire fed itself, a creature of pure, voracious energy.

Darien compelled his horse toward it.

The gelding wanted to balk, so he wrapped its eyes in shadow and silenced the sound of the blaze in its ears. The heat did not touch them as they moved into the flames, but the wind of the fire did. It savaged his cloak and whipped his hair, rippling his horse's long mane. Engulfed by the flames and yet unconsumed, Darien leaned his head back and savored the rapturous wonder of the magic field surging like a torrent through his mind.

They passed through the heart of the fire and emerged again on the other side. Releasing his hold on his horse's senses, Darien let the blaze behind him slowly die. Ahead, the men of Faukravar's army stood as if dazed, weapons lowered, staring with mouths slackened.

No one moved to confront him as Darien directed his mount down the hill and out onto the Field of Tol-Ranier. Men stepped back as he moved past them. Their eyes followed him as he rode by, keeping his horse at a swaying trot right through the heart of Faukravar's army.

When at last he reached the small group of mounted officers on the far side of the field, he drew up beside the man wearing a general's insignia on his uniform. The soldier's face was ashen gray, his expression sagging. Darien regarded him for a long, silent moment. Then he informed him:

"You are relieved of your command."

The general blinked.

"Which one of you is his second?"

A young, aristocratic man with a contemptuous sneer nodded his head at him. "That would be me."

"You're relieved, as well."

The officer's stare glared hatred as his hand darted for his blade. Darien's eyes caught the motion. With a cry, the young officer retracted his hand, staring in horror at the glowing red hilt of his sword. Bringing his hand up, he gaped at the angry burns that covered his fingers.

Confident that there would be no further resistance, Darien backed his horse up until he could take in the small group of men together as a whole.

"The Enemy is advancing in numbers not seen since the fall of Caladorn," he said. "Which man of you has the courage to lead this army in a battle that will decide the fate of everything you know and everything you love?"

For a long moment, no one moved. Finally, a young man near the back looped the reins of his horse over the pommel of his saddle and dismounted. Walking forward, the young officer looked up at Darien with wide brown eyes that held no fear.

"I do, Prime Warden."

The young man dropped to his knees in the snow and leaned forward until his face was pressed up against the loose powder that covered the Field of Tol-Ranier. He remained there as his fellows stared down at him contemptuously.

"You may rise," Darien said. "What is your name?"

"Lieutenant Malcolm Wellingford, Prime Warden." The young officer stood up. He drew his sword and offered it to Darien hilt-first.

Darien received the sword, holding it up to inspect it. It was a common piece of steel, not elegant or ornamented in any way. The blade had seen much use, but it still held a keen edge. Extending it forward, he noted that the balance was good.

Darien nodded, handing the sword back. "This blade will serve me well. Do you swear on the honor of your house to follow wherever my lead should take you, deferring to whatever order I give immediately and without question?"

"I do so swear, Prime Warden."

Darien nodded solemnly. "General Wellingford, please issue the command to form ranks."

He waited as his new general darted back to recover his horse.

Darien turned back to address the remaining officers:

"Any man not wholly committed to me should leave right now. Otherwise, if you choose to desert later, such an act will be considered treason. You shall be hunted down and slain without mercy."

He waited as the men before him exchanged nervous glances. Faukravar's former general turned his horse around with a quick jerk of the reins. He withdrew from the field, back stiff with injured pride, followed by three others.

The remaining officers stared after the departing men. But when they turned back to Darien, each man's expression was hardened with fresh resolve.

As the soldiers spread out across the field drew together and assembled, their officers dismounted and knelt silently in the snow. Darien accepted their oaths gravely. Then he rode out before the ranks of gathered men, and there drew up his mount. As he did, he sent his mind outward on the tides of air above the field, weaving shadows overhead to cover the face of the sun.

Night fell across the Field of Tol-Ranier, the daylight fading into darkness. An eerie stillness descended upon the plain as all motion ceased and all eyes were drawn toward him. Darien surveyed the soldiers before him, measuring the mettle of the men. Then he raised his voice to be heard above the compressed, silent tension.

"Greystone Keep has always held the Pass of Lor-Gamorth, and the pass has always held the North against the Enemy. But Greystone Keep has fallen. The North will soon fall also, unless we make a stand.

"We march to Orien's Finger, where we will be faced with two of the greatest Enemy hosts ever assembled. You do not go friendless and alone; the forces of Emmery will be with you.

"And I will be with you, as well. I am Prime Warden Darien Lauchlin, Grand Master of the Eighth Tier. I am the last surviving Sentinel of Aerysius, and I am also Unbound.

"We are all that stands between our homeland and the fate that befell Caladorn of old. Should we fail, then our lands will be desecrated, and our families enslaved by the Enemy. But if we succeed, then all of you will go to your graves knowing that it was by your courage alone that every last nation of the Rhen survives in the light and hope of the sun."

He released the gathered shadows and allowed the morning to dawn again, the sun emerging to glare brilliantly above in a clear morning sky. A thunderous cheer went up as the ranks before him collapsed. Discipline abandoned, the men swarmed forward around him like a breaking wave.

Darien closed his eyes and, smiling quietly, bowed his head.

He woke before the break of dawn to the sounds of the encampment already stirring. Darien dressed in the darkness, not even bothering with simple magelight. It had been hard to awaken. The air of the tent was cold, and his blankets warm. Sleep crusted his eyes, and he found himself terribly groggy.

It was still dark when he emerged and stood gazing out across the snowy field. Already, the men had most of the camp broken down. His own tent was one of the few still standing.

Darien opened his mind to the magic field. Ever since Naia had left, it was the only thing he seemed to take comfort in. He groped for it constantly, for no real reason other than the contentment it brought. Sometimes Darien fought with himself, knowing that the allure of the field was starting to become something of an obsession. But often he reached for it unconsciously, not even aware he was doing so until it was too late.

Arriving at the command tent, he found his young general busily poring over a list scrawled across a strip of parchment. At least the boy could read. That was more than he'd hoped for. He really didn't care, one way or the other. Darien hadn't accepted the young man's oath because he was in need of a strong commander. He had accepted Wellingford because he needed someone biddable.

Strolling up behind him, Darien looked over his shoulder and studied the first few lines of the list. "I see your King finally came through with the provisions I ordered."

Wellingford looked back at him, seeming a bit startled. Handing over the parchment, he said, "We received the wagons in the night. But His Grace only sent enough supplies to last us twelve days. That will do little more than get us there."

Darien nodded, scanning down the list appraisingly. "That's all I requested. We'll need to travel swift and light." Handing the list back, he started to turn away.

"But, Prime Warden, what are we going to do about supplies for the march home?"

Darien shrugged. "We'll just have to worry about that when the time comes."

The boy's brow wrinkled up. "You don't think we'll be coming home, do you?"

Darien didn't respond. Instead, he turned and strode away.

He walked over to the edge of the encampment, where he stood silently observing the last details being completed. In a short amount of time, the camp was entirely broken down, the men forming up in a long column for the march.

Movement on the ridge caught his eye. The King was riding toward them, surrounded by his knights, pennants fluttering from their lances. Faukravar himself was suited for battle, his thin frame covered with gleaming black plate. The King of Chamsbrey rode with his plumed helm in his hand.

Faukravar's party drew up, the King gazing down into Darien's eyes with rigid contempt. After a long moment, the man stated in a somber voice:

"Ever have the Kings of Auberdale ridden to war with the armies of Chamsbrey."

Darien nodded weary acceptance. There was little he could do about it. "As you like," he said, then added, "Just don't get in my way."

Chapter Twenty-Eight
Dreams

Pass of Lor-Gamorth, The Front

Traver awakened to a sharp, stabbing pain in his hand matched only by the throbbing ache in his head. He squinted up into the flickering lights of the clouds, wondering how he wasn't dead. The pain flared like a knife thrust. Traver recoiled his hand. As he did, he saw the beak of the scavenger bird that had mistaken his warm flesh for a piece of meat.

"Go away, damn you!"

The vulture spread its wings and hopped backward. Traver threw a small rock at the thing to get it gone. It flapped into the air a few feet before alighting back again, this time even nearer. Apparently, the thing didn't have the common decency to wait until he was dead.

Traver wanted to scream in frustration.

"All right," he said. "I'll tell you what. You go snack on somebody else for a while. Come back in a few days, and if I'm still here, you can have as much as you like. I won't even make a fuss about it."

When the bird bobbed its head, Traver took it for a sign of agreement. Turning his face away, he made one last attempt to pull his legs out from under the dead horse's carcass. But he couldn't get enough traction in the crumbled dirt. All he succeeded in doing was clawing sand into his face.

When he felt the bird's beak again, this time on his shoulder, he did scream.

"I told you to go find somebody else!"

"There isn't anyone else," responded a somber voice. "At least, no one else alive."

Startled, Traver craned his neck enough to take in the miracle of Corban Henley's face. He wanted to laugh. That thick red beard was such a beautiful sight. But instead, he found himself weeping.

"There, lad," Henley soothed, patting his shoulder. "It's good you like to hear the sound of your own voice so much. Otherwise, I never would have found you."

Traver beamed up at him. But then it occurred to him to wonder what Henley was still doing there. The skirmish was over, the rest of their fellows fled back to the camp in the canyon, or perhaps moved on by now.

As he stared at Henley's face, Traver thought he saw the answer. The big Valeman sitting beside him was scraped up, and there was a tightness around his eyes. Henley was in a lot of pain.

"What happened to you?" Traver asked.

Henley scowled, reaching down to pat his leg. "Broken. Snapped right clean. I guess neither one of us will be going anywhere."

Traver's cheerful mood took a plunge. "But, you can walk, right? You found me, didn't you?"

Henley shook his head. "I can hop a small distance, but that's as good as I can do. I'm sorry, lad, but I can't lift that carcass off you."

Traver grimaced. A snowflake fluttered down through the air to alight on his cheek. "So what are we going to do?"

"We go to sleep." Henley's voice was calm. "Maybe we'll dream a bit. If we're lucky, they'll even be good dreams."

Traver nodded. He could do that. It didn't sound so bad. He just wished it didn't have to be so awfully cold. He drew his cloak around himself as tightly as he could as another snowflake settled on his skin. At his side, he heard Henley coughing, a weak and rasping gurgle.

"Three feet of snow, or thereabouts," Craig grumbled, gazing out on the miraculous change that had transformed the Shadowspears overnight. No longer black, the sharp peaks above him glistened a deadly white. The men had scarcely enough blankets and cloaks for the summer months, and the onset of winter was like a harsh and bitter death grip.

The force commander had put the men to work as the blizzard broke over them, using their shields to pile the drifting snow up around their tents. Only eleven men had been lost during the night. It should have been much worse. The cover of snow around the tents created an insulating barrier. His own tent had been almost uncomfortably warm with twelve other men packed inside. In the middle of a raging snowstorm, Craig had woken up three times during the night dripping wet with sweat.

But now the camp was struck. His men stood shivering, their sockless feet crusted with ice that fell down into their boots. Craig staggered as he walked toward them, his own feet breaking through the treacherous surface, sinking down through the snow at every step.

He jerked his foot up with a rain of ice and grunted in dismay to find that his boot hadn't come up with it. Glaring down into the dim blue hole of the track he'd just made, Craig was forced to bend down and dig his hand around in the snow to retrieve his boot.

Behind him, Garret Proctor stared out vacantly across the white canyon, his cloak plastered against his back by the wind. As Craig inverted his boot to dump the snow out of it, he risked a quick glance back at the man.

"The path will have been sheltered in the night," Proctor said. "Get the men down to it, and you'll find the way ahead clear. Leave behind the dead and wounded."

Craig stared at him, appalled. "We can't leave living men behind for the Enemy—you know what they'll do to them!"

"Then don't leave any living men behind."

To Craig's horror, Proctor withdrew his dagger from its sheath and pressed it into his hand, squeezing his limp fingers tightly around it. Craig gazed down at the misery knife, sickened by the cruel feel of its narrow hilt in his palm.

⊛

Proctor was right, yet again. When they finally found the road in the narrow gap of the pass, it was covered with just a thin sprinkling of snow over a slick layer of ice. The high walls of the canyon had protected it from the storm.

Craig had done his duty with the dagger. It had been tempting to delegate that order, to hand the blade off to one of the men, as Proctor had handed the task to him. But it had to stop somewhere.

They left the dead behind in the ravine, dark and tattered shapes adrift in a calm white sea. Craig hadn't looked back as he turned his horse around and rode away, the beast lunging forward through the snowdrifts.

Somehow, they were still ahead of the advancing Enemy column. Craig could see where they were camped, just a few ridges behind in the twisting coils of the pass, their presence revealed by thin trails of smoke from their fires.

Proctor's mind had not been idle in the night. Somewhere in the dull haze the commander moved through, a tangled skein was unraveling.

At Craig's command, a single fire arrow shot into the sky. A roaring thunder echoed from high above on the cliffs behind them.

Kicking his horse forward at a gallop, Craig tried not to think about the dead men who had stayed behind to light those charges. He rode on as a mountain's weight of snow fell to choke the pass.

"Dig through that, you damned filth," he spat, jabbing his heels into his horse's sides.

Wolden, The Rhen

Wolden was deserted.

At least, it appeared that way to Craig's eyes as he rode at the head of the long column snaking down off the spine of the foothills. Proctor was with him, riding at his side on his dark and rugged stallion. The commander's eyes were narrowed and watering in the brilliance of a sun that, in over fifteen years, his face had seldom looked upon. The men trailing behind rode with their heads lowered, hunched forward in their saddles, their faces tightly drawn. The relative warmth of the afternoon did little to cheer their spirits; they had seen too many horrors.

When they reached the outskirts, it became clear Wolden was indeed abandoned. Not so much as a chicken foraged in the snow in front of the scattered, ramshackle huts. It was a bizarre and haunting sight, rendered even more distressing by the lingering silence that clung to the place. The squeak of an ancient windmill broke the tension of the quiet. Somewhere, a wooden gate squealed open on rusted hinges, pushed by a gust of wind.

"What's this?" he breathed, glaring at the gate that had startled him. To Proctor, he asked, "Is this your doing?"

"Not mine."

"Whose, then?"

Proctor didn't respond. Craig sat forward in his saddle, looking from house to house. Ahead, the lane widened as they approached the town wall. He could see the gate wide open before them. There was something else there, as well. A sign was posted beside the entrance.

Proctor dismounted and strode toward the gate. Craig followed him, glancing sideways at Proctor to find that his commander's eyes had become suddenly, piercingly intent. The old soldier tore the sign down from the wall and strode forward with it. Craig jogged after him through the gate and down a wide, snow-covered street, hurrying to catch up.

Wolden was just as quiet and vacant as its outskirts. Not a soul stirred on the street. The doors of the shops and houses stood shut, many of them barred with beams of wood that looked to have been just slapped up and nailed haphazardly to the frames. The town had been emptied in a hurry.

They turned at an intersection. There, Proctor came to a halt, eyes scanning the buildings that bordered the street. Craig glanced around to see what the man was looking for. The street was empty, except for a fine coating of ice powdered with snow.

The only difference he could see was that many of the doors were standing open to the elements, not closed and boarded up like the rest.

Proctor strode toward the first open doorway. Craig pressed ahead of him, keeping one hand within easy reach of his hilt. The door stood slightly ajar, so Craig pushed it the rest of the way open with the toe of his boot as he moved into the room.

Dozens of unstrung bows lay spread across the floor, arranged in overlapping bundles along with bunches of arrows, hundreds of them.

Craig knelt and lifted a bow from the first pile by his feet, holding it up to inspect. The horn bow had a rustic look about it, though Craig could see that the workmanship was sound. He looked at the strange letters carved into the wood of the bow.

It was a poem. *Song of blood, song of heart.* Turning the bow around, he saw that the poem continued on the other side. *Fly true, true heart, die true.*

Craig found the simple lines powerfully stirring. He started to set the bow back down atop the pile, but hesitated. Instead, he drew it close, feeling an odd surge of sentiment toward the elegant weapon with its poignant verse.

"Horn bows," he muttered. Then he threw his head back and bellowed a whooping battle cry. *"Do you know what this means?"*

The force commander nodded, eyes once again staring fixedly ahead. "We'll hit them hard and break away fast. We will harry them all the way down the corridor."

Chapter Twenty-Nine
To Threaten a Queen

Rothscard, The Rhen

Kyel's last memory of Rothscard hadn't been a pleasant one. The last time he'd looked upon the walls of Emmery's capital, it had been in the company of a pack of condemned convicts and their guards. Then, Rothscard had seemed loathsome and dark, a stinking swelter of dirty people living in trash and filth.

But now, for some reason, the Rothscard he entered seemed altogether different. The stone of the city walls looked pure and white, the towers graceful and soaring. Vibrant banners billowed in the air from the tops of the turrets. The rolling band of hills that embraced the city looked like immaculate, emerald gems.

His horse took the last stretch of road at an eager lope, passing scattered groups of travelers. Kyel let the gelding have its head, waiting until they were almost at the walls before easing back to a trot as they reached the end of the road.

Rothscard's east gate was a tall arch cut into the wall between two fortified guard towers. Kyel guided his horse toward the middle of the passage. On either side of the gate stood groups of Rothscard Bluecloaks who seemed to be doing little of anything besides staring dully at the clusters of people moving through their gate.

As Kyel rode through, he heard one of the guards exclaim, "Isn't that a mage's cloak?"

To his chagrin, Kyel found himself the sudden focus of attention. The guards stared at him with wide eyes, necks craned at the sight of the Silver Star at his back. Kyel was reminded of the scene in Wolden, when the people there had made such a commotion over Darien's appearance. He hoped it wouldn't be like Wolden. Kyel didn't want that sort of trouble.

"Hold up there!" someone shouted.

Kyel sighed and pulled back on the reins, slouching in weariness. He shouldn't have worn the cloak. He should have taken it off, wadded it up, and thrown it away. Now, it was simply too late.

"That's the bloody Silver Star!"

Ringed by more than a dozen guardsmen, Kyel sat back in his saddle and raised his face to the sky. Why couldn't anything ever be easy? Why did every task always have to be so difficult? The gift of the cloak was going to turn out to be another one of Darien's damnable lessons. Just like the vortex or the Temple of Wisdom.

A guard reached up and, taking his horse's reins in his hand, said, "Pardon, Great Master. We're going to have to ask you to hold up for a minute."

"Fine," Kyel muttered, frowning as he realized what the man had just called him. They took him for a full Master, which he supposed was an easy mistake to make.

The guard turned to someone behind him. "Neville, go fetch the captain. Run along, now, lad!"

"What's the problem?" Kyel asked, watching the young Bluecloak dart off, disappearing in the turmoil of the crowd moving around them through the gate. He knew exactly what the problem was but wanted the satisfaction of hearing someone say it.

"Oh, no problem, Great Master," the man said, a wary look on his face. "Just that the likes of you'd be expecting an escort to the palace."

"Oh. Sure. That sounds good."

Hearing his response, the group of men ringed around him exchanged dubious glances. Kyel supposed he probably hadn't sounded very mage-like. He would have to try adopting a more confident air in the future, or no one was bound to believe him. Squaring his shoulders, he tried to strike a more assertive pose as he waited on his horse but found the attempt almost embarrassing. It was hard to look confident when there was a group of brawny men with swords ringed about.

Kyel waited uncomfortably as his horse stood there, swishing its tail at the flies. The guards stood silent, the crowd around them keeping their distance. He was drawing stares from the passersby, a mixture of looks that only made him feel more uncomfortable.

"Do you mind climbing down off that horse?"

Kyel flinched. He twisted around and found himself staring at a man who'd come up behind him and was now examining the longbow that hung from his saddle. The guard's interest in his bow made Kyel feel nervous, even protective. He didn't like the way the man was fingering it, his touch almost a lingering caress. But he did as he was asked, lowering himself to the ground on stiff legs.

The guard walked around his horse, a hand stroking the gelding's coarse winter coat. He was a tall and muscular man. He wore his chin-length hair parted in the middle. His face was exceptionally angular, his eyes stern and discerning. The man moved with an easy grace that reminded Kyel of a cat stalking a bird, precise and deliberate. It also reminded him of the way Darien moved. The similarity was almost uncanny.

"Mages are forbidden to carry weapons, are they not?"

Kyel didn't like the way the guard was standing so close to him, scant inches from his face. It was intimidating. He could feel the man's breath on his cheek.

Trying to meet the guard's eyes, Kyel nodded. "I'm no Master, if that's what you're thinking. I'm just an acolyte."

"What's your business in Rothscard?"

Kyel had rehearsed this line enough times, but actually saying it was a different thing entirely. "I'm here at the request of the Prime Warden. My business is with your Queen."

The guard smiled cagily and shook his head. "The Prime Warden's dead, son. I've seen her corpse myself. I was part of the Queen's entourage when Her Grace went to view it."

Feeling uncertain, Kyel couldn't help looking down. This was the part where it was going to get tricky. From his experience in Wolden and again in the Temple of Wisdom, he was going to be forced to do a lot of talking. Whenever his master's name was mentioned, there was always something to explain.

"There's a new Prime Warden. Darien Lauchlin."

The man's expression creased to an uncertain frown. It was not the reaction Kyel had been expecting. Warily, the guard said, "I've met Darien Lauchlin. Describe him."

Kyel had no idea what to say. "He's tall. Dark hair." He shrugged. That was the best he could do.

The guard tilted his head slightly, moving even closer to Kyel. "When I knew him, Darien was an acolyte, the same as yourself. But there was something different about him that set him apart, something he shared in common with you, actually. Can you tell me what that is?"

Kyel didn't have to think about it long. The man's fascination with his longbow brought the obvious answer to mind. "His sword," he said. "You know of it?"

A slow, arrogant smile bloomed on the guardsman's shadowy face. "Know of it? I'm the one who taught him how to use it." He extended his hand. "Nigel Swain, Captain of the City Guard. Formerly of Aerysius, and formerly of the Arms Guild."

Kyel found himself clasping the man's hand automatically, too stunned to think. "Kyel Archer," he mumbled, impressed by Swain's firm grasp. "I'm Darien's acolyte."

"So the boy thinks he's Prime Warden, now, does he?" Swain delivered a scoffing sigh that fanned his oily hair back from his face. "Aerysius must have fallen on his head. Come on, mount up. I'll get you to the palace. Ever been to Rothscard before?"

Kyel winced, quickly shaking his head. "I've only passed through."

The last time Kyel had visited Rothscard, he'd been in chains. That was scarcely something he wanted anyone to know, even if the man was a friend of Darien's. He wondered what the captain would think of him if he ever found out. It certainly wouldn't help with his current assignment as an ambassador to the Queen.

He waited for Swain to bring his horse around, a dark gray

beast with a scruffy coat. The look in the animal's eye reminded Kyel of its owner.

He couldn't keep his eyes off Swain as they rode, noticing the way the man sat his horse, a reflection of his casually deliberate stride. Kyel was also having trouble dismissing the longsword slung at the man's back. It looked like a copy of Darien's. Or perhaps it was the other way around. Kyel felt almost in awe of the man. Swain had professed an association with the Arms Guild, so he was probably a blademaster.

They turned onto a broad, cobbled street lined with rows of houses stacked one against another. The city was already decorated for Winter's Eve, with bows and bells hung from almost every door, and ribbons wrapped around every lamp post. Even the bare limbs of the trees were bedecked with colored lanterns. The feel of the city made Kyel homesick.

And then Emmery Palace itself came into view. When he saw it, Kyel felt like he'd been there before. In a way, it was almost as though he had. The palace was practically the image of the mayor's home in Wolden, only on a far grander scale.

Swain had him dismount in front of a span of wide marble steps. Two liveried footmen came forward to take their horses, but Kyel was hesitant about handing his over. He reached for the smooth curve of his longbow, wondering if it would be possible to bring it inside. He didn't want to leave the bow there, attached to his saddle.

"Go ahead, bring it along. You may as well enjoy it while you still have the chance."

"What do you mean?" Kyel wondered with a frown.

"Well, once you become a Master, you can't very well have a longbow around, can you?" Swain said with a knowing grin.

But Kyel still felt confused. He knew it was traditional for mages not to carry weapons, but he figured that if Darien was going to prohibit him from keeping the bow, then his master would have done so long ago.

He said, "Darien still has his sword."

"He does, now, does he?" The captain's smile retreated from his face. "Maybe you'd better leave that bow behind, after all."

Kyel didn't like the fleeting look of concern that crossed the man's eyes. Swain had taught Darien the art of the blade, so why should it matter to him if the mage still carried it?

But Kyel thought he knew the answer. There was more to be had in learning a skill than the obvious result. Suddenly apprehensive, Kyel wondered what the man would think if he found out that Darien had gone much further than simply refusing to relinquish his weapon.

He didn't like the feeling he was getting in the pit of his stomach as he followed the captain up the steps. The man led him down a long hall to a circular foyer graced by an enormous vase. Rich tapestries hung from gilt staves, many having an antiquated look. Again, Kyel was reminded of the mayor of Wolden, of the man's obvious passion for art.

They found the Queen in her solarium, standing before a canvas with a paintbrush in her hand. It was not the image Kyel had been picturing, and neither was Romana herself. From Darien's description, he had envisioned the Queen of Emmery as pompous and aloof, a gilded monarch on an ivory throne. But the woman he found in her place defied his expectations. For one thing, she was far younger than he'd anticipated, perhaps even close to his own age.

And she was lovely, in a common sort of way that caught Kyel off-guard. Her gown was silk, but simple, lacking any fancy embroidery or jewels. She wore her dark brown hair in a loose twist that spilled fine curls down her neck, softening her appearance. As Romana turned toward the sound of their entrance, she paused with the paintbrush in her hand.

Nigel Swain swept into a low bow that Kyel tried his best to emulate.

"You may rise."

Her voice was a sweet soprano. Again, quite unexpected.

Swain said, "Your Grace, may I present Kyel Archer, acolyte of the new Prime Warden, Darien Lauchlin."

Romana's eyebrows shot up. Her gaze took in Kyel, lingering on his cloak, then swept back to Swain with a questioning look. Carefully, she set the paintbrush down on the tray of the easel and walked across the room to a small mahogany desk. Rifling through the papers on it, she produced a letter. She held it up for Kyel's inspection, waggling the parchment in the air to draw his attention to it.

"I received this note from one of my most loyal subjects, Mayor Blake Pratson of Wolden. It has been often on my mind of late. In it, Mayor Pratson details a rather bizarre encounter he had with a mage, his acolyte, and a priestess of Death. He failed, however, to mention anything about this Darien Lauchlin aspiring to the office of the Prime Warden."

Kyel found himself taken aback. Thrown off by her appearance, he had almost forgotten that Romana was ruler of one of the largest and most prosperous nations of the Rhen. He couldn't let himself be fooled by the innocent appearance of her face. This was a woman to be reckoned with.

And she had opened their conversation with a direct attack on Darien's right to the title he had claimed. But Kyel had learned from his experience with the clerics of Om. It was just a tactic, a way of trying to put him on the defensive right from the start.

Not wanting to let her strategy succeed, he took a step forward and said, "Begging your pardon, Your Grace, but there was no one else to fill the position." A month ago, he would have never had the nerve to say such a thing to a queen, and certainly not in such a tone.

But Romana did not seem offended in the least. Rather, she actually looked a bit impressed. She went on, unruffled. "This letter addresses some issues I find quite troubling. I assume by your presence here that you were sent to enlighten me?"

Kyel took a deep breath, trying to remember the rest of the speech he had rehearsed all the long way from Glen Farquist. But as he opened his mouth to speak, his mind drew a complete blank. He would have to improvise.

"I really don't know what to tell you, other than what you already know from that letter," he said, with a hastily added, "Your Majesty." Then he summed up the situation with the two Enemy armies, including as many details as he knew.

"Darien believes they'll continue south to Rothscard if not

stopped. He is aware that you have a standing army, and he asks that you yield over command of it to him."

There. It was out. Now there was nothing to do but wait for the tidal wave to break. Glancing sideways at Swain, he saw the man staring at him in astonishment. Romana herself looked stunned. Holding up her hand, the young Queen shook her head, closing her eyes.

"Allow me a moment to try to understand this. You are telling me that I should be expecting an imminent siege any day, and in the same breath asking me to give over my only means of defense?"

He'd known he was asking a lot. But the way she had just summarized his request made it sound downright ludicrous.

Swain stepped forward, inserting himself between Kyel and the Queen. "If I may?"

Romana nodded.

"I know Darien, or at least I used to," Swain said. "He's impudent, he's brash, he's stubborn as a goat, and he marches to no drummer's beat but his own. He's also one of the smartest men I've ever met in my life. I don't know what he has in mind, but I would urge you to hear his man out."

The Queen frowned. But with a graceful dip of her chin, she allowed, "You may continue."

"Thank you, Your Highness," Kyel said, feeling bolstered by Swain's unexpected support. "Darien didn't tell me all of his plans, but I think I've figured out some of it. He would never leave Rothscard defenseless. He plans to use the Circle of Convergence at Orien's Finger to turn back the Enemy."

"By himself?" Romana looked appalled at the very notion.

Kyel gulped. "Well, yes." He shrugged. "And your army."

The Queen whirled around, pacing back toward the window. "This is absurd! Who does he think he is, another Orien?"

Swain nodded, looking confident as he said, "I'm sure that's exactly what he's thinking."

Romana rounded on him with a furious look, demanding, "How do you know this man?"

He reached up and tapped the hilt of his sword. "I trained him in the art of the blade. He was an acolyte at the time, but I agreed to go along with it under his mother's nose. He studied under me for nine years. I probably know him better than he knows himself."

Romana looked aghast. "And what is your opinion of all this?"

The conviction drained from Swain's face. "My opinion?" he echoed, looking unsettled. Slowly, he shook his head. "All I can say is, I wouldn't want to be on the wrong side of Darien Lauchlin if he's got his back up against a wall. And if he never gave up his sword..."

His voice trailed off. His eyes shot up, fixing on Kyel. "He's broken Oath, hasn't he?"

Kyel found himself with no option. He admitted a grudging, "Aye."

The Queen of Emmery gasped. Her hand rose to her mouth as she turned back to Swain. "Then the man is just as rabid as his brother. And if the portrait you have just painted of him is accurate, then he is probably thrice as dangerous."

She seemed to be taking a moment to collect herself. Finally, she turned back to Kyel. "Take this answer back to your 'Prime Warden.' Tell him I have declined his request to yield command of my army. I may yet decide to send my forces northward, but if I do, it will not be to aid his cause—it shall be to hunt him down and destroy him."

Kyel just stared at her. He had expected argument. He had expected refusal. But it never occurred to him that the woman would actually threaten Darien's life.

"But, what of the Enemy?"

Romana merely shrugged. "Thank you for your concern, but these walls have survived sieges in the past. We will survive again; we always do. It is your own kind, young Kyel, that is endangered. Perhaps you should think about that and return to me again in the morning."

It was a dismissal. Kyel just stared at the young, seemingly-innocent Queen for a long moment before turning to leave. He even started walking toward the door. But then he stopped, turning back to her.

"I'll come back in the morning, Your Grace. And when I do, I sincerely hope you've changed your mind. You see, my Prime Warden gave me another message for you: either hand over your army or hand over your crown. Because Darien's back *is* up against a wall. And believe me, he'll do anything it takes to protect your kingdom's future, even if that future doesn't include you in it."

Chapter Thirty
The Jenn

The Cerulean Plains, The Rhen

The dream ended, and there was only darkness. Terrible darkness. And cold. So bitterly cold. He couldn't stop shivering. Traver ached all over, but the worst of the agony was in his hands. He knew he was hot enough to be sweating, but for some reason all he could do was lie there wracked with violent chills that chattered his teeth and rattled his body to the bones. If only he could stop the shaking. It had awakened him from his dream.

He remembered the dream. He wanted desperately to go back there, become a part of that dream again. The dream was important, more important than any reality he could ever know. He had to see them again, to tell them, to warn them…

When he awoke again, the chills were gone, but the pain in his hand was terrible. Traver tried to open his eyes, but all he could see was darkness. He wanted to get a look at his hand, to find out what was wrong with it. His fingers throbbed, sending shooting pains lancing up his arms all the way to his shoulders.

Gradually, it was coming back to him. The dream, the pass. Corban Henley. He remembered falling asleep. At least, he thought he did. And he'd been right; it hadn't really been so bad. It was waking up that was terrible.

He made an effort to sit up. It wasn't much of one. He'd tried to use his hands to push himself up. He realized immediately what an awful mistake that was.

"Don't move," a female voice admonished him from the darkness.

Traver had no problem complying. He lay back, clenching his teeth as he waited for the stabbing pain to fade back to a dull, throbbing ache.

"Drink," the voice said, and he felt a cup pressed against his lips.

The water was cold, and it tasted wonderful. He hadn't realized how thirsty he'd been. Traver gulped it quickly, not caring that he wasn't getting all of it in his mouth. He felt the water running down his chin, dribbling down his neck. When the woman took the cup away, he felt disappointed.

"That's enough, for now," said her calm, easy voice.

"Who are you?" Traver asked, wishing there was light enough to see her face.

"My name is Kayna."

"Where am I?"

The voice hesitated. "You are in the tent of my husband."

He didn't like the sound of that. Especially since he was naked beneath the blankets. That's all he needed: some woman's husband coming home enraged at finding a naked man in his bed. Wouldn't that be just his luck? He could hardly defend himself the way he was. It occurred to him to wonder if maybe the woman's husband was responsible for saving his life.

"Where's Henley?" he asked, remembering the Valeman.

"I don't know who that is. You are the only one we found alive on the killing ground."

Her words brought a pang of remorse. It wasn't fair. Henley was one of the best men they had. He should have been the one to survive. Traver found himself wondering what kind of dreams the Valeman was having. He hoped they were good dreams.

"You're lucky we found you." The woman's voice drifted through the darkness.

He asked, "What were you doing in the pass?"

"One of our herds strayed away a few nights back. We followed their tracks up into the Mountains of Shadow. When we found them, the beasts were already slain and slaughtered.

But my husband found you instead."

"I suppose I owe him."

"You owe him your life. When he found you, you were almost frozen to death. The vultures had already been at your meat."

The thought was repulsive. Traver remembered the bird, the one that had mistaken him for a piece of carrion. "Am I whole?" he whispered, though he wasn't sure he wanted to know the answer.

There was a long pause. "Nearly. The frost and the birds got to your hands. We had to cut off two of your fingers."

"*No.*" It couldn't be. He wouldn't have a chance of gripping a hilt with two fingers missing. In the space between horror and grief, he felt his anger rising.

"You had no right!" he raged at her. "I *need* my fingers, damn you!"

"Well, they're gone, so get used to it. Just be grateful for the eight you still have."

He'd gone back to sleep after that. It was not a peaceful sleep; the pain kept waking him. When he opened his eyes, he could see dim light coming in through a smoke hole in the roof. Kayna was gone. Looking around, Traver tried to figure out his bizarre circumstances.

When the woman had mentioned they were in a tent, he had taken it to mean some type of portable shelter. But this had the look of something more permanent. It was large, framed with wooden stakes and covered with tanned leather. Designs had been painted on the walls and over the flap that served as the door. There was a fire pit in the center, and the floor was covered in skins mounded into pallets. The tent even had its own peculiar smell, like a strange blend of spices mixed with smoke.

He thought about trying to sit up, but the idea was still daunting. His hands still hurt, but the texture of the pain was different, more of a stinging sensation. Hesitantly, he pulled his left hand out of the blankets and held it up. His whole hand was wrapped in strips of animal skin that had been soaked in water and then dried on stiff. The way the bandages were arranged, he had no idea what kind of damage was concealed beneath.

The flap of the tent parted, and a man stepped in. He moved across the space toward him, kneeling by Traver's side. The fellow was dressed in fur and tanned leather. He had long, greasy hair, and a beard that looked to have soaked up every drip of fat from his breakfast. And he *smelled.* The stranger fairly reeked of horse.

Without speaking a word, the man snatched up Traver's left hand and started peeling off strips of bandage. Traver closed his eyes, afraid to see what was under those hardened leather strips. With a crack, the entire casing fell away, and Traver found himself staring up at his naked, ruined hand.

The last two fingers of his left hand were gone. Only swollen, bloody tissue remained in their place. Traver just gaped at the ghastly wound. He still had his thumb and his first two fingers, which were the three best fingers to have. Traver couldn't stand it. He had to turn and look away. He felt ill, his stomach twisting.

"The wounds are healing nicely," the man said.

It sounded like a sick jest. Wanting to scream in frustration, Traver growled, "You had no right to cut off my fingers."

"Your fingers were already dead," the man said. "If I had left them on, the rest of you would be following."

It was small comfort. What was he going to do without the use of his hand? Certainly not soldiering.

"My name is Ranoch."

Traver looked up at him. The man had a kind face beneath the filth. In a way, Ranoch reminded him a little of Corban Henley. Just a darker, wilder version.

"Traver Larsen."

Looking around the tent, Traver couldn't help wondering what kind of people he had fallen in with. They were obviously nomads of some type, and from the looks of the skins, they were probably herdsmen. Staring at the fur of Ranoch's heavy winter robe, he couldn't resist asking, "You people are horse herders?"

Ranoch nodded, looking proud. "We are the Jenn."

The man reached down by his side and produced a plain

earthenware cup, which he proffered in both hands. Traver stared at the cup suspiciously, wondering at the steam that was rising from it.

"What is it?"

"Hot mare's milk," Ranoch informed him solemnly.

"That's revolting." Traver grimaced, trying to turn his face away as the herdsman lifted the cup to his lips.

"Drink it. You need the strength."

Holding his breath, Traver opened his mouth. The milk was heavily spiced, and much sweeter than cow's milk. The fatty texture made him want to gag. Swallowing, he muttered bravely, "Not bad. It would do better with a chaser though."

Ranoch chuckled, tilting the cup again as Traver tried hard not to spit the foul liquid right back in his face. The second gulp went down worse than the first one. But the herdsman was insistent and made Traver drink the whole cup before putting it down.

"A crier came through our camp over a week ago," Ranoch said, leaning forward on his knees. "All men were asked to bring their bows and offer Horseright to the Callas Greathe. It is said that the Dakura are invading the plains. I was wondering if you knew anything about it, since you've fought them."

Traver stared at him blankly, hardly understanding a word. Slowly, he asked, "You mean the Enemy?"

Ranoch nodded. Traver struggled to sit up, using his elbows to shimmy himself forward. Ranoch caught him by the shoulders, easing him up the rest of the way. Traver felt suddenly faint, his body trembling with the effort. But it was a small victory, one he was proud of. He would have to get used to small victories.

"We've been trying our best to slow them down," he said. "The keep's fallen. There's just too many."

"Greystone Keep is lost?"

When Traver nodded, the man shook his head sadly.

"How did you know they were coming?" Traver asked. It didn't make sense. Proctor and the rest might be down from the pass by now, but that didn't leave enough time for word of their arrival to circulate around the plains.

Ranoch rubbed his eyes wearily. "I told you. A crier came

through our camp."

"How did he know?"

The man shrugged. "There are two ways the cry can be taken up. It can come from the Tiborah, the spiritual leader of our people. Or a Sentinel might raise the cry, but that would indeed be rare."

Traver's eyes widened in understanding. "Lauchlin."

"What?" The herdsman stared at him in confusion.

"He's a Sentinel I know."

"You know a Sentinel?" Ranoch exclaimed.

"Aye, I do."

The herdsman shook his head, a look of newfound respect in his eyes. "I offer you my food, my fire, and my protection for as long as you wish," he said solemnly. "After you heal, if the Dakura have not yet blighted the plains, I would be honored to offer you Horseright."

Traver blinked at the man, thoroughly confused. "Sounds great," he muttered.

Chapter Thirty-One
Chains

Rothscard, The Rhen

His guest room at Emmery Palace was the most luxurious Kyel had ever seen. It was more than just a room; it was an entire suite. The sitting area had a warm fire already glowing in the hearth, with three plush chairs gathered around in an intimate setting. There was also a tiled washroom with a large marble tub. The bedchamber itself was draped in silk, the bed almost scandalously large.

It didn't take him long to discover a rope pull by the door that summoned a liveried servant. A boy arrived with a sharp knock and listened to Kyel's request for warm water with a bewildered expression on his face. But it was Kyel's turn to be confused when the boy strode into the room instead of going to fetch a bucket.

Perplexed, Kyel followed him to the washroom, where the boy leaned over the tub and threw a valve. A gush of water came out of a pipe that he hadn't even noticed, spilling out of the wall and into the tub. Amazed, Kyel put his fingers in the stream and was surprised to discover it already warm.

"How?" he gasped.

"The water comes from hot springs under the palace," the boy explained. "Don't drink the warm water. It tastes sort of funny. But the cold water comes from the river, and it's good to drink."

"I've never heard of such a thing."

The boy went to fetch towels down from a shelf. When he was gone, Kyel found himself neck-deep in the most soothing bath he'd ever experienced in his life. He lay with his head against the sloping back of the tub and scooted down until the water came up to his chin. Then he closed his eyes and relaxed, listening to the muffled thuds of his heartbeat.

He lay there until the water grew cold, then let some out and drew more fresh. Finding a brush, he scrubbed his body until he felt sure he had most of the grime off. When he was done, he dried off and shaved, then ran a comb through his wet hair.

He dug into his cloak pocket, bringing out *Treatise on the Well,* then crawled into the bed. It was the first chance he'd had to open the text since leaving Glen Farquist. He skimmed the first chapter, which was just another description of the creation of the Well. It wasn't until he got to the third chapter that he finally found something of interest.

Spread out across two pages was a diagram of the Well, drawn painstakingly in ink. The diagram showed the Well from two different perspectives. Kyel raised the book, flexing the spine back carefully as he studied the drawings. The Well of Tears looked just like any other well he had ever seen, with the singular exception of the odd markings that encircled its rim.

Turning the page, he saw the same markings expressed in a series, some circled and numbered. Unfortunately, there was no explanation as to what the numbers could mean.

Intrigued, Kyel flipped forward a few chapters and stopped when his eyes caught a glimpse of a heading that read, SEALING OF THE WELL. He read the entire passage, letting his eyes scan rapidly across the page with a growing uneasiness that increased with every word:

> *Resealing the Well requires two mages working in cooperation. The Well itself must be manipulated in its chamber by deactivation of the rune sequence in reverse order. Concurrently, the Well must be sealed on the side of the Netherworld, which requires a Grand Master of no less than the fourth tier to enter the gateway. This is, by definition, a sacrifice, as any person entering the Netherworld would become there entrapped by the collapse of the gateway, condemned body and soul to the*

Netherworld for all eternity.

"Merciful gods," Kyel whispered.

As soon as he said it, Darien's words came back to haunt him: *the gods have no mercy.* Kyel snapped the book shut and set it down. He didn't understand half of what he'd just read, but he understood enough.

It would take the two of them working together to seal the Well of Tears, and Kyel knew he wasn't remotely prepared to put the Soulstone around his neck yet. He might be in for years' more training before he would be ready to tackle something like the Well.

And then either Darien or himself would have to enter the gateway to become the sacrifice the Well of Tears demanded. Kyel knew he could never, ever summon enough courage to do that, knowing the repercussions. Sacrificing his life would be bad enough, but condemning his soul to hell on top of it? The very thought was horrendous, unspeakable. But how could he ask Darien to do it for him? The mage had already suffered enough. He deserved an eternity at peace.

But at least he'd be with Meiran.

As soon as the thought occurred to him, Kyel wanted to hit himself for even thinking it. He was being selfish, and cowardly on top of it. His mind was just groping for comfort, trying to reason its way out of the guilt he was already feeling. Thoroughly disgusted with himself, Kyel resolved not to think about it again. Maybe there was another way, maybe Darien could figure something out. Perhaps he was just getting himself worked up over nothing.

A knock at the door startled him from his thoughts.

Rising from the bed, Kyel crossed the room, expecting another servant as he cracked open the door. Instead, he was surprised to find himself looking into the face of Nigel Swain. Kyel let the door swing fully open, his heart skipping a beat as he took in a hallway full of blue-cloaked guards.

"Didn't anyone ever tell you never threaten a queen?" the captain asked.

As Swain moved into the room, Kyel found himself wondering why Darien had made it all sound so easy. He'd thought it was going to be just another one of his master's tests, this one a lesson in diplomacy. Well, if this was a test, then he'd just failed it.

Swain drew Kyel's hands behind his back and locked a set of iron chains around his wrists. It was only his second time in Rothscard, and both times he had found himself in chains.

Damn you, Darien.

The only thing he'd ever wanted was just to go home. Every day it seemed the chances of that happening were growing more dismal.

"What are you going to do to me?"

Swain directed him by the arm out into the hall.

"The Queen wishes to have a word with you."

"She had but to ask," Kyel grumbled.

He hadn't meant it as a jest, but his words inspired a cheerless smile on Swain's angular face. Guards fell in around them as Kyel was guided forward.

He was scared. Swain was right. He shouldn't have threatened Romana. He wondered what the punishment for something like that was. They'd already shipped him off to the Front once and, anyway, Greystone Keep had probably already fallen. The way things were starting to look now, the Front might even be right here in Rothscard in another week or so. Then they wouldn't have to ship him anywhere.

The thought almost made him want to laugh, though it would have been a bitter laugh indeed. Instead, he swallowed and tried not to stumble as they guided him down a flight of polished marble stairs. It was hard, walking down the steps with his arms chained behind his back. If he tripped, he wouldn't be able to bring his hands up to catch himself.

At the bottom of the stairs, Swain led him to a large white door. The chains on his wrists were starting to chafe, and the small gaps in the links kept pulling at his arm hairs. His shoulders ached from the way they had him trussed.

Kyel felt ill when he realized he was being taken to the Queen's formal audience hall. Romana sat on a raised throne at the far end of the room, and there was nothing commonplace about her now. She wore elegant blue layers of silk, embroidered and bejeweled. Her dark hair was arranged in a coif caught up by the Sapphire Crown of Emmery. She held a gold scepter in one hand. Romana was now the very image of a queen. Kyel found himself thinking that if she'd looked that way earlier, he would have never found the courage to say what he had.

Swain's grip on his arm forced him down into the bow that Kyel had forgotten to make. He resented the gesture. It was one thing, abasing himself before a pretty girl with a paintbrush in her hand. It was quite another when that same girl had transformed into the image of a glorious but wrathful monarch who had issued the order to have him restrained.

"Rise." Her clear soprano voice carried the commanding ring of authority.

Kyel obeyed, though there was little grace in his movement. The captain's grip remained painfully firm on his arm. Kyel waited nervously, wondering what sentence the Queen would pronounce. He thought Darien had greatly underestimated the woman's boldness. He waited, but the Queen said nothing. She seemed to be waiting for him, gazing down at him from her elevated throne with distaste in her wide blue eyes.

Not knowing what else to say, Kyel asked her, "Why did you have me placed in chains?"

Romana's eyebrows arched, as if she was surprised by his straightforward question. She moved her hand to the arm of her throne, brandishing the scepter as she replied:

"I had you placed in chains because I wished for you to experience what they feel like."

Kyel frowned, almost as disgusted as he was shocked by her answer. "I fear I don't take your point."

Swain's grip flexed on his arm, sending a shooting pain stabbing into his shoulder. Romana glared down at him, but her tone was even as she pressed, "Tell me, how do they feel?"

Kyel knew exactly what she was getting at, and he didn't appreciate it one bit. Shrugging, he told her, "Heavy. They chafe."

"And how do *you* feel, wearing them?"

"Vulnerable," he replied honestly. Her questions were becoming tedious. He wished the Queen would just make her point.

Romana gazed at him intently as she asked, "Can you tell me the purpose of chains?"

Angry now, Kyel growled, "I can think of several."

"Such as?"

"To constrain someone, to confine. To control."

"Exactly," Romana pronounced as if leveling a death sentence. "The mages of Aerysius chose to live their entire lives shackled to the confines of the Oath of Harmony. Even though the weight was heavy, and it chafed at times. Some of the most powerful men and women the world has ever known spent a lifetime feeling just as vulnerable and constrained as you do at this moment. And yet many sacrificed their lives to preserve that Oath; they felt it was that important." She paused. "What are your thoughts on this?"

Kyel could have answered that question the moment he'd walked in the door, without playing her infuriating game.

He told her in all honesty, "I am aware of its importance. I believe the Oath is a necessity."

The Queen of Emmery nodded. "What I require is your word that when you receive the Transference, you will swear the Oath of Harmony and uphold it throughout your entire life."

"You have my word."

The insult she was dealing him grated to the bone. Who did she think she was, to demand his word on something that should have never been any of her business in the first place? He wished Darien was there. The Sentinel would have been outraged by this little queen's temerity.

Romana looked supremely pleased with herself. "Very well. I would like you to know that I have reconsidered your entreaty. I have decided to send my army northward, after all."

Kyel was shocked. He hadn't expected this, not at all.

"I thank you, Your Highness," he said in a much calmer voice.

He waited, but she said nothing further. "Now would you please take these chains off me?"

"No."

"What do you mean, *no?*" Kyel's face flushed hot with anger. "Why not?"

Romana raised her hands expansively. "Because you are my assurance."

"Assurance against what?"

The Queen sighed, setting her scepter down across her lap. "I have spent much time today contemplating a great many things. I have come to realize that, though desperate, this plan is probably the only chance of success we have. If your master wishes to play the part of Orien, then so be it. But he must agree to abide by the rest of Orien's script, right up to the very end."

At first, Kyel didn't take her meaning. Then, slowly, it dawned on him. She was talking about…

"No," he gasped, feeling utterly revolted and enraged. "I won't do it."

"Those are my terms." Romana leaned forward, gripping the arms of her throne. "If Darien Lauchlin uses the vortex, then he must follow Orien's example and kneel at your feet when the battle is done. You will keep your word and swear the Oath of Harmony the moment after you receive the Transference from him. Then that will be the end of this ghastly business."

"No," Kyel whispered, shaking his head. "There's more. He needs to help me close the gateway, seal the Well of Tears. And then there's Aidan—"

But Romana wasn't listening to him. Silencing him with a furious glint of her eyes, she uttered, "That is the purpose of legacy, is it not? When your master falls, you may take up his banner for him. But you will do so Bound."

Kyel tried to back away from her, but he was held fast by the steel grip of Swain's fingers. "You can't ask that of me. *I won't do it.*"

"Then you will spend the rest of your life with *my* chains on your wrists." The Queen of Emmery turned to her captain and ordered, "Take this young man to a cell where he can think over his options carefully."

Swain hauled him around by the arm, wrenching Kyel's shoulder as he did. Stumbling, Kyel careened after him out of the throne room, head reeling in fear and revulsion. A contingent of guards fell in behind them as Kyel was compelled forward down the long halls of the palace and out into a dismal afternoon.

As he walked, Kyel tried to think of what he could do to get himself out of this. Romana's threat had scared him. It scared him even more because he thought he knew what Darien would do when he heard of it. Everything seemed to be pointing in one direction, and he could feel the numbers starting to total themselves together in his mind.

Darien would make Romana a counteroffer. He would insist on surviving long enough to reach Aidan and the gateway. With one decisive stroke he could fulfill his Bloodquest, seal the Well of Tears, and follow the example set by Orien that Romana demanded. And then, when it was over, all parties involved would be satisfied.

It was sick. It was also perfect.

Just like the rest of Darien's plans. As the cell door slammed shut behind him, Kyel realized with a gut-twisting wrench that this must have been his master's intent all along.

Sleep was impossible. And yet there was nothing else to do, so Kyel tried his hardest. But with his arms chained behind his back, there was no position that he could find that was comfortable. The hours dragged by as guards came and went, sometimes with prisoners and sometimes not. Sometimes they glared at him or whispered taunts. Often, they raked their swords along the metal bars of his cage as they strode by, a jarring sound that rattled his nerves.

It was hours before he finally had a visitor. And then, it wasn't who he'd been expecting. Appalled, Kyel watched as a blue-cloaked guard sifted through his iron ring of keys, throwing back the bolt of his cell door to admit a brawny, bald old man with the smell of the forge on his clothes. In his hand he carried a forger's hammer, wielding it upright like a club. An apprentice trailed behind him, lugging a small but heavy anvil into the cell, which he all but dumped down on the floor with a resounding *thud.*

Kyel stared at the anvil with a feeling of dread. Romana was carrying her point much too far if she was willing to drive it home with a blacksmith's hammer. To his disgust, three more guards surged into the cell in the wake of the forger's apprentice. Two came forward to restrain him while the third edged behind him and unlocked the chains on his wrists. Kyel's shoulders spasmed with relief the moment they were off. But the relief did not last long.

The guards wrenched him forward and down, one catching his head in a lock while another seized his arm and forced it down on top of the anvil, pinning it there with the full weight of his body. Kyel tried to struggle as he saw the blacksmith lifting his hammer over a fresh length of chain. But the guard who had him by the neck tightened his hold until there was nothing Kyel could do but watch and desperately pray that the blacksmith didn't miss his mark.

The hammer rose and fell with a sharp ring that made Kyel flinch. There was no pain, at least; the blacksmith's aim was true. In moments, the vile work was done.

As the guards released him, Kyel held his hands up before his face, staring down in revulsion at the lengths of chain wrapped around his wrists like a matching set of crude iron bracelets. The woman had gone too far. Much too far. He didn't care if she was a queen; Romana had no right.

The blacksmith looked back over his shoulder with sympathy in his eyes as he left. Kyel sank down on the cot, staring at the Queen's chains. There had to be something he could do. She couldn't get away with this. It was an insult, not just to him personally, but to every Master who had ever lived and died by the Mage's Oath.

If Aerysius still existed, Emmery's Queen would be bent over her knees for this, he felt certain. But Aerysius didn't exist anymore. And the man currently calling himself Prime Warden was not there to help him, even if he had the inclination to do so.

There was only one thing to be done about it—there simply was no other choice. He was fed up, and not just with Romana. Darien had known damned well from the beginning what he would be facing. Yet the mage had sent him anyway. This was all another one of his schemes, one of his twisted lessons. Perhaps he hadn't foreseen the chains, but Darien must have known how Romana would react. He had planned for it all along. It was just another stepping stone on his path to Aidan and the Well, to surrendering himself to Orien's fate.

Kyel had no intention of letting him go through with it. He was afraid of Darien's wrath, but someone had to save the man from himself.

Reaching into his pocket, Kyel pulled out the Soulstone and gazed deeply into its glimmering facets. It was terrible. And terrifying. The strange red light flickered and throbbed, pulsing like a living heartbeat. Knowing that he had no idea what he was getting into, Kyel spread open the silver bands of the collar and held the medallion up against his chest. It felt sinisterly cold.

His hands trembled as he brought the bands up around his neck, fumbling at the clasp with his fingers. At first, he didn't think it was going to work. The clasp seemed stiff and frozen. But then he heard a faint, metallic click.

As the stone's raging torrent gushed through his body and into his mind, Kyel squeezed his eyes shut and tried his best not to scream.

In the end, his best wasn't anywhere near good enough.

Chapter Thirty-Two
Fly True

The Cerulean Plains, The Rhen

The ancient copse of cypress trees stood stiff in the midst of a rolling expanse of white, their evergreen branches unmoving. The air was still, lacking even the suggestion of a breeze. Beneath the trees' gnarled limbs, an uneasy tension was brewing. It moved over the snow-fed ground like the probing fingers of an inquisitive hand.

The men could sense it. The horses did, as well. The animals worried at their bits, shifting and stomping uneasily. Craig's own mount stood trembling, eager for the charge. It was bred for the fight; the love of battle ran hot in its blood.

Craig kept a firm grip on the reins. He raised his other hand over his head, clenched in a tight fist. The tinkling of chain mail rattled under his cloak as the stallion beneath him danced in place. He waited, the eyes of twenty men behind him riveted on his fist.

In the distance, a single arrow arced upward into the sky, a red ribbon affixed to its shaft, fluttering in its wake. The arrow and ribbon reached the apex of their flight, curved, then plunged swiftly down toward the earth.

"NOW!" Craig bellowed, dropping his fist.

The horses broke into an all-out charge, emerging from beneath the cover of the trees. Craig's heels pumped his stallion's heaving sides, urging it faster. The warhorse swept forward with a great surge of speed, putting all of its heart and muscle into the race. Like the horse beneath him, Craig was eager for the fight.

Filled with the thrill of battle, he raised his horn bow as his mount crested the rise of a hill. He held the curve of the bow parallel to the ground and nocked an arrow to the string. The men behind him did the same.

Before them, the forces of the Enemy sprawled across the plains like a dark and dangerous sea. Craig kicked his mount faster, drawing the arrow back. Just as the black wall of Enemy ranks collapsed and broke toward him, he let the bowstring sing.

"Fly true," he whispered, quoting the verse inscribed on his bow.

Reaching to the quiver fixed to his saddle, he withdrew another shaft and launched it after the first, three more following. The air around him hummed with the hiss of arrows and screams of death.

Craig tugged at the reins, wheeling his horse around before a charging group of infantry that broke away from the main force. Enemy arrows whispered in his ear as they flew past him, finding purchase in the backs of his own men who fell, slouching sideways from the saddle. Craig leaned forward, pressing his face against his stallion's neck in an effort to make himself as small a target as possible.

He turned in the saddle and, raising his bow, sent a steady stream of arrows back in the direction of his pursuers. In front of him, he could see the green limbs of the cypress grove beckoning. Branches reached out for him, clawing at his helm and swiping at his cloak.

Behind, he heard the screams of outrage from hundreds of Enemy throats. They were quickly overpowered by the war cries issued from five hundred Greystone archers that ran out from under the cover of the trees.

Craig barked a laugh as he watched the Enemy fall, the air itself singing with the deadly whisper of shafts. The remaining Enemy soldiers struggled to retreat as Greystone soldiers charged forward with weapons drawn.

Craig watched from the edge of the skirmish as his men finished off the last few nodes of resistance. His leg throbbed fiercely. Looking down, he saw that an arrow had buried itself deep in the muscle, perhaps even to the bone. Swearing, he cursed his luck.

Soon, it was done. The swelling cries of triumph that rose from the battlefield drowned out even the stabbing ache in his thigh. Craig barked out a laugh as he gazed upon the fallen remains of black-armored bodies, hundreds of them. Once again, Proctor's tactics had worked.

The force commander himself came up beside him on his mount. Proctor's eyes were grimly pleased, until they fell on the black fletching that pierced Craig's leg. A frown of concern stiffened the hard planes of his face.

"Just a nick," Craig reassured him, grinning against the pain.

But then his expression fell. He recognized that distant look in his commander's eyes, noticed Proctor's hand absently stroking the hilt of the dagger at his side.

Grimly, Craig swallowed. Since their retreat from the pass, Proctor had been consistent with his policy that no living man should be left behind for the Enemy, while at the same time refusing to allow the wounded to impede their mobility. The commander's sinister knife had seen more use in the past week than ever since its forging.

Staring now at that ebony hilt, Craig realized the meaning of the stony look on Garret Proctor's face.

Chapter Thirty-Three What Hurts, Teaches

Rothscard, The Rhen

His screams had brought the guards.

They had found him lying on his side, unconscious on the floor of his cell. Kyel remembered little of it, or of the frantic apothecary who'd been summoned to force a draught of some terrible liquid down his throat. He'd lain in his cot the rest of the night, shivering violently, fading in and out of sleep pierced through with disturbing and sometimes even shocking nightmares. The two times he'd managed to drag himself up enough to pass water into the foul bucket, he had barely managed the act. It reminded him of when he'd taken ill with Mountain Fever when he was a boy. His body felt the same: wracked and abused, and horribly weak.

Kyel had been utterly unprepared for the agony of Transference. He had never read anywhere or heard mention that it was supposed to be so excruciating. Somehow, he didn't think it was. Perhaps it was because he wasn't ready for it, or maybe it was because of the nature of the Soulstone itself. Kyel had never imagined so much pain could be compressed into such a short period of time.

Somehow, he'd managed to get the damn thing off his neck. He didn't even remember doing it, but he couldn't stand thinking about what might have happened if he'd left it hanging there. He remembered Luther Penthos' warning about how the stone, when black, had the effect of sucking the gift right back out again. The thought was particularly nauseating.

The stone was black now. The light had passed out of it, into himself, Kyel imagined. As he lay back in his cot staring up at the medallion, it was hard to believe that, only last night, the same stone had glowed with a dazzling inner radiance. It no longer even looked like a gemstone. Just a dull and lifeless clump of rock. It reminded him of some of the obsidian stones he had seen in the Pass of Lor-Gamorth.

He didn't like looking at it anymore. The sight of it filled him with a dread that made him think twice before shoving it back into his pocket. He wanted the thing as far away from him as possible, but there was nothing else to be done with it. Darien had called it an heirloom of power, and Kyel knew it was his responsibility to keep it safe. There couldn't be many such objects left in the world. Most had probably been lost in the destruction of Aerysius. For all Kyel knew, the Soulstone was the last of its kind, an obsolete relic of a dead civilization that existed now only in one man's memory.

No. Now there was yet another remnant of Aerysius' shattered legacy: himself.

Kyel stared somberly down at the iron chains on his wrists, contemplating them quietly in the dim light of the cell. He was a Master now, though Romana's chains did nothing to bind anything except his dignity. He had given his word to Emmery's Queen that he would swear the Oath of Harmony as soon as he came into his power, but Kyel didn't even know the words to say. Darien had never told him.

Which really was not a problem. At least, not yet. He had no idea how to use his newfound strength.

He could feel it moving within him, the vibrant power of Emelda Lauchlin's gift. It felt strange, being the recipient of an inheritance that wasn't his own. He might be a Master in name, but that was as far as it went. He didn't even know what tier he was, or what title he might someday come to use. Was he a Master or a Grand Master? He didn't know. He had no order to call his own and was trained to none. He had the cloak, the chain on his left wrist, and the beautiful quiescence of the magic field moving sweetly in the back of his mind. But that was all.

Sighing, Kyel sat up and rubbed his eyes. At least he was

starting to feel somewhat normal again. His body was still a little weak, and the muscles in his legs kept cramping. But his head was clear, the fever-like symptoms gone.

He sat on his cot until a guard finally arrived with his breakfast and a ripe taunt on his lips. Kyel ate the scraps of bread in silence, gulping down the stale water with much more enthusiasm. He wasn't hungry. But he was beginning to grow bored.

For something to do, he lifted his hand and tried concentrating on the chain on his wrist. He had no idea what he was doing. He tried to imagine one of the links bending just enough to slide the thing off, attempting to visualize it in his mind. Nothing happened. He had known it wouldn't be that easy.

Yet, he couldn't resist the urge to explore his new talent. He had the feeling that he'd better learn its use, and quickly. He didn't have Darien there to show him, but he could almost hear the sound of the man's voice muttering in his mind. Just like they had in the vortex, the Sentinel's words kept echoing back at him like a refrain: *Try again.*

This whole business reminded him of the vortex. Then, all he'd needed to feel the current of the magic field was knowledge of the trick. It had taken him awhile to find the right technique, but once he had it down, the rest had been almost too easy. This had to be another trick. If only he could just discover it.

As he had in the vortex, Kyel reached out from within and felt the rhythm of the field, opening himself to it. That had to be the place to start. Otherwise, Darien wouldn't have bothered teaching him that skill. The mage had known what a short period of training he was likely to have and would have omitted any part of the normal lessons he didn't deem necessary.

Still, it didn't work. The chain remained fixed to his wrist, unaffected. Kyel squeezed his eyes shut, sighing in frustration.

Try again.

Biting his lip, he obeyed. Again, he reached out for the magic field, this time pulling at it instead of just groping along the currents. Instantly, a wondrous sensation swelled within him, a feeling of sweet contentment. Startled, Kyel released the field, looking up in amazement. He had done something right.

The chain was still there, the link yet unbent, but the feeling of bliss had been like no other he had ever experienced. It was a startling reaffirmation. He tried it again immediately, practicing the technique of filling his mind with the wonder of the field without another thought spared for the chains. That was all he did the remainder of the morning, until a voice startled him from his exercise.

"Good. You're not dead."

Kyel started, flinching back from the magic field as he turned to find Nigel Swain glaring at him through the bars of his cage. He sat up straight, suddenly afraid of what the man had seen. Hopefully, the wonder of the magic field had not been written on his face. Kyel rose to his feet, taking a few hesitant steps toward the man.

"So, do you mind telling me what all that ruckus was about yesterday?" Swain demanded, steel gray eyes peering through the oily strands of his hair.

Kyel lifted his hands, shrugging. "I had a nightmare."

"A nightmare." The captain shook his head. "I don't think so. Try again."

Try again. Kyel wanted to groan. He would have to come up with something much better. He had never been a good liar. It wasn't difficult to look as uncomfortable as he felt as he told Swain, "I was practicing something Darien taught me. It went wrong."

Those cold eyes just stared at him, making his flesh prickle. Softly, the captain said, "Acolytes are forbidden to practice without the guidance of a Master. At least, they were. Darien must have given you that directive."

"No," Kyel said. "He never told me any such thing. In truth, the last time he had me learn something, he dumped me down in the middle of a vortex and left me there to figure it out on my own."

"What?" Swain clutched the bars of his cage as Kyel took an involuntary step backward. "He's breaking you?"

"I don't know what that means."

"It means he's forsaken a lot more than his Oath," the captain snarled, eyes raging. "If Aerysius still existed and Darien was found to be using such methods, he'd be the subject of a Grand Inquiry."

Kyel shook his head, not knowing what to say.

"What I want to know is why," Swain demanded. "What's making him feel so pressured that he'd be compelled to go that far? I want an answer. And this time, it had better be a straight one."

Kyel felt like he was back in the Temple of Wisdom. Swain's threatening glare seemed all too much like the perceptive gaze of the high priest, taking the bare facts he admitted to and inferring much more than he ever intended.

"He's eighth-tier," Kyel found himself confessing. "If you don't know what that means—"

"I know damned well what it means!" With a growl, Swain wrenched himself away from the bars and swiped out at the air with a fist. "By the whoring mother of the gods, *why didn't you tell us this before?*"

"You know why I didn't!" Kyel shouted at him, appalled and scared by the man's reaction. "Your Queen already has it in for him. Darien's in enough trouble already without—"

"You stupid, ignorant boy. You don't even know what kind of man you've placed your trust in. Think about it! We're talking about an *eighth-tier* Grand Master who's foresworn his Oath, shouldered the weight of the world, and on top of it all, he's already lost everything! Plus, he's Sentinel-trained, which means he has every piece of knowledge he needs to corrupt what he's learned into something deadly wicked. You're apprenticed to a madman, Kyel. You'd better open your eyes before it's too late to do something about it and we have the next Zavier Renquist on our hands!"

Kyel's mouth dropped open. He stood there, shaking his head in denial. Swain unlocked the door to his cell, leading him out. Kyel went along complacently, staring at his boots as he walked, filled with a desperate sense of unease. Swain couldn't be right. Darien was a good, decent man. Sure, he had his moments and, sure, they seemed to be growing more frequent, but…

Kyel stepped out of the building into the glistening white sheen of fresh snow. Blinking, he forgot his train of thought as his eyes gazed upon the sight of what looked like every Rothscard Bluecloak that existed all assembled in front of the palace steps in neat, orderly files. And, before them all, the Queen of Emmery was seated in a sedan chair born on the shoulders of four enormous men, her golden scepter in hand, the Sapphire Crown on her lovely head.

Kyel couldn't believe his eyes. The scene looked like something out of legend. He waited with Swain as the ranks formed up behind the Queen's chair. A guard walked toward them leading two horses. One he recognized as his own. With a sigh of relief, he saw that his longbow was attached to his saddle. He had been worried that he'd never see it again.

The guard offered him the reins of his horse, but as Kyel stepped forward to take them, Swain jerked them out of his hand. The captain traipsed back to the saddle and snatched the bow from it, wielding it up before Kyel's face. With a look of contempt, he took it in both hands and brought the shaft down viciously over his knee, snapping the bow clean in half.

"No!" Kyel screamed. But it was already too late.

Mortified, he stared at the broken shards of his longbow in Swain's merciless hands. That single stave of wood had been his only friend, his constant companion, all through the long, dark months at Greystone Keep. It had been such a beautiful piece of wood, so elegantly simple, at the same time so comfortingly effective. Practicing with it had been the only thing he had taken pleasure in at the Front, and his developing skill had filled him with confidence and a blooming sense of pride. As he watched Swain throw the shards of the bow down like scraps of filth at his feet, Kyel felt like bending over to pick them up, wanting to run his fingers over the golden yew just one last time.

But he made himself stop. Deep down inside, he knew the captain was right. Mages were forbidden weapons, and there was a reason for it. Kyel couldn't help but tremble as he thought of Darien's sword. He wondered if things would have turned out differently if the Sentinel had cast the blade away as he should have or, better yet, never picked it up in the first place. He wondered if Darien would still have yielded his commitment to the Oath, or if he would have found the strength to rise above the temptation.

Kyel turned away from the sad remains of his bow. He was a mage now. Even if he hadn't sworn the Oath of Harmony, he would live it in his heart. In a way, he was glad Swain had done what he had. It made accepting the constraints of the Oath that much easier. Even if he didn't know them, not really.

When the captain approached with his horse, Swain lay a hand on Kyel's shoulder. His hard face held no sympathy. But there was another expression there, one that Kyel was thankful to find. When Swain placed the reins in his hand, he did so with a faint trace of understanding in his eyes.

"The hardest thing to learn about a weapon is knowing when it's time to give it up," the blademaster said.

"'What hurts, teaches,'" Kyel quoted, staring down at the reins in his hand.

Swain's brow creased. "That's the motto of the Arms Guild. Did you learn it from Darien?"

"Aye. He said it applies to most lessons in life."

Swain nodded, patting him on the shoulder. "Well, at least he remembers something I tried to teach him. Come on. We don't want to keep the entire army waiting."

Kyel glanced back over his shoulder at the ranks of men formed up behind their Queen. "That's not the army?"

Swain barked a laugh. "That's just the city guard, son. They go wherever the Queen goes, and right now she's coming to see us off. The real army is waiting outside the walls. Now, let's go, before the men get hostile."

Kyel nodded. He tried to resist taking one last glance back at his bow as he mounted up and rode away from it, but he just couldn't help himself. It was hard to part from it. But it was better this way.

And, in the end, he was even thankful.

Chapter Thirty-Four Orien's Finger

The Cerulean Plains, The Rhen

He was vulnerable.

It was a loathsome, despicable feeling Darien had suffered for two and a half days. His very skin crawled as if infested with a thousand writhing maggots. No matter how many times he raked his ragged nails across the surface of his flesh, still the feeling persisted. His main source of solace was gone, the rapturous song of the magic field silenced in his head. That was the worst. Walled away from the raging torrent of Orien's Vortex, he could take no comfort in what had become his only source of solace.

The field's absence darkened his mood and fouled his temper. Those who dared come close enough to see the raging intensity that seethed in his eyes turned and shied away, often with great haste. The day before, he had almost taken Wellingford's head off for no greater crime than startling him.

Which was another problem entirely. The anxiety inspired by the field's absence was becoming too much of a distraction. He was starting to lose focus. A blundering fool like Wellingford should never have been able to catch him by surprise, even if the boy had sneaked up behind him intentionally. Within the turbulent fury of a vortex, such distraction could easily prove fatal. If the King even suspected he was so helpless, Faukravar would not hesitate to move against him. Fortunately, the King had never taken an interest in magic or mages, or the man would have schooled himself enough to know what a vortex meant for him.

And Faukravar was really the least of Darien's worries. If Renquist and his demons knew he was alive, then this would be the place they would try to take him. Not with the strength of their power; they were just as helpless within a vortex as he was. But their pets were as darkly potent within the torrent of a vortex as they were without.

If Arden Hannah suspected he'd survived her fire, he might find himself confronted with such a fate. But Darien didn't think she had any reason to believe he was still alive. By the time Craig's charge had driven her away, he'd been hanging over that blaze for minutes, slowly searing like meat on a spit.

What a surprise he had in store for her. Darien sincerely hoped Arden would be traveling with her army. He had read about Bryn Calazar's Battlemages lending their support in the theater of war. If Arden showed herself at Orien's Finger, Darien had prepared something special with her in mind. Like a solicitous suitor, he'd put a great deal of thought and effort into selecting the perfect little something, a gift personalized just for her. He hoped she would find it just as stunning as he thought she would. If she didn't, then he would just have to keep trying until he got it right.

He was glad now that he'd sent Naia back home. The coming battle was going to be terrible. It would be no place for a priestess and certainly no place for a lover. Darien couldn't guarantee her safety, just as he couldn't guarantee his own. But it was more than that. He was glad she wasn't there to see him, to see the black, festering place where he had once kept his heart. He'd noticed the look on her face in Auberdale, when she'd seen him covered in the blood his sword had so eagerly spilled. The sight of him had repulsed her, but she had quickly forgiven him.

Naia would not be so quick with her forgiveness if she could see him now. There was little blood on his hands yet, but he felt as though he had already bathed in a river of it. He might as well have. Over the course of the past week, he had rehearsed his part in the coming battle hundreds of times in his head. At first, he had quailed. But then he'd forced himself to go over it one small step at a time, visualizing every graphic image again and again in increasing detail, until at last he felt numb enough to actually go through with it.

Which was another reason for his foul temper. Already that day, he'd killed hundreds of his own men scores of times in his head. He made himself visualize each dying face, hear every scream of anguish. Each time, it got a little easier. And it was still early in the day.

He rode in the middle of the drawn-out column, eyes focused on the backs of the men ahead. He'd let Faukravar take the van, and not out of deference to Chamsbrey's King. Because of his vulnerability while within the vortex, Darien felt reassured only with a ring of armored men around him. He had even moved his tent. The first week of the march he'd pitched it out away from the encampment, prizing his solitude above all else. Already, too many eyes were growing too wary, fixing him with questions he had no intention of answering. But the last two nights they had spent within the vortex, and he had positioned his tent in the center of camp.

Still, he'd had a hard time getting to sleep. The crawling feeling of his skin bothered him, and his heart kept beating a thundering tempo in his chest, not wanting to slow its pace even for sleep. He lay there for hours staring up at the roof of his tent, feeling more isolated and alone than ever before in his life.

More than anything, he missed Naia. But he was glad she was gone. So very, very glad.

Up ahead, the sharp ridge of a mountain groped upward from the snow-covered plain. They had made good time. He could scarcely believe they had made it all the way from Auberdale to the Cerulean Plains in only eight days, even if it was according to his own plan. He'd calculated the pace of the march himself from scaled charts in the command tent. It was a harsh pace, yet the well-disciplined soldiers had handled it well.

Even Wellingford was proving true. The youth had a small but laudable charisma that went over well with the men. He was still far from a great commander, but the boy did seem effective at getting things done.

Darien saw him riding up now, his young general's horse

working its way back from the front of the column. Wellingford's eyes scanned over the faces of the men, a frown of concentration on his face. When he spotted Darien, the frown intensified. Directing his horse into a gap between ranks, he turned his mount to ride beside him.

"The King is wondering why you're not inclined to accompany us," Wellingford said. He added, "I'm wondering also. It is not the Prime Warden's place to breathe the dust kicked up by an army of men and their horses. People are starting to ask questions."

"Let them ask," Darien growled, not willing to address the reasoning behind his choice of position. "But if anyone has the temerity to openly speak out, then send that man to me. I will not have my judgment questioned the day before the battle."

"But, Prime Warden, it would be wise to keep up appearances—"

"*What did I just say?* Now, go back and tell that pathetic wretch of a King that if he really desired my company, then he shouldn't have conspired to have me killed. *Go!* Or I'll make you my first example."

Wellingford paled. Darien watched him depart, silently seething. He didn't notice the gap that widened between himself and the men that marched at his side, or the looks of dismay in the eyes of the soldiers within hearing distance of his outburst. Instead, he summoned yet another image to mind, an image as grisly and appalling as it was comforting.

To the men around him, the new Prime Warden they had sworn to follow seemed to be riding in a kind of trance. He sat slumped on his horse with eyes closed and arms slack as his face, gloved fingers maintaining only a flaccid grip on the reins. His long, unbound hair stirred in a breeze, playing forward into his face, unnoticed. Once in a while, he would give a slight flinch, as if in the throes of a bad dream. Perhaps he really was asleep and dreaming.

Or perhaps, more likely, he was mad.

It was late afternoon when they had their first glimpse of Orien's Finger. It rose slowly up from behind a jagged ridge, a narrow column of dark gray rock. Its surface was strangely textured, cracked and age-worn, with lighter patches of lichen speckling its sides. About a quarter of the way from the top, a wide, diagonal crack had the appearance of running all the way through the stone. The summit looked in danger of slipping off at any time, given but a chance breath of air, or even a whim.

To Darien, the crag had the ominous portent of destiny. It looked much as he had imagined. Subtly different: taller, darker. Eminently more sinister. The shadow it cast fell across the horseshoe-shaped valley behind it, the angle of the shadow bending across the smooth face of the surrounding cliffs, where its tip touched a carved, numeric rune. Orien's Finger was an enormous natural sundial, and the ancients had taken advantage of it. Only, Darien had no idea how that sundial was meant to be read.

Darien left the center of the column and sent his horse toward the edge. From there, he kicked the animal forward at a lope, his pulse quickening as he closed the distance between himself and the slender pillar of rock. He rode past the head of the column, right up to the King's entourage and beyond.

At the base of the dark tower, he came to a halt and climbed down from the saddle. Confident that he stood within the eye of the vortex itself, Darien opened his mind and groped for the magic field like a blind man tantalized with the promise of sight.

It was rapturous. Darien gasped, collapsing to his knees in consummate relief as he immersed himself in the field's soothing intensity. Here in the eye, where the lines converged together, the sweet savor of the field was like no other.

Darien filled himself with it, saturating his body completely. He drew on the field, soaking it in, like a man dying of thirst trying to drown himself in a pool of water. He pulled in more, until agony blended with ecstasy. The sweet song in his head became an anguished scream.

Reluctantly, Darien released his hold on the wild energies, letting the power drain out of him and slip away. He held just a little back to hoard jealously, unable to distance himself from the field completely. His head ached, and his body trembled with weak spasms, but he paid them both no mind. Wondrously complete again, he rose, shaking, to his feet.

And saw an army of men gaping at him in dismay. Faukravar was staring with eyes wide and full of disgust, his face a pallid shade of gray. At his side, Wellingford looked crestfallen and bitterly ashamed.

Darien turned his back on them. What had they seen? Something they never should have. What had he looked like, there in the cold shadow of the spire, writhing in the field's anguished ecstasy? Probably mad.

He should have never succumbed to the temptation of the magic field. Now, he had much to atone for. From the looks on their faces the damage was extensive, and there was simply not enough time to fully repair it. Solstice was only a dawn away. In his moment of weakness, he had just lost the respect of every last man that followed him.

Worse, they probably thought him dangerously insane.

Ignoring the fatigue that yet lingered from his struggle with the field, Darien turned and forced himself to face his men. They must see him as strong. If he played this right, he might be able to convince them that he was some kind of troubled martyr, casting himself in Orien's image. It was not a persona he would wish to emulate if he had a choice. He didn't see himself as even approaching the nobility of Orien's legend. He was creating an altogether different legend for himself, one trenched in infamy.

But if the men needed to see him as Orien, then he would have to play the role.

Taking his horse by the reins, Darien led the gelding back toward the column, testing the field as he went. Later, he would need to make certain he knew where the eye of the vortex ended, and the cyclone of power began. But for now, he was satisfied with the feeling of contentment brought to him by the eye, the calm within the storm.

He stopped in front of Faukravar. Pretending that he didn't notice the disgusted look on the King's face, Darien dredged forth a somber smile.

"It's a good day," he told the King. "Tomorrow will see the dawn of a better one. The banners of Chamsbrey shall wave triumphant over the field."

To Wellingford, he ordered, "Set up camp on the south side of the ridge. No fires. The smoke will give away our presence. Use up as many rations as it takes to make certain every man has a good meal."

"Aye, Prime Warden," his general responded. His face looked perhaps a bit less pale, but he was still gazing at Darien with an expression of doubt.

Darien thought of the character of Orien they so desperately needed for him to imitate. With that in mind, he decided to elaborate with a little added mystery.

"I'll be up there." He nodded his head in the direction of the crag. "Allow no one to disturb me. I'll need to prepare myself, and I must do so alone."

Darien dropped the reins of his horse as he turned away, noting in satisfaction that the looks on their faces had once again changed. His strategy had worked, it seemed. The doubt and dismay were gone, absent even from Faukravar's eyes. Instead, he left them staring at his back, eyes wide in wonderment.

Darien hid a grimace as he walked away, feeling disgusted by the lie. He felt shamed that he'd brought himself to stoop so low, forced to win back their trust with a vulgar display. But if that was what it took to win the battle ahead, it was just another sin to add to the long list of them he was already accruing.

He wouldn't need the closing of the gateway to condemn his soul to hell. He was getting there just fine on his own.

Stone steps wrapped around the face of the dark column, a narrow and winding stair. It had broken and collapsed in many places. In other spots, the steps had been worn down to nothing more than a ramp. Darien took his time, picking his way carefully. It wouldn't do if he slipped and fell to his death on the eve before the battle. And eve it was. Already, the sun was beginning to slip behind the snow-clad mountains in the west. Tomorrow was Solstice, the shortest day of the year.

Darien kept his eyes averted from the edge. Once, heights had never bothered him. Now they did. The memory of his fall from Aerysius was kept fresh in his mind by the constant nightmares that plagued him almost every night. As he moved up the treacherous steps, he kept one hand braced against the rock face at his side, the other extended in front of him.

He slipped once, his fingers raking over the stone until they caught on a crack in the rocks, the only thing that saved him. Trembling, Darien pressed forward on legs that seemed suddenly less stable.

Before his fall, he could have skipped up this path. He had the balance taught to him by a blademaster, but it did him little good when his vision reeled, and his knees turned to jelly. He tried to will the path ahead to stabilize, but he could do nothing about the sweat that glazed his palms and ran trickling into his eyes.

More than once he came to a place where the steps had crumbled away completely. There, he was forced to gather his courage before making a staggering step across the break. Fortunately, it was never more than just a few feet. He tripped attempting the last gap, roughening his palms on the stone. But he drew himself up, feeling the bite of a cold breeze inspired by the height.

He was almost there, hundreds of feet above the horseshoe-shaped valley. It was getting dark. Darien shivered as he staggered up the last few steps, hands groping at the rock wall for stability. The stairs made a quick turn then leveled out.

Darien paused, closing his eyes and bracing himself. Then he stepped cautiously out over the snow-traced markings of the Circle of Convergence. He crossed the circle, stirring the slight dusting of snow that covered one of the lines with the toe of his boot. Walking across to the far side, Darien stepped off and moved toward the cliff's harrowing edge. There, he drew up, still yet paces away, but unable to move another step.

The view was awe-inspiring. And it was also terrifying. The sun had set completely, its light only the palest gray on the horizon.

The snow-covered plains swept out away from him, glowing in the soft light of the rising moon. Above, the stars were strung across the heavens like innumerable glittering crystals. Their myriad glows were cast in red reflection below, slightly to the north, where the campfires of the Enemy seemed to outnumber even the light of the stars.

A breeze reached out, whipping his hair and chasing his cloak. The feel of it was brisk and chill, stimulating. Slowly, he lowered himself to the flat summit of the crag, pulling his legs up to his chest and wrapping his arms around them.

Once, as a boy, he had tried counting the stars. He'd given up not long into the endeavor after reaching several hundred in just a trace amount of sky. The remainder of the heavens lay yet unnumbered above him. He had come to realize that such a task would probably take him the rest of his life.

This time he was determined to number them all, no matter how long the chore would take. It was imperative he know their total. Darien stared down at the red-orange lights below that twinkled brighter than the stars and started counting.

He knew Wellingford was behind him. He'd heard the scraping of his travel-worn boots crest the summit. The boy hadn't startled him this time, which was good. Darien hadn't moved from where he'd been sitting, gazing down at the fires below. He'd finished counting some time ago but was unwilling to leave his perch.

Staring out across the plains, his thoughts had drifted to Naia. He'd let the hours wear away, quietly savoring the image of her in his mind. It was very late, or perhaps very early; he wasn't sure. Whichever the case, Wellingford had no business being there. The boy should have been asleep hours ago.

His new general said, "I know you wanted to be left alone, but you did give the order that every man must have a good meal."

"So I did." Darien turned to glance over his shoulder.

Wellingford approached cautiously, a small sack in his hand. Remembering his own trouble with the broken and nerve-wracking stair, Darien found himself looking at Wellingford with new respect.

The young man seemed hesitant. Darien took the sack and, opening it, discovered that it was filled with dried meat, slices of bread, and even some cheese. Wellingford produced a waterskin and handed that to him, as well. Darien accepted it with a muttered word of thanks.

The boy stared out at the flickering lights, his cloak stirring behind him. Softly, he whispered, "Is that the Enemy?"

"Aye." He watched as Wellingford stepped forward, stopping right at the edge of the cliff. Just seeing him there made Darien shudder. Wellingford didn't seem bothered by heights in the least. He stood motionless, gazing outward across the plains, one foot slightly ahead of the other.

"Mother of the gods," he whispered.

Looking up at him, Darien asked, "Have you been taught how to estimate an army's strength by counting campfires?"

Wellingford turned back around, taking a step away from the cliff's edge. "Yes, but...there's too many. It would take all night."

"Not all night." Darien shook his head. "Judging from the lights, I estimate their numbers at somewhere near fifty-two thousand."

The boy swept a hand back through his hair, shaking his head as his eyes glistened in the moonlight. "I never thought there would be so many," he said, lowering himself to sit at Darien's side.

"There were more, once. I can only assume that the men under Garret Proctor's command have put their courage and their horn bows to good use."

Wellingford just stared at him blankly.

Darien raised his hand, pointing toward the dark swell of a ridgeline. "Look there." He indicated a patch of starless sky hanging inches beneath the moon, slightly above the rolling hills that sloped upward into the Craghorns.

"I see nothing."

"The stars above the ridge," Darien specified.

"There are none." Wellingford shook his head in puzzlement.

"I don't understand. What could be obscuring them?"

"Smoke. From campfires."

The boy drew in a sharp gasp of breath. "The second army," he whispered. When Darien nodded, Wellingford's face seemed on the verge of collapse. He had that crestfallen look again, although this time it made his face seem older instead of younger.

"Do we really stand a chance? The forces from Emmery you promised us never arrived."

"I won't be expecting them till the morrow." Darien stared hard at Wellingford's face. The boy needed reassurance, needed it desperately. "Why don't we go over strategy? I was thinking to wait, but seeing that you're here…"

"That would be good," Wellingford said eagerly, leaning back with his gloved hands in the snow. His fingers sank deeply into the icy powder with a crunching noise, exposing a wide, man-made crack in the stone below. Perplexed, he brushed away the snow with his fingers to reveal a curving line.

"What's this?"

"You're sitting on a focus line of the Circle of Convergence."

Wellingford stared down at it, frowning. "I'm afraid I don't understand."

"You don't want to," Darien assured him. "Just listen, do your part, and leave the rest to me."

Chapter Thirty-Five
Black Solstice

The Cerulean Plains, The Rhen

"Time to get up."

Kyel groaned, wondering what hour it could possibly be. Squinting into the darkness, he made out the form of Nigel Swain, a mere shadow against the other shadows within the tent. Outside, it appeared to be ink black through the open flap, and cold. Terribly cold. Why hadn't Swain closed the flap when he'd entered? Probably a tactic to get him up and moving faster.

Then he remembered: Solstice. Dawn. Today. Feeling suddenly wide awake, Kyel threw his blankets back and shot up from the covers.

"What time is it?"

"Too damn early," came Swain's acidic growl. "Come on, I brought you some of that fodder they're serving in place of food."

Kyel shook his head even though he knew the man probably couldn't see him in the darkness. The thought of eating curdled gruel within scant moments of waking was frankly nauseating. Besides, his bladder was so full it ached. He dragged himself up from his pallet, moving toward the opening. "I need to go out for a minute."

He was stopped by the captain's warning growl. "Better be *just* a minute."

Kyel nodded, taking the man's point. He had spent the entire first day of the march making frequent trips into the bushes before he was finally able to bend one single link of his chains. Then, it had taken him another day and a half of side trips to close the same link back up again. He'd practiced opening and closing the link at every chance he found, until the presence of the vortex had given him other things to think about. That was all the practice he'd had. And it was all he was going to get.

That was precisely what Swain was grumbling about. After the first two days of Kyel's prolonged excursions afield, the captain had caught on that he was up to something, though he never figured out what. But after that, Kyel had found his movements strictly watched. If he didn't make it back quickly enough, Swain made certain he missed his next meal.

He made his water then returned to the tent, the first light of dawn still absent from the sky. The moon was setting, though, which meant sunrise couldn't be that long in following.

The captain met him outside, waiting for him. As Kyel strode up, he could feel Swain's eyes looking him over, lingering a moment on the chains. Kyel pretended he didn't notice.

"How long will it take us to get there?" he asked. They couldn't be that far away. Most of the camp still had to be broken down, and he'd told Blandford that Darien was expecting them by sunrise.

Swain transferred his bowl to his left hand, wiping his mouth with his sleeve. Pointing, he said, "See that ridge?" He indicated a jagged patch of blackness against the slightly grayer sky. "Orien's Finger is about two more ridges north of it. We'll be there about an hour after sunrise, so that's about a two-hour march."

Kyel felt stunned. Betrayed. "But Darien told us to be there *at* sunrise!" He rounded on Swain. "We can't arrive an hour after the fighting starts—it might be too late!"

The captain just shrugged. "Blandford wants the Enemy bloodied a bit before we engage."

Kyel couldn't believe what he was hearing. What did they expect Darien to do, take on both armies by himself? Or was that exactly what they intended? Feeling a sudden, searing anger, Kyel took a threatening step toward the captain.

"This has been your plan all along, hasn't it?" he accused. "You intend to just bide your time while he wears himself down, then sweep in when he's no longer a threat to you."

Looking at the coldly gleaming hilt of Swain's sword, Kyel felt his rage swell to scalding. "That's why you're here," he realized. "You're captain of the *city* guard. You don't even belong with the army! Romana just sent you along because Darien trusts you—you're the one who trained him. That's it, isn't it? You're here to kill him!"

Swain looked at him sideways, a dangerous glint in his eyes. Then he took a step back and, tossing aside the flap of the tent, ducked inside. Kyel wanted to scream in rage. Not bothering to bite back the curse on his lips, he followed Swain into the tent. He wasn't going to let him get away, not without an explanation.

In the darkness of the tent, he saw the captain's shadow as only a blur. Then hands were on him, restraining him from behind. He felt the warm brush of Swain's breath at the back of his neck as the captain warned, "Don't press me further."

But Kyel couldn't help himself. "I don't understand you. You must have been his friend. How can you do this?"

The hands eased their pressure on him gradually. Kyel turned around, peering intently into the shadows of the man's angular face. Swain's eyes glared at him with a dangerous intensity, his chest heaving with every drawn breath.

"I knew a *boy* named Darien Lauchlin, once," he said. "But that was a long time ago. The man up there on that mountain, now…I don't know him anymore. I don't want to know him. And if you had any brains in your head, you wouldn't want to, either."

Sunrise.

Darien had spent the hours after moonset pacing the circumference of the circle, stirring the dusted snow off with his boots and with the power of his mind. He dared not use too much. There were creatures that could sense such stirrings of the field. But a trickle here and a tad bit there gradually revealed the deeply-hewn lines that ran inward from the margin of the circle, forming an exactingly rendered copy of the star he wore on his back, only many times larger.

Two stars, one offset against the other. He knew the pattern of the circle was not a star at all. At least, not by intention. The rays were a focus that directed the lines of power in the eye of the vortex, merging them together in one place, one single point in space at the circle's center. That was the power of the Circle of Convergence. All the energy of the vortex could be gathered here. The rays of the star functioned like lenses to bend the lines of the magic field together and filter them, rendering that tremendous well of power safe to use.

But like glass lenses, each circle had its flaws, its little imperfections. Even minuscule faults had an impact on its ability to focus the surrounding vortex. Orien's was a lesser circle, which meant its flaws were more problematic than the greater circle that had existed in Aerysius, now buried beneath the rubble of the Hall. Darien was not sure what impact those flaws would have on the circle's use. Only time would tell. All he could see from his cursory study was that Orien's Circle was still functional after its long sleep of over four hundred years. All he had to do now was awaken it.

Gazing down from the rim of the crag, he could see the gray sky in the east giving way to vivid hues of gold and vermillion. Sunrise had always been his favorite time of day. The colors of the sky seemed more saturated than they did at sunset, especially when there was just a splattering of clouds on the horizon, as there was today.

But there was no joy to be had in this sunrise, this dawn, this day. Darien ignored the timorous beauty of the wakening sky as if it didn't exist. To him, nothing existed in the world except for the vast black wedge approaching from the north, that and the Circle of Convergence beneath his feet. It was almost time.

This dawn, this day, this purpose.

Steeling himself, he walked to the tip of the nearest ray and drew upon the potent rapture of the magic field, a wonder far more stirring than any daybreak. He felt the power moving through him, a bliss unlike any other. The magic field had never felt this way, not until lately. Not until he had clothed his heart in ashes and cloaked his soul in apathy. But now it seemed the tranquil stirring of the field was the only thing keeping him going, the only thing keeping him alive.

Beneath his boots, the ancient stone-carved lines began to glow with a silvery light that ran like quicksilver down the length of the ray to the circle's focal point. Unnoticed, the first rays of the sun broke above the white rolling plains in the east.

His back to the sunrise, Garret Proctor contemplated the advancing army before him. He had worn their numbers down considerably. But it had hardly made a difference.

So many dead. All for the trust he had placed in one man. One man who he still had no guarantee would come through for them.

He sat his horse and waited. His new captain, a man by the name of Wade Tarpen, was at his side. Tarpen had Craig's horse and Craig's gear, but none of the other man's spirit. Proctor grimaced as he looked to the east, toward the sunrise, despising the wait.

Today, he knew, he was going to die. He doubted Lauchlin had even known it at the time, but the mage had sentenced them all to death with a few simple words uttered at the base of the tower at Greystone Keep.

Draw the majority of their strength into the eye of the vortex, and I'll see to it you get your wish.

Proctor wondered if Lauchlin had realized at the time the hone of the blade he'd let fall that day. Because there was only one way to draw both Enemy hosts deep enough into the eye of the vortex for Darien's purpose to succeed.

He had missed the break of dawn. It had been over fifteen years since his face had last gazed upon the rising sun. Garret Proctor savored the warmth of daybreak, knowing there would never be another. Death was always cold, just as the grave was always dark and stale. He knew; he had buried enough friends to be certain.

⊛

Darien heard someone approaching up the steps. It could have been Wellingford, but he knew it wasn't. It might have been any number of people, but he already had a very good idea who it would be. He recognized the sound of her footsteps even before she came into view. It was a noise firmly ingrained on his mind. The sound of her slippered feet moved often through his nightmares.

He turned to face her as Arden Hannah came into view, picking her way over the last treacherous step to emerge at the glowing summit of the crag. Her creatures must have sensed the ripples in the field he'd created by awakening the circle.

Dark forms swept out from behind her, gliding past her to line the edge of the rim, six in all. Necrators. Darien had begun to feel the effects of their approach minutes before. He had known they were drawing nearer when the song of the magic field had started to fade in his head. It was almost gone now. Almost, but not quite. He could still feel the pulse of it dimly, like the tremulous echo of a dying heartbeat.

He wasn't there yet. There must be something further he needed to do.

Arden stood regarding him with sparkling eyes, resplendent in an intriguing mixture of blue silks and silver chain mail. Slowly, a smile bloomed on her lips. It was a triumphant smile, and its radiance swept upward to gleam in her eyes.

There was a low growl. Darien's eyes were drawn behind her, to the beast that glared at him with glowing green eyes. The thanacryst was black and large with matted fur. It had a rabid look. Its mouth was open and panting, a wide and cavernous hole that drooled thick saliva to the stone. Revolted, Darien felt an instinctual impulse to draw away from it.

"You're so full of surprises, my dear."

Her voice was like silver droplets of moonlight. She took a step toward him, placing a slippered foot inside the margin of the glowing circle. Tilting her head slightly, her eyes narrowed as she considered him.

"Oh, my, but you've changed. When we first met, you were just a little sweetling. My fire must have scorched your soul." Gazing into his eyes, she said in a voice full of conviction, "Look at you. You're positively glorious."

Darien shuddered, the silken tone of her voice eliciting memories he had struggled to forget.

Behind her, the thanacryst uttered a low, guttural growl of yearning. Its nose quivered as it sensed the proximity of its prey. Arden placed a hand on its head, soothing it with the liquid texture of her voice.

"Easy, my pet. Not yet."

Turning back to Darien, she brought a hand up. Her fingertips stroked the pale flesh of her neck.

"Come to me," she commanded. "There is nothing in the world so erotic as two mages united, naked bodies and unrestrained power intertwined. I can give you a little taste of what it would be like, if you were mine."

Standing there on the margin of the circle, offering herself up to him like a sacrifice, her seductive energies took hold of him with an influence that was overwhelming. This time, Darien allowed it. He did nothing to resist the electric tension that shuddered down his nerves. It was almost like the longing ache he felt for Naia, though shockingly more feral. It filled him with a desperate urgency he had no inclination to ignore.

His eyes took in the shape of her figure, the sleek curves of the chain mail draped over her hips. He found the sight of her as enticing as it was repulsive. But, strangely, the dichotomy just added to her attraction.

He needed to take her. And he needed to enjoy every hungry second of it.

Moving forward, he kept his gaze fixed on Arden's as he reached up and grasped the platinum locks of her hair. Consumed with untamed rage, he scoured his lips over the silken crease of her neck, the intensity of his assault driving a gasp from her lips.

He reached his hand up and released his cloak. Drawing it from his shoulders, he spread it out over the glowing lines of the circle's rays with the star facing downward, pressed against its larger counterpart.

He pulled his shirt off over his head and drew her toward him, dragging her down with him to the ground. Her power flowed over him, through him, the electric intensity of her gift searing like wildfire through his mind.

Conscience forsaken, Darien gave her everything she asked for, everything he had, everything he was. Most important, he gave Arden exactly what she wanted from him most.

There on the flattened summit of Orien's crag, Darien surrendered to Arden Hannah all that remained of his tortured soul.

His raised fist a silhouette against the red disk of the rising sun, Garret Proctor himself bellowed the command to send his men forward to their deaths. He kicked his boots into the flanks of his horse, drawing the cold length of steel he had not wielded in battle since Meridan. The hilt felt good in his gloved hand, the balance of the sword excellent. He had never favored a fight from horseback, but a man had to eat from the plate the gods served him, even if the fare was cold and bitter.

With a grim smile on his face, Garret Proctor swept his blade downward, sheering through the end of an Enemy spear. Pressing his mount forward with his legs, he raised his shield and warded off the attack of a mace as he wheeled his horse around, charging back out of the thick of the fight.

Darien rolled over to lie gasping on his back, staring upward into the sky. He felt Arden's hand caress his chest, heard the silken texture of her voice as she whispered in his ear, "I think I'll make you my pet. Yes. For a little while, at least."

Darien closed his eyes, the sound of his pulse ringing in his ears, the song of the magic field a sudden, rapturous symphony in his head. Reaching up, he took her hand in his.

The raging current he sent through her took Arden by surprise.

Twisting in agony, her mouth drew into a rictus as she screamed, blue lightnings of power clawing into her flesh. Darien watched in fascination as her pale skin glazed and then crisped, cracking to ooze boiling fluid that ran like tears down her face.

He let the crackling energies die with the sound of her screams. Leaning over her, he smiled in satisfaction.

"The necrators…"

Startled by her voice, Darien drew back. Somehow, she was still alive. But not for long; the sound of her breath was but a gurgle in her throat.

"They have no power over you."

"Because my heart is black," she whispered as she died.

Darien nodded, staring down at her charred corpse. He felt no sympathy for her whatsoever, absolutely no remorse. The only thing he felt was a satisfying sense of vindication.

"So is mine, now," he assured her.

He rose to face the ring of necrators who stood regarding him with acute disinterest. They had no reason to challenge him. If they looked deeply into his heart, the only thing they would find was an ally.

Proctor raised his sword to block the blade that cleaved down at him as his stallion reared and attacked the Enemy with its hooves and teeth. He clung to his shield, warding off blow after blow from one soldier as another worked furiously to get his blade inside his guard. He parried the thrusts, then changed through to a downward cut that took his opponent in the neck. The man crumbled as Proctor swung his sword around to ward off a glancing slice from the opposite direction.

He spun his horse away, angling the destrier back toward the charging horde.

Darien gazed down from the rim of the summit, his boots scant inches from the edge. He was no longer troubled by the reeling vertigo he had experienced earlier. Many things he had been afraid of before had ceased to be a problem. Arden's thanacryst sat on its haunches at his side, nose quivering as it scented the wind, drooling an awful fluid that slicked its dark fur and dripped, viscous, to the stone. The necrators at his back remained silently at their stations. He paid them no mind. They would linger there until he deigned to send them away. He was their master, now.

Darien gazed down, considering the view below with calm indifference. To the north, he could see the wedge of the first host, dispersed now as they rushed to harry what was left of Proctor's men. To the west, he could see the van of the second host emerging from behind the ridge. There was still no trace of Emmery's support, but now he doubted he would need it. Orien's Circle glowed behind him, pulsing to the cadence of the magic field.

He waited, watching as below him, men of Proctor's command were swept under by a breaking tide of death.

He waited and did nothing.

Reaching down, he ran his fingers over the coarse fur of the thanacryst's head. The beast had been anxious, ever since he had dumped its mistress' corpse off the edge of the cliff. He soothed it with quiet, whispered words, hand ruffling the slathered fur of its neck.

Garret Proctor felt the arrow take him in the chest, piercing through his armor even as his sword smashed through the visor of an Enemy pikeman. Gritting his teeth, he brought his blade up again. Hacking his way out of a thicket of shields and swords, he sent his mount at a gallop across the snow-covered plain. Ahead, he could see the tall spire of Orien's Finger like an ancient and decrepit pillar thrusting upward into the sky.

All he had to do was reach the pillar's base. After that, his final duty would be consummated.

The thanacryst growled. He thought perhaps it might be hungry.

Patting its head, Darien took one last look down at the flagging chase below, then turned away from the edge. Under the silent watch of the necrators, he strode calmly to the center of the circle, taking his place at the focal point of the glimmering lines of the star.

It was time.

Darien closed his eyes, shrouding his mind in concentration as he felt the Circle of Convergence through his feet. The lines of power pulsed once, harkening to his call. Gathering the energies of the focus, Darien summoned the strength of the magic field, offering himself as a conduit for the vast intensity of the vortex.

The battle below forgotten, he opened up his mind. The surge of power flooded into him, filling him, consuming him utterly.

The lines of Orien's Circle glowed, glimmering, increasing to a white brilliance unequalled even by the sun. A breeze stirred, playing with the strands of his hair. The wind swelled, became a vibrant gust of air that moved along the perimeter of the circle, slowly rotating. Almost stately, the spinning column of air grew, groping upward into the sky as the new-found morning began to darken.

The thanacryst threw back its head and howled.

The necrators looked silently on, their dark forms unaffected by the first strains of the grand resonance forming around them, groping upward to choke the sky.

Chapter Thirty-Six
Grand Resonance

The Cerulean Plains, The Rhen

Garret Proctor fought the reins of his horse, wincing as his arm grazed the arrow in his chest. The entire front of his padded gambeson was stained a dark burgundy sheen. Fighting had enlarged the wound, and the battle-rage that quickened his heart only served to pump the blood out faster. He had seen such wounds before and knew it was mortal.

Grasping the arrow, he snapped off the protruding end of the shaft and flung it away. The pain was fierce, almost incapacitating. His vision swam, and for a moment the pillar of rock before him wavered and grew dim. Looking down, he could see his lifeblood now coming in spurts timed to the rhythm of his heartbeat.

Orien's Finger reared sharply overhead, jutting upward into the sky. As his horse took the hill at the base of the crag, Proctor drew back on the reins and wheeled his mount around. Behind him, what was left of the men under his command were embroiled in a desperate race. There were so few left. Two more fell from their horses even as he watched. The writhing mass of both Enemy armies flooded behind them, churning like an ocean at the place where two swift currents meet.

The hurling onslaught slowed to a halt. His back to the rock face of Orien's Finger, Proctor brandished his sword over his head as the men that were left formed up at his side. Before them, the front ranks of the Enemy pierced the air with a resonating cry.

The cry was taken up like a wave through the ranks, sweeping out from the crag like a deafening riptide. The clamor rose even further as the second host joined in, over fifty thousand fresh voices adding their thunder to the din.

And then every voice suddenly silenced in unison as all eyes were drawn upward to the sky.

From horizon to horizon, the dawn went abruptly, alarmingly gray. Proctor saw a shadow slip across the face of the sun, rendering its disk pale and colorless, like a face taken by the pallor of death. The new white sun glowed like an ill omen in the sky, its veiled face emitting little warmth and little light. The day turned rapidly, sinisterly cold. The air seemed almost to congeal, became stiff and still.

A dreadful calm descended on the plains, silent and impassive. Even the dark ranks of the Enemy stood motionless, like a frozen black sea. His own men glanced around fearfully, faces as pale as the dim sun overhead.

Garret Proctor did not need to look up. He knew what was coming. Instead he closed his eyes, fondly remembering the few friends he had known in life and praying the gods would forgive his sins.

The sky grew dark as the sun paled to a ghostly hue. Staring up at it, Malcolm Wellingford knew his face only reflected the ghastly shade. The summit of Orien's Finger could be seen looming high above the ridge behind them, encased in a circulating mass of black clouds that expanded even as it rotated, groping out across the sky.

"The signal," Wellingford whispered to himself through the fear that gripped his heart. The turmoil above surpassed anything his nightmares had ever conceived. He had been expecting something big, perhaps even terrible, but nothing as darkly *evil* as the sickness above that infected the sky.

The boy still in him wanted to turn his horse and flee, gallop away as fast and as far as he could. But the new-found man within him knew he had a duty to perform. A duty that, at all cost, had to proceed.

General Wellingford drew his sword, striving to keep the point of the blade steady as he held it skyward over his head. Raising his voice, he addressed his men:

"Ring them in to the line, push them up against the pillar as close as you can! They'll try to run but accord them no escape! We have but one chance at this. There'll not be another. *Do not fall back!*

"Now, *FORWARD!*"

With a downward slash, he leveled his sword in the air. The blade did not waver in his hand, so unlike the heart that faltered in his chest. He was but a boy, but he was also a man with a homeland to defend.

He held his breath as twelve thousand men rushed out from behind the cover of the ridge, the sound of their charge shaking the very ground and trembling the air around him.

As Swain had promised, they were exactly an hour late. Kyel had fidgeted in the saddle the entire ride, terrified of what awaited them up ahead. He strained for a view of Orien's Finger, but the sight of it was still blocked by a range of hills that stretched out in front of them to the north. What he did see ahead was disconcerting.

"What is that?" He pointed at a dark patch in the distance that was almost hidden from sight by a small grove of trees.

Swain squinted, a frown of concentration on his face. A look of surprise dawned in his eyes. He whispered, "It looks to me like a bunch of fools. Something tells me you held back a few bits of Darien's plan."

"I told you what I knew," Kyel said defensively. "He's the one who didn't share everything with me."

Swain looked skeptical. "So you're telling me you had no idea an army from Chamsbrey was going to be meeting us here?"

Kyel shook his head, wondering what on earth Chamsbrey's presence could mean. He didn't wonder long. Looking up into a sky suddenly dark and gray, he saw with dread that the sun had gone a pasty shade of white.

And then the crag came into view. At its summit was a spiraling mass of black clouds. Appallingly unnatural, they spread outward like a rotating saucer that was rapidly increasing in size. Kyel stared up at it, horrified.

At his side, Nigel Swain drew up his mount. "Not dangerous, you say?"

Kyel barely heard him. He gaped at that writhing mass with acute disbelief. That couldn't be Darien. It couldn't be. The thing in the sky was *evil.* There was no other word for it. And the sun…whatever had been done to the sun was repulsive. Something malevolent was taking place ahead, something both hideous and terrifying.

"What is it?" he whispered.

Beside him, Swain never took his eyes off the abomination in the sky. "I have no idea."

Kyel pulled his horse up, transfixed by the view ahead. In the distance, he could see Orien's Finger with its black, swirling crown. At its base was almost the mirror image of what was taking place above in the sky.

The dark mass of the Enemy host was ringed by a thin line of infantry desperately fighting a pitched battle to hold their line. The scene was as heartrending as it was appalling. The army from Chamsbrey had no chance. Their numbers were like a child's dike of sand trying to hold back the rising flood of a river.

In the sky above, the black clouds rumbled. A low, resonating thunder built gradually until Kyel could feel it in his chest. The sound of it swelled, unrelenting.

His horse reared, almost throwing him off, and still the echoing thunder rose. Kyel jumped down and grabbed his mount by the bridle, holding it with one hand as he tried to cover his ears. The rumble became a deafening vibration.

And then the entire world went black. Looking up, Kyel saw that the racing clouds had utterly consumed the sky. They swirled overhead, raging. The only light to be seen was at the summit of Orien's Finger. There, a white brilliance gleamed from out of the darkness, pulsating with thrumming vibrations that shook the air and trembled the very foundations of the earth.

Kyel's horse reared again, knocking him to the ground. The gelding bolted, galloping away, but he hardly noticed. His eyes were fixed on that pulsing beacon of light.

An explosion of orange-yellow flame shot upward from the summit, blazed there for a span of seconds, and then turned and swept back down upon itself. It poured over the sides of the crag, spilling like a ferocious, glowing waterfall to rush outward in an expanding cloud that whipped across the plains. There was a brief, blinding flare of light. Kyel screamed, throwing his hands up before his face.

Then it vanished, as if stopped by an invisible and impregnable wall. The noise of it hit, a terrible, air-splitting thunder like the sound of all the heavens collapsing straight into hell. Then the sound was gone, dying almost as abruptly as it came. A warm wind like a summer breeze drifted toward them from the crag, billowing great clouds of dust up high into the air.

Kyel watched from the ground, mouth gaping, unable to believe what his eyes had just seen, what his ears had just heard.

It had taken seconds. Only seconds. Nothing could have survived that.

At the summit, the white light faded to a dim afterglow, then died away completely. Overhead, the sky was still encased in darkness, though the clouds seemed to be slowing. Below on the plain, nothing moved. An appalling stillness had taken hold of the morning.

Kyel looked out into the darkness, his mind numb, his heart heavy with tears.

Darien opened his eyes to find the demon-hound nuzzling its head against his face, whimpering. His vision blurred, and for a moment there seemed to be two beasts leaning over him. The images wavered, gradually blending into one. The thanacryst crouched at his side, its forelegs sprawled across his chest. Doglike, it reached its head out and slathered the side of his face with its black and oozing tongue. The smell of the creature was foul, like moldering death.

The sky was not as dark as it had been. The unnatural night had given way to an overcast sky. The clouds above were drizzling, a gentle sprinkle that was warm and comforting.

"Move," Darien told the beast, patting his hand on the stone by his side. The thanacryst whined a complaint but shifted its weight off his chest. It lay down beside him, its muzzle between its paws, looking dejected.

Darien rolled onto his side then pushed himself up weakly. He was sitting near the edge of the summit, though he didn't remember getting there. Before him, the circle was quiescent. Sadly, he realized it would never again awaken. Orien's Circle was ruined. The stone itself seemed to have liquefied and run, then cooled once more in rippling pools of slag. The star itself was grotesquely distorted. The lights of its rays would never shine again. The abusive torrent of power he had subjected it to had destroyed the circle completely.

It was a waste, one of a great many wastes that had come from this day.

He tried to push himself to his feet but found he lacked the strength for it. So instead Darien leaned back, resting his head against the thanacryst's heaving side. He gazed upward at the gray, overcast sky and let the rain drizzle down on his face. Dimly, he could see the dark shadows of the necrators still present at their stations around the summit's rim, silent guardians watching over him sightlessly. He found their presence strangely comforting.

He closed his eyes and let his mind wander toward sleep. But almost as soon as it came, his rest was disturbed by a fragile sound from below. Sitting back up, he stared warily at the place where the stairs met the summit's rim. Behind him, the thanacryst uttered a low growl.

Darien did nothing; there was nothing he could do. If it was one of Renquist's darkmages, then they would have him. The bone-weary exhaustion that filled him prevented him from touching the field. He had a suspicion of whom it might be, and he wasn't prepared for that challenge, either.

But he was wrong. To his horror, it was Naia's veiled face that crested the rim.

She froze as she took in the vision of the necrators and the thanacryst at his back. Face pale, she looked at him, slowly shaking her head. She was the last person in the world he wanted to see. He had wanted Naia to remember him the way he was. Not like this.

She crept forward, gaze wandering over the melted circle at her feet. Then she stopped, eyes drawn to the necrator that glided forward to confront her. Darien frowned, not understanding the demon's sudden motion. Naia's presence should not have provoked it; she was no mage.

"Visea," he whispered, and watched as all six shadows melted downward, disappearing into the stone.

She pressed forward again, crossing the ruined circle to stand before him, eyes on the thanacryst that stood growling from deep within its throat. Darien put a hand on the beast, stilling it. Then he looked down, not wanting her to see the shadows that he knew consumed his eyes.

She knelt beside him, reaching out a hand to touch his face. He shrank away from her touch, wincing as if in pain. Her hand found his hair instead, running through it soothingly.

He closed his eyes, wishing to the gods he was dead. If he were dead, she wouldn't have to see him this way. Better that she gaze upon his corpse than be witness to the decayed corruption that had become of his soul.

"Easy," she whispered, trailing a hand down his cheek.

He suffered her touch. A week ago, he had longed for it. But Naia's hand was pure and wholesome, and it had no business touching such a filthy thing as his face.

"I'm here," she whispered. "I won't leave you again."

But that wasn't what he wanted. He needed her to leave, right now, before it was too late.

"Can you stand?" she asked. "We must go down from here. It's not safe."

He couldn't understand why. The Enemy was no longer a threat. Or, at least, they shouldn't be. Darien felt confused. His senses were jumbled, and he was feeling even fainter now than he had before, as if Naia's soft touch had sapped away the last vestige of his strength.

She stood up and pulled him to his feet. Darien staggered as the world seemed to lurch, but he managed to remain standing with Naia's support. He had to lean on her heavily as she guided him across the destroyed circle to the stairs.

He could hear the sound of the thanacryst's paws padding along behind, dutifully following its new master.

Kyel walked at Swain's side over the blackened ground. The blast from the circle had created an almost perfect ring of devastation that extended out about a league from Orien's Finger, where it suddenly just stopped. After that, the plains continued off to the horizon, untouched.

Kyel didn't understand it. But apparently, someone else had. The remains of Chamsbrey's army were wandering in dazed shock on the other side of the boundary, not daring to set foot within the ring of scorched earth. Someone had known where that boundary would be and had positioned most of the soldiers on the other side of it during the battle, saving their lives.

But the Enemy hosts had not been so lucky. Kyel picked his way around what remained of the two armies, now reduced to twisted lumps of melted armor. There would be no graves dug here; there was nothing left to bury. Not even bones had survived the tremendous heat of the blast. The black soil that crunched beneath his feet glittered where it had been melted into glass.

The sight was appalling. Swain walked in silence, face constricted in a grisly scowl. Kyel didn't know how to feel. In a way, he was almost as dazed as Chamsbrey's soldiers. A victory had taken place here today, though it had more the feel of a bitter defeat.

War had been waged, but what kind of war? There was no honor in what had happened here, only cold inhumanity. His homeland was safe, but at what cost? A price had been paid, and it was more than the sum of the souls that had been taken so brutally out of life.

Orien's Finger loomed overhead, its sides scorched black, its summit appearing dangerously offset. A crack had widened near the summit, and the stone itself had slipped forward. The entire top of the pillar seemed in danger of toppling at any moment. Kyel shivered, almost hoping to see it go.

They reached the base of the column, feet still crunching on glass that looked like dried and cracked pools of mud. Kyel stared down at one such puddle, wondering how hot the sand must have been to melt like that. It was beyond imagining.

A hand on his arm made him look up.

Swain had stopped, fingers reflexively going for the hilt of his sword, though he didn't draw the blade. Kyel looked ahead to the base of the crag.

Naia sat at the opening of a narrow stair carved into the side of the cliff, Darien's head resting on her lap. His eyes were closed as if in sleep. Naia's hand stroked gently through his hair. Behind them, a hideous beast sat on its haunches, panting. It looked almost like a dog—a dog exhumed from the grave. It drooled long strings of saliva that dripped to the stone.

Kyel felt stunned by fear. He wasn't sure what provoked it—whether it was inspired by the repulsive beast or the sight of Darien lying cradled in Naia's lap. Kyel couldn't tell whether he was dead or asleep, and he wasn't sure which would scare him more. This was the man responsible for the atrocity that had turned even the very sand to glass, and the fell beast that lingered above him only affirmed Kyel's fear.

Swain started forward and Kyel followed, stopping as the captain knelt at Naia's side. The priestess looked up at him through her veil, an unspoken question on her face. As Swain moved a hand to Darien's arm, the mage opened his eyes.

Kyel turned away. He couldn't bear to look at him. The shadows that had once wandered across the Sentinel's eyes had since utterly consumed them. Darien's face was a mask of pain.

"I thought you'd come," he whispered, staring up at Swain. The words didn't even sound like his own. The beast above him whimpered, edging closer. Naia encircled him in her arms, looking fiercely protective.

"Then you know why I'm here," Swain muttered softly.

Darien nodded.

"I can't leave you Unbound," the blademaster said, sitting down next to him on the step below. "You're too dangerous now."

Darien shook his head. "There are some things I have to do first."

Swain drew back, a considering look on his face. Almost kindly, he assured him, "Kyel is perfectly capable. He's come along well. You've done what you had to do, now leave the rest to him."

Naia stared at Swain with a contemptuous look in her eyes. Darien grimaced, pushing himself up with effort. He squeezed his eyes shut as he leaned on the step above to stabilize himself. Kyel wanted to go to him, but something held him back.

"It takes two mages working together to seal the Well of Tears," Darien said. "Kyel can't do it alone."

The captain shrugged indifferently. "Then leave the damn thing open. Come on. You knew the price before you started any of this. Don't try to wheedle out of it now."

Darien glared at him. "You know me better than that."

"I don't know you at all anymore."

Darien brought a weary hand up to rub his face. "Aidan must be stopped. He's using the Well of Tears to coordinate the Eight with the strength of the Enemy. If you leave him be, everything I've done here today won't matter. They'll just keep coming."

"I don't know," Swain muttered, looking around at the charred earth that surrounded them. "If you're asking me to choose between you and your brother, I'd have to pick Aidan. From what I'm seeing, he's the lesser of two evils."

"Do you think I enjoyed this?" Darien demanded, eyes narrowing.

"I don't know, Darien. Did you?"

Behind them, the beast growled, standing up. The hair on the back of its neck raised, its mouth open and cavernous. Darien put a hand out. The creature sat back down, closing its mouth with a snap.

Swain sighed, shaking his head. "Look, Darien, I'm not here to argue with you. Either Transfer your gift to Kyel, or I'll be forced to end this myself. You're the son of Gerald and Emelda Lauchlin. Honor their memory and die with some dignity."

Naia gasped, and even Kyel felt his anger rising. Staring down at the iron chains on his wrists, he remembered the resolution he had made, back in Romana's cell. The reason he had put the Soulstone on in the first place. He wasn't supposed to be letting this happen.

"You can't touch me," Darien said, spreading his hands. The sleeves of his faded shirt fell back, revealing a set of fresh pink scars that encircled both his wrists where the marks of his Oath had once been. Kyel found the sight of them appalling, and not just because of their appearance.

Swain sneered down, unconvinced. "Look at you. You're wiped out. You couldn't even think of touching the field in your condition."

Darien raised his eyes to Kyel. "Show him."

"Show him what?" Kyel frowned.

Darien's eyes hardened. "You know damn well what I mean."

Kyel thought he did. Only, it took him completely aback that Darien already knew about it. Still, he found himself holding his breath as he reached out with his mind and did the only thing he knew how to do with his ability: he bent a link on each chain.

The iron bracelets slid off his arms, falling to the dirt with a clinking noise. Swain stared down at the chains, stunned. Kyel just hoped it would be enough.

In front of him, Darien pushed himself up, rising to his feet. He still looked unstable, but the dark shadows in his eyes compensated for any weakness his stance implied.

Glaring down at Swain, the mage said, "You can take your chances against two of us, Unbound. Or you can listen to my offer."

Still gazing at the chains, the blademaster said, "I'm listening."

"Come with me to Aerysius. Let me finish what I've started. After that, you can do whatever you desire with me. You have my word. I'll do nothing to resist."

Nigel Swain appeared to be thinking, his eyes considering the beast behind Darien. "I don't know if I trust your word."

"Do you trust mine?" Kyel asked him, stepping forward.

The captain turned to regard him. "You came to me claiming to be an acolyte. That doesn't do much for my trust."

"I was." Reaching into the pocket of his cloak, he withdrew the Soulstone, letting it swing by one of the heavy silver bands. "The stone contained his mother's gift," he admitted. "I put it on and received the Transference in the cell."

He took a deep breath, wondering how far he dared go. Glancing at Naia with a look of apology, he turned back to Swain.

"Darien will no longer be a threat if we close the gateway. The Well of Tears demands a sacrifice in order to seal it. He's known about it all along. It's always been his intent to offer himself."

Naia surged up, demanding, "Is this true?"

Darien nodded, turning to fix Swain with a look of rigid contempt. "When the gateway collapses, my soul will be trapped in the Netherworld. Is that end dignified enough for you?"

Kyel looked down. He had seen this coming all along. He had been hoping Darien had found another way. But there was no other way. Swain was right; one look at the hideous beast confirmed it. Darien had planned this well. He had known from the beginning about the Well and had known the price of giving up his Oath. He had devised a perfect strategy to pay both tabs with a single coin.

Swain never took his eyes from the creature as he grated, "I guess it'll have to do. You've already damned yourself anyway."

Naia's hand shot up and slapped him on the face.

The captain stared at her for a long moment then turned and strode away. Kyel glanced after him, wondering what Swain was going to do. But the sound of Naia's voice made him turn back around.

"Darien, *no,*" she pleaded, reaching out for him.

But the mage jerked his arm out of her grasp. "You should never have come back."

Darien took a lurching step down the stairs, followed by another. Not knowing what else to do, Kyel rushed forward to support him, glancing back at Naia in sympathy. He helped Darien down the last few steps as the priestess stared at his back, looking just as devastated as the surrounding landscape.

They hadn't gone far when the sound of Darien's voice halted him. "Give me the Soulstone."

Kyel looked at him, taken aback. But nevertheless, he drew the medallion from his pocket and handed it over. Darien clutched the stone tightly, holding it against his chest for a moment before dropping his hand. His body trembled with the strain of just staying upright.

Darien reached up and removed Kyel's hand from his arm. "Now, repeat each word I say, exactly as I say it: 'I swear to live in harmony with all of creation.'"

Kyel gulped, realizing his master's intent. Numbly, his lips moved, uttering the phrases of the Oath of Harmony:

I swear to live in harmony with all of creation,
To use my gift with temperance and wisdom;
Always to heal and never to harm,
Or my life will be rightfully forfeit.

When he heard the sound of his own voice trail at last into silence, Kyel looked down at his right arm, reveling in the beauty of the shimmering chain that had appeared, graven into his skin by the conviction of his words.

Chapter Thirty-Seven
A Deeper Look

The Cerulean Plains, The Rhen

Kyel pulled back the flap of the tent and ducked as he entered. It was dim, though still bright enough to see by the ambient light. Once inside, he was able to stand upright, letting the flap swing back into place.

Naia turned to look up at him, her veil rendered almost opaque in the poor lighting. She was kneeling on the floor, fingers resting on Darien's hand. The mage was curled at her side in a bundle of covers, for all appearances deep in sleep. A sleep that had lasted for three days.

In all that time, the priestess had never left Darien's side. Kyel had come often to look in, making sure she didn't need anything. Each time he did, he was reminded again of Luther Penthos, the High Priest of Death. Naia's father. Kyel had almost confronted her about it. But then he'd thought better of it.

Her presence stirred his hopes. If anything could possibly save Darien from himself, it was Naia's willing love. From Kyel's perspective, the priestess was the last, best chance Darien had of salvaging his soul before he died.

"How is he?" he asked.

"The same." The priestess sighed. "He still hasn't awakened."

Kyel could tell by the sound of her voice that she was worried. Naia was fiercely protective of him, especially when Swain was around. Whenever the captain came to glance in, Kyel could almost see the priestess' hackles raise. It was a reflection of the way that strange beast looked whenever Kyel came too near it.

"The sleep's normal," Kyel assured her for what seemed like

the hundredth time. "He did the same thing the last time he wore himself out."

From its place at Darien's feet, the hideous creature stirred from sleep, awakening with a wide, cavernous yawn. Kyel found the thing revolting. Like Naia, the beast hadn't moved from the vigil it kept at Darien's side. Whenever Kyel came near it, the thing uttered a low growl, its nose wetly quivering. Kyel felt certain the creature would have attacked by now, if it wasn't for Darien's presence holding it at bay.

"What is it?" he asked, giving voice to the question that had echoed so often in his mind.

"A thanacryst."

Kyel glanced at Naia in surprise. She had never mentioned knowing anything about it, and he wondered where she had come by the knowledge. The thing made his skin crawl, especially the way it was always studying him with yearning interest.

"It doesn't like me," he muttered, staring at it.

The priestess nodded, her face pensive. "I think it's hungry. It senses food."

Kyel didn't like the sound of that. He had the feeling there was something inside him the beast desperately wanted to feast upon. The creature turned away, laying its head across Darien's legs with a desolate whimper.

The mage stirred, groaning and tossing in his sleep. Naia's hand moved to fix the blanket that had slipped down. As if comforted by her touch, Darien's face immediately relaxed. Almost, Kyel thought he could see the man he remembered from Greystone Keep.

Naia's veiled face was the first thing Darien saw when he opened his eyes. He had been drifting in and out of sleep, each time coming a bit closer to full wakefulness. It was difficult. His body resisted even the most fundamental impulse to stir from the heavy weight of the covers and the soft pallet beneath him. He stretched, for a moment basking in the soothing warmth of

Naia's tender smile.

And then he saw the thanacryst. And remembered.

Her smile was anathema, as poisonous to him as deadly nightshade. If he succumbed to it, he would lose every advantage he had gained by consummating his sins between Arden's legs. Then he would be prey once more for the necrators. Even the thanacryst would turn on him to slake its ravenous thirst for the life force of a mage. He would lose the only opportunity he had to prevail against his brother. No. Love was a luxury his impoverished heart could not afford.

He could barely stand to look at Naia after what had passed between Arden and himself. There had been no love in the act, but there had been passion. Desperate passion. It was a requirement. If he hadn't enjoyed the moment to its fullest, then his ploy would have failed utterly. The necrators would have probed his heart and found him still wanting. He would have never regained his perception of the magic field and, in all likelihood, he would be dead by now. That, or on his way to Bryn Calazar in chains. Nevertheless, the guilt plagued him fiercely. He could never expect Naia to understand or to forgive him. Darien doubted he could ever bring himself to ask. He didn't want to.

He had to find a way to make her leave. Her very presence was a corruption, a temptation he knew he didn't have the strength to fight. The part he had left to play was going to be difficult enough. If she stayed, he doubted he could go through with it at all.

"I thought you'd be gone by now," he said. He didn't have to work hard at instilling the cold dispassion that came through in his voice. It was there naturally now, a brittle outgrowth of his twisted soul.

"I'm not leaving you again," she assured him, ignoring the cruelness of his tone. "You need me by your side."

He seemed to recall her saying something similar once before, though he couldn't remember when. Grimly, he shook his head. "This is no place for you."

But Naia just smiled down at him, a poisonous, rapturous look.

Taking his hand, she said, "In Auberdale, I asked you to make a decision that was not yours to make. I didn't realize it at the time, but it was my decision all along."

"Naia, that makes no difference—"

"It does," she insisted firmly, her voice ringing out above his own. "I told you I can either be a priestess or your lover, and I've made up my mind."

"No," Darien growled, jerking his hand back and sitting up. "I've made up *my* mind. I don't want you here. Go home."

"Darien—"

"Go home, Naia," he raged coldly, feeling frustrated and lost. "I want you to leave. *Just go.*"

"No."

Her eyes trail down to the thanacryst at his feet. The creature noticed her attention, growling softly as it rolled over on its side in a submissive posture.

Holding fast to her quiet smile, she told him, "I've sat here for three days looking down at this wretched beast. People come and go. It ignores everyone. Yet, strangely, it doesn't seem to like me. It's appalling, really, the way it keeps sniffing me, almost as if it's hungry."

"Perhaps it is," Darien said, staring at the thing.

"It doesn't seem to like Kyel, either. Every time he comes here to look in on you, that creature stares at him and growls dreadfully."

Darien frowned as the meaning of her words slowly sank in.

The priestess continued, "I found myself starting to wonder, isn't it odd that the beast ignores the presence of every other person, with the exception of Kyel and myself? And then I began wondering, what in the world could Kyel and I possibly share in common?"

Any feeling Darien had left was drained away by the time she had finished speaking. He stared at her, his mind and heart utterly bereft. It was impossible. And yet…it also made sense.

"Look at me," he commanded.

Naia did. Her dark eyes were wide and clear through the fabric of her veil, those eyes that before had consumed his dreams, his hopes and desires. He must believe they held nothing for him now. Naia's eyes were perfect in every way, wide and glinting with the fierce spark of intelligence he found so compelling. Compassion was there, too. Her gaze was suffused with it, along with a caring tenderness that made him ache. But if there was anything else in her eyes, the translucent fabric that hung between them obscured it from his sight.

"Without the veil," he commanded.

What he asked was tantamount to ordering Naia to strip naked there in front of him. Before, it had been a wondrous gift she had shared with him willingly. Now, with all that had transpired, asking her to remove her veil felt like a transgression.

As if to torture him, Naia smiled tenderly as she lifted both hands and drew the fabric back from her face. He found himself confronted by the unconstrained radiance of her gaze, unable to look away. It was wondrous, mesmerizing. Her face held an irresistible solace, an unconditional promise of hope and commitment.

Naia's dark eyes promised him everything he'd ever wanted and more. He could never have any of it.

"Put it back," he whispered.

She obeyed, lowering the veil back into place. As she did, it seemed as if the last light faded quietly from his world. He looked down, squeezing his eyes shut against the pain. Her presence was torture enough. He never should have allowed this. He couldn't stand it.

"I have the potential, don't I?" Her words stirred across the bleakness of his heart.

It took him a moment to answer her. "I never saw it before."

But it was there, undeniably. He didn't even need to test her to be certain. There could be no mistaking it.

"Perhaps you didn't want to see it," Naia said. "Or perhaps you weren't looking deep enough."

But he already knew why he'd never noticed it there before. Her veil obscured the shine of the potential in her eyes. And the two times he had seen her face in its absence, his mind had been on other things. Near her, he was blinded to even the blatantly obvious. Her presence befuddled his senses, fouled his edge. Another potent reason why she had to go.

"This changes nothing," he said.

"Yes, it does. Kyel is no longer your acolyte. You need someone who can inherit your gift."

There, she was wrong. The power within him was a monstrous legacy too potent for any one mage. He would never condemn her to such a fate. It would be too much for her, even as brightly as she burned. He could never do that to her, even if he had a choice. Which he didn't.

"I'm sorry, Naia, but my gift dies with me."

Her face paled, her expression faltering. With a look of desperation, she fiercely shook her head. "I won't accept that. You always find a way."

He whispered, "Not this time."

"You're not even going to try, are you?".

He wasn't. There was no point. "You heard Swain. Mages were never meant to exist Unbound. Look at me. I'm living proof of the reason for the Oath."

"There has to be a way," she insisted. "Can't you just say the words again?"

"Once forsaken, the Oath can never be reaffirmed."

Naia's brow creased in frustration, her eyes wet and glistening. "So you're just giving up?"

Her grief only served to provoke him. This was exactly why she had to leave. Now. Before the sight of her tears softened his heart. He told her in a tone devoid of mercy:

"Now do you understand why you have to go? We have no chance, you and me. No future. *Look at that thing.*" He nodded at the thanacryst. "That is my soul, Naia. Do you know how I came by that creature? I killed its former mistress—right after I lay with her."

He ignored her sharp gasp and pressed on. "I don't deserve you, and you sure as hell deserve better than me. Now, take your things and get out. *Leave.*"

She was sobbing. Her shoulders were shaking, her hands pressed against her face over the fabric of her veil. Darien watched, unmoved. She could spill every last tear in her body, but it was better this way. Much better.

Still, she didn't go.

In the end, it was he who left the tent, the thanacryst jogging dutifully behind in his wake.

Kyel was bored. There was nothing to do in the encampment, at least nothing for a mage. The soldiers seemed busy enough, scurrying here and there about their duties. The camp of Faukravar's army had an entirely different feel to it than Emmery's. It was easy to tell a Chamsbrey soldier without looking at the uniform. They all seemed to be going through the motions of their various labors in a daze, their efforts halfhearted. There were far fewer men wearing black and violet uniforms than blue and white. What Chamsbrey did have was a disproportionate supply of tents. Counting tents, Kyel had figured that Faukravar's army was now roughly half the size it had been before the morning of Black Solstice.

That's what they were calling it now. He'd heard the words often throughout both camps. It seemed apt. Black for the clouds that had darkened the sky, black for the charred earth beneath Orien's summit. Black for the lives that had been so cruelly ripped out of life, both friend and Enemy alike. And black for the atrocious means used to attain such a one-sided victory.

He knew what to call it now, the awesome and horrendous undertaking Darien had performed alone on the summit of the crag. According to the priestess, Darien had created a grand resonance, something conceived of in theory but never before employed. Not even Orien himself had worked such appalling devastation. Darien's desperate act on the summit had far surpassed even the most notorious feat of Aerysius' most infamous Grand Master. Orien couldn't have even accomplished such an act; he'd been only fifth tier.

Only.

The sound of raised voices startled Kyel out of his thoughts, and he hurried forward out of curiosity. As he moved past rows of tents, men noticed his cloak and stepped away from him with looks of fear. Kyel didn't blame them. What they had seen on Black Solstice had given them more than enough reason to fear the sight of a mage.

Rounding a group of tents, Kyel saw the cause of the commotion. To his surprise, he recognized Nigel Swain standing beside General Blandford in what looked like a heated argument with the King of Chamsbrey.

The King was seething, face red and eyes scalding. One white-gloved hand was fingering the pommel of the sword he wore at his hip, the other twisting one of the points of his goatee.

"Who do you think you are, to presume to gainsay me?" the King growled.

Swain stood in a fighting stance, his body at an angle to the King. He said, "There's another army headed this way, and I'm not about to let you just pack up your toys and leave."

Kyel frowned, walking closer. Swain's words shocked him, the vehemence in them nearly as outrageous as the news of another army. If the captain wasn't careful, he was going to wind up with his head on a block.

"How dare you," spat Faukravar, face turning an even deeper shade of red. "General Blandford, I want this man scourged!"

Blandford looked at the King dully, lifting one of his long-whiskered eyebrows. "I'm sorry, Your Grace, but my Lady Queen would be most put out if I consented to scourge her fiancé."

Kyel stopped in his tracks. Looking at Nigel Swain, he felt like hitting himself over the head for not seeing it before. Romana had all but deferred to the captain, back at the palace in Rothscard. And Swain had been passionate in his devotion to her.

Faukravar's face melted through several shades of red into pasty white. "What?"

"That's right." Swain grinned smugly.

Faukravar's gloved hand dropped from his goatee as he struggled to compose himself. He said, "It would seem that Romana has even worse taste in men than she does in wine."

Swain shook his head. "My Queen has excellent taste in wine. She just has better sense than to waste a good vintage on a coward like you."

Gasps issued from the small crowd of onlookers as Faukravar's face turned a glaring purple. Tugging the glove from his hand, he threw it down in the snow between them, visibly trembling in outrage. Swain stared down at the white glove, eyes coolly considering.

It was time to intervene, Kyel decided. Surging forward, he bent down and retrieved the King's glove, holding it up and offering it back to him. Faukravar's eyes took in the glove then moved to linger on Kyel's black cloak. His face looked ready to burst from the amount of blood that engorged it.

"I'd take it, if I were you," Kyel urged him, indicating the glove in his outstretched hand. "Unless you have a champion eager to duel a Guild blademaster."

Faukravar stared at the glove, stared at Swain, then glared at Kyel. His lips curled, revealing a set of chipped and yellowed teeth that had the look of worn daggers. He snatched the glove out of Kyel's hand and stalked off, followed by a small group of lackeys, muttering something about "contemptible mages" under his breath. When he was gone, Kyel turned back to face a still-grinning Nigel Swain.

"What's this about another army?" he demanded.

The grin disappeared from the captain's face. "Thirty thousand, coming from the Gap of Amberlie. They'll be here by evening." He sighed, blowing a greasy lock of hair back from his mouth. "It seems Darien was right, after all. They'll just keep coming."

"Rider approaching!"

Kyel turned at the sound of the outcry, glancing across the blackened terrain. He saw the exhausted horse before he saw the rider, recognizing the man from the color of his cloak. It was the first gray cloak he had seen south of the Pass of Lor-Gamorth. The rider was from Greystone Keep, and by the looks of it, badly injured.

Kyel ran toward him, Swain following at his heels as he

captured the spent horse by its bridle. The soldier was already sliding out of his saddle when the captain caught him up in his arms, easing the man to the ground.

Kyel leaned over him, placing a hand on his chest and desperately trying to probe the man with his mind, the way he had seen Darien do before. An image came to him, fleeting and unintelligible. But his eyes saw enough to tell that the man was dying. His face already wore a pale mask of death, the shirt beneath his mail vest saturated with blood.

"Archer?" the soldier muttered weakly, looking perplexed.

Kyel frowned, staring down at the man, trying to see under the caked blood and grime that splattered his face. He thought he might recognize him but couldn't be certain. It didn't matter anyway. His own name was the last word the soldier would ever utter.

Kyel grimaced as Swain bent down to close the dead man's eyes. If only he knew enough of his gift to do something useful with it, he might have been able to save him. Darien could have done it. But Darien wasn't there.

"What's this?" Swain whispered.

Looking down, Kyel saw what the captain referred to. The dead man's hand clasped a piece of rolled parchment that was stained brown with dried blood. Swain had to fight the man's death grip to retrieve it. Unrolling the scroll, he scanned the page harshly before shaking his head and crushing it into Kyel's fist.

"Here," he grunted. "I can't read."

Kyel found himself staring at the captain in mute disbelief. If he was going to be a royal consort, Kyel figured the man had better learn how to read. Turning to the wadded scroll, he uncrumpled it, smoothing it against the palm of his hand. Letting his eyes trace over the neat, embellished script, he felt his heart lurch to a halt in his chest. He had to start reading the note all over again, taking it from the top. The last line he scanned at least five times before he finally believed it.

"Well?" Swain pressed. "What does it say?"

Kyel felt too stunned to speak. His hand violently clenched the parchment, wadding it up into a ball in his fist.

"It's a summons," he said finally. "Darien's presence is requested at a parley tonight under flag of truce. It's signed 'Zavier Renquist.'"

Darien backed away from the crowd of onlookers that lingered over the body of Wade Tarpen, a soldier from Greystone Keep he'd known from the two years he'd spent there. He had arrived too late to save the man. Intent on the corpse, no one paid him any mind. No one noticed as he quickly bent to retrieve a wadded ball of parchment off the ground and then silently slip away.

Without his cloak, he was harder to recognize, and few people did. They were used to marking him by the white emblem of the prime warden. But the cloak was gone now. After the transgression he had committed on its fabric, he hadn't been able to put that cloak back on. Instead he had wrapped it around Arden's body and sent it over the cliff with her vile remains.

He was clothed only in his black breeches and a shirt that he'd borrowed from one of the empty tents, his baldric tossed over it. The shirt was part of an officer's uniform, the insignia of Chamsbrey embroidered on the breast, bars of rank stitched onto the shoulders. The fabric wasn't nearly warm enough. He shivered as he strode toward the place where he'd bid the thanacryst wait.

The creature was still there, stationed in the exact spot he'd left it in front of an abandoned tent. The beast loped over to him, froths of spittle flying from its jowls. Its green eyes glinted banefully as it stared up at him, looking expectant.

"Ceise," Darien whispered, spreading his fingers at his side.

The thanacryst obeyed, falling in to heel beside him as he walked toward the margin of the camp. With the beast at his side, Darien no longer had the luxury of anonymity. Men stared, first at the thanacryst and then at him, with expressions of fear and repugnance.

The mood of the men toward him had altogether changed. It was easy to see why; Chamsbrey's army had been decimated. From what he could judge, there were perhaps a little over half the number of soldiers as had left with him from Tol-Ranier. Still, it was better than he had anticipated. Wellingford had heeded him well and had managed to keep a good number of his men out of the eye of the vortex. The boy had turned out to be a decent commander.

He trudged by a group of soldiers lingering around a fire. Darien felt their eyes upon him, heard the quiet, whispered words uttered behind his back. He could almost smell their hatred and fear. They blamed him. They were lucky to be alive to blame him. If he'd held back even a fraction, they would all be dead. He almost felt like turning to confront them, their reproach kindling a simmering fury.

As if sensing his mood, the thanacryst growled. Darien dropped his hand to steady it, feeling the beast's wet tongue licking the tips of his fingers. As he moved out of earshot of the group, he heard one of the soldiers mutter the word "darkmage" under his breath.

So that's what they thought of him, did they? Darien felt his bile rising as his temper cooled to an arctic chill. He groped for the solace of the magic field, tugging at it sharply with the full force of his mind. He took in too much, too quickly. The excess energy bled off his body in crackling blue tongues that drew stares from everyone nearby. Soldiers gaped at him, backing away. Darien paid them no heed, suffused with the soothing ecstasy of the field.

Comforted, he released it slowly.

He turned and stared out into the blackened ground that spread before him. The amount of devastation was overwhelming, beyond anything he had expected. Everything within the eye of the vortex had been reduced to char and ashes. The land itself seemed tortured.

Orien's Finger was blackened. The stone had a glassy, molten appearance. The summit looked dangerously detached, shoved to the side and leaning precariously atop its dark pedestal. He had been lucky that it hadn't given way completely.

The crunch of boots told him Wellingford was approaching. Darien had the distinctive sound of the boy's footsteps memorized. He was vaguely surprised that anyone would have the temerity to seek him out. He pretended not to notice the young man's approach, letting his general come to stand at his side unacknowledged.

"Prime Warden." Wellingford's voice was hesitant. "I didn't know you were recovered. Are you sure you're well enough to be about?"

Darien felt a mild stir of resentment that anyone would care about his health. Hadn't the boy looked out on the devastation that surrounded him? Hadn't he seen with his own eyes the injury that had been dealt here? And the dead; could he not hear the silent screams of the tortured dead that lingered in the air? So much horror could never occur in a place without leaving a lasting imprint behind. A thousand years from now, the grief of those who had died here might still be heard, a telltale whisper on the wind.

"How many total casualties?" Darien asked, wanting a number he could use to scourge his soul.

"Estimates are over a hundred thousand," Wellingford replied after a moment's hesitation. "Six thousand of our own."

Darien stared out across the blackened land, searing the numbers into his mind. "Have there been any survivors from Greystone Keep?"

"Only three, Prime Warden. All infantrymen."

Darin bowed his head, overcome. Devlin Craig had been the staunchest, most loyal friend he'd ever known. And though he still held some resentment toward Garret Proctor, Darien understood him better now. Neither man had deserved so cruel an end. Craig especially; the captain had risked his own life to save him from Arden's fire, only to be immolated by his own.

"What is the situation with this third army?" he asked in a deadened voice.

"Our scouts have reported thirty thousand on the march, coming by way of the Gap of Amberlie."

Darien nodded. His brother's work, again. "There's a darkmage with them," he informed Wellingford. "At least one. You'll need to meet them outside the eye or be faced with a magical assault."

"Where will you be?" his young general asked, looking at him anxiously.

Darien raised his hand, pointing toward the slopes of the Craghorns, his eyes seeking out the summit of the highest peak. The one surrounded by a faint green nimbus that was barely visible through a veil of white haze.

"I'll be up there. If I can seal the Well of Tears in time, it ought to neutralize their darkmage."

Wellingford looked at him in mute incomprehension, but Darien didn't explain. Instead, he said, "We'll meet tonight in the command tent to discuss strategy. Come with your officers at the turn of Third Watch. I want the officers from Emmery there as well."

"Aye, Prime Warden." Wellingford sounded doubtful. As well he should.

Darien turned his stare back to the devastated earth, imprinting its scorched features on his mind. He asked, "Have you ever seen the Black Lands, Wellingford?"

"No. I haven't."

"Well, now you can say you have."

He found Kyel and Swain together, sitting by a fire in front of a blue tent. Neither man saw him approaching. Swain looked occupied with honing his blade, while Kyel seemed to be contenting himself with picking lint off his black cloak. The cloak suited him, Darien decided. It made him appear taller, stronger. More confident. Or perhaps it wasn't the cloak at all.

The boy he had met at Greystone Keep had grown. He wasn't a boy anymore, Darien realized sadly. His innocence had been the price of those chains. It was a shame. Kyel's innocence was something Darien had always admired and even envied.

Swain glanced up and scowled. The noise of the whetstone became a shrill scrape, grinding down the length of his blade. The sound made Darien's neck prickle. He understood the threat.

"I'd like to speak with Kyel. Alone," he added, glaring at Swain.

The man shrugged, slamming his blade home in its scabbard as he rose to leave. He kicked out at the thanacryst as he stalked past, but the beast didn't seem to mind. Its attention was riveted on Kyel, its ears laid back and hackles raised.

"Theanoch!" Darien snapped at it. The thanacryst whined, slobbering furiously.

Kyel frowned up at him. His hands fell away from his cloak, the markings on his wrists gleaming metallically in the sunlight. Darien stared down at them, his interest captivated. He had found another thing about Kyel to envy.

"You're awake." Kyel sounded surprised, but not necessarily pleased.

Darien gestured toward the tent behind him, hoping that the pain he felt didn't show on his face. The young man had every right to hate him, just the same as everyone else. But it hurt, all the same.

"It's time for your last lesson," Darien said, avoiding his eyes as he moved past him into the tent.

Inside, he waited for Kyel. He wished things could have been different. In a different world, Kyel might have been his friend. In a different world, he could have married Naia, even raised a family. In a different world, his hands would not be stained in a river of blood, wiped dry on a bed of ashes. His conscience would be clean. He could be the man he'd always wanted to be, was meant to be. Not this.

But there was no other world, no easy escape. Darien staggered as he lowered himself to the ground, reaching out his hand to steady himself. Kyel stared down at him in concern. The thanacryst in the doorway sounded as if it were purring.

"You're not well," Kyel observed.

Darien ignored him, gesturing at the ground. "Have a seat."

"Darien, you need to listen to me—"

"Sit down."

Kyel obeyed, but his expression was anything but compliant. When he was settled, Darien considered him a moment before saying, "You put on the Soulstone against my command."

Kyel shrugged. "You knew all along I was going to do it."

It was true. Nevertheless, he couldn't let the slip in obedience go unmentioned. Kyel was no longer his acolyte, technically, but he was still far from being ready to assume the mantle of a full Master. There was little Darien could do for him now. The remainder would be up to Kyel himself. He could choose to make himself as great as he wanted or settle for much less. It all depended on how much effort he was willing to invest.

"I figured Romana would leave you little choice," Darien admitted.

Kyel scowled and shook his head. "I'm so tired of your games. That's all I've had, ever since I agreed to become your acolyte. I don't know the first thing about using my gift. All you've ever done is set hurdles in my path, then sit back and watch me go over them. The vortex, the Temple of Wisdom, Romana…all just more of your games. I'm tired of them. I don't wish to play anymore."

Darien sighed. "Whether you agree with my methods or not, you've learned from them."

"*What?* What have I learned?"

"For one thing, you would have never stood up to me like this a month ago. And I wager you gave Romana quite a headache."

Kyel glared at him. Slowly, his anger seemed to fade, and he dropped his stare to the ground.

"I was in awe of you," he said. "When we first met, back at Greystone Keep. You were everything I wanted to be. You seemed to know so much, you were so confident, so committed to what you believed in. But now…I don't know if it's losing your Oath, or the Bloodquest, or if your gift's just eating you up inside. Perhaps it's everything. But you're not the same anymore. I think you're sick, Darien. The truth is, you scare me."

Darien nodded, reflecting on Kyel's words. More gently, he said, "Then learn from my example. Always hold to what you believe in, fix your sight on what's most important, and you'll do fine. Everything else doesn't matter at all." With a quiet smile, he added, "I wish I could have done so many things differently. Now, it's too late."

"But it's not too late," Kyel insisted. "Forget about Aidan. Leave the Well of Tears open, like Swain said. Just go someplace quiet and marry Naia. Settle down in a village and make a life for yourself. Give yourself a chance to heal."

The idea was tempting. But he shook his head. "No. We're leaving for Aerysius on the morrow."

"You're making a mistake."

"It won't be my first." He left the implied corollary unsaid. "Now. I came to tell you one last thing. You can do almost anything you want with your gift, within reason. There is a natural order that governs everything. Even magic obeys it. If you know how something works, then you know how to manipulate it. But you must be utterly committed to the task. Never mire yourself in doubt.

"And you need to broaden your knowledge. When this is over, set yourself to the task of study. Learn everything you can about everything there is. Only then will you truly earn those chains."

Chapter Thirty-Eight
An Unexpected Offer

The Cerulean Plains, The Rhen

The evening was clear and furtively still as Darien directed his horse across the threshold of the vortex. Nose to the ground, the thanacryst loped along at his side, its enormous paws making deep tracks in the snow.

Darien felt reassured by its vile presence. The beast was small comfort, but its strange devotion was the only protection he retained. Under the torrent of the vortex, the solace of the magic field was once again denied him. Into the night he rode alone, unarmed, and utterly powerless. It was a despicable feeling, but necessary. All weapons were proscribed by the ancient conventions of parley.

In his right hand, Darien clutched a white banner improvised from a torn bedsheet. The strip of cloth was much longer than it was broad, and he carried it draped over his hand, its frayed edges trailing almost to the ground. The banner was large enough to be seen from a distance. Darien could only hope that any sentries ahead would see it before loosing their shafts.

His life now depended exclusively on the honor of a demon.

He rode in thoughtful silence, reflecting on his decision to obey the crumpled summons in his pocket. He'd convinced himself the parley was a necessary risk. He needed to look Zavier Renquist in the face and take the measure of his enemy. But now that he was fully committed, Darien realized he had been prompted by an underlying motivation much more reckless in nature: he was fascinated by the man.

In legend, Zavier Renquist had been the greatest Prime

Warden the Lyceum had ever produced, vastly potent and passionately committed to duty. Renquist's treason had been as unexpected as it was devastating. Meeting the man face to face, Darien thought perhaps he could gain some insight into what had driven the most esteemed Prime Warden in all of history to become the most reviled.

And it burned, the desire to know what the man wanted of him.

Ahead, there was movement in the snow. Darien slowed his horse, raising the banner to be certain it was duly marked. Squinting, he made out the forms of four riders approaching, their armor as dark as the mounts they sat astride. As they drew nearer, he saw that the men wore full battle plate, tassels swaying from the tips of their spears. If he were in any other place, and these were any other soldiers, he would have taken their strange presence for an honor guard.

He could hear the jingle of their tack as they approached. Darien waited, the white cloth held in his outstretched hand. The thanacryst stood by his side in the snow, head cocked and ears erect. Its grisly tail began to wag, hesitant at first, then eagerly.

"Theanoch," Darien hissed at it. The creature obeyed instantly, whining as great globs of slobber dripped from its mouth.

One of the soldiers reined his mount around, backing the horse up and drawing abreast of him. Darien peered into the grate of the helm, trying to make out the dim features of the face beneath. He raised the banner in his hand, offering it out across the distance between them. The Enemy soldier lifted a chain-gloved hand and accepted the fragile badge of truce.

"Demas tur narghul, nan ledro." Darien said. *I have come, as agreed.*

The soldier tipped his dark helm approvingly. *"Nan ledro.* Come. Follow."

The man jerked the reins out of Darien's hand, riding forward with them held high enough to clear the Tarkendar's head. The others closed in around him, encircling him tightly as the first soldier led his gelding forward through the snow.

He sat straight in the saddle, wondering about the significance implied by the tight formation the soldiers were assuming. He had come willingly enough. They had no reason to fear he would try to bolt. It was almost as though the men were arranged defensively, forming a living shield around him.

Darien wondered what they felt he needed protection from. Perhaps the discipline of the Enemy was faltering, if Renquist feared betrayal from within his own ranks. Of course, Darien had to consider, he was personally responsible for the slaughter of a hundred thousand of their fellows. That could breed resentment despite any amount of discipline, in any army. Renquist was probably just being prudent.

Darien found himself missing the comfort of the magic field with a desperate sense of urgency. And he missed his sword, the familiar weight of the baldric on his shoulder. Even with his guard, Darien felt more vulnerable than since he'd entered the vortex. He couldn't stop his eyes from wandering over the snow, alert for sign of treachery. The soldiers that surrounded him rode in silence, but he noted that all four men were examining the surrounding terrain just as avidly as he was.

Behind him, the thanacryst whined. Darien had forgotten it was there, faithfully jogging along on the heels of his mount. Every so often it paused, scenting the air, and uttered an eager growl.

They crossed a long, crescent-shaped fold in the land where a frozen stream ran its course. They followed the streambed until a dark object came into view. It was a pavilion, Darien realized, erected in a solitary location at the summit of a snow-draped knoll. Darien took heart in the sight. He'd feared he was being led into the thick of the Enemy encampment. But he also felt a wary sense of apprehension. It seemed Renquist was taking no chances.

They led his horse up the hill to the front of the pavilion, where the soldiers that ringed him halted together as one. Darien dismounted as two figures emerged from the tent. They were the first men of the Enemy he had ever seen unhelmed, with the sole exception of the dead. Both wore long robes of the same indigo blue, an insignia embroidered on the breast. Darien frowned, trying to make out the features of the emblem, but his view was blocked by a soldier who stepped in front of him.

"This way." The man gestured with his hand.

As Darien moved toward the entrance of the tent, he managed a glance at the two robed men guarding the doorway. The insignia on their chests glared at him, igniting a spark of outrage as he recognized it.

It was the Silver Star, or something so similar that it made little difference. Darien felt a cold rage in his chest. The two men were mages. That they would dare emblazon themselves with the star of fallen Aerysius took him beyond ire, well past contempt.

One of the two, a dark-haired man with a cruel scar on his face, glared at him fiercely. Darien almost missed the significance of the white cloak draped over his robe, the cloak of a Prime Warden. Darien stopped, staring at the man in patent astonishment. There was only one person it could possibly be: Cyrus Krane, ancient Prime Warden of Aerysius, now one of Renquist's fell companions.

His guards stopped short of the tent's entrance. The two mages stepped forward, Krane's eyes coldly examining him, scouring up his body from his boots, lingering on Darien's eyes. He didn't appear to like what he saw.

In contrast, the red-haired man was wearing an almost amiable expression on his face. For some reason, he reminded Darien of Corban Henley, and it was more than just the color of his beard. The man had Henley's way about him, a cool and deliberate air. He nodded slightly, a look of intrigue in his eyes.

"Byron Connel," he gave his name without preamble. "This is Cyrus Krane. Come inside. We've been expecting you."

He turned, sweeping back a flap of fabric and holding it open for Darien as he ducked to enter. Krane fell in behind them, the hem of his cloak rustling over the snow-covered ground. The warm air that hit his face made Darien feel almost relieved.

Within, the interior was dark, lit only by softly glowing lanterns set about on a floor covered with lavish rugs. Otherwise, the tent was empty. There was no furniture and, more disturbing, no one waiting within.

Darien paused, his frown deepening as he felt a sudden stab of panic. He had expected to find Renquist inside the tent. Casting a sidelong glare at Connel, he turned to find that Krane had halted, bodily blocking the only exit.

"Is this how you honor a badge of truce?" Darien demanded, taking a step back away from the two demons. He should have been more afraid. But the anger he felt overshadowed even his fear.

"Be at ease," issued a low voice from behind him.

Darien spun toward the sound. There had been no one there. But suddenly, inexplicably, there was. Zavier Renquist stood and moved toward him, emerging from the shadows of a corner.

Darien stared, too frozen to draw breath. He felt Renquist's stare moving over him. He found himself unable to do anything but stand and be measured, feeling that his every nuance was being probed and exposed.

Renquist paced slowly forward, hands clasped behind his back. He was tall and exceptionally broad of shoulder, his figure imposing. He wore his long, brown hair pulled back from his face, gathered in a braid at the crown of his head. The white cloak of a Prime Warden hung down his back. He had the look of a raptor, one poised in the air with claws and wings extended.

Shoulders relaxing, he said at last, "You're not remotely what I was expecting. Come. Have a seat." He extended his hand, indicating the rugs thrown over the ground as he lowered himself down upon them, cross-legged.

Darien struggled to collect himself as he sat across from him. Renquist had caught him off-guard. He had obeyed the summons thinking it an opportunity to evaluate the nature of this legendary man, but instead had become himself the object of scrutiny. Darien tried to swallow the rigid lump that was rising in his throat, threatening to claw its way out. Now that it was too late, he realized he had made a serious error in judgment.

He should never have come.

Trying his best to maintain his composure, Darien leaned forward and stared unblinking into the ancient demon's eyes. What he saw there was harrowing. Renquist's eyes were sinister pools of shadow that perfectly mirrored his own.

"What were you expecting?" he asked.

"A twisted and pathetic wretch like your brother. But you're nothing like him, I see."

Darien hesitated before stating, "No. We are nothing alike."

Renquist's eyes bored into him, probing. It was as though he were considering Darien with sinister intent and was only too pleased at what he was finding. He leaned back, knitting his fingers together, his elbows resting on his knees.

"The truth is, I find myself rather fascinated by you," Renquist admitted. "You are the first mage in all of history to ever successfully employ a grand resonance. And it seems you have bested one of my own. I take it that is Arden's thanacryst?"

Darien followed his stare, finding the beast curled up behind him in a corner of the tent. He gave a slight nod, wondering what Renquist had to be implying from his possession of the creature.

To his astonishment, the ancient Prime Warden's smile broadened. "I thought I recognized it. An unusual pet, for one such as yourself."

Darien shrugged. "It seems to like me well enough."

"So it seems," uttered Renquist. "Though I must caution you: thanacrysts have a tendency to turn when you least expect it. They make unreliable pets, at best."

"I'll take my chances."

Renquist nodded, looking down at his hands. "I brought you here to make a proposition. My army is twice the strength of your own. I still have six mages at my disposal, along with some unusual pets of my own. Orien's Circle has been reduced to a lump of slag by your abuse of it. I was up there myself this morning. I've seen it. You are left with very few options."

Darien shook his head. "If that were the case, then you wouldn't have bothered with this parley."

The demon's stare was beginning to unsettle him. Darien could feel himself becoming unnerved, cold beads of perspiration collecting on his brow.

Renquist raised a hand. "What I propose is this: I will withdraw my forces back into the Black Lands and agree to refrain from hostility for a period of two years. All I ask is that you agree to my terms."

Darien asked suspiciously, "What are your terms?"

"You. I want you to surrender yourself to me."

Darien glared at him contemptuously. He had seen this coming. It made perfect sense. If he was taken out of the equation, then Renquist could afford those two years to sit back, bide his time, and replenish his armies. He would not want to risk another Black Solstice.

"I'm no fool. My father was murdered in your fires, and Arden already gave me a taste of your flames. I have no desire to repeat the experience."

But Renquist only smiled. "It is not my intent to kill you. You have impressed me, and that is no easy thing to do." He paused for a moment, his gaze slipping to the side as if in thought. Then his eyes snapped back to lock on Darien's with rigid intensity.

"What I propose is this: I want you to accompany me back to Bryn Calazar as my apprentice. I seem to be down a mage, and our number has ever been Eight. You would make a formidable *nach'tier.*"

Darien blinked, taken completely aback. *Nach'tier* was an ancient term for darkmage. Renquist was offering him Arden's place at his side. He would make a demon of him, a minion of Chaos such as himself. Darien was utterly unprepared for the suggestion. The very notion made his skin crawl. Yet, at the same time, it was almost flattering.

Behind him, the thanacryst purred.

"No."

It was only a moment's hesitation, but Renquist hadn't missed it. Black eyes gleaming, he seemed to be savoring the gloating smile on his lips. "Why not? You are almost there already. I can sense it in you. It would take only the lightest brush of a finger to push you over the edge."

His words were like a whispered omen of damnation. Darien felt them slithering over his skin like the cold coils of a serpent. He couldn't deny the truth of those words, which made it all the more critical that he deny them urgently.

But there was no conviction in his tone as Darien mumbled

softly, "I'm nothing like you."

He felt dazed, the cold sweat on his brow now running in icy rivulets down his face. The dim lighting of the tent seemed suddenly darker, the air cold and atrociously stale. The sound of his own shivering breath hissed like a gale in his ears.

The smile on Renquist's face was almost fatherly. "We have so much in common, you and I. A thousand years ago, I sold my soul for a price that, to this day, I've never regretted paying. Tell me, Darien. What is your price?"

Darien squeezed his eyes shut as he fought to gather his scattered thoughts, whispering, "You could never afford it."

"Can't I?" Renquist challenged ominously. "Then let me sweeten my offer. In addition to the withdrawal of my forces, my Master has agreed to relinquish the spirit of Meiran Withersby, reuniting her soul and body, and returning her to life. It is within His power. What do you say? Commit your soul to Xerys. With one simple word, you would save thousands of soldiers under your command and give them a chance to live to fight another day. And you would be saving the mother of your only child from an eternity of despair and pain."

Renquist's words hit with the force of a deathblow.

It was impossible. Meiran would have found some way to get word to him. But he had been at the Front two long years, where news was scarce. Only two birds had arrived from Aerysius the entire time he had been there, both from his mother's private coops.

Darien whispered, "I have no child."

"That's not what your brother told me."

"Aidan's lying." He silently pleaded it was so, even as he knew it was too much to hope for.

"You have a son, Darien," Renquist insisted. "His name is Gerald, after your father."

"No…it can't be."

Even as he said the words, he realized he was wrong. Aidan was simply not creative enough to come up with something so clever. His brother had a knack for taking the ideas of others and corrupting them to fit his own particular needs. But actually devising something so perfectly cruel? It was as beyond him as the stars.

Aidan would have known that he would never accept Renquist's offer for any advantage to himself. But this was about Meiran. For months, he had dreamed of her, sometimes falling, sometimes screaming, sometimes writhing in tortured agony. At other times, she was simply smiling at him, the green light of hell shining in her eyes. She had meant everything to him. She had been the singular passion of his life.

And, together, they had made a son.

Aidan had chosen the one leverage he knew Darien could never endure. He had passed along the information knowing it was exactly the fatal brush Renquist would need to send him hurling over the edge.

But Darien had already taken that step himself. At the cliff's edge in Aerysius, he had looked his brother in the eye and denied him then.

Somehow, Darien found the strength to stand. Staggering, he backed away, shaking his head. As he moved to duck under the low opening of the tent, he heard Renquist's voice behind him:

"I'll leave the offer open. Should you decide to change your mind, you'll know where to find me."

Chapter Thirty-Nine
The Edge

The Cerulean Plains, The Rhen

Kyel was tired of waiting. And he was growing increasingly apprehensive as the long minutes dragged by. Everyone was, especially Swain. The blademaster had a look on his face like curdled death, his oily hair stringing forward into his eyes. The interior of the command tent seemed almost charged with the compressed tension in the air. Even Wellingford was pacing, every so often slapping a pair of white gloves against his thigh with a resounding *crack*.

"We're here to discuss strategy," Blandford said finally. "Let's get on with it."

Wellingford shook his head. "We can't hold this meeting without the Prime Warden. We need his input. He told me there is a darkmage with the approaching army, and only he knows how to counter them."

Swain grimaced at Wellingford's use of Darien's self-proclaimed title. But that was nothing compared to the fury that sprang to his eyes at the mention of the word 'darkmage.'

Fixing his glare on Kyel, Swain demanded, *"You told him about Renquist's summons?"*

At the mention of that name, the tent fell abruptly silent. Kyel glanced around to find every man there standing with faces paled in astonishment. Wellingford stood shaking his head, lips moving soundlessly. Even Blandford's usual composure was shattered. Emmery's general slouched with mouth slack and eyes glazed as if poleaxed.

"No!" Kyel gasped. "I tossed it away!"

"Where by all the graceless gods did you toss it?"

Kyel's mind spun furiously. He didn't know what he'd done with the note. He remembered crumbling it up in his hand, but after that…

"I don't know," he admitted. "I can't remember."

Swain's oath was lost in the clamor that exploded in the tent. Everyone was shouting, bandying words like "Renquist" and "darkmage" in panicked voices. Things were deteriorating rapidly, Kyel realized, taking in the faces of the officers around him. Someone was going to have to get the men back under control.

He was about to raise his hands to get their attention when the commotion suddenly silenced. Every man in the room stood rigid, attention rapt on something behind him. Kyel turned to look over his shoulder and froze, taking in the form of a man who had appeared behind them in the tent's entrance.

It was Darien. But not the Darien he knew.

The mage's face was ghostly white, eyes squinting and bloodshot. He stood as if wracked, arms clutched across his chest, shivering. His black hair was spilled over his face, but nothing could hide the look of tortured devastation written there. His eyes were dull and blank, absent even a trace of the presence that was his signature. He looked well past grief, well beyond torment. To Kyel, he looked like a man utterly destroyed.

Swain surged toward him first, grabbing Darien by the arm and swinging him around, maneuvering him out of the tent. Kyel followed, only dimly noticing Wellingford stepping in behind to block the exit. Outside, he followed as Swain dragged Darien into a space between tents. There, the captain seized him violently by the shoulders.

Kyel ran toward them, fearing that Swain was going to start tearing into him by the look on his face. But as Kyel stopped behind him, he realized Swain's strong grip was the only thing keeping Darien standing. His knees were slack, his body wilting like a droughted stem.

Swain gripped Darien's face, demanding, *"What did he do to you?"*

Darien didn't respond. He just stood staring dimly into Swain's eyes, sweat trickling down his brow. Kyel looked on as the captain increased the pressure of his fingers, squeezing them mercilessly into Darien's skin.

"By the whoring mother of the gods—*what did he want?*"

With a growl that sounded like an injured wolf, Darien broke away from him, twisting his face out of the blademaster's grasp. He bent over, hands on his knees, glaring up at Swain through the sweat-plastered strands of his hair. His eyes were red pools of scalding hatred.

"He wants me."

It took Kyel a moment to understand Darien's whispered words. His voice was so low and broken it was almost unintelligible.

Swain demanded, "What terms did he offer?"

The Sentinel ignored him.

"His terms, Darien!"

Without looking at him, the mage drew himself up and uttered flatly, "He offered to withdraw."

"What else?"

Darien looked at him, eyes imploring. To Kyel's horror, he saw the mage's eyes were filled with tears that spilled freely down his cheeks. The sight struck Kyel with alarm. In the entire time he had known him, through every trial and every sorrow, he had never once seen Darien break down.

"He told me I have a son…and he told me he could bring Meiran back."

Swain spun away from him with an oath.

Renquist had found the one thing certain to tear Darien apart, the one temptation his nature would never allow him to refuse. Yet, somehow, he had. Somehow, Darien had scraped up just enough strength to refuse him and walk away from that meeting.

But, Kyel realized with dismay, Renquist may have achieved his goal, nonetheless. Darien would never be able to bear the guilt that decision had cost him. One look at his anguished face made it clear the mage believed he'd damned Meiran all over again, just as surely as if he'd thrown her into the pit himself.

And the part about his son…Kyel groaned. What was worse, Darien thinking he had a son somewhere that he could have chosen to bring a mother home to? Or the closure of knowing the boy was dead?

If it were his own child, Kyel decided, he would rather know the truth.

"You don't have a son, Darien," he said softly.

"What?" The Sentinel stared at him in bleary confusion.

Kyel shook his head, fighting back tears of his own. "The boy's dead. I'm sorry."

"How do you know?"

"They had a book about your family in the Temple of Wisdom. I read it."

Face constricted in grief, Darien collapsed to his knees. Kyel looked away, glancing to Swain for help.

The captain shook his head. He said in a voice impassively calm, "This is sick, Darien. I'm going to end it right here. Kneel."

He drew his sword with a shivering scrape of steel and brought it back over his shoulder. The oiled blade gleamed in the moonlight as he adjusted his grip.

Darien just stared at that glistening length of steel as though it was the one thing he desired most in the entire world. His face relaxed, and for a moment he looked calm, almost relieved. But then, firmly, he shook his head.

"No. That sword you're holding would be a *mercy*. But I have to finish what I started. There's no one else left to do it."

Swain's blade held fast. He regarded Darien with a level stare that Kyel found impossible to read. There was no trace left in his eyes of the hostile contempt that had been there whenever he had so much as glanced at his former student. Nor was there the barest hint of compassion, or even clemency. But the blade faltered. Swain took a step back and dropped his sword to his side, nodding his head.

"All right," he allowed, sheathing his blade. "We leave for Aerysius at first light. Come on, Kyel."

Kyel followed him as Swain turned and strode away. He couldn't help chancing a glance behind, which revealed Darien kneeling with his head thrown back as if gazing up at the sky. Fine ripples of blue energy coruscated over his body, bleeding off into the night. It was a sad and eerie sight, one Kyel didn't think he would ever forget. He turned away, leaving Darien alone to silently shed his grief.

He wandered back to the command tent, where he found Swain shooing the collected officers out the back, sending them off without a word of explanation. Wellingford was the last to leave, following the others with a look of intense concern.

"He's gone," Swain said when they were alone. He tossed himself down in one of the scattered chairs, bringing a hand up to his brow. "Renquist pushed him too far."

"I don't think he'll make it to Aerysius," Kyel said softly, thinking of the strange blue light he had seen welling from the mage's body like lifeblood from his soul.

"I should have ended it back there. This is just cruelty, now. And what if he changes his mind?" Swain sighed, shaking his head. "Can you think of anything that can hold him together, just long enough to get him up the mountain?"

Kyel didn't hesitate with his answer. "Naia."

Swain grimaced. "Go ask her."

He found Naia alone a short distance from the camp, knelt in prayer before a small statue of her goddess. Two small votive candles flickered in the blackened soil just in front of the cloth the priestess had spread over the ground. Sensing his presence, Naia straightened, turning. She didn't appear surprised.

Kyel felt profoundly sorry for her. He walked toward her, hands clasped together in front of him, and knelt at her side.

"We're leaving for Aerysius on the morrow," he said.

The priestess looked down, her eyes trailing back toward the statue. It was hard to tell through her veil, but Kyel thought perhaps she'd been crying.

"I want you to come with us," he said. "Darien needs you."

"Did he send you?"

"No." Kyel shook his head. Something must have happened

between them. Darien had probably treated her wrongly, the same way he seemed to be treating everyone. Kyel didn't want to hurt her worse than she already had been. But there didn't seem any way around it.

He drew a deep breath and said, "He met with Zavier Renquist tonight."

"What? Why?"

"I don't know. But Renquist really got to him, Naia. I don't think he'll make it to Aerysius without you."

Bowing her head, Naia said, "I don't think I'm the answer, Kyel. I'm not important to him."

"Is that what he told you?"

The priestess nodded, pressing her lips together tightly. Kyel didn't know what else to do, so he reached out and took her into his arms, lending her what small comfort he could. Naia accepted his gesture, laying her head on his shoulder and closing her eyes.

"I've seen the way he looks at you," Kyel said. "He's just trying to push you away because he doesn't want to see you hurt."

"I wish I could believe that." Naia pulled back from his embrace.

He didn't want to, but he had to tell her. "Renquist offered to bring Meiran back. He told Darien she gave him a son. The child's dead, Naia."

She gasped, bringing a hand up to her mouth. "How can he stand it?"

Kyel sadly shook his head. "I don't think he can anymore. That's why he needs you. Without you, I'm afraid we'll lose him."

Naia bowed her head against her chest and sighed weakly. "I'll come."

"Thank you," Kyel whispered, standing up. As he moved away from her, he glanced back to see Naia knelt once again in prayer. The small, wavering lights of her candles had died, drowned out by the melted tallow. The same tallow that, when solid, had once kept the delicate flames alive.

Kyel couldn't sleep. It was getting on toward morning, anyway, so he rolled out of his blankets and dressed. He occupied his time before sunup by leafing through the text he had brought back with him from Om's temple, *Treatise on the Well.* After all he'd gone through to acquire it, Darien had never once asked for it.

Kyel read and reread the passage about sealing the Well. But he found he understood it no better now than he had back in Emmery Palace. The book said something about 'deactivation of the rune sequence,' which made no sense to him. He didn't know what a rune was, how it was activated, or what it would take to deactivate the thing.

And, besides, he found he couldn't concentrate on that part. His eyes kept jumping down to the bottom of the page, to the last sentence that described the sealing of the gateway.

Kyel finally closed the book with a sigh. It was useless. And it was also time to leave.

He scooped up a bowl of millet gruel on the way to the command tent, throwing back his head and trying to hold his breath as he swallowed it down. The clumps stuck in his throat, making him gag. He couldn't finish it.

Not knowing what else to do with the bowl, he handed it off to a soldier who sat alone at a campfire looking hungry. The man took one look at his cloak, another at the bowl in his hands, then tossed it on the ground.

Kyel tried not to let the soldier's display of resentment get his temper up. It was galling, though, the way these men were always staring at him. Before Aerysius' fall, a black cloak had commanded immediate respect wherever it was seen. Now a mage's cloak seemed more like a badge of iniquity. Somehow, when this was over, he was going to have to work at changing that.

Kyel arrived at the command tent to find Swain already there, waiting beside his horse. The captain didn't look like he'd gotten much sleep, either. Kyel greeted him sullenly.

"Is she coming?" Swain asked.

Kyel nodded. At least, he hoped Naia hadn't changed her mind. He shivered. It was a bitterly cold morning, and the wind was coming up. Freshly fallen snow covered most of the blackened ground, except in places where men had trampled through it, reducing the fine white powder to ashen-gray sludge. The sky was still overcast, the sun only a pale glow. Looking up, Kyel wondered if it might not snow again before the day was through. That would be just their luck, to get mired in a blizzard.

He heard footsteps behind him and turned to see Darien approaching. The mage looked a little better than he had the previous night, but there was still a pall of gloom lingering about him. He was dressed all in black with his hair tied back for once, the hilt of his sword protruding over his shoulder. Somehow, he had found himself a new black cloak to wear, though Kyel doubted there would be a Silver Star on the back of it.

His attention was drawn to the thanacryst that followed at the Sentinel's heels. The creature jogged along with its tongue hanging out, drooling avidly. Kyel averted his eyes in disgust.

Darien stopped in front of Swain, slouching, his eyes downcast. That wasn't like him at all. Just yesterday, he had been trudging around the camp shooting glares at Swain. Now it seemed he couldn't look the captain in the eyes.

Swain put his hands on his hips. "Just out of curiosity, have you thought about how we're going to get up there?"

Darien nodded, hand tensing on the leather strap of the baldric slung across his chest. "We'll need to go through the Gap of Amberlie. After that, there's only one way up the mountain. We climb."

The blademaster appeared exceptionally unconvinced. "That's a three-thousand-foot cliff, Darien."

The mage shrugged. "We'll take the stairs."

Swain cast a glaring stab of doubt at him. "I was captain of the guard there for nine years. I don't remember any stairs."

"Do you recall the system of passages beneath the city?"

The captain nodded.

"Aidan showed them to me. We used to go down there sometimes when we were both still acolytes. We got along occasionally, if you can imagine it. There's a stair that goes all the way down inside the mountain and comes out somewhere at the base. Aidan told me about it. He used it all the time."

"So you don't know where this stair comes out?"

"No. But I'll know it when I see it. It's the only way."

With a surge of excitement, Kyel threw his pack down on the ground and started rifling through the contents, his fingers at last closing around the leather cover of *Treatise on the Well.* Righting himself, he flipped the book open to the page he'd marked with a folded piece of parchment that had completely slipped his mind.

"Here." He stuffed the paper into Darien's hand.

As Darien looked down at it, Kyel thrust the text at him, as well. "And here's this book you wanted so badly. You never even asked me for it."

Darien refused the book with a shake of his head, gazing down at the map in his hand. "I have no need of it," he grumbled absently. "You're the one who'll be sealing the Well, not me. Wait. Where did you come by this?"

Kyel felt a surge of resentment. "I found it in a text down in the vaults. I was *supposed* to be researching ways to help us, remember?"

Darien ignored him, eyes poring over the map in his hands. He whispered, "This is *exactly* what I need."

Kyel nodded, feeling smug as Darien continued his fervent examination of the map. The mage stood there for minutes, just staring down at it, eyes scouring the page. Then, at last, he let his hands drop, fingering the parchment as he turned to glance behind them with a bewildered expression.

In a voice just as slack and stunned as his face, he said, "The entrance is on this side of the mountains. It's just behind Orien's Finger."

Kyel glanced up at the blackened rock pillar, his face doing an unintentional imitation of Darien's. "It couldn't be." His gaze darted to the line of the Craghorns jutting away into the distance. "The Vale's yet leagues from here. Isn't that Aerysius over there?"

He pointed at a bank of clouds that hung against a jagged line of tall peaks. To his eyes, the gray gloom of the thunderheads seemed to be tinged distinctly, unnaturally green. Seeing Darien's slight nod, Kyel stared even harder at the summit beneath the cloudbank. It was leagues to the north, beyond even the Gap of Amberlie.

"We'll place our trust in your map," Darien muttered, a strange expression on his face as he folded the paper back up, running his fingers along the crease.

Kyel wondered what thought had occurred to him. Before he could ask, he was distracted by the sound of an approaching horse. He looked up to see Naia leading her small roan mare across the field toward them.

The priestess was dressed for travel, a coat thrown over her white gown. She wore a new veil he had never seen, one that glimmered with hundreds of tiny crystals worked into the fabric. She smiled as she saw them. But her expression wilted as her eyes sought Darien.

The mage turned to Swain with a look of fury. To Kyel, he seemed ready to reach for the blade at his back.

"No."

If Kyel hadn't heard it, he would never have believed it possible that one simple word could be infused with such resentment. Darien took a threatening step toward the captain, looking like a wolf moving in for the kill. Kyel could see Swain's hand drawing slowly toward his sword as the air around Darien fairly crackled with blue energies.

The captain stated firmly, "That's the condition. Either she comes, or we're not doing this at all."

Kyel backed away a step as the strange energies that writhed over Darien's body condensed into a brilliant aura that completely enveloped him. With a cry, Kyel threw his hands up to cover his eyes from the intensity of the light. The air itself seemed disturbed, a whistling wind that ripped at his hair and tormented his cloak.

"Darien," Naia called over the sound of the wind, "Is this truly your wish?"

The brilliant light collapsed into glowing filaments that wavered for a moment in the air before burning out completely.

Where the light had just been, now only the Sentinel remained. He stood with his head bowed, eyes focused dimly at the ground between his boots.

"Damn you, Swain."

Without looking up, he moved away toward the horse pickets, shoulders slouched and feet scraping the ground with every step. When he was gone, the captain let out a slow, lingering breath.

"That was close."

Chapter Forty
Absolution

The Cerulean Plains, The Rhen

Darien let the black warhorse pick its own path toward the west. Ahead, Orien's Finger looked nothing more than a cracked and blackened log dug up from the ashes of an abandoned fire pit. Its summit had slipped even further off its charred pedestal than he remembered and had twisted slightly askew. Someday soon, the entire mass of broken rock was going to come crumbling down.

Darien looked toward the green glow above dead Aerysius. He tried to dredge up a picture in his mind of that terrible pillar of light, but the image was dim and bleary. It had been months since he'd last seen it, stabbing into the foundations of the ruined city like a spike through the heart.

Then, the sight of the gateway had terrified him. But now he was almost eager to view that dreadful column of power again, anxious for the promise of release the gateway could afford him. He gazed ahead toward the bank of storm clouds that hung over the jagged mountain peaks, a look of distant yearning in his eyes.

He was finally going home.

The sound of hoofbeats made him aware that a horse was drawing up alongside his. Not in the mood for conversation, Darien turned to glare at whoever had the temerity to invade the one, small moment of privacy he had claimed for himself. Expecting either Kyel or Swain, he was surprised to find himself glaring at Naia instead. His anger diffused instantly. Feeling ashamed, he glanced away.

"Can we talk?"

Out of the corner of his eye, he could see her peering at him through the sheer fabric that covered her face.

"I don't know what there is to talk about," he muttered in reply.

"Stop it."

The ferocity of her words took him aback. He almost pulled his horse up as he turned to look at her. Naia's dark eyes were filled with resentment, her cheeks red with ire that could be seen even through the mist of glittering crystals before her face.

"Stop trying to intentionally hurt me," she told him. "It's unkind. And it's not getting you anywhere."

As always, she had seen right through his walls as if they were made of glass. To her, his defenses were as thin as the translucent drape of fabric she always wore. She was becoming expert at tearing right through them, rendering him naked and exposed.

He didn't know what to say to her. He rode in silence, trying to ignore her presence. It was impossible. He longed for her, missing her company more now that she was here, riding at his side, than when he had thought her leagues away in Glen Farquist. He let his gaze trail back to the light of the gateway in the clouds above Aerysius, thirsting for the comfort of its promise.

Softly, she said, "I know what you're trying to do. You think that by distancing me, you can protect me. But you're wrong. You have a lot of audacity if you think you are responsible for my feelings. You are not. You have no right to treat me this way. What you're doing is cruel. And it hurts."

She was right, of course. She had looked into his soul and seen for herself the bleakness that was there. Why wasn't she riding away? She was still there, still at his side. And she was waiting for a response, he realized.

He had no idea what to tell her that wouldn't hurt her more.

"Talk to me," Naia insisted. "You owe me at least the truth."

He didn't know what version of the truth she wanted to hear.

"Do you care for me, Darien?"

He whispered softly, "Aye."

"Look at me."

It was hard. Naia's eyes were more beautiful than ever, burning with a fierce compassion he hadn't earned and would never deserve.

"I love you. And I forgive you," she said.

It was the last thing in the world he wanted to hear. Kicking his heels into the Tarkendar's sides, Darien sent the warhorse forward at a gallop.

Kyel's eyes followed the sight of the black gelding racing ahead, feeling a fresh swell of resentment. He regretted asking Naia to come. He should have left her behind with her votive candles and her goddess. Her presence didn't seem to be making a bit of difference anyway. Rather, it seemed to be having the opposite effect. Naia's company seemed to be instilling in Darien an even deeper melancholy.

The ruined crag towered over them, its shadow obscured by the gloom that still hung overhead in the sky. Looking ahead, he saw Darien's horse disappearing behind the dark column of stone.

When Kyel's own mount finally trotted around the circumference of the pillar, he found Darien sitting cross-legged in the snow, staring upward at the shattered summit. The hideous creature he'd adopted sat beside him. Kyel felt like uttering a choice word from Swain's extensive vocabulary of curses. Had Darien done nothing in the time he'd been there? Dismounting, Kyel scowled as he led his horse up behind him, further embittered by the fact that his arrival went completely unacknowledged. Darien still sat there, staring up at the sky, eyes dark and distant.

"Well?" Kyel demanded.

He glanced around at the curving walls of the small valley, finding nothing but burnt and ruined stone. If there had ever been a stair, it was gone now. The full force of the grand resonance had hit this area the hardest of all. Still, the mage just sat staring up at the dilapidated pillar, unblinking.

Kyel wanted to throttle him.

But then Darien stood up and lifted his hands as if trying to hold some enormous weight. Kyel felt a sudden surge of fear as he realized what the Sentinel was readying himself to do. He turned to find Naia and Swain approaching on their horses.

"Go back!" he yelled.

The captain frowned at him for the briefest moment then followed Darien's gaze upward to the summit of the crag. Eyes widening, he leaned over and grabbed the reins from Naia's hand, swinging both horses around and sprinting away.

The entire summit of Orien's Finger shuddered, rock and debris raining down. Kyel threw his arms up to cover his head as, with a horrible, grating noise, the broken mass of stone twisted on its pedestal, righting itself. The summit shifted forward, grinding as it slid slowly back into place. Kyel looked up, dropping his arms as he realized that not so much as a grain of dust had touched him.

Darien was not yet finished with his work. He was still staring upward, concentration bent on the column overhead. He extended the first two fingers of his left hand, angling them upward toward the restored cap of stone. White light burned, hissing, along the crack in the rock face. The stone melted from within, running outward from the crack and reforming again whole.

When it was done, Darien lowered his hand. Kyel stared in wonder, realizing he hadn't even broken a sweat. How many tons of rock had Darien shifted, using nothing more than the force of his mind? And he made it look so effortless. Kyel couldn't even think about performing such a feat himself. It was inconceivable. As he stared up at the intact pillar of stone, he found himself wondering why Darien had performed the task at all.

When he asked, the mage just shrugged, replying, "I needed to know the time."

Kyel stared at him blankly as Darien sat back down in the snow and stared out across the canyon.

That's all he did for another hour. Only, this time, the mage's attention was focused at the cliff walls behind. Kyel stared at them until he had their every feature seared into his mind, but he saw nothing to warrant such scrutiny. So he paced, growing increasingly impatient, as Naia and Swain stood silently looking on.

It was getting frustrating, and every time he asked Darien what he was doing, the Sentinel would only reply, "Just wait."

At last, Darien stood back up from the ground. His pants were soaked through from the snow, but he went through the motions of dusting them off anyway. The thanacryst bounded to his side, jumping up and pawing at his shirt. Darien whispered something to it that Kyel didn't catch, and the thing lowered itself to its haunches and sat there, panting like a dog. To his disgust, Darien reached out and ran a hand fondly through its wet, matted fur in praise.

"What now?" Kyel demanded.

"Just wait." Darien turned away and stared up into the sky.

A gust of wind rose from behind him. It increased in strength until it blew over the valley with the force of a gale. Above, the gray clouds moved quickly by overhead, increasing their speed until it seemed they crossed the sky at an impossible rate. Gradually, a break formed between the thunderheads to reveal blue sky between.

Kyel stared in amazement at the golden beams of sunlight that slanted down from the gap in the clouds, even as the air around him remained dark and chill. He was almost afraid; the whole scene reminded him too much of Black Solstice. But then he realized the darkness that encased them didn't come from some dread power blotting out the daylight. It was the shadow cast by Orien's Finger, revealed only now by the dramatic appearance of the sun.

The wind stopped. Overhead, the clouds ceased their motion as Darien turned and walked toward the blistered cliffs, following the dark shadow cast by the crag. He paced up the exact center of the broad line drawn across the ground, stopping only when he came to the blackened wall of rock. There, he muttered something under his breath that Kyel couldn't hear.

But something heard him.

Above his head, the outline of a marking glowed from the

seared rock of the cliff face, glistening with a golden light. The rock ahead of them dissolved, a dark opening appearing in its place. In the dim light beneath the shadow of Orien's Finger, Kyel could just make out the beginning of stairs angling upward into the cliff.

"I'll be damned," Swain muttered, staring ahead.

Darien glared at him.

The Craghorns, The Rhen

They had to leave the horses behind. Darien had a hard time turning away from the Tarkendar. Craig had given him that horse. Watching the black gelding wander away with its nose to the wind, he felt almost as if he was giving up the last part of his old friend that still remained. But there was no other choice, so he shouldered the weight of his pack and, collecting Naia's without asking, turned toward the darkness of the opening he'd created.

As soon as the sole of his boot found the first step, he knew something about it was peculiar. The step didn't seem formed of solid rock, but rather of a strange, spongy material. It was almost like stepping off the ground onto a cloud. When he reached the fourth step, he was hit by an intense revelation.

"Kyel." He whirled around, searching desperately back through the opening. But he could see no trace of his former acolyte, or any of the others. He waited. Presently, Naia came through. Then Swain. It was strange. The opaqueness of the opening reminded him of the entrance to the Catacombs. It might have been the same, peculiar spell. Kyel appeared, looking past him into the darkness beyond.

"Shield yourself," Darien warned, appalled he hadn't thought of it sooner. He had almost made a lethal mistake that could have killed them. "The stair is spelled."

"Like the Catacombs?" Naia asked.

Darien nodded. "In the Catacombs, time and distance have no meaning. I feel the same principle at work here. I wouldn't be surprised if we reach the level of the Well far sooner than we'd thought.

"But," he said to Kyel with a look of dire warning, "that means we'll be walking into Orien's Vortex at any time. And then the vortex that surrounds Aerysius. We won't know when one ends and the other begins. No magelight," he added with a sigh.

"You want us to climb in the dark?" Swain asked. "That's insane."

Darien shook his head. "It shouldn't be long. It makes sense. Acolytes had a very strict curfew. Aidan said he followed this stair all the way down to the bottom and back. Aidan was a model acolyte. He was never caught out past curfew."

"It's a bad idea," Swain grumbled.

Darien looked down at him, almost finding it within himself to smile. In the years since he'd seen him last, he had missed Swain's abrasive temperament. The captain was one of the few constants he knew he could depend on. Swain could always be counted on to say what he meant and do what he believed. His personality was as economically efficient as his signature style with the blade: he never embellished, and he never sought to soften a blow.

He was glad Swain was with him. He was glad to have them all. Sweeping his gaze around at his companions, Darien realized that, unwittingly, he had surrounded himself with every friend he had that was still alive. He wished Craig could have been there, and even Proctor. Even Royce. So many others, all gone on ahead of him. Looking now at the friends that remained, Darien realized how grateful he was to have them there.

Feeling better than he had in a long time, Darien turned and started up the dark flight of stairs. And, as he cut himself off from the solace of the magic field, he found that he didn't need it so desperately, after all.

Kyel groaned, trying to keep his concentration focused on the next step ahead of him. They had been climbing ever upward in darkness for what seemed like hours. The journey was grueling, made even worse by the fear of falling Kyel felt at each step.

He was at the rear of the party. There was no one to catch him if he fell. The blackness that surrounded them was consummate, as if he'd been rendered completely blind. He could see nothing, not even the fingers of his own hand.

He groped forward tentatively, probing the step ahead with the toe of his foot before transferring his weight to it. He dared not take more than one step at a time. If not for the intermittent sounds of voices, he wouldn't have known any of the others were still with him.

As the long minutes dragged on, the fear that he was being left behind grew stronger. He started humming, the sound of his own voice making up a little for what he lacked of his perception of sight. And he hoped the sound would alert the others if he started trailing too far behind.

More than once, he bumped into Swain's back as the captain came to a lurching stop in front of him. Naia was having trouble with her dress and had to keep pausing to collect it out from under her feet. After several halts, Kyel heard Swain mutter something under his breath, followed by the distinctive sound of ripping fabric. There were no more dress problems after that, though Kyel wondered about the results of Swain's hasty tailoring job.

His legs ached, not used to so rigorous and prolonged a climb. He was afraid his calves were going to start cramping. At least the stair was not as steep as it could have been, and the steps were decently wide.

At last, they came to a narrow corridor where Darien called a halt. When Kyel moved to sit down, he found himself squatting in a puddle of water. Or something like water. In the darkness, it could have been anything.

"Can we not have a light yet?" he asked, sick of the gloom and anxious to find out the nature of the substance he had just stuck his hands in.

Darien's answer was long in coming. "We must be at the bottom of the cave system by now. I'll wager it's safe enough to risk it."

And then, miraculously, a hazy blue light bloomed from out of the ground that instantly revealed the forms of his companions. Kyel sighed, feeling relieved to be out of the darkness.

Darien consulted the map while they rested, a diffuse orb of magelight casting its glow above the page. The thanacryst sat dutifully by his side, its eyes glowing in the darkness. When it was time to go, Darien folded the map and shoved it back into his pack, staring ahead at the narrow passage before him. The magelight ran forward over the wet ground, following the motion of his eyes.

Fascinated, Kyel tried to form a glowing ribbon of his own. A faint golden tendril appeared briefly before winking out. It was the best he could do. He didn't think he could manage anything bigger. Maybe with practice, but not yet.

Darien said, "The Well of Tears is up three levels."

"Great. So how do we get there?" asked Swain.

Darien pointed down the corridor in front of them. "We take this straight ahead. We'll come to a series of rooms. One has a winding stair that will take us up to the level of the Well."

"Doesn't sound too bad," the captain muttered, staring ahead with his hands on his hips. "We'll have this done and over with by nightfall."

But Darien shook his head. "No. We should wait till dark, on the chance Aidan is using the caves. He pushed himself up from the wet floor. "We'll stop for a rest in one of the rooms up ahead."

That sounded good to Kyel. He could use a rest after that climb. They moved forward again, following Darien's glowing mist down the corridor. As Kyel walked, his feet splashed through dark puddles.

The cave seemed saturated with water. It dripped from the ceiling and ran, oozing, down the walls. The roof overhead was covered in creamy bumps that collected water on their ends until a full droplet was formed, then released it to splash down to the puddles below.

After only minutes, the corridor opened into a good-sized chamber. Unlike the passage they had just emerged from, the room had more of a man-made appearance, or at least it had been man-altered. There, Darien and Swain spread out, each taking a doorway, the captain moving cautiously ahead with his steel bared. Kyel waited with Naia as the priestess stared at the doorway Darien had disappeared through. At last, both men returned through completely different passages.

"It's clear," Swain announced.

Darien nodded his agreement.

They settled down together in a dry corner of the room. Kyel broke into his pack, rummaging through it for a bite to eat. All he had managed to pack was stale bread, so stale bread was what he had. Darien produced an apple that looked only a few days too old. He handed it to Naia, who smiled her thanks.

After the short and meager dinner, Kyel decided he'd better ask Darien the questions that remained unanswered. Removing *Treatise on the Well* from his pack, he opened it to the page he'd been fretting over.

"I still don't understand what I'm supposed to do," Kyel said, moving over to sit beside him. "It says to deactivate the rune sequence in reverse order. How do I do that?"

"What's the order?"

Kyel had no idea. Flipping to the runes listed a few pages back, he handed the book to Darien. "Here. Have a look."

Darien stared at the page for a moment, increasing the intensity of magelight that surrounded him. "This isn't the true sequence. It's a cipher."

Kyel frowned, not understanding him. He watched as Darien bent over the book, tracing the line of markings with a finger. *"Metha, calebra, noctua…benthos…"*

He paused, brow wrinkled in concentration. His finger moved back again to the beginning of the line, squinting down at the page. Then he sat back, eyes narrowed, his gaze lowered in thought.

Above him in the air, a faint blue line sprang into being. Kyel scooted back, startled at the line's sudden appearance in front of him. Twisted branches grew out from the line, until Kyel realized he was staring at one of the strange characters from the page. The rune moved, circulating upward, as a different character appeared where the first had just been.

Soon, the air was filled with glowing runes that formed a circle that hovered, floating above them. Naia and Swain both crept forward, staring in fascination. Slowly, the runes moved to form a line that crossed the length of the chamber. Kyel recognized the order of the characters. It was the sequence from the book.

But then the runes began rearranging themselves. The first one slid upward and to the right, settling into the space between two others that moved over to make room. Then another character near the end of the line slid all the way across the chamber to the beginning of the sequence.

As Kyel stared in awe, the glowing blue figures began moving, sliding in and out of sequence, spiraling up from their positions and dropping back into new ones. He glanced at Darien and saw the mage's eyes rapidly sliding back and forth, tracking the motion of the runes.

And then all movement abruptly stopped.

Kyel let out a breath as he stared at the glimmering chain of characters that hung above them in the air. He almost flinched when the entire line suddenly condensed, shrinking and falling at the same time, rotating once as they fell onto the open text in Darien's hand. Kyel heard a faint, sizzling noise as the markings scorched themselves into the page.

"Here's the reverse sequence," Darien said, handing Kyel the book as if nothing had happened. Kyel could only stare at the fresh markings that had inscribed themselves across a previously blank portion of the page as Darien went on, "Progress left to right, just as you would reading. Begin with this one, *dacros*." He indicated the first rune of the sequence. "*Ledros* will be on the far side of the rim. Work counterclockwise around the Well, following this progression."

Kyel looked back up at him, dumbfounded. "What do I do? How do I deactivate the runes?"

Darien scowled. "They were activated with Meiran's blood. You must purify each rune, one by one, in that order."

"How do I do that?"

Darien looked down at the markings scorched into the page, a solemn and resolved expression on his face. "Fire should work best," he answered in a voice strangely gruff. "Burn them clean."

Kyel swallowed. Then he nodded. "I'll try."

Darien's shook his head. "No. There can't be any halfway with this. You know fire. You know how it's made. Your doubt is the only thing holding you back. You'd better start believing in yourself. Otherwise, all of this is for naught."

Swain broke in, "What exactly do we do if this doesn't work?"

Darien turned toward him, eyes adamant. "Then there's nothing you *can* do. Renquist wins. He's a demon—he's *dead.* When he died, his gift was Transferred to another mage or lost to the air. His power over the magic field comes only through his link with the Netherworld, through the Well of Tears. The only way to stop him is to seal the Well. That's the only thing that will cut him off from his power."

Swain nodded, sucking at his cheek. "So if this doesn't work, then we're left facing that Enemy host down there as well as Renquist at full strength."

"And six more just like him," Darien reminded him. "You won't have a chance." He turned back to Kyel. "Do you understand, now, how much of this depends on you? Once I walk into that gateway, I won't be able to help you anymore. You'll be completely on your own."

Kyel dropped his gaze to the floor, feeling suddenly shamed. At last he nodded, unable to look Darien in the eyes.

"I understand," he whispered softly.

Darien stared down at the scars on his wrists. He sat with his back against one of the rough walls, listening to the steady sound of Kyel's breathing. The others had chosen to try to get some sleep. They hadn't had much the previous night.

Darien had offered to stand watch. There were too many things on his mind, too many emotions churning inside his head. And he didn't want to face the dreams he knew would come. He'd had enough of them.

The sound of Naia stirring broke him away from his thoughts.

Lowering his hands, he looked up and saw her moving toward him. Swain had done a number on her gown. It came to only knee-length now, with frayed threads hanging off where the captain had ripped it. Darien appreciated the look. Naia had beautiful legs. He found it hard to shift his gaze away from them.

"I can't sleep," she complained, sliding down the wall to sit at his side.

"You ought to go back and try," he said.

But Naia shook her head, leaning back against the rough wall and looking at him through the fabric of her veil. "No. I want to be with you."

Her eyes held his own, capturing him. Slowly, he reached his hand up and drew the glittering fabric off her face.

"You are beautiful," he said, gazing into her eyes. "Thank you for everything. I should have told you that before." He looked back down at his wrists, feeling suddenly very sad. "You should try to get some sleep," he whispered.

The feel of her lips on his made him forget the scars, forget what could not be. For one, brief moment, he closed his eyes and forgot everything but her. He reached up and pulled her into him, holding her close.

Chapter Forty-One
The Well of Tears

The Craghorns, The Rhen

"It's time to go."

Kyel hadn't realized he'd fallen asleep. Stretching, he sat up and stared around the dim chamber that glimmered in the quiet tendrils of Darien's magelight. The others looked like they were already prepared to set out again. Swain walked toward one of the exits, his pack swung over his shoulder.

Darien had burdened himself with the weight of both his own pack and Naia's. They were standing together in the middle of the chamber, Darien's clasped around her slender fingers. For once, Naia was without her veil. Kyel couldn't help but stare openly at her face, feeling moved. He was glad for them. But also very sad. Stuffing his blanket into his own pack, he pushed himself up off the ground.

"It's not far," Darien said as he led Naia toward one of the doorways.

Kyel fell in behind them, limping on legs that ached even worse than they had before. Swain followed, drawing his blade.

The magelight lit their way, trailing ahead as Darien led them through a series of adjoining chambers, each one just as dark and empty as the last. After minutes, they came to the stair Darien had told them about. Kyel followed him up the rough stone steps that wound around into blackness.

The stairwell almost reminded him of the tower of Greystone Keep, but infinitely darker. It smelled of old mold and wet rock. Water dribbled under his feet, running over each step in thin streams before trickling down to the one below it. The water spilled over the side of the first landing they came to, falling like a thin waterfall to the floor below.

"Stop," he heard Darien's voice echo in front of him.

Kyel stood motionless, staring up into the pale glow cast by the magelight. The Sentinel groped along the wall with his hand. Kyel heard a faint clicking sound that emanated from deep within the wall.

"What was that?" he asked.

"A trap." Darien pointed out a small circle recessed into the wall. "Thanks to that map you found, I knew to look for it. Otherwise, we'd all be dead."

Kyel stared at the small but lethal circle, shivering. "Are there more?"

"Two more up ahead before the chamber of the Well."

"How do you know there aren't others? Ones not marked on the map?"

The mage shrugged as he started forward again. "I don't."

Kyel kept his gaze angled at the wall from that point on. But Darien didn't stop again until they reached the third landing on the stair. There, he did another quick inspection of the wall, this time beckoning Kyel forward to point out the circle he found before depressing it.

"You're going to need to remember where these are for when you come back this way."

Kyel nodded, swallowing, as Darien pressed his finger against the circle. Again, there was a faint click. Then Darien moved on, clasping Naia's hand as he led her beside him through an opening.

Kyel followed, glancing both ways as he stepped into a long and narrow corridor. The passage ran perfectly straight, angling slightly upward. Ahead, Kyel could see a faint green glow. Darien paused, disarming yet another trap, then moved forward toward the source of the light.

"We're nearly there," he announced grimly.

The passage brightened gradually as they drew ever closer to that strange and sickly glow, until Darien was able to release his magelight altogether. They turned a corner, moving cautiously toward a doorway that flared with a brilliant spill of light.

Kyel followed him toward the opening with an unfolding sense of fear. He didn't like the look of the light, was repulsed by its unnatural hue. He stopped within the stone frame of the doorway, holding a hand up before his face to shield his eyes against the glare coming from a column of terrifying brilliance at the far end of the chamber.

He stared at it with a mingled sense of awe and horror, eyes taking in the surging energies that swept upward from the column's base, from a ring of stone that rose from the floor. Beyond it, he could make out the black silhouette of what appeared to be a stone table or altar with sinister-looking chains. His eyes went back to the circle of stone, then looked to Darien for the confirmation he was dreading.

"Is it…?"

"The Well of Tears," the Sentinel affirmed.

Kyel stared, transfixed by the writhing light stabbing upward from the Well. The air of the chamber crackled with energy. A low humming sound echoed off the walls, intermittently disturbed by a sharp hissing noise. The air was permeated with the pungent scent of decay.

Kyel let his eyes trail down the terrible pillar of light to the rough stone of the Well itself. There, along the rim, he could see the glowing runes. It came almost as a shock when he realized he could actually read them. The first rune glared out at him with a piercing brilliance that seemed to want to inscribe itself into the backs of his eyes: *dacros*.

Mesmerized, Kyel moved forward, his boots sloshing through dark puddles of water collected on the floor. He wasn't aware of the others behind him, knew nothing but the glaring markings that looked like claw marks raked into the stone of the Well's rim. He knelt beside the character of *dacros*, his hand reaching out until he could almost touch the luminous marking with the tips of his fingers. He traced the rune's outline in the air above it, lips moving silently to form the syllables of its name.

"You know what to do," he heard Darien's voice from behind him. Looking up, Kyel found the Sentinel standing over him.

"Remember—believe in yourself. Be steadfast, and do not doubt."

As Kyel looked up at him, Darien nodded slightly, confidently, then turned away. Suddenly dismayed, Kyel realized that it was Darien's way of saying goodbye. Kyel didn't want him to go, didn't want to be left without the comforting scaffold of his presence.

Kyel watched Darien cross the chamber away from him, his heart sinking as he realized he would never see him again. He suddenly realized that in the entire time he'd known him, Darien had shown only confidence in him. Through every test he had prepared, every trial, Darien had never doubted him once. Kyel understood then what he hadn't been able to understand before: that the mage had been his friend all along, and he had just never realized it.

Darien stopped beside Naia, turning to regard her with a softened expression on his face. "Stay here," he said. Reverently, he traced his fingers down her cheek.

"Darien—" she began.

He shook his head, silencing whatever it was she had started to say.

To Swain, he uttered, "Take care of them."

The captain nodded. "I will."

The thanacryst padding at his side, Darien strode out through the chamber's dark opening, disappearing into the shadows on the other side. Kyel stared after him into the darkness beyond, profoundly saddened.

He turned back to the Well. He had a part to play, and he couldn't falter. He owed it to Darien not to fail.

First, he needed to locate the rune progression. Then he could wait, giving Darien the time he needed to accomplish his part of the task before them.

Lifting his fingers back to the rune, Kyel muttered, *"Dacros."* Moving around the rim, he located the next marking in the sequence. *"Ledros."* He found he didn't need to refer back to the text to remember the pattern. The sequence was already established in his mind. With growing confidence, he hunted down the next vile marking. *"Noctua."*

Darien moved through the darkness of the caves, a pale azure glow of magelight revealing the path before his feet. If he remembered correctly, somewhere up ahead was another trap. This one, he intended to trigger. He needed to draw Aidan's attention to him. He didn't have time to go hunting through the rubble of Aerysius to find his brother.

Somewhere deep below, Kyel would be preparing to start his work on the Well of Tears. There wasn't much time. He would have to find Aidan before Kyel finished his task. Otherwise, his brother would be alerted to the threat to the gateway. Swain was an accomplished blademaster, possibly the best, but he was no match against a mage. And, Bound and inexperienced as he was, Kyel would be all but defenseless.

The corridor he moved through was narrow and dark, its walls wet and covered with spongy secretions from the rock. The magelight groped along just ahead of his feet, lighting his way. He tried not to let his thoughts wander back to his companions at the Well, but they kept slipping back that way despite his efforts. It had been hard to leave them. But what awaited him ahead, he had to face alone. Where he was going, his friends could not follow.

The magelight revealed the shadows of an intersection just ahead. There, Darien paused. His eyes scanned the walls to either side as the magelight traveled up the stone, following the motion of his gaze. He found a small circle in the wall that depicted the nature of the trap: the button was inscribed with a small pictogram.

The marking was so worn by the constant trickle of water and the passage of years that it was almost indiscernible. It took him a moment to interpret the symbol. Thankfully, it was just the type of device he needed. Any movement through the intersection would trigger it, unless the circle was depressed.

This time, Darien stayed his hand, walking purposely into the trap.

He hadn't known what to expect. An alarm of some kind, a screeching wail or distant tolling of a bell. But there was nothing. No evidence the device had even been triggered. It was possible the mechanism had failed after so many years of disuse and neglect. Possible, but he doubted it. Aidan would have made certain his defenses were well maintained. His brother had always been one to err on the side of caution, if not downright paranoia.

With a sense of conviction, Darien knew his presence had been made known. All he had to do now was wait.

Waiting was never easy.

He roamed forward, pacing slowly, casting the magelight ahead and brightening its intensity. He would give them a luminous trail to follow, so there would be no guessing his location. Already, he felt too pressed for time. Not daring to move far from the trap he'd sprung, Darien stopped, bending over to pet the thanacryst. The beast whined, its tail beating against the wet stone as Darien passed his fingers through its fur. However dreadful, the beast was a faithful companion. Its eyes gleamed in the darkness, wide and eager.

Abruptly, the motion of the tail stopped. The thanacryst lifted its head, nostrils quivering as it scented the air.

Darien straightened, alerted by the sudden change that had come over the demon-hound. He closed his eyes and listened but heard nothing. No distant echo of footsteps, no rush of armored bodies. Of course, whatever might be coming may not tread on legs and feet. He opened his eyes, scanning the narrow path ahead.

The necrators that rose up from the floor all around him came as no surprise. Darien merely regarded them, releasing the magelight and letting complete darkness settle in. He felt no trace of the awful dread their presence had once inspired. The rhythm of the magic field continued on in his mind, uninterrupted.

They were no threat to him. He had rendered himself immune to their influence. His meeting with Renquist had taken him beyond the point of return. Now even the indiscretion of his feelings for Naia was not enough to lessen the sickness in his heart. Darien smiled, knowing he was now free to feel anything he wished. There was no going back, not anymore. Not ever.

The necrators had not been a surprise. But the sight of Cyrus Krane striding toward him gave Darien a shock. He had not expected the darkmage, and the significance of Krane's presence was alarming.

The demon drew up before him, his gaze lingering on the thanacryst that stood at Darien's side, purring and drooling profusely at the same time. Krane's stare roved upward as a smile came to his lips, distorting the dreadful scar on his face into a jigsaw pattern that made his appearance seem even harsher than it was already. His eyes were satisfied, perhaps even gloating.

"We had a feeling you might try something like this," he stated. "My Master will be well-pleased."

Darien refused to be intimidated. The advice he had given Kyel held true, especially now. He had to remain steadfast. To doubt was to die. He held no white banner in his hand this time.

"Which master are you referring to?" he taunted. "Aidan or Renquist?"

"I have but one Master," was Krane's terse reply. "Now, so do you."

Darien made no effort to resist as the necrators pressed in around him, surrounding him with their shadowy forms. Krane turned away, striding back down the long corridor the way he had come as the necrators moved to follow him, gliding like shadows over the ground. Darien allowed himself to be herded forward, moving in the wake of Krane's flowing robes.

Strange, how Krane felt comfortable enough to walk with his back to him, as if he considered him no threat at all. Perhaps the demon felt confident enough that the necrators had eliminated any possibility of his resistance. Or, perhaps, he really did pose no threat to the ancient darkmage, which was a thought altogether more disturbing.

The corridor wandered upward, turning back on itself as they approached the surface. There, a narrow stair was carved into the rock, curving as it rose. Krane mounted the steps first, his magelight a crimson mist pouring up the stairs. Darien followed, walking within the confines of his shadowy guard. After what seemed like minutes, the stair opened up, emerging at the base of the ruined city.

As he stepped out of the darkness of the warren, Darien realized he was once again finally home. Only, Aerysius was no longer as he remembered it.

There were no structures, no crumbled ruins, no traces of the devastation he remembered from that dreadful night. There, on the cliff face high above the Vale, the slate had been wiped completely clean. Except for the soaring arches that rose like a forlorn and obsolete monument over the snow-covered square, only empty terraces remained. The ruins were gone, scoured away. The arches were all that remained, and the terrible column of light striking upward into the heavens.

Darien craned his neck, gazing up at the towering pillar of the gateway. The sight of it filled him with a mixture of dread and anticipation. The glowing spear of light inspired nothing of the terror he'd experienced the night it had first appeared. He understood its purpose better now. He had internalized it, making it his own. With that strange sense of ownership, he allowed Krane to guide him toward it, out into what had once been the ornately tiled square. Now just a flat expanse of snow and rock.

Looking around, he realized there was nothing left for him here. This desolate mountain face no longer held even the memory of his home.

"Darien?"

So transfixed was he by the barren foundations of the city, he had almost missed the small, dark figure kneeling in the snow only a few steps away.

Like Aerysius, his brother was nothing as Darien remembered. Indeed, his face was more of a devastated wasteland than the city he had brought to ruin. Aidan was gaunt, the flesh sagging on his pale face, eyes but dark hollows above the sharp ridges of his cheekbones. His hair had gone completely gray, almost white, and had receded dramatically. He knelt on the ground, arms bound behind his back by bonds of red light that twined about his arms in a grim parody of the scars hidden beneath Darien's own sleeves.

Darien froze, forgetting the presence of even Krane. He wanted to look away but found it impossible to do anything but stare at the sad, twisted man that had been the object of his hatred for so long. Almost, Darien thought he could feel sorry for him. Almost. But then he reminded himself of Meiran, of the Hall of the Watchers, of the mother he had lost. That was just the beginning of the long, blood-written list he wanted to hold this man accountable for.

"They want to remake you," Aidan rasped, staring up at him with wide, startled eyes. "Why did you come?"

Confused, Darien felt a terrible, growing sense of dismay. Aidan was insane. It was written on his face, gaped out from his reddened, tortured eyes. The realization came as a startling shock. Darien could feel the hatred he had nurtured so carefully for so very long simply dissolve. In its place, he felt only an emergent sense of pity.

Turning to Krane, Darien silently implored the man for an explanation.

"He drained too many before the Hall of the Watchers fell," the demon stated, glaring down at Aidan as if he were some abject and broken tool to be discarded. "There is only so much power the human mind can endure."

Not knowing what to feel, Darien gazed down on his brother somberly. Slowly, he moved toward him. As he lowered himself to kneel at his side, Aidan shrank back, turning his face away. But not before Darien caught a glimpse of the tears that streaked his ruined cheeks.

Peering intently, Darien searched the man before him, trying to find something left within him to hate. But he found nothing. Just a pathetic, miserable creature that cowered from his presence. Darien found himself instead searching his own heart, wondering if he had it within himself to deliver the justice he had sworn in blood to mete.

Sighing, Darien reached out with his mind and unmade the bonds that constrained Aidan's wrists. His brother sagged visibly, chin falling against his chest, eyes staring vacantly at the ground. Tears fell from his cheeks, dribbling to the snow.

Wretchedly, he whispered, "Forgive me."

Darien almost wished he could. The sight of his brother's tears brought back memories of their boyhood together. For once, not all of those memories seemed so terribly bad. There had been times when he'd enjoyed Aidan's company. Not often. But times. For a long period of his life, his brother had been the only connection he'd had with his family. He had never been fond of Aidan as a person. But, once, Darien had loved him as a brother, the only brother he'd ever had.

"Take my hands," Darien whispered. "Let's be done with this."

"What are you going to do?"

Darien shook his head. "I can't forgive you, Aidan. Mercy is all I have left to offer you."

Behind him, he heard the soft footsteps and shivering robes of Cyrus Krane.

"Yes," the demon hissed at his back. "Take his life. That is the first step."

"The first step of what?" Darien turned to glare up at him, resenting the intrusion.

"Your new life as one of us." Krane smiled down at him: a gloating, sinister grin.

Darien shook his head, feeling suddenly uncertain. "I declined Renquist's offer."

"You were under the protection of truce last night. Not so, now."

With a shiver of dismay, Darien realized Krane was right. Aerysius was a snare, with his brother set out as bait. After their meeting, Renquist had anticipated he would come here. It was a trap, and he had fumbled blindly into it.

Darien rose from his brother's side. "I'll never be one of you."

"But you already are." The confidence in Krane's tone made Darien take a step back, consumed by a cold numbness that eclipsed his every perception.

"What do you mean?"

"The thanacryst." Krane nodded at the creature. "Such a beast cleaves only to a soul already damned. You are a Servant of Xerys. You have surrendered yourself to Him freely. You belong to Him, now."

"No."

He refused to believe it could be that heinously simple.

But Krane seemed very certain it was. He dismissed Darien's denial with a curt wave of his hand. "You already made your choice. There is no going back. Now, go. Do your duty by your brother. I wish to depart this vile place."

Darien glanced up at the gateway. The beacon throbbed, beckoning, its slithering ropes of energy calling out to him with a promise of hope and release. There was no chance he could reach it. Krane stood before him, physically barring his path.

There was only one thing to do. Dropping back to Aidan's side, Darien reached out and took his brother's hands in his own. As their fingers touched, Darien felt a pulling sensation from deep within, a strange and distant tingling. Startled, he realized that his brother was establishing a conduit between them, locking them together in a treacherous link. Reviled, he tried to pull back.

But Aidan clenched his hands, a look of hungry desperation in his eyes. Darien fought as the pulling became a tearing ache that grew into a tangible pain. The pain swelled, increasing to a wrenching agony. Darien threw his head back, gritting his teeth and clutching his brother's hands as he fought to turn the conduit back around.

A lightning spear resolved from the sky and stabbed into Aidan. Darien felt the conduit slam closed with a force that hurled him backward.

He rolled onto his side, looking up to see Aidan writhing on the ground, red energies crackling as they clawed over his body. The sounds of his shrieks were terrible, and they seemed to go on and on. Finally, Aidan collapsed back to lie in the snow, his tortured body limp and still.

Darien looked away, horrified. Cyrus Krane moved toward him and, to his amazement, reached down and offered him his hand. Darien accepted it, allowing the ancient darkmage to help him to his feet. His legs trembled as he walked over to where Aidan lay motionless on his back. Darien bent down over the body of his brother, laying his head against his chest to listen for a heartbeat. Unbelievably, he heard a faint stirring, weak and irregular, but undeniably there.

"I don't understand. He summoned you. I thought you were required to obey him."

Krane shook his head. "Only until the initial purpose of our summoning was fulfilled. Since then, we've been under our own recognizance."

Darien looked back down at his dying brother, not quite certain how to feel. Aidan had been responsible for the tragedy of Aerysius, but everything that had happened since had been Renquist's doing all along. All this time, Aidan had been merely the demon's pawn, nothing more.

Feeling strangely weak, Darien struggled back to his feet. He was unable to take his eyes off his brother, watching the shuddering rise and fall of his chest.

"Come, now," Krane commanded, extending his hand with a welcoming invitation on his lips. "Renquist is expecting us down the mountain."

Darien shook his head, the demon's cool assurance distilling a cold anger within him. "I'm not going anywhere with you."

Krane only shrugged. "I'll compel you if you leave me no choice. But I must warn you: our Master exacts harsh punishments from his Servants. And you must also think of Meiran. Her soul will be made to suffer along with yours."

Darien gaped at him, appalled, feeling his anger chill to a frozen sea of contempt. He couldn't accept that. Not Meiran. Too many souls had already paid the price for his decisions. Meiran was innocent and had already suffered far more than she ever deserved. Looking at Krane, he narrowed his eyes and coldly shook his head.

"Your master can go to hell."

He reached out from within, summoning the fatal potency of his rage. A shaft of fire bloomed from his hand, hurling viciously at Krane. The demon seemed to shrug slightly as a wall of red light appeared in front of him, neatly absorbing the lance of flame. Krane smiled, black eyes gleaming with sinister promise as he reached his hand upward to the sky.

Darien dodged, but he wasn't quick enough. A writhing net of living energy fell, draping over him and tugging him to the ground.

The searing fibers of the net burned, scorching his skin with blistering heat as he struggled to free himself. Through the web of glistening light, he could see Krane's robe trailing toward him over the ground, through his groans he could hear the demon's malevolent voice:

"Is it your wish to spend an eternity in such pain?"

The net lifted, dissolving into threads that slithered away into the air. Darien lay on his back, shuddering as he healed the burns the ghastly thing had made. He struggled to sit up, but no sooner had he accomplished the motion then a series of rings appeared around him, constricting. The rings tightened inexorably, compressing his ribs a little more with each breath.

Soon, even breathing became impossible. Frantic, Darien reached deep inside the mage. He clasped his mind around the demon's heart, envisioning it shuddering to a standstill in his chest.

But, as he groped for that blackened and twisted organ, he discovered to his horror that Krane's heart was already dead.

With a laugh, the ancient Prime Warden threw out his hand. The rings fell away as a ferocious blast of air hit Darien full in the face. He sagged to the ground, feeling the sharp stab of a sword thrust take him between the ribs.

He looked down to see blood welling over the hand he held clutched against his side. He could hear Krane's laughter, almost drowned out by a clamorous ringing in his ears. He groped within, trying to get enough sense of the wound to heal it. As he did, he felt a shooting lance of pain descend like an axe through the middle of his head.

Abruptly, the magic field was gone. He couldn't even sense it.

Darien looked up and saw Krane moving toward him as if

through a fog, a dim silhouette backlit against the brilliant light of the gateway directly behind him. The demon seemed to be moving impossibly slow as he knelt at his side, smiling that baneful grin, fingers roving over him scant inches above his body.

"Your first lesson, my acolyte," Cyrus Krane pronounced. "Never seek to defy your masters again."

He pressed his hands to Darien's chest, wielding vicious, searing agony. Darien convulsed, the noise of Krane's harsh laughter drowned out by the sound of his own screams.

Kyel figured he had waited long enough. It was time.

He moved back to the first rune in the sequence and raised his hand. Behind him, he could feel Naia leaning over him, looking on over his shoulder. Her presence made him suddenly self-conscious, and he clenched his hand into a fist. He couldn't doubt. He had to believe. He knew fire, knew how to summon it from flint. All he needed to do was transfer that knowledge to the air.

Raising his finger to the glowing rune, he muttered its name and willed the air above it to warm. At first, there was nothing. Then, slowly, he could feel the heat. But it wasn't enough. He steeled his mind in concentration, consuming his thoughts with a determined, singular intent. A fine dagger of flame flared toward the rune, hissing as it came in contact with it. Kyel almost fell backward into Naia in alarm, staring up at the rim of the Well to see the unholy light of *dacros* suddenly dim and fade out.

"That's it," Naia whispered. "You can do this."

Kyel nodded. He moved around the Well, swiftly finding *ledros*. Kneeling beside the vile mark, he quickly conjured the tiny knife of flame. Within seconds, the next rune turned a dull, lifeless black.

He repeated the task, working counterclockwise in the sequence Darien had given him, wandering in circles around the Well of Tears until, at last, he found himself kneeling before the pale light of the final marking. Raising his hand, Kyel seared the last vestige of Meiran's blood from the dark stone of the rim.

The column of light shivered, white energies crackling through it. Kyel stared up at it, terrified, as the gateway seemed to throb, its form suddenly unstable.

The Well of Tears was sealed, at least in this world. But the awful energies of the gateway still shivered, throbbing in the air like a dilapidated pedestal on the verge of collapse.

"The rest is up to Darien, now," he whispered.

The gateway shivered, pierced through by white streaks of energy that shrieked violently upward. The whole pillar throbbed, shuddering fiercely.

Cyrus Krane turned toward it, an expression of horror on his face. On the ground beneath him, Darien squinted up, admiring the beauty of the white streaks that tarnished the vile perfection of the green column of light. He smiled a small, sad grin. Then he drew in a long, wheezing breath that sent a lancing pain from his ribs.

"Crenoch!" he shouted.

The demon-hound obeyed, springing up from the ground in a great leap, catching Krane in the chest with its paws and shoving him backward with the force of its weight.

Krane staggered, arms pinwheeling, as the thanacryst's huge mouth closed on his throat. Together, beast and demon tumbled into the gateway, disappearing in a brilliant flash of light.

The smile slowly faded from Darien's lips. The pulse of the magic field was still nothing more than a faded memory in his head.

He struggled to roll onto his side, shaking and weak from Krane's vicious assault. Clenching his jaw, he pushed himself up and crawled painfully toward his brother.

Aidan still lay where he'd fallen. Reaching his side, Darien collapsed on top of him, laying his head on his brother's chest. Surprisingly, there was still a heartbeat in that ruined body.

Darien grasped Aidan's limp form in his arms, clutching him tight as he struggled to rise. His body trembled, refusing the effort he was asking of it.

Darien groaned. He heaved himself onto his knees, then rose, locking his arms around Aiden's middle. His legs shook as he took a lurching step backward, dragging his brother after him.

"Darien…"

He looked down, surprised to find Aidan's blue eyes cracked open.

"It hurts…"

Darien gazed down into his brother's wretched face and assured him, "It'll be over soon."

He took another step backward toward the pillar of light. The pain in his side was like a fiery brand that flared with every motion of his body.

"I'm scared," Aidan whispered in a weak, trembling voice.

Darien took a last, long look up at the towering pillar as he whispered, "Me too."

Gripping Aidan under the arms, he crossed into the ethereal light.

The Gateway

At first, he saw only mist. A hazy green bleakness that unfolded before him, expanding outward in swirling clouds of vapor. Beyond the mist, there was darkness. This place had the feeling of closeness, as if there were walls all around he simply couldn't see. This couldn't be the Netherworld, Darien decided. Somehow, he must still be within the gateway.

And he was alone. His brother had gone on ahead of him.

Darien collapsed to his knees, raising his hands before his face. Appalled, he took in the sight of the aura that surrounded his fingers and emanated from his skin. It was the same awful glow he remembered from the Catacombs. The aura was brighter, now, writhing up his arms, very visible against the darkness and the mist.

This time, he knew exactly what it meant.

Dropping his hands, he raised his voice and called out into the bleakness, "I accept your offer. Now, make good on your end."

The mist around him continued to swirl, unaffected by his words. Scowling, Darien realized what he had to do. Somehow, he'd known it all along. He closed his eyes in dread and forced himself to utter the same infamous phrases spoken by Zavier Renquist a thousand years before:

I commit my soul to Chaos. From this day forth,
I will be the obedient servant of Xerys.
I will serve faithfully all the days of my life…
and may not even death itself release me.

His voice trailed off into silence. Still, the haze that enveloped him yet lingered, swirling. Darien wondered if he had been heard at all, or if his proffered oath had been rejected entirely. Only silence surrounded him. Only silence and the mist.

But then, a soft light spawned before him, a pale and wondrous glow that confronted the mist and turned back the darkness. To Darien, it was the most beautiful sight he'd ever seen.

Mesmerized, he crawled toward the radiant promise of that glow. Before his eyes, the light assumed definition, solidifying into the image that for months had haunted his waking memories and his dreams. He reached out toward it, his trembling fingers tracing the soft profile of the face that glowed before him like the first light of a rising moon.

Meiran lay beside him on the ground, dark waves of her hair spread out at her side. The gown she wore was stained and tattered, her eyes closed as if sleeping. But then, as he watched, those lovely eyes fluttered open.

For a moment she stared up at him vacantly, as if waking from the depths of the deepest slumber. Dim confusion nettled her features. Then, slowly, her expression changed. Meiran's lips parted, dark eyes widening.

She was even more beautiful than he remembered. She was gazing up at him with such a look of joy it wrung his heart. Clutching her against him, Darien held her close in his trembling arms. He closed his eyes and kissed her, his nostrils filled with the sweet fragrance of her hair.

With effort, he forced himself to draw back away. He took her face in his hands, cupping her cheeks, as he told her gently, "I need you to be strong for me."

The joy in her eyes collapsed, replaced by a look of shadowy confusion. Darien shook his head, grimacing through the sorrow in his heart. He wished he had time to explain. He wished he had time to hold her longer in his arms.

Shaking, he brought the Soulstone up, encircling the bands of the collar around his neck as his fingers fumbled at the clasp.

"As soon as I'm dead, get this off me."

The look of confusion on Meiran's face dissolved into terror.

He let the clasp of the necklace snap closed.

The onslaught of pain was instant and terrible. Darien fell back against the ground, shuddering in agony as the talisman around his neck stirred awake with a deep inner glow.

Meiran held him in her arms as his soul was ripped out of life. Her beautiful face was the last thing Darien saw as he died. It was all he wanted to see. It was enough.

Chapter Forty-Two
Wiped Clean

The Craghorns, The Rhen

The chamber shuddered, the whole world lurching under Kyel's feet.

"Quick, get the cover on!" Naia screamed.

Swain was already bent over the enormous circular slab of stone, heaving against it with all his might. Kyel saw the captain didn't have near the strength it would take to budge it.

"Stand back," he commanded. He raised his hand as Swain released the cover and backed away. It was just a push, that's all. He could not doubt.

The cover of the Well of Tears rose silently from the wet floor, dripping liquid filth as it hovered, sliding stately through the air, at last lowering to a gentle rest on the rim.

Then there was only darkness. Kyel tried to see through the emptiness that surrounded him, but all he saw was the red afterglow of the gateway. Confused and scared, it took him a moment to realize what had just happened.

The Well of Tears, finally, had been fully sealed from both sides.

"He did it." Swain's voice echoed through the darkness.

As if from somewhere very distant, he heard the soft sound of Naia weeping. The noise made Kyel's heart feel heavy with sorrow. Moving toward it, he groped through the darkness until his fingers found the silken texture of her gown. He folded his arms around her, pulling her close and wishing there was something further he could do.

But there wasn't. So he stood there, holding her, as long

minutes dragged by. Through the darkness, her voice whispered, pleading, "I want to go up there."

He couldn't say no, even though he wanted to. He knew it was the wrong thing to do.

Kyel produced a soft, misty glow around his feet. The magelight drifted out away from him, coursing in glimmering tendrils of burnished yellow-gold. He had read that every mage produced their own signature color. This was his, and Kyel stared down at it with a sense of pride.

In its pale warmth, Naia's face looked very young and incredibly fragile. Taking her by the hand, he let the golden magelight spill before them as he guided her out of the chamber. He didn't turn back. He had no desire for a last glimpse of the Well.

Instead, he followed the long corridor, eyes scanning the walls for the tiny circles that indicated the presence of the magical traps Darien had pointed out to him. He found only one and disarmed it with a click. Letting the ribbons of magelight spill before them, he moved ahead, leading his two companions up a wide, curving stair.

At the top of the steps was an opening that revealed a gray expanse of sky. Overhead, storm clouds were gathering. Kyel mounted the last few steps with growing unease.

He didn't know what to expect at the top of that stair and wasn't sure if he wanted to see it. He had never known Aerysius, but he harbored a long-established and cherished image of what he thought it must have looked like. Wanting to hold onto that vision, he was hesitant to see the reality that confronted him over the top of the steps.

What he found surprised him. There was no city at all. Only empty terraces on a high mountain face, barren rock covered by a thin layer of snow. And, to his amazement, it was snowing still. Soft white flakes drifted down from the sky, alighting on his shoulders and clinging to his face. Kyel moved out into the white haze, Naia at his side.

It was hard to see anything through the falling snow and swirling mist. He could make out the shadow of a tall and thin arch, but there was virtually no other trace that people had ever lived in this place. The wide terrace he stood on could have been a natural indentation in the cliff. Perhaps, one day, it would go back to nature, be reclaimed by the mountain face that had nurtured it for so long.

Aerysius was truly gone. Except for the soaring arch, not a vestige of the city remained. There was no trace of the gateway. The sky above the mountain had been released from the grip of that unholy light.

Kyel stared straight ahead into the falling snow, feeling Naia's fingers tighten around his own. He wished he hadn't brought her. There was nothing for them there, nothing but hurt. It was time to go.

Swain placed a comforting hand on Naia's shoulder. "We should leave, now."

The priestess nodded, bowing her head.

Kyel moved to turn away from the stark and lonely terrace. As he did, his eyes caught a motion ahead in the drifting snow.

He peered through the mist, seeing what looked like a shadow moving toward them through the obscurity of the haze. He hesitated, a muddled turmoil of hope and fear choking his heart. Eyes fixed on the shadow ahead, he watched it resolve into the features of a woman.

Kyel felt Naia's fingers trembling in his hand, heard the sound of her moan as she threw her head back. Then she broke away from him, stumbling forward through the snowdrifts. Kyel started after her as the strange woman staggered forward. He reached her just in time to catch her before she fell.

"Who is she?" Kyel all but whispered.

Swain knelt beside him and brushed matted strands of dark hair from the woman's face. Her skin was ashen pale, her body shivering violently in Naia's arms. Tears ran down her cheeks, falling from her chin to land softly in the snow. She gazed up at Swain with a look of uncertainty.

"Captain?" she muttered.

Nigel Swain nodded, his face sad and solemn. "Hello, Meiran."

Kyel gasped, filled with sudden understanding. Renquist had

delivered on the promise he had made to Darien.

A glimmer of light in Meiran's hand captured his attention. She raised her trembling hand from her side, offering out the necklace clasped in her fingers. Kyel felt an urgent flair of grief when his hand closed around the glowing medallion.

He held the Soulstone up before his face, marveling at its myriad facets. The gem pulsated with a radiant inner life, brighter than he remembered it being ever before. A sad sense of finality rushed over his body like a wash of cold water. This was legacy he was holding. Now more than ever before, he fully understood what that meant.

But this legacy was not his own. Wordlessly, he offered the medallion to Naia. She received it from him timorously, her expression a mixture of sorrow and awe. She held the medallion in her open palm, fingers trailing over the gem's smooth texture.

"He left this for me," she whispered.

Kyel nodded, though he knew she was partially wrong. The power in the Soulstone was an inheritance that would have to be shared. The heritage of Aerysius was in that stone, the power it contained too great for just one person. Looking back down at Meiran, his eyes confirmed what his heart had already guessed.

There were no chains on Meiran's wrists.

It was then that Kyel fully understood the nature of the gift. Deep within the gem's glowing facets moved the same inner power that had moved through Darien. It was a part of him that would be with both women always, would never grow old and fade, never sicken or falter.

Kyel wrapped his arms around both of them as he bowed his head, thoroughly overcome.

The Cerulean Plains, The Rhen

Traver watched the wild man on his buckskin horse galloping away, smiling a crooked grin of thanks after him. It had been downright decent of the herdsman to ride with him all this way. Reaching down with the three remaining fingers of his left hand, he ruffled the mane of the horse Ranoch had given him. It was a tough beast, although an ugly and temperamental one. Ranoch had given him the pick of his herd, and Traver had chosen the piebald. He liked the stallion's one, glaring blue eye.

He rode bareback; the Jenn didn't see the need for saddles or tack. The horse was guided by a simple rope, using pressure to guide its movements instead of a bit. Traver was beginning to consider himself a decent rider after all the time he'd spent on the piebald's naked back.

Ahead, he could see the encampment of two armies, and he thought he recognized the blue colors of Rothscard. He didn't want to get involved with *those* again. He'd had enough of Rothscard Bluecloaks to last a few lifetimes.

There had been a third army that had concerned him more, the black armor of its warriors standing out as a deadly barrier between himself and the forces of his countrymen. But that army was heading in disorganized retreat back toward the Gap of Amberlie. Traver watched them go, wondering what had prompted them to leave. There was no sign a battle had been fought, nor even a skirmish. Something strange was going on down there.

He kicked the piebald to a gallop, leaning forward as they raced over the snowy fields. Ahead, he saw a thin tendril of smoke and, drawing back on the ropes that served for reins, decided to go investigate. The smoke was coming from a small fire built under the bare branches of a tree.

Squinting, Traver made out the form of a man leaning up against the tree trunk, appearing quite asleep. But as Traver came nearer, the man's eyes shot open. The man reached for the black hilt of a knife at his belt.

Traver almost went for his sword. But then he remembered he'd lost it. He had lost more than just the blade. He'd lost the ability of ever wielding a weapon again. At least the man on the ground looked like he'd changed his mind about attacking him. He sat up straight, head cocked to the side, a look of disbelief on his face.

At the same moment Traver recognized him, Devlin Craig said

wonderingly, "Larsen?"

Traver threw back his head, laughing as he slid down from the back of his horse. "What are you doing here?"

Craig scowled, pointing to his leg. Traver grimaced as he saw the bandage wrapped tightly around the man's thigh. It was ironic, actually. He raised his hands, wiggling the fingers he had left.

Craig cracked a grin, chuckling and shaking his head. "We're two fine soldiers, aren't we?"

Traver laughed and clapped him on the shoulder as he knelt at his old captain's side. Nodding in the direction of the departing Enemy army, he asked, "What's happening down there?"

"I don't know." Craig shrugged, picking up a fallen branch and pointing with it. "They've been sitting down there for two days, then this morning they just packed up and began withdrawing."

Traver frowned. "I wonder what happened."

With a grimace, Craig leaned his weight on the branch, using it to help push himself to his feet. Limping a step forward, he offered, "Let's go down there and find out. I'm starving."

Traver moved toward him and helped support the man's weight, wondering how, with only eight fingers, he was ever going to get Craig's big bulk onto his one-eyed horse.

Darien's story continues in 'Darklands'...
...but will he be the same?

Preview of

Darklands

The

Rhenwars Saga

Chapter One
Infernal Commission

Aerysius, The Rhen

The old man wandered the dark corridor toward his death, the girl trailing after him.

The girl's right hand clutched a thin-bladed knife, the sort of knife once used by hunters of the clans to scrape the flesh of beasts away from bone. But the girl had encountered no such beasts in all her short years of existence. The knife in her hand wasn't meant for the flesh of animals. It thirsted for the blood of the old man.

Azár glared ahead at her master's life-weary gait with a scowl of derision on her face. Zamir was selfish, and his selfishness had imperiled all the clans. He should have made this last journey months ago, back when his death might have actually counted for something. Now, too late, Zamir's belated gesture of sacrifice was just as wretched and irrelevant as the old man himself.

"Here," Zamir grimaced, bringing a trembling, rheumatic hand up to trail down the weeping surface of the stone passage. In the darkness, his damp and gnarled fingers resembled the tangled roots of trees. Azár's gaze lingered on them, apathetic, her hand compressing the hilt of the knife in her palm.

She waited, staring dully, and said nothing.

Azár watched in silence as her master shambled forward through the nebulous tendrils of magelight that churned at his feet. Her eyes remained fixed on the scraps of colorless fabric that clung to his emaciated back. She made no move to follow him into the shadowy chamber beyond. Not until his voice called out from the darkness to rebuke her. Azár forced herself to move forward through the doorway.

She stopped, mouth agape. Her hand on the blade fell limply to her side. Her eyes wandered slowly over the images that confronted her, searing themselves like caustic brands pressed against the backs of her eyes. To one side of the chamber was a dark stone altar set with ancient, rusted chains. To the other side of the room stood a sinister ring of man-carved stone.

Azár watched with morbid curiosity as Zamir sat himself down upon the worn surface of the altar that rose from stagnant pools of water collected on the floor. He lay himself back, adjusting his position, folding his arms across his chest. His age-leathered face gazed upward into the shadows, eyes fiercely introspective.

"Recite the forward sequence," he instructed her in a gravelly, old-man voice.

Azár's gaze swept across the room in the direction of the Well.

The Well of Tears appeared exactly as she'd expected, exactly as she'd feared. It was made of staggered granite blocks stacked as high as her waist. Carved all around the rim were runes at once both ominous and familiar, sad vestiges of a lost heritage one thousand years dead. The runes themselves seemed to beckon to her, compelling her to approach.

Azár scowled at the markings, resenting them. It was the fault of the runes they were here, such a far and dangerous distance away from anywhere they were supposed to be. The runes were a key that unlocked a door, a door between worlds. Azár had spent the past two years preparing for this journey. Even still, she felt horrendously ill-prepared. This was a path she had never desired for herself, would never wish upon anyone.

"Sistru, qurzi, calebra, ghein, vimru…" Her voice faltered. Azár cleared her throat, edging cautiously forward as she continued reciting from memory the order of the ancient cypher: *"Ranu, benthos, metha, zhein, noctua…ledros. Dacros."*

She dropped to a crouch beside the Well of Tears as her voice trailed off into a festering silence. She lifted a finger to trace reverently over the first of the sacred markings to confront her:

dacros. The final rune of the sequence. Ancient symbol of Xerys, God of Chaos and Lord of the Netherworld.

"You make me proud," the voice of the old man affirmed from behind her. "What will be is better than what is gone."

Azár didn't turn back around to look at him. Instead, she remained squatting in a tarry pool of stagnant water with her hand upraised before her face. Her dark brown eyes considered the rune *dacros* that seemed to glare out at her like a brand seared into the Well's stony hide. Slowly, Azár lowered her hand and cast a wordless glance back over her shoulder in the direction of the old man.

Zamir yet lay on his back on the stone altar, arms folded across his chest. His tired eyes stared ostensibly upward at the ceiling, or perhaps straight ahead into eternity. He made no further effort to instruct her. There was no need.

Azár rose to her feet and stalked back across the chamber. From the woven belt at her waist, she produced a small pewter cup, which she set down on the rough surface of the altar rock at her master's side.

Face utterly impassive, Azár took Zamir's arm into her hand. Wielding the thin-bladed knife, she slit open the underside of Zamir's arm all the way from his elbow to his wrist. Azár stared down at the blood that welled from the gaping incision. As she watched, the dark fluid coursed over her fingers and ran dribbling down her arm. Gradually, she became aware of the sound of the old man's voice muttering the phrases of the *Dhumma*, the prayer that is spoken with the last breath before dying.

Azár studied Zamir's face, gazing with curiosity into the old man's dimming eyes. She set the knife down and centered the pewter cup beneath the running trickle of blood to better collect the spilt offering. The vessel filled quickly to the brim. Azár took Zamir's frail hand into her own in a final gesture of compassion, gazing down into his face as his lifeblood drained out of him.

The girl said nothing. She stood there, holding her master's hand, watching as the last light faded quietly from his eyes. As it did, Azár felt the warm stirring of power that grew within her fingertips. Her eyes went wide, her breath catching in her chest.

The swelling warmth of the Transference swept up her hand into her arm, spread outward through her chest, raging like a firestorm through her veins. The power coursed through her, filling her, penetrating every fiber of her being.

Then, abruptly, Azár felt the conduit slam closed.

She cried out, cringing back away from the emptied husk of the old man. Her eyes wide and bright with alarm, Azár took a staggering step away, her breath coming in sharp and panicked gasps. Her gaze darted wildly around the dark chamber, her brain struggling to make sense of the confused perceptions that assaulted it. Tears wrung from her eyes by the violence of the Transference streaked her face, dribbled from her chin. Her whole body was shaking, weakened from the deluge of powerful energies.

Panting, Azár summoned a faint glow of magelight. AI shimmering mist was inspired into being, roiling tendrils exploring the wet floor around her feet. The magelight pierced the shadows of the chamber, driving them back against the recesses of the walls. By the light of her own newfound power, Azár's eyes were drawn once again toward the Well of Tears. She glared at the portal, despising it utterly.

Steeling herself, Azár reached for the life-warm pewter cup at her side. Taking it into her hand, she made her way across the chamber. She knelt beside the Well, holding the cup of her master's blood up before her face in trembling hands. She dipped a shaking finger into the cup and then held it up before her face to consider. She turned her finger slowly, observing the wet sheen of blood in the skirling tendrils of magelight. Strengthened by resolve, Azár leaned forward and applied Zamir's spent lifeblood to the first rune of the sequence. The blood absorbed quickly into the porous stone as if sucked inside.

Before her eyes, the ancient rune *sistru* awakened from sleep and began to glow with a green, ethereal light. Nodding in satisfaction, Azár moved around to the far side of the Well, to the next marking of the sequence. She brought that rune, too, to life. Then she moved on to the next. Calm and deliberate, Azár took her time, working meticulously all around the rim until, at last, all of the ancient markings glowed with their own inner life, the pestilent hue of the Netherworld.

When Azár was finished, she stood up and backed tentatively away. She regarded her work, satisfied. The Gateway was unlocked in this world. But someone else would have to unlock it from the other side.

Azár rose and used her nascent powers to slide the cover off the Well of Tears. The thick granite slab lifted of its own volition and glided smoothly aside. It hovered for a moment in the air, as if suspended from invisible strings, before lowering the rest of the way to the floor.

Azár turned warily back toward her master. Zamir had one last journey to make. The Well of Tears demanded a sacrifice, and the old man's soul would be the final gesture that would unseal the Gateway.

Zamir had been a frail old man, but the dead weight of his corpse was still too much for Azár's slight build to manage. So she closed her eyes, aligning her thoughts with the rhythmic pulse of the magic field, allowing the power of her mind to supplement the strength she lacked in her flesh. Azár used her newfound power to speed Zamir on his final journey. She lifted his body up over the Well's rim, giving him a shove.

With the slightest scraping noise, the corpse slipped into the gaping shaft and tumbled downward into darkness.

Azár turned her face away. It would take some time for Zamir's spirit to complete the final task he had set for himself. There was still yet time to ascend the long flights of steps to the level of the surface. She would have to hurry; her part was still far from complete.

Azár sent her magelight roaming forward, her feet following its glowing trail out of the chamber and into the dark passage beyond. She knew exactly which direction to turn; her master had made certain she would not falter in her task. The dark corridor she traversed was part of a larger warren of passageways that infested the mountainside below what had once been proud

Aerysius, city of the mages. Now just a sad and desolate mountainscape that stood forlorn three thousand feet above the Vale of Amberlie.

Following the map she had committed to memory, Azár let her feet carry her up a dark and narrow stair, moving through a glowing trail of magelight that spilled ahead of her. Her eyes reveled in the texture of the light, awed by the magelight's warm, summery glow. It was her own creation, her very first. A lifegiving thing of wonder and graceful beauty.

Azár sent her mind out, sampling the pulse and rhythm of the magic field in this place. It was soothing and vibrant, gentle and stately. It was hers, now, to command as she pleased. She could feel Zamir's power moving within her, a wondrous and potent legacy.

She emerged at last from the depths of the mountain into a cool, clear night. She gazed out upon the bare terrace that stretched before her, captivated by the stark austerity of Aerysius' bare foundations. Azár gazed upward into the sky, tilting her head back as an abrupt gust of wind seized her long, dark braid.

Before her, violent energies erupted upward from the ground, piercing the heavens like a turbulent, ethereal lance. The sinister column pierced the sky, penetrating the dome of the heavens with a violence that was alarming. Lightning licked down to assault that awful spire, crackling sharply overhead.

Confronted with such a daunting vision, Azár felt her courage start to falter. She lowered her gaze, biting her lip. She concentrated on the sound of her breath, willing her mind to focus. When she opened her eyes again, she regarded the Gateway with newfound resolve.

Azár gasped in shock. There, from out of the dazzling brilliance of the column, dark figures had already begun to emerge. Stirred by the site of them, Azár's heart quickened its pace. She stood her ground with fists balled against her sides, feet apart, her back rigid. Eyes widened with excitement tempered by awe, Azár watched as the first man-shaped silhouettes drew forth from the glaring wash of light to converge on her position.

Recognition dawned slowly across Azár's face. The man who approached first was easily identified by the spiked weapon he bore: Byron Connel, ancient Warden of Battlemages, wielder of the legendary talisman *Thar'gon*. To his right strode an elegant woman in a flowing white gown, dark of hair as well as skin. A demon-hound with menacing green eyes stalked at her side. Azár had heard enough tales of the Eight to recognize Myria Anassis, ancient Querer of the Lyceum. Another woman with loose chestnut hair was walking toward her. She strolled alongside a man just as sinisterly handsome as the woman was deceptively beautiful: Sareen Qadir and Nashir Arman. The pair approached slowly, cautiously. The woman's eyes seemed to glisten, a smile of excitement growing on her lips.

So distracted was she by the pair that Azár almost didn't notice the two men approaching her from the opposite direction. She turned, startled to find herself confronted by the imposing forms of Zavier Renquist and Cyrus Krane. The two ancient Prime Wardens drew up together before her, both in flowing indigo robes with the white cloaks of their office billowing behind them, inspired by the wind displaced by the Gateway. Cyrus Krane regarded Azár with a sneer rendered all the more cruel by the jagged red scar that bisected his face. His dark eyes were murky pools of unveiled threat.

Zavier Renquist paused before her, arms behind his back, feet spread apart, gazing down upon Azár with an expression of somber esteem. His dark hair was pulled back from his face, gathered into a thick braid at the top of his head. He was staring at her expectantly, as if calmly awaiting her to address him first. Had he been any other man, Azár might have considered it.

Appearing satisfied, Zavier Renquist lifted his chin and addressed Azár in a deep and resonant voice:

"Our Master extends to you His gratitude. In you, Xerys is well-pleased. He commits to you the services of the Eight and His army of the night until the initial purpose of our summoning is fulfilled. So, my child, it is time to speak your desires. What shall be your command?"

Azár swallowed, unable to look away from the mesmerizing cauldron of authority that simmered in Zavier Renquist's eyes. She held his gaze with her own as she summoned her own fragile voice, praying her words would not falter and betray her fear.

"I command you to save my people." Azár channeled every scrap of assertiveness she could muster into her tone. She drew herself up, lifting her chin. Her fists were still balled tightly at her sides. "Deliver us from the darkness. Raise us up from the ashes. Return to us our birthright – this is my command!"

Zavier Renquist stood there regarding her for a prolonged, searching minute. It was impossible to read his expression; the ancient demon's face was altogether blank, without any hint or trace of emotion. He stared deeply into Azár's eyes as if scrutinizing her worth, contemplating the fabric of her soul, weighing the meddle of her character. At last, apparently satisfied, he gave a terse nod.

"Then it shall be as you command," he said, shifting his weight over his feet. His indigo robes swayed with his motion. He turned to cast a predatory stare across at Cyrus Krane then turned again toward Azár. Very formally, he spread his hands and assured her:

"Malikar's deliverance is long overdue. And this time, there will be nothing in this world that can deter us from our goal. Allow me to introduce to you the man whose responsibility it shall be to reclaim the light and heritage that was lost so long ago when Caladorn fell into darkness."

He gestured with his hand, indicating a man who had drawn up silently behind the others and now stood with hands clasped in front of him, head bowed against his chest. As Azár's attention focused on him, the man glanced up through matted strands of long, black hair that had fallen forward over his face. His yellow-green eyes locked on hers with an intensity that was frightening.

Azár felt herself taken sharply aback; she had no idea who this man was. He fit none of the descriptions she had ever heard spoken of the Eight. The look in his eyes chilled her very soul.

She frowned in consternation, her brow nettling. "I don't understand," Azár whispered. "What has become of our mistress? Who is this man? How is it that he alone is expected to accomplish what all Eight of you could not achieve before?"

Zavier Renquist clasped his fingers together in front of him: a gesture of patience. "Your mistress failed. Her soul has been consigned to Oblivion." He fixed Azár with a flat, significant stare. He extended his hand, indicating to Azár the stranger across from her with the haunted eyes. "This is the man who bested your mistress in combat and has replaced her at my side. He has assumed all of Arden Hannah's rights, privileges, and obligations."

Azár fixed this newcomer with an incredulous stare, shaking her head in confounded dismay. "Who *is* he?"

Zavier Renquist explained, "Darien Lauchlin is the lone Sentinel who laid waste to Malikar's legions at the base of Xerys' Pedestal."

Azár's mouth dropped open. She had not been present at the massacre, but she had heard of the atrocities committed by Aerysius' Last Sentinel, his final act of desperation. Thousands of brave warriors had not returned from that campaign, their bodies reduced to charred ash scattered on the wind. Azár shivered as she regarded the disquieting man before her, coming to the slow conclusion that Zavier Renquist had to be telling the truth about him. It was the only explanation for the depths of torment in those harrowing eyes.

"This is impossible!" Azár managed at last. "The man you speak of is dead!"

"As am I," the prime warden reminded her with a shrug and a smile. Spreading his hands, he went on to explain, "Darien Lauchlin committed his soul to the service of Xerys. He is now one with us in purpose. He has assumed all rights, responsibilities, and covenants of the Servant he replaces. So Darien is, in every respect, the overlord your people have been so long awaiting. Your request is his singular purpose to fulfill."

Azár turned her head and spat upon the ground. Whirling away, she exclaimed in anger, "I will not suffer the company of this man! He is not even a man—he is a demon, a monster!"

"Perhaps." The ancient prime warden raised his eyebrows. He did not appear affronted in the least by Azár's accusation. "But I would strongly advise you to reconsider, and think very carefully before declining Darien's assistance. Because, considering the nature of your demands, it sounds like a monster is exactly what you need."

Azár gazed at him with dread in her eyes, knowing deep down in her gut that Renquist's assessment was probably accurate. She sighed, giving in, heart heavy with dismay.

"Go with her," Zavier Renquist commanded his newest Servant in a voice suffused with arrogance and ice. "You heard her demands. Go forth and fulfill them."

The dark-haired demon nodded slightly. "I will do my best, Prime Warden." His voice sounded terse, strained. He strode forward.

"Stop."

Renquist's sharp command halted him in his tracks. As Azár looked on in fascination, Darien Lauchlin turned back around with weary patience in his eyes.

Zavier Renquist promised him, "Your best isn't going to be good enough. Instead of your best, *I demand your worst.* You must let go of your past and embrace your destiny. Unchain your inner demons. Conquer your own ghosts just as you once conquered my armies. Transcend the constraints you have used to shackle your conscience and experience firsthand what true freedom feels like."

Darien Lauchlin nodded, dark strands of hair swaying forward into his face. "It shall be as you ask, Prime Warden."

"It had better be. For your sake. And for hers."

Azár stared long and hard at the two men, her brow furrowed in consternation. Renquist's threat had not been directed toward herself. She let her gaze linger on the man trudging toward her, a demon-hound jogging behind in his wake. Frowning, she wondered which woman's life Zavier Renquist had just threatened. And why that woman's life mattered so much to this tormented monster of a man.

Glossary

acolyte: apprentice mage who has passed the Trial of Consideration and sworn the Acolyte's Oath.

Acolyte's Oath: first vow taken by every acolyte of Aerysius to serve the land and its people, symbolized by a chain-like marking on the left wrist.

Aerysius: ancient city where the Masters of Aerysius dwell.

Amberlie: town in the Vale of Amberlie below Aerysius.

Anassis, Myria: ancient Querer of the Lyceum, now a Servant of Xerys.

Archer, Amelia: wife of Kyel Archer.

Archer, Gilroy: baby son of Kyel Archer.

Archer, Kyel: apprentice merchant of Coventry Township.

Arms Guild: institution for the study of blademastery. Also called the School of Arms.

Assembly of the Hall: the Masters of Aerysius, as a collective entity.

Athera: Goddess of Magic.

Atrament: the realm of Death, ruled by the goddess Isap.

Auberdale: capital city of Chamsbrey.

Battle of Meridan: famous battle in which the Enemy was turned back in large part due to the efforts of the Sentinels.

Battlemage: order of mages who accompanied armies into battle in ancient times before the Oath of Harmony.

bittern: demonic creature that has the ability to sense disturbances in the magic field.

Black Lands: what was once Caladorn, now the desecrated home of the Enemy.

blademaster: title awarded to graduates of the Arms Guild.

Blandford, General: general of the Emrish Army.

Bloodquest: ancient rite of vengeance condoned by the goddess Isap for righteous causes.
Bluecloaks: slang for the Rothscard city guard.
Book of the Dead: ancient text wherein the Strictures of Death are inscribed.
Bound: describes a mage who has sworn the Oath of Harmony.
Broden: Guild blademaster employed by the Mayor of Wolden.
Bryn Calazar: ancient capital of Caladorn.
Cadmus: Voice of the High Priest of Wisdom.
Caladorn: ancient empire to the north, now known only as the Black Lands.
Catacombs: place of burial that exists partly in the Atrament.
Cerulean Plains: large grassland region in the North.
Chamsbrey: Northern kingdom ruled by Godfrey Faukravar.
Circle of Convergence: focus of magic designed to draw on the vast power of a vortex.
Connel, Byron: ancient Battlemage of the Lyceum, now a Servant of Xerys.
Corlan, Finneus: first tier Master of the Order of Sentinels.
Coventry: town in the kingdom of Lynnley.
Craghorns: mountains that border the Vale of Amberlie.
Craig, Devlin: captain of Greystone Keep.
Cromm, Cedric: author of *The Mysteries of Aerysius.*
Cummings, Chadwick: advisor to the King of Chamsbrey.
darkmage: a mage who has made a compact with Xerys.
Death's Passage: *see* **Catacombs**.
destrier: various breeds of large warhorse.
Dreia: Goddess of the Vine.
Eight, the: the Eight Servants of Xerys.
Emmery: Northern kingdom.
Emmery Palace: the Queen's palace in Rothscard.
Enemy, the: collective name for inhabitants of the Black Lands.
eye: area at the heart of a vortex where the lines of the magic field run almost parallel.
Faukravar, Godfrey: King of Chamsbrey, also known as the Vile Prince.
field lines: currents of the magic field.

Field of Tol-Ranier: ancient battle site near Auberdale.

Flynn, Tyrius: fourth tier Grand Master of the Order of Sentinels.

Front, the: area bordering the Black Lands.

gateway: portal to the Netherworld.

Glen Farquist: holy city in the Valley of the Gods.

Goddess of the Eternal Requiem: statue of an aspect of the Goddess of Death; her face of Righteous Vengeance.

Grand Master: any mage of the fourth tier or higher.

Grand Resonance: theoretical acceleration of the magic field that produces a cataclysmic chain reaction.

Great Master: title of honor applied to any mage.

Greystone Keep: legendary fortress in the Pass of Lor-Gamorth.

Hall of the Watchers: Stronghold of the mages of Aerysius, where exists Aerysius' Circle of Convergence.

Hannah, Arden: ancient Querer, now a Servant of Xerys.

Henley, Corban: formerly of the Vale, now a soldier of Greystone Keep.

high priest: title of the religious leader of one of the ten Holy Temples.

Isap: Goddess of Death.

Jenn: nomadic horse culture of the Cerulean Plains.

Kayna: woman of the Jenn, wife of Ranoch.

Krane, Cyrus: ancient Prime Warden of Aerysius, now a Servant of Xerys.

Landry, Clement: Minister of State to the King of Chamsbrey.

Larsen, Ellen: wife of Traver Larsen.

Larsen, Traver: friend of Kyel Archer.

Lauchlin, Aidan: first tier Master of the Order of Empiricists. Firstborn son of Gerald and Emelda Lauchlin.

Lauchlin, Darien: second son of Gerald and Emelda Lauchlin.

Lauchlin, Emelda: Prime Warden of Aerysius. First tier Master of the Order of Chancellors.

Lauchlin, Gerald: *(deceased)* father of Aidan and Darien Lauchlin, fourth tier Grand Master of the Order of Sentinels. Murdered by ritual immolation during the Battle of Meridan.

Lyceum: ancient stronghold of the mages of Bryn Calazar.

Mage's Oath: *see* **Oath of Harmony**.

magelight: magical illumination that takes on the hue of the mage's signature color.

magic field: source of magical energy that runs in lines of power over the earth.

Maidenclaw: one of the two mountains that mark the entrance of the Black Lands.

Master: any mage; more specifically, a mage of the first through third tier.

Meridan: *see* **Battle of Meridan**.

Mysteries of Aerysius, The: authoritative text on the subject of the Masters of Aerysius.

***nach'tier*:** word for darkmage in the language of the Enemy.

Natural Law: law that governs the workings of the universe that can be strained by the application of magic, but never broken.

necrator: demonic creature that renders a mage powerless in its presence.

Nelle, Lynnea: first tier Master of the Order of Querers.

Netherworld: realm of Xerys, God of Chaos.

node: place where the lines of the magic field come together in parallel direction but opposite in energy and cancel out.

Nordric, Ezras: fifth tier Grand Master of the Order of Sentinels.

Norengail, Romana: Queen of Emmery.

North, the: the Northern kingdoms of the Rhen, including Emmery, Chamsbrey and Lynnley.

Oath of Harmony: oath taken by every Master of Aerysius to do no harm, symbolized by a chain-like marking on the right wrist.

Om: God of Wisdom.

orders: different schools of magic.

Orguleth: one of the two mountains that mark the entrance to the Black Lands. Also called the Spire of Orguleth.

Orien Oathbreaker: infamous Grand Master who used the Circle of Convergence on Orien's Finger to turn back the Third Invasion almost single-handedly.

Orien's Finger: crag on the edge of the Cerulean Plains where Orien Oathbreaker made his stand.

Pass of Lor-Gamorth: pass through the Shadowspear Mountains that guards the border of the Black Lands.

Penthos, Luther: high priest of the Temple of Death.

Pointer Stones: ancient standing stones in Glen Farquist that mark the location of sunrise on the morning of Winter Solstice.

potential: ability in a person to sense the magic field.

Pratson, Blake: Mayor of Wolden.

Prime Warden: leader of the Assembly of the Hall. Literally, the 'First Guardian' of the Rhen.

Proctor, Garret: legendary Force Commander of Greystone Keep.

Raising: Rite of Transference, during which an acolyte inherits the legacy of power from another mage.

Ranoch: man of the Jenn, husband of Kayna.

Renquist, Zavier: ancient Prime Warden of the Lyceum, now a Servant of Xerys.

Rhen: name of the collective kingdoms south of the Black Lands.

Rothscard: capital city of Emmery.

Royce, Sutton: captain of Greystone Keep and Guild blademaster.

School of Arms: *see* **Arms Guild**.

Seleni, Naia: priestess of Death.

Sentinels: order of mages chartered with the defense of the Rhen.

Shadowspears: mountains that border the Black Lands.

Silver Star: symbol of the Masters of Aerysius, indicative of the focus lines of the Circles of Convergence.

South, the: Southern kingdoms of the Rhen, including Creston, Gandrish, and Farley.

spire of the Hall: tower of the Hall of the Watchers where the Masters keep their residence.

Strictures of Death: laws of Death.

Structural Resonance: acceleration of the magic field that produces a harmonic instability in the field capable of destroying large structures.

Superposition: within a vortex, where several lines of the magic field combine and produce a vast well of power.

Swain, Nigel: Guild blademaster, formerly Captain of the Guard in Aerysius, currently Captain of the Guard in Rothscard.
Tarkendar: breed of destrier, or warhorse.
Tarpen, Wade: soldier of Greystone Keep.
temples: various sects of worship. Each temple is devoted to a particular deity of the pantheon.
thanacryst: demonic creature that feeds off a mage's gift.
thar'tier: word for Battlemage in the language of the Enemy.
tier: additive levels of power among Masters. The higher a Master's tier, the greater that person's ability to strain the limits of Natural Law.
Torrence, Edric: third tier Master, also known as the Bird Man to the local peasants.
Transference: process by which an acolyte inherits the legacy of power from another mage, resulting in the death of the Master who gives up his or her ability.
Treaton, Lance: Minister of the Treasury to the King of Chamsbrey.
Trial of Consideration: rite by which the potential to perceive the magic field is tested in a person.
Ulric: soldier of Greystone Keep.
Unbinding: the act of forswearing the Oath of Harmony.
Vale of Amberlie: long, narrow valley in the North.
Valley of the Gods: valley where exists the holy city of Glen Farquist.
Vile Prince: *see* **Faukravar, Godfrey**.
vortex: cyclone of power where the lines of the magic field superimpose and become vastly intense.
Well of Tears: well that unlocks the gateway to the Netherworld.
Wellingford, Malcolm: soldier of the Northern Army of Chamsbrey.
Withersby, Meiran: sixth tier Grand Master of the Order of Querers.
Wolden: town in the North, in the Kingdom of Emmery.
Xerys: God of Chaos and Lord of the Netherworld.

The Eight Orders of Mages

Order of Arcanists: order of mages chartered with the study and creation of artifacts and heirlooms of power.

Order of Architects: order of mages chartered with the construction of magical infrastructure.

Order of Chancellors: order of mages chartered with the governance of the Assembly.

Order of Empiricists: order of mages chartered with the theoretical study of the magic field, its laws and principles.

Order of Harbingers: order of mages chartered with maintaining watch over Athera's Crescent.

Order of Naturalists: order of mages chartered with the study of Natural Law.

Order of Querers: order of mages chartered with practical applications of the magic field.

Order of Sentinels: order of mages chartered with watching over and protecting the Rhen in a manner consistent with the Oath of Harmony.

Acknowledgements

Thanks to my editor, Morgan Smith. And thanks to my family for putting up with me.

Connect
Facebook.com/MLSpencerAuthor
Twitter.com/MLSpencerAuthor

Milton Keynes UK
Ingram Content Group UK Ltd.
UKHW011820190923
428965UK00001BI/127